Liars' Games

To Linda,
Best wishes,
Susan Finlay

Liars'

Games

A Project Chameleon Novel

By

Susan Finlay

Liars' Games is Copyright © 2014 by Susan Finlay.

First Edition

Cover Design by Ken Dawson

Paperback ISBN-13:978-1500328092

Published in the USA

AUTHOR'S NOTE

This is a work of fiction. All of the characters, the events, the Front Range School District, its schools, and Weymouth University are fictitious. A significant amount of research was performed for this book and series, but as this author has never been in Witness Protection and never worked in a school, author creativity and license filled in the gaps.

CHAPTER ONE

DR. JULIET POWELL gazed expectantly out the side window of the parked SUV, sitting with its engine idling and heater humming. Brad Meyers and three seriously dangerous looking unnamed men, who had joined them this morning in New Mexico for the long trip, were checking out a new hiding place for her and her three-and-a-half-year-old son, Aidan. She knew the drill well, having suffered through the occurrence twice before. She hoped this move would give her a better outcome than the previous moves.

"Mom . . . mmy, I want to get out!" Aidan shouted suddenly, interrupting her reverie. He squirmed and pulled on the straps of his car seat, trying to unfasten them.

Juliet leaned over and smoothed his hair. "It shouldn't be much longer, little man. Why don't you play with your toys until they return, all right?"

He quieted for a couple of minutes and then squirmed harder than before. "I want to get out, Mommy. Let me out!"

Trying to ignore the pleading of her impatient son, she glanced at the digital clock on the dashboard. It showed 6:15. Fifteen minutes had passed since Brad and his men had left the car and still no word. She didn't blame Aidan for wanting out of the car. She wanted out, too. More than eight hours stuck in this vehicle, with only two bathroom stops and one twenty-minute lunch break at a fast food restaurant, was too much. Her eyes shifted to the dangling keys in the ignition.

She got out of the back seat, slid into the driver's seat, started the SUV and rammed the engine into reverse, tires squealing, Brad running to stop her. Before he was half way to the vehicle, she shifted the clutch into drive and tore out of the parking lot and onto the street, stomping on the accelerator and careening away from the men screaming at her in her rear view mirror.

Brad's door jerked open, making Juliet jump and bringing her imaginings to an end. Aidan squealed in surprise.

"I just got the all-clear signal," he said. "Come on, we can go in now."

She nodded, but Brad didn't see her because he'd already turned around and walked away. She sighed, then reached over, unfastened Aidan's child-seat restraints, and helped him out. Aidan, clutching his small bag of toys to his chest, jumped quickly to the ground.

Exiting to the sidewalk, Juliet picked up her son and walked to the large complex of modern two-story condominiums, each in a different style yet sharing common adjoining walls, and each with a single-car garage attached. Brad and one of the men stood in front of one of the units. A third man walked past Juliet, back toward the car. She noted his holstered half-hidden gun as he passed, and shivered. The guns the men carried were necessary in their line of work, and she knew they were for her protection. Still, they made her more than a bit nervous.

She caught up to Brad and said, "I'm ready."

"Before we go in, I want to reiterate that we can't keep moving you. Do you think you can manage to blend in this time and not blow it? Remember, you're supposed to be a chameleon.

2

And you've got to get better at lying and sticking to your cover story. My superiors are losing patience."

She gave a feeble nod, unable to promise in words, since she wasn't especially sure she could do any better this time.

"Put me down, Mommy. I can walk. I'm not a baby."

She didn't argue. He was getting squirmy again and becoming rather heavy. The early evening air was breezy, cool, and dry—early autumn weather—and she could hear a lot of traffic noise.

"We're in Edgewater, a suburb of Denver, Colorado," Brad said. "We've found you a job nearby. I've also arranged for a nanny to come to your condo tomorrow, eleven-thirty. Name's Kate Townsend. She comes highly recommended by a friend of mine who lives here in the Denver area. But she still can't be told anything about your situation. Interview her. If she's not acceptable to you, shop around for another candidate."

"I hope she'll work out," Juliet said. "Thanks for setting up the appointment."

Brad held open the front door. "It's the best we could do on short notice."

"I'm sure it will be fine."

Aidan pulled his hand loose from his mother's and hopped around. "Gotta go to the bathroom," he said, holding the middle of his pants.

"Bathroom's next to the kitchen," Brad said, pointing.

Juliet followed Aidan, who was halfway there already. When she bent down to help him with his trousers, he shook her hand away. "Mommy, no. I can do it."

She smiled and left him alone, closing the door behind her.

The condo smelled of fresh paint. White paint. Oak flooring in the entry gave way to beige carpet that looked reasonably clean and smelled as if it had been shampooed earlier in the day. She squatted down and touched it. It seemed to be dry. The kitchen was modern yet basic. The bedrooms were evidently upstairs. Although it wasn't the kind of place she'd lived in back in Massachusetts or in England, it was better than the last apartment. She was becoming accustomed to living with less.

After finishing a quick tour of her new home, she said, "You said you found a job for me? What will it be this time?"

"Okay, here's what I know," he said, handing her a piece of folded paper. "You start work on Wednesday. That'll give you four days to get settled-in. Report to the Administration Building of the Front Range School District. Ask for the HR Manager, Helen Jackson. She'll have all your paperwork, including your employment contract. As far as I know, you'll be teaching math at Redding Middle School. Obviously that shouldn't be a problem considering your skill with numbers. It's all on the paper I just gave you."

"Teaching? I thought I wasn't supposed to be in that profession anymore."

He shrugged. "Don't ask me. My boss arranged the job and left me out of the loop."

Juliet detected a note of bitterness in his voice. It wasn't the first time. On a few other occasions he'd hinted at dissatisfaction with his superiors. When she asked him about it once, he'd brushed it off like it never happened. That was months ago, back when he was easier to talk with. She used to be able to joke around with him sometimes. But something had changed since then. She didn't know what and decided she shouldn't ask.

"Just do what Ms. Jackson tells you," he said, "and don't blow it this time. And whatever you do, don't keep calling me and asking what you should do. It's been almost ten months. I can't keep holding your hand. You've got to stand on you own. Now, do you remember your new name and Aidan's new name?"

She nodded. "What about furniture?"

"Sorry. Couldn't get a furnished apartment or condo on short notice. You'll just have to sleep on the floor tonight and go shopping tomorrow." Brad walked to the front door and opened it. "We'll be in touch."

"Wait! How will I get around here without a car? Is there public transportation?"

Brad stopped halfway out the door, turning his head to look back at Juliet. "Oh, sorry, I forgot. Someone will drop-off a rental car and your new I.D. later this evening. You have some cash, right?"

"Yes."

"You'll get new bank account info in a day or two. Okay, then, you know how to reach me if there's an emergency." He turned and left, closing the door behind him.

Juliet went to the front window and watched despondently as the SUV drove away, once again wondering at her plight. How the hell had she gotten into this mess, she asked herself for the umpteenth time; but of course she knew the answer. Was her life ever going to be safe? Would she and Aiden ever have a normal life again? It seemed doubtful. Sighing, she locked the front door and made a mental note to buy a deadbolt first thing in the morning. Although the men had checked out the condo, she went through it again herself and checked all of the windows to make sure they were locked.

While Aidan played with his stash of toy cars and miniature dinosaurs, the only things he was allowed to take with him from New Mexico, Juliet inspected the kitchen appliances and cupboards. She started writing a shopping list in a small notebook she kept in her handbag. As per regulation, she and Aidan had left everything else behind, including their clothes. Her shopping list would grow exponentially, she knew, especially in an unfurnished apartment. The problem was that if they got moved again, everything she bought would get left behind again.

Was it really worth stocking up the house with more than the bare minimum?

THE FOLLOWING MORNING first thing, she found a hardware store in the phone book and, using the map Brad had left, drove there in her new rental car and purchased deadbolts and tools for installing them. It took her two hours to finish just that small project, giving her and Aiden barely enough time for a quick lunch before the nanny interview. At eleven-thirty, a young clean-cut Kate Townsend arrived. Juliet introduced herself as Claire Constantine, and her son as Marcus. Kate seemed nice. She'd been working as a nanny for two years, and was taking evening courses at a local community college. Kate said she hoped to do some of her homework during the day, when it wouldn't interfere with her job as nanny. Juliet agreed. Aidan seemed to take to her right away. That cinched it.

Over the next three days, Juliet kept frantically busy purchasing clothes, food, towels, groceries, furniture . . . basically all the necessities of living for Aiden and herself to settle into their new home. She managed to finagle the mattress store into same day delivery, saving a second unbearable night on the rock hard floor, but had to wait until the third day for the rest of the furniture to be delivered. Somehow she managed. Aiden took it all in stride and seemed to treat it, in his own words, as a 'fun adventure'.

ON WEDNESDAY MORNING, her scheduled start date, Juliet dressed in one of her new outfits, served breakfast to Aiden, made coffee for herself and waited nervously for Nanny Kate to arrive. No matter how many new jobs she started, she always got jitters her first day. When Nanny Kate arrived, Juliet went over the specific rules and details regarding care for 'Marcus' and gave Kate her cell phone number and told her to call if she needed anything.

During her drive to the school district's administration building, Juliet practiced introducing herself by her new name. She'd remembered fine when she met Nanny Kate, but as they'd told her over and over when she first entered the program, 'practice makes perfect'. She really had come to hate that phrase.

By the time she entered the Human Resources office, Juliet's hands felt clammy. Still, she managed to introduce herself to the HR Manager, Helen Jackson, as Claire Constantine without a problem. So far, so good.

Ten minutes into their meeting, sitting across from Helen, Claire stared dumbfounded at the contract the woman had presented her after delivering a verbal bombshell, describing the job she was being offered. Claire tried to still her shaking hands, yet the paper rattled despite her efforts. "This—isn't the position I was expecting."

"Is that a problem, Ms. Constantine?"

Before she had a chance to respond, the woman's phone rang, interrupting them. Ms. Jackson excused herself, taking the call. While Ms. Jackson talked, Claire studied her momentarily. Immaculate clothes, lovely jewelry, perfect make-up. But her hair, close-cropped spiky gray, simply didn't match her attire and made her look a bit like a porcupine.

Claire shook her head and refocused on her current problem. Logically, based on her background, she might be capable of handling the position of high school principal—maybe—but the real issue was whether someone in her situation should be in such a high profile position. From what she knew, that was usually ill-advised, possibly not even allowed. On the other hand, Brad did say his boss had arranged the job. The back of her neck felt tense and she rubbed it.

After 'Porcupine' replaced the receiver in its cradle, she said, "Since you don't seem to want the job, I guess we're done here." She reached across the desk and snatched the papers out of Claire's hands.

"No. Wait." Claire sat up straight and placed her hands in her lap. *Be careful*, she told herself. *It's about asking the right questions.* "I didn't say I don't want the job. I just have a few questions. I just came in thinking I was being offered a position to teach math. Are you sure there is no mistake. I—"

"Look, I didn't make the decision. Neither did our hiring committee. This came from the school board." She pursed her lips and studied Claire with icy eyes for a few moments, then said "Midland High's principal resigned unexpectedly. The position they're offering you was his. The board President, John Richmond, bypassed our normal hiring procedures.' Staring daggers, she continued "Of course you already know that."

"Uh, actually, I don't know—" But if Brad's boss had spoken with the school board, that could explain it, she thought.

Porcupine peered over the rim of her rectangular glasses. "Do you want the principal's job or not?"

Claire twisted her hands in her lap. Normally, she would call Brad but she couldn't do that now. Not after his complaint and cautionary words during their last conversation. Sighing, she said, "Yes, I want it."

Porcupine returned the offer papers she had retrieved earlier and said "Fill out these forms. I'll need photocopies of your I.D."

Claire pulled her new social security card and driver's license from her handbag. She glanced at the documents—they looked real enough—and she supposed they were, in a way. Holding her breath, she handed them over. While the HR Manager left to make copies, Claire filled out the forms. For better or worse, she would stick with her decision, but something else still bothered her. She couldn't quite put her finger on it.

She heard a copy machine working in the background somewhere and a few minutes later, Porcupine returned, giving back her I.D. Claire asked, "Is there anyone around with whom I can speak about the school?"

The woman pursed her lips, then without a reply, stood up and trudged out of the office again.

Claire turned her attention back to the forms. Fifteen minutes later, as she was completing the last form, tell-tale high heel sounds alerted her that Porcupine was on her way back. A man followed her into the office.

"I can't stay long," he told Porcupine. "I have another meeting in fifteen minutes."

"Well, let's get on with it then. Claire, meet District Superintendent Steve Jensen. Steve, meet Midland High's new principal, Claire Constantine. She's just moved to Colorado."

He raised his eyebrows, then walked to her and extended his hand.

The woman walked around her desk and plopped back into her chair, clearly dismissing them while also clearly indicating she wasn't giving up her office.

Trying not to show uneasiness, Claire stood up and shook his hand. He didn't speak, and she became acutely aware in the silence that ensured that he was studying her. *Fine. If he can do it, so can I.* She studied his appearance: brown hair, beard, and mustache, pleasant face. Instead of a suit, he was attired more informally in a plaid blue and black shirt with the sleeves rolled up, khaki trousers, and black-suede shoes.

Steve broke the silence. "I must admit you're not what I expected."

Well, he isn't what I expected of a superintendent, either. She kept that to herself and asked, "Oh? What do you mean?"

"You look young, more like a student than a principal."

"I'm thirty-five. Is that a problem?" The moment the words came out, she realized she was blinking more than usual the way she always did when she lied; don't volunteer too much, they'd taught her. She closed her eyes for a second, and when she reopened them, Steve was staring at her. Her heart rate quickened, and she automatically reached up and rubbed her neck.

He squinted, and curved his lips ever so slightly—a gotcha smile. She'd only added five years to her age, and her fake documentation would confirm the number. Still, if his suspicion was aroused because of this, she could imagine herself getting fired before even getting started. Then where would she be? In big trouble with Brad and his superiors, that's where.

"If there's a problem . . . ."

"No. I guess that's what happens when we hire someone sight unseen."

"I'm sorry. Your HR Manager informed me that normal hiring procedures weren't followed in my case. I guess the circumstances were unusual."

Had anyone told him why the school board needed to hire her? From the way he scrutinized her, she didn't think so. She paused, and tried to gather her wits. "Well, at any rate, I hope you won't be disappointed in my work."

"No, I'm sorry. It's not your work that worries me." He sighed. "Do you have any idea what you're getting into, Claire? Aren't you concerned or afraid to work at Midland?"

"What? Should I be? What's wrong with Midland? I haven't been given any details about the school yet."

He twisted his mouth and shook his head. "Crap! Oh, sorry. What I meant to say was that you should have been told what this job entails before accepting. This school and those kids are going to eat you alive."

"Is that what happened to the former principal?"

Steve shrugged. "I have no doubt. He didn't say specifically, just left without giving notice. Said he'd had enough."

She opened her mouth, intending to speak, but snapped it shut. So that's why Porcupine had seemed evasive. Well, too late now. Grin and bear it as her father used to say. The muscles in the back of her neck tightened more and she unconsciously rubbed at it again, to no avail.

"If you're having second thoughts, we can void your contract. Don't worry."

She tried to keep her face blank as she pondered her response. What would Brad tell her to do? She could almost hear his voice: 'convince him you aren't afraid'.

She tilted her head, and gave a slight teasing smile, then said, "No, no, that's fine. I've dealt with cannibals before and I haven't been eaten yet."

Steve peered askance at her for a moment and then chuckled. "I like that. You've got spunk and a sense of humor. God knows you'll need it."

The muscles in the back of her neck relaxed slightly, and she smiled at him.

Steve smiled back and then said, "I hear you're from out of state. How is your move to Denver going? Are you getting settled in yet?"

"I guess so. Only been here a few days and had a lot of shopping to do to get settled in. I do have a question while you're here though. I haven't the faintest idea where Midland High School is located."

"Where do you live?"

"Edgewater, near Redding Middle School where I originally expected to work."

"Ah. I think you're in luck. The two schools are only about five miles apart so I doubt it'll affect your driving time much.

11

They're both roughly twenty minutes from this central admin building. Didn't Helen give you a map for getting to the school?"

"No, not yet. Well, anyway, that's a relief. I noticed traffic here seems to be quite heavy during rush hour. I didn't relish the thought of driving across town to get to work. I'm glad that won't be an issue."

"Traffic can be quite heavy, and I'm afraid you'll soon discover driving can also be a bear during winter and during snow storms. They don't use salt on the roads here, just crushed granite which tends to embed itself either in the ice or in your windshield, neither result improving the situation." Smiling pleasantly again, *he definitely had a nice smile*, he continued "Other than that, what do you think of Denver so far?"

"Oh, the mountain vistas here are breathtaking. I can't wait to explore, visit downtown, the museums, and go to the mountains." She stopped and smiled back at him, tucking a loose strand of hair behind her ear. "Unfortunately, I'm not good navigating unfamiliar places. I probably need a tour guide."

He grinned and then opened his mouth to speak. At the sound of papers rustling on the desk, he glanced over at the HR Manager. A subtle change came over him and he held out his hand to Claire and said, "Well, welcome to Denver and to the school district."

CHAPTER TWO

WELCOME TO DENVER! Before that, welcome to Albuquerque. Before Albuquerque, welcome to Portland. Before her ordeal had begun, she'd been welcomed to Boston and Weymouth University as a professor. Claire sighed. So much for moving to the U.S., the land of opportunity, she thought as she placed her paperwork in her laptop bag and walked to the exit. *If Callum and I had stayed in England, I wouldn't be in this mess.*

She left the central administration building and entered her rental car. Once settled in, she typed Midland High School's address into the car's GPS system and waited for a satellite connection. The on-screen map appeared along with a decidedly Brit computer voice, telling her to 'drive the highlighted route'. As she began driving, Claire operated on auto-pilot, her mind busy replaying the earlier scene. What a mess. She'd already made a spectacle of herself before her new boss. Worse yet, she'd practically flirted with the man. Her only hope was that he hadn't interpreted it that way.

She sighed, stopping at a red light. At least she recognized her faux pas this time; an improvement over her usual track record. She tapped her fingers on the steering wheel, dissatisfied. What good was recognizing mistakes when you couldn't fix them? That was analogous to closing the barn door after the horse has bolted. "Must do better," she muttered out loud.

She shook her head at her own shortcomings, which admittedly were greater than they should be for someone as highly educated as she was. And it wasn't only her knack of messing up in social situations, especially when nervous, but that she was too transparent, as well. When Claire was young her mother had often advised to practice her facial expressions before a mirror and develop an opaque veneer. She could kick herself now in hindsight for disregarding her mother's words.

The light changed and she drove forward, checking her rearview mirror frequently to see if anyone was following her. It had become a habit ten months ago back when her troubles had begun. The voice in the car's GPS interrupted her musings, telling her to keep right and turn onto Kipling in 0.4 miles. She switched lanes, sped up to get through the light before it changed, and ended up jamming on the brakes. While she waited, she tried to distract herself from her thoughts by studying the looming foothills of the Rocky Mountains. A light snow layer already covered them and this was only early September. *Going to be an early cold winter.*

She was too close to the foothills now to see even the tallest mountains of the Front Range—Longs Peak, Mount Evans, and Pikes Peak if she was remembering right—but she'd seen the tops of them in the distance several days ago while driving on Interstate 25 through Denver in search of furniture. The mountains rose sharply behind the foothills and provided a spectacular backdrop to the city. She wondered if she might fare better if she hid in those mountains. She could buy a cabin, grow her own food, and home-school her son. That begged another question: Could she live with the isolation? And if she was in isolation, what if her enemies found them? No one would hear their screams, let alone rescue them. She shivered involuntarily at the picture that popped into her mind.

Claire shook her head. She couldn't take the chance. Whatever problems she had with the people who were controlling her life now, she knew her best chance of protecting her child was with them. Besides, her son needed socialization, and normalcy, if that was even possible for a child prodigy. Her own childhood had been far from normal, and as a result, she'd always considered herself a misfit. She might as well have had SUPER-NERD engraved on her forehead.

Someone tooted their car horn at her and she jumped, looking up at the light. Green. She turned the corner quickly and then her mind wandered back into retrospect.

Her parents had always told her she was lucky to 'be gifted'. What they hadn't told her, she began to slowly comprehend after one particularly emotional day. Her dad had picked her up from school, and they'd driven past by a homeless man holding a sign 'Will work for food'. She had cried and screamed until her father took her to buy food for the man. Her supposed gift apparently came with additional baggage—over excitability, an 'extra emotional antenna' which made her far more permeable to feelings.

Like most kids, as she'd grown up she'd learned to apply filters to the world around her so life's dramas didn't affect her with such intensity. But her emotions still topped the charts on most days.

She arrived at the school and parked in the faculty car park as Porcupine had instructed, and then walked around the school building to where the students parked. Music poured from multiple car radios cranked up to full volume, resulting in a mash of rap, reggae, and Chicano. A dozen or so students sat atop cars, a few others were dancing. One particularly dangerous looking kid shoved another one who had apparently made the wrong remark.

She looked at her watch. Ten o'clock. Why weren't they in class? Shouldn't staff be monitoring the school grounds?

She continued walking. A few students took note of her and she was immediately accosted by wolf whistles and obscenities. She could feel her face grow hot as coals. Out of the corner of her eye she saw two teenage boys wearing orange bandanas walking toward her. When they were three feet away, one of them said, "Hey, Mama. Take off your jacket. Let us have a better looksee at that beautiful ass."

Ignore them, she told herself. Stay calm. Keep walking. Moments later she sensed someone close behind and then a hand grabbed her bottom. She spun on her heels so fast that the boy stumbled backwards in surprise.

"Shouldn't you be in class?"

"Hey, if you be a teacher, I'll follow you anywhere," he said. The other boy laughed raucously as they exchanged a fist-bump.

She swung back around and hastened toward the double doors.

The school's entrance hall was dark and mostly deserted, not particularly safe, but decidedly better than it had been outside. She swallowed and exhaled, being able to walk right in without anyone stopping her. Come to think of it, that didn't seem right. Shouldn't there be metal detectors and security guards? Or was she overreacting to Steve Jensen's earlier inference? She had googled the U.S. education system after Brad told her about the teaching job. Metal detectors weren't used everywhere—only in some large urban districts with a history of chronic weapons offences. Should she assume, since Midland didn't have the equipment, the school wasn't so dangerous? It already seemed dangerous to her. Either way, letting anyone walk into a school building unchecked seemed risky and wrong. She shivered.

As she walked down the hall, a few students were milling around lockers, and stared at her as she passed.

She picked one, and said, "Excuse me. Can you direct me to the administration office?" The student pointed to his left.

Walking in the identified direction, she quickly found and paused outside the door labeled Administration, took a deep breath and opened the door. Two students sat in a corner, heads bent together, whispering. She didn't see anyone behind the reception desk.

"Good morning. Can I help you find someone?"

Claire turned toward the voice and saw a youngish lean black man, but obviously older than a student and certainly better dressed, with a stiff, unbending posture.

"Well, yes, I hope so. Actually, I'm looking for the principal's office."

"Principal's not here. Quit two weeks back. I'm the acting principal, Ron Baker. Are you here to enroll?" He stood, smiling, his hands behind his back—probably clasped from the looks of his stance—his eyes fixed on her face.

"Oh—no. I'm not a student." She hesitated as heat again climbed up her neck. Crap. Should have projected confidence and authority. Too late to start again. "Uh, sorry. I should introduce myself. I'm Jul—uh, El—uh, I mean Claire. Claire Constance." She bit her lip and started again. "I'm Claire Constantine. I'm the new headma . . . principal." She looked down at the laptop bag she held up close to her chest as a shield. When she looked up again, his face was empty as though someone had taken a blackboard eraser and wiped away every expression.

He said, in a cool tone, "Nice to meet you." He took a step towards her, shook her hand, and stepped back again. "Helen Jackson called and told us you were coming."

She bit her lip. So he had been expecting her and was deliberately giving her a hard time. Just great. "I'm happy to meet you. I look forward to working with you."

He nodded without speaking. Then he turned and watched as three more employees exited an office. Ron motioned to them.

"Meet our new principal. Claire. Hmm, what was the last name again?"

Claire thought she detected a sneer after his question. "Constantine," she said.

A pudgy man with graying hair said, "Jorge Perez. Spanish. I mean I teach Spanish."

She made a move toward him, intending to shake his hand. He crossed his arms and stood with his legs apart, his lips pursed, and his eyes squinting. He could probably intimidate students into submission with that look alone. She gritted her teeth and tried not to show her feelings.

"I'm Nancy Palmer," another voice chimed in.

Turning slightly, Claire saw a slender woman standing nearby.

"Head of the English Department," she said, extending her hand.

At least someone here is friendly. Claire smiled and shook Nancy's hand. The woman met her eyes and smiled.

"You remind me of my first day here," Nancy said. "It was a disaster. I wanted to dash away like a diner who couldn't pay her tab but the principal had placed the school in lockdown that day and trapped me. Bill here can tell you."

The third employee grunted, then said, "I'm Bill Wilson, Guidance Counselor."

Claire reached out and shook his hand and he squeezed her hand hard. She looked into his face. He was staring at her, his jaw bricklike.

She opened her mouth. It was dry as a desert, and when she tried to speak, the words caught and stuck and scratched in her throat. "Maybe I should . . . will you please direct me to . . . uh, my office?" She could almost feel her blood rising up from her neck as if someone were filling a beaker. Trying to recover, she said, "Sorry, a bit parched."

They all stared at her. In her mind's eye she saw herself back as the scrawny twelve-year-old sitting in her old high school, her golden-brown hair fashioned in two long plaits. She wore her favorite red and white and black striped woolen skirt and a soft red cardigan, her legs shrouded in black tights, swinging back and forth. Around her, older students stared at her as though she were an alien from Mars.

"Are you all right?" Bill asked.

Jerked back into the present, she glanced at the staff members and tried to force herself to smile, then looked away. "Forgive me. I guess I have a bad case of first-day nervousness."

Bill smiled and nodded in understanding, but when he glanced at his companions, and his smile twisted into a faint snicker, Claire knew better. Not a counselor in whom she would want to confide.

"Ron, could you arrange for the faculty to meet in the—uh—"

"Faculty lounge?"

"Yes, thank you. Immediately after school?"

"Certainly."

"Well, then, if you'll excuse me, I think I can find my office." Claire turned, looked around and found a door marked 'Principal', and strode toward it, aware of four pairs of eyes watching her. She switched on the light, closed the windowless door behind her, and leaned back against the door. She shook her head, then placed her hands over her face. She really wasn't trying to look like an idiot, but she'd certainly done so, even stumbling over her own name. Couldn't they have given her an easier last name? Although Constantine wasn't bad, it certainly didn't spring to mind or roll-off her tongue. Still, someone with a near-photographic memory should have no trouble remembering a new name, even a difficult name. It hadn't been a problem back at Human Resources. So what happened when she arrived here? First-day nerves self-sabotage? She shook her head again, frustrated with herself.

Don't worry, you can learn management skills. It's the bloody lying you have to worry over. Sure, you'll get used to it. Probably get used to looking stupid, too. Well, big surprise, at least you don't have to worry about blowing your cover by showing that you're a genius.

Chills ran up her spine as she realized she wouldn't be able to see who might be lurking outside her office. Not good from a principal viewpoint or for that matter from a witness-in-hiding viewpoint either. She waited, but hearing nothing else, she focused her attention on her new office, immediately noting its cheerless dingy grayish-brown walls and its lack of windows to let in outside light.

On one side of the office stood an oversized beat-up walnut desk stacked with papers, with an old worn green leather swivel chair between it and the side wall. Two cluttered bookcases stood next to the desk on the back wall, their dusty shelves in disarray, books lying every which way, as if someone had just thrown them on the shelves. On the other side of the office, the stuffing oozed from gashes in the fabric of a tattered beige sofa along the wall. An ugly chrome and glass coffee table stood in front. Four unmatched waiting-room style chairs, probably rummage sale rejects, seemed haphazardly placed around the room. The room's ugliness, combined with the lack of window and the lingering smell of old cigar smoke, reminded her of a prison cell and made her shiver again. "Just lovely, kill me now!"

Plopping onto the swivel chair, she placed her elbows on the desktop and looked down. A gasp escaped her as she read dozens of graffiti messages etched into the wood. Disgusting messages. Hopefully the work of students and not the previous principal. *Well, at least they can spell.* Fingering them, she felt the deep grooves that told her they'd meant to leave a lasting impression and knew she would keep the desk with its flaws as a reminder of the low-caliber of students she should expect to encounter. Clearly, the prison atmosphere in here wasn't the only reason the principal had quit. She sighed and shook her head. *Might as well get started reading files. Maybe I can learn something from them.* She thumbed through the first stack of papers and folders. It would take her days to get through it all. No, more likely weeks, if the eight metal filing cabinets on the opposite wall flanking the door were full. *Please let those not be full.*

A peek inside confirmed the drawers were not only full, but were a disorganized mess—files out of order, multiple folders jammed inside of others, loose papers on the sides of the metal frame. She began pulling out about ten folders at a time and set them on the desk. As she worked, she came across a complaint lodged by a teacher against the former principal, claiming he'd been promised a promotion to department head, however, the principal gave it to a brand new teacher instead. She searched for paperwork indicating the reasoning and outcome. She found nothing. Not surprising. People lie and make promises they don't intend to keep. They do whatever they want to get what they want, and the more powerful they are, the worse they are. Chances are, the superintendent never received the complaint.

The next few hours were spent studying everything she could find documenting the most recent happenings at the school. She jotted down notes, and mentally prepared herself for her first staff meeting. She thought she was almost ready until she glanced at the clock. It was already time to go to the faculty lounge, and her stomach was knotting up the way it used to do when she was a teacher's aide in college and was terrified to speak to the students. The last thing she needed was to re-live those past insecurities. She closed her eyes and willed herself to relax, but her heart continued its flip-flopping. How could she meet the entire faculty when she couldn't even meet four employees without bumbling? She held out her hands and shook them to try to shake out her nerves.

Take a deep breath, let it out. Don't stammer so much and don't slip back into Oxford English.

Her American mother, after living in England for fourteen years, had learned to switch back and forth but had chosen more often than not to parade her Americanisms and American pronunciation in defiance of her British husband.

Claire had copied her sometimes. Neither of them would have guessed it would come in handy one day. She'd done pretty well during her second new identity until a few weeks ago when two Brits had visited the accounting firm where she worked in data entry. They'd stopped near her cubicle and were discussing a news report from London. Without thinking, she'd turned round and asked for details, letting her full Home Counties accent out for everyone to hear. The boss summoned her into his office and questioned her about it, and she'd panicked and couldn't think fast enough to cover her blunder. She'd told him the truth.

Claire trudged to the faculty lounge and selected a place to stand. No one was there yet. All right, that would give her time to gather herself. She waited in the empty faculty lounge for ten minutes and kept checking her watch. Hadn't they received the message about the meeting? Finally, fifteen minutes late, the faculty started filing into the room. As they walked past her, she caught snippets of gossip about herself. She intercepted glares, too, and the phrase 'if looks could kill' sprang to mind.

Once everyone was seated, she began, "Good afternoon. For those of you haven't met me yet, I'm your new principal, Claire Constantine. I'm looking forward to working with you." Sullen faces stared back at her. She cleared her throat and continued, "I—"

"Why would you pick this school?"

It was Bill, the school counselor she'd met earlier. She should have known.

"Well, I—I don't exactly know how to answer. I mean I—I didn't really pick it. The porc—I mean, it's the position the HR Manager offered."

"So either you got stuck with us, or we got stuck with you. Does that about sum it up?" another man asked.

She opened her mouth, intending to speak, but closed it again. Teachers looked at each other and snickered. She struggled for words. What could she say? The room was quiet except for the loudly clicking clock on the wall straight ahead and the clicking of keys on mobile phones. Were they texting each other?

Before she had a chance to compose an answer to the man's question, a bell rang and her staff stood up and hastened toward the door.

"Wait," Claire said. "We aren't finished." Everyone ignored her except for Nancy Palmer who stopped and looked at Claire with pity in her eyes.

"Thank you for staying, Nancy. I tried. Are they always like this?"

"Pretty much. They didn't like Carl, either, if it's any consolation. Nor do they like Porcupine. She's a pain."

Claire's mouth gaped open for a moment.

"You call her Porcupine?"

Nancy shrugged. "A few of us do. Not to her face, of course. Don't want to make her angry. She can be a real bitch."

Claire nodded.

"Carl was the latest in a long string of incompetent principals at Midland. I guess the staff here doesn't have high hopes for you, especially—" She stopped and looked toward the door.

"Especially what?"

Nancy turned her head back toward Claire. "Nothing. Forget it."

Oh, God. They'd probably all heard about her bumbling entrance this morning. Deciding to let it drop, she said, "One other question. What was that bell for?"

"The after-school activities busses will be here in a few minutes. That's when most of the staff goes home."

On Claire's drive home she tried to keep her mind on the traffic, but thoughts kept intruding. Why hadn't she waited until morning to conduct a full-faculty meeting? She could have prepared herself better and come at it with a fresh face and renewed energy. Instead, she'd blustered her way through, and it had taken only five minutes to see no one wanted her in their school.

At home, Nanny Kate left while Claire was still hugging Marcus. He squirmed when she hugged him a fraction longer than he wanted. She released him, and he hopped and twirled across the living room floor in a silly dance he called his froggy gyro.

"I know you're probably hungry. Unfortunately, I really need a quick shower before dinner. You don't look as if you're starving."

Marcus laughed and wrinkled his nose. "You need one, Mommy. Yucky smoke."

"I'll only be a few minutes. Are you going to continue dancing or shall I put something on the telly for you?"

"Telly? TV, silly." He picked up a toy car and rolled it along a make-believe road on the wood floor in the entryway. "Zoom-zoom."

She locked her front door, latched both deadbolts, and double-checked the windows to make sure they were secure in case the nanny had opened one.

After her shower, Claire cooked dinner and tried to forget about work. Listening to Marcus chatter while they ate, made her smile, and she finally felt some of her tension dissipate. Even cleaning up the kitchen helped lighten her mood. After she finished that task, she slumped onto the sofa and listened to the six o'clock news. Although today's high was forty-three degrees, tomorrow's temperature was expected to reach only twenty-three, with a chance for flurries. Claire winced. A twenty degree drop in temperature—and snow. Snow in the high country this early in the season was typical she had heard, but here in the Denver Basin? She groaned, thinking this was not going to be an easy winter.

At Marcus's bedtime, she carried him into his bedroom piggy back style, with him giggling all the way. His pale gold walls, or his 'happy color' as he'd called it when he picked it out at the hardware store three days ago, made her smile. They'd gone shopping for his new quilt, and she'd suggested one with dinosaurs. He'd shaken his head and reached for a light yellow one with daisies and butterflies. 'I can have summer all the time,' he'd said, grinning from ear to ear.

She helped Marcus change into his pajamas and drew back his quilt. He climbed into bed and she sat on a bedside chair and read the next chapter in his Harry Potter book, their new nightly ritual. She closed the book, kissed his cheek, and said, "Goodnight, sweetie."

"Goodnight Mommy." He gave her a goofy smile that made her wonder what he was thinking.

"I forgot to ask you earlier. What did you do today?"

"Watched Sesame Street. And Nanny Kate read of my story books."

"Did you have a good time?"

He nodded, and pulled his covers up to his chin, and then his face crinkled. He cocked his head alerting her that something was amiss.

"Do I need to look for a different nanny?"

"I dunno." He bit his lip and said, "She won't play alphabet game. It's easy. Take turns. Make words startin' with same con . . .so . . . nants, in alpha order. She said I pulled her leg. I didn't touch her."

"You know, most kids don't know about letters or consonants until they start school. Nanny Kate's here to look after you, keep you safe. She's not a teacher."

"But I wanna learn. She says little kids can't read. I wanna read my story books to her. I think I can. I know my letters and sounds."

Claire smiled and patted his soft brown hair. "I know you do. I'll talk to her. Soon."

"She thinks I'm a baby." He shook his head vehemently.

"Of course you aren't. She's just getting to know you. It takes time."

He pouted. Oh, please not a tantrum. Not that he had many. But he had them often enough. Tonight, she didn't have the energy to deal with that. "For now, Marcus, why don't you try reading them to me?"

His face lit up and he discarded his covers and jumped off the bed. "Now? I get book."

"Oh, no you don't. You and I both need to sleep. Tomorrow night, I promise. Right after dinner, you can read to me."

"Okay," he said. His shoulders slumped, and then he crawled back under his covers and sighed.

How easy it would be to indulge him, especially considering her guilt about whisking him away from his home so often. The problem with reading to him now was that once he became immersed in a book, he'd get over excited and wouldn't be able to sleep. He might not need the sleep, but she certainly did.

She reached out and hugged Marcus. "I love you," she said and then switched off the light and pulled the door closed, and then rechecked the locks on the front door again, the way she did every day. Back in the living room, she picked up her mobile phone and flipped between the phone number listings that would connect her to several of her so-called protectors. Then, remembering Brad's words from her first day in Denver, she set her phone down and went to bed.

CHAPTER THREE

STEVE JENSEN RUBBED his temples to ward off a headache. After reading the fifth weekly report from the district's high school principals, he looked through yesterday's emails for the last one—the one from Midland High. Huh? Nothing. Had he deleted it by mistake? He grimaced, then picked up the telephone receiver to call Carl Robinson. As he punched in the third digit, he remembered why no one had sent a report. Carl had quit two weeks earlier. The Assistant Principal didn't know how to prepare the report, and the new principal had only started work yesterday. *Man, I need more coffee. Not awake enough.* He shook his head. What did that say about those five reports he'd just read? Sometimes he really hated this job; actually that was more often than he liked to admit. He'd come to work for this district, thinking he could make a difference. Instead, most of what he did was put out fires, attend meetings, and deal with bureaucrats.

The thought of Carl Robinson and hating jobs reminded him of the last phone call he'd received from the man.

"We've got big trouble," an unidentified caller said. "Better get over here. Now!"

"Huh? Over here? Where? Who is this?

Distracted by the caller, Steve didn't notice the traffic light change to red until he was about to enter the intersection. He slammed on his brakes and screeched to a stop, then sighed in relief that no one was behind him, until he noticed that the abrupt stop had caused his full coffee cup to tumble out of the cup holder. Damn, he muttered. Hot coffee covered the leather car seat and the floor of the car. Fortunately, only a small amount had splashed onto his suit pant leg.

He dabbed the spot on his suit with napkins leftover from his fast-food breakfast. The larger spills would have to wait.

In the background on the hands-free telephone he heard noises, but no one had answered his questions. "Are you still there?" he asked the caller.

"I won't be for long," the man snapped. "I've had enough of this hell-hole you call a school. Now get your ass moving."

Carl Robinson. He should have known. Who else would talk like that to their boss? He opened his mouth to say something scathing, then decided to wait until he had more details of the situation. "Am I to assume you're asking me for help?"

"Damn right. You administrators sit on your rear-ends in your cushy offices and leave the rest of us to do the dirty work. It's about time you got into the trenches yourself."

Steve clinched his jaw. Carl was an irascible man in his late sixties who, over the past two years, had caused a dozen of his employees to file complaints against him for his leadership skills, or lack thereof. But neither Steve nor the school board could fire Carl, even though the man had been the major cause of the deterioration of his school. Who else would want Carl's job now that the school was a disaster?

"Okay, Carl. Calm down and tell me what's going on."

"Same kind of garbage that always goes on here. You know what I'm talking about. If I'd called and told you we'd gotten a mysterious note or letter from some punk threatening to blow someone away like those kids at Columbine, you'd jump into action. But blatant acts of violence you ignore. I'm sick of drug dealers, gangs, and juvenile delinquents."

"I don't ignore Midland's problems. I'm trying to hire security guards and buy surveillance cameras. Even metal detectors. It takes time. Money, too. School hasn't even been in session two weeks. Bear with me."

"Bear with me, bear with me. And what do you mean two weeks? We had the same damn problem last school year. What am I supposed to do? Wait until the bastards kill somebody."

"It isn't easy to get the school board to agree on anything, especially when we're talking about huge outlays of cash, which we don't have, as you well know. I'm doing the best I can."

"Right. Just the same old runaround."

"Take it easy. Tell me what happened. Did a student try to kill someone? Or even threaten to? Because, I've gotta tell you, I haven't heard any reports like that. Everything you've told me has been worrisome, yes, but nothing that's called for immediate action."

"Oh, so having hoodlums break into the building before school and trash my office isn't drastic enough to warrant immediate action? I caught them in the act and chased after them, swinging my briefcase like a machete."

Steve sighed and rubbed his forehead. "You could have started off this conversation with that information." He shook his head in disbelief. "Anyway, I'm in my car. I'll be there in twenty minutes."

"Hey, you're early!" someone said, pulling Steve out of his memory. He looked up to see Frank Lawrence leaning into his office. Frank was one of the assistant superintendents, and the one whom Steve trusted the most.

"Yeah, I need to catch up," Steve said, "and I have a committee meeting shortly. Yesterday I had no time for anything and had to skip lunch again. Fire-fighting as usual. Sometimes I wonder why I stay in this job. Certainly not because it's a kick-back kind of job. What's on your schedule today?" He picked up his coffee cup and sipped his now tepid coffee.

Frank said, "I've got a pile of paperwork to take care of, but I think I'll drive over to Midland High first. I heard from Helen Jackson that the new principal started work yesterday. Have you met her yet?"

"Oh, yes, I met her."

Frank raised his eyebrows. "And? What'd you think?"

"Damned if I know. She's nice on the eyes. But there's something fishy. I haven't decided if it's her or the school board."

"What do you mean?"

Steve hesitated. Normally, he would be careful talking with employees, but Frank wasn't like most employees. He was a life-long friend. Steve and Frank had grown up together in California and Steve had helped his friend get this job because he knew Frank was someone he could trust. "This is between the two of us, okay?"

Frank nodded.

"Do you know who the new principal is? Did Helen fill you in?"

"She gave me a name. That's all."

Steve smiled and leaned forward. "Well, you know I was pissed when the board bypassed my hiring committee and took on a new employee, a teacher from out of state, without explanation. I told you about that, didn't I?" He paused, and Frank nodded. "It turns out they went and offered her the principal position. They didn't say a damned word to me. I found out when Helen introduced us. I remembered the name."

"Holy cow! What are you going to do?"

"Not much I can do. But I need to find out more about her. Let me know what you think about her after you meet her."

CLAIRE PARKED IN the faculty car park and walked around the left side of the building as she'd done yesterday, this time observing the school's grounds: weeds, trash, grass unmowed, graffiti on the walls. She looked at the overgrown bushes abutting the building and wondered how many dirty needles might she find dumped behind them? Did she even want to know? An equally disturbing thought entered her head: this was a perfect hiding place for a mugging. As she reached the front of the building, where there weren't any bushes, she relaxed. A red leaf dropped onto her shoulder, brushing her cheek, and she glanced up. The tall oak's leaves glistened as they twisted in the breeze and the crisp air whipped her hair into her eyes, reminding her of autumns in England.

Forget about the past and your home, she told herself. But when she stood facing the four-story building, she could almost imagine ivy, and believe this was Balliol College. It was a long time since she'd been in Oxford. She shook herself and continued walking, studying the building. A lovely ornate Clock Tower featuring the signs of the zodiac around the dial, beginning with Aries at one o'clock and running anticlockwise, was inset in the brick near the roofline above the entrance. An equally lovely ornate doorframe surrounded the main entrance. Not something she would have expected here. But looks were quite often deceiving, she thought with a wry smile. Directly above the doorway, an elegantly engraved plate bore the date "1935". *This must have been a lovely school at one time.*

She paused. She didn't know what hiding places there might be around the other side of the building. Around the corner, an indentation in shrubbery caught her eye. Cautiously she approached it and was surprised to find an overgrown courtyard guarded by four winged lions. The lions were mostly hidden by vines and weeds, and the ground itself was littered with empty soda cans and beer bottles. *This garden must have been lovely back in the early days—like a cozy little terrace.*

Claire headed back to the main entrance and dug the key ring out of her handbag. After several attempts with different keys, she opened the door and entered. The door swung rapidly closed behind her with a deafening crash, making her jump. *Well, I guess the closing mechanism needs some work. Must be more careful in future until I have it fixed.*

All was hushed in the dark entrance hall, when suddenly a radiator began to hiss and rattle, making her jump again. Moments later, it quieted to a murmur as it began pumping warmth into the hallway. Searching the entry area in the dark, she lucked out and found a light panel, opened it, and flipped the switches. As the fluorescents illuminated her way, she appraised the dingy scene around her. The walls, originally painted off-white, had deteriorated over the years to a dirty yellowish gray. The dark brown industrial vinyl tiles on the floor were dull and filmy. Old and plain. No color. Nothing inviting. But then she turned around and there was a large colorful mural covering the front wall on either side and above the entry doors. Peeling paint, cracking and faded colors in a few places gave evidence that it was probably painted years ago, perhaps when the school was first built.

She walked up to the second story and arrived at a long hallway lined with lockers in graffiti-covered gray metal. Some of them looked as if someone had beaten them with baseball bats.

The corridor was ghostly quiet, except for the clicking of her own high-heels on the linoleum. Trying several classroom doors and finding them locked, she peeked through the narrow windows in a couple rooms. More of the same dilapidated dinginess. She came across a wide set of concrete stairs leading to the third story and as she climbed, she noted at least one place where the railing was loose, requiring immediate attention.

Continuing on to the fourth floor, she was unable to shake that feeling someone was following her. Chills trickled down her spine, and she spun around to look, but could find no one.

Get a grip, Juliet! You aren't a little girl frightened of the dark, checking for monsters under the bed.

Still, she couldn't shake the feeling and ended up dashing down the three flights of stairs bound for the safety, if you could call it that, of her office. Once inside, she looked around and picked up a file folder marked budget reports. Far off she heard the front door bang again. A glance at her watch told her it was still too early for teachers and students. Probably nothing. Forget about it. But when she tried to resume her work, her ears were prepped and then she heard another sound. Was it the door to the admin office?

She felt her heart pounding. Should she sit here and wait, or investigate? She closed her eyes momentarily, then stood and walked over to peer into the corridor. No one in sight. Thinking Ron might have come in early, she stepped into his office. Empty. As she turned round she collided with something—with someone. She gasped as large hands grabbed her by the shoulder. Her mind told her to pull away and run, but instead, she turned her head and looked up at a man, unsure what she expected to see. Claire gasped again. "Who—who are you?"

"Sorry. Didn't mean to scare you. I'm Frank Lawrence, one of the district's assistant superintendents. I'm your supervisor. Thought I should stop by and meet you."

"Oh lord, you gave me a start." Claire exhaled and bit her lip, studying him momentarily. He wore a brown suit with a beige dress-shirt and had hair the color of a sandy beach with a hint of gray, pale blue eyes, slim build and around mid-forties—not a threatening sort of guy at all. She knew looks could be deceiving, though, and with people hunting for her, she couldn't take any chances.

"I—I'm sorry to ask, but I need to see your district I.D. badge." She resisted the urge to look away so he wouldn't see her embarrassment over asking her boss to prove his identity.

He chuckled and unbuttoned his suit jacket, then grabbed hold of the lanyard holding his I.D. badge and displayed it for her.

Claire read his name and verified the photo. Relaxing a bit more, she said, "Thanks. I guess I don't need to introduce myself. Obviously you already know who I am."

He nodded and gave a lopsided smile.

"I'm glad you aren't a vandal. After reading and hearing about the problems here, one can't be too cautious."

"Ah, you must've heard what happened here the morning Carl Robinson quit. It can be scary working in this place alone. Guess I should've called first, let you know I was coming. I'm glad to see you haven't abandoned ship quite yet."

"I'll be here until someone throws me overboard." She smiled with false bravado.

He laughed and stuck his hands in his pockets. "What's on your agenda for today?"

"I've assigned myself the task of getting familiar with this place."

"Can I help? Answer any questions? I'd be happy to share with you the school's history, if you're interested."

"I would love that. You're the first person around here to volunteer information and sound friendly. We should go to my office. It'll be more comfortable there."

He followed her and sat down in a chair facing her desk. "I'm probably the easiest guy in the district to get along with. Funny, laid-back, goofy. People call me a big ham."

She smiled. "That's cute, and much better than being called a turkey. I've worked with a few of those."

Frank chuckled again. "We're gonna get along well together, I can already tell."

She joined in his laughter.

"So, where do you want to start?" Frank asked.

"Uh, well, I've noticed teachers, and even principals, seem to come and go at an alarming rate around here."

Frank gave a sheepish smile. "Guess no one told you that being assigned to this school isn't exactly a prize."

Claire struggled to keep her face blank.

"Mostly, it's gang activity, drugs, and general lack of enthusiasm among the students that chases away the good employees. It's kind of a Catch-22. When faculty and administrators don't care enough to motivate these kids, you know, make them believe they can make a difference in their own lives, the kids drop out of school, the good employees leave, and it goes round and round."

"None of that is particularly uncommon in inner-city schools. But doesn't the school district do anything to help, such as provide training to teachers so they can better reach these kids?"

Frank nodded. "We do, but it's useless if the teachers don't care."

"Are all your schools like this?"

"No, not at all; most are good. Midland's pretty much an outlier, in terms of violence and in test scores."

"Violence?"

"Oh, nothing as bad as Columbine has occurred here," he said, waving his arms and speaking faster. "Didn't mean to alarm you. You'll see fights, threats, and bullying in school. Get familiar with lockdown procedures. Most of the gang violence occurs off campus in the neighborhoods, on the streets. I wouldn't suggest going for a long stroll around here."

"Why isn't the school equipped with metal detectors and security cameras? Wouldn't those deter trouble? Or does this school not need them?"

He shrugged. "I don't have a good answer for you. I'm not in charge of that area. I supervise the high school principals."

"Haven't the administrators considered security measures? Steve Jensen made it sound like this school has many issues." *Good grief, don't I have enough safety concerns of my own?*

"You'll have to talk to Steve about that. I know he's been trying to get more security here, however, it's a hot-button issue."

"Why is that?"

He shrugged. "Don't quote me, but the logical guess is money. The school board controls things around here. You might have sensed it if you'd interviewed with them."

An awkward silence filled the air. She thought about Brad Meyers and his boss. "I thought there was a hiring committee. Your HR Manager told me. The school board doesn't interview candidates, do they?"

"Well, no." Frank folded his arms. "Not the whole board. The board president and another board member are on the hiring committee, as is Steve."

"Oh, I didn't know," she said, suddenly understanding the slight edge in Steve's attitude toward her yesterday. She looked away, and fidgeted with the top button of her suit jacket. "I met the Superintendent briefly yesterday," she said. "Would you advise I arrange a longer meeting with him?"

"Not necessary. In a week and a half Steve will hold his bi-weekly round table luncheon. This one will be at Cameron High

School. He'll be there, along with a couple of the school board members, and the six high school principals. You'll get an email from him."

Claire nodded.

"Have you explored the building yet?"

"Yes," Claire said, "I started to, but haven't seen all of it." She wasn't lying. She just wasn't going to admit she'd let her imagination scare her half to death and had hidden back in her office.

"Well, if you want, I can show you around."

"Or I can."

Claire and Frank spun around to see who had spoken. Frank looked surprised, then grinned. "Hey, what are you doing here, Steve? I thought you were meeting with your new committee."

Steve Jensen said, "I did. Now it's your turn."

"What?"

Steve laughed. "Change of plans. We decided you'd be the best administrator for that committee, so I came to switch places with you."

Claire bit her lip.

Frank raised one eyebrow. "You're kidding, right?"

"Afraid not."

"Gee thanks, friend," Frank said. "Sounds like someone didn't wanna be on that committee."

Steve grinned. "RHIP, buddy."

"Okay, where's the meeting?"

After Frank left, Steve said, "I'm somewhat acquainted with Midland. Come on, I'll show you around."

Claire took a deep calming breath. Keep your attention focused, she told herself.

She was compelled to peek at him out of the corner of her eyes as they walked. He was more attractive than she remembered from the day before, and still as casual in corduroy black trousers and cream polo shirt, with a burgundy sweater over it. He was taller than she remembered, too, perhaps six feet tall, trim and well-groomed although something about him reminded her of a woolly teddy bear—perhaps his brown hair, beard, and mustache, combined with his semi-gruff voice.

When they reached the main hall, Steve said, "At one time this hall was open to a South Courtyard similar to the courtyard on the side, the one with lions."

"Oh yes, I saw that one."

"Great hangout for drug deals," he said. "Gotta keep an eye on that area."

She thought, 'yes, and a great place for a hired assassin to hide out'. She said, "Should we close it off?"

"Probably wouldn't do much good unless you seal it up with concrete."

At the unexpected comment, she turned her head to look at him askance. He was watching her and grinning, which made her laugh.

He said, "The auditorium originally had windows looking into the hall. They've been bricked and plastered over, and pieces of statuary adorning various rooms have been removed."

"I wish I'd seen it back then."

"I know what you mean. I wasn't here, either, but I've seen photographs. Midland's gone through many changes, such as reorganizing space, for one. Most of these changes occurred decades ago. The front of the second floor was originally planned as a teachers' lunchroom. Insufficient funds made it necessary to use it as a study hall instead. Later, the study hall was lost too when it had to be divided into three much needed classrooms."

Steve stopped a moment and physically backtracked, then turned and led her down a different corridor. By now, the faculty was beginning to arrive for work and teachers were unlocking classroom doors. "Sorry. Even though I know the school fairly well, I still get a little lost now and then."

He stopped once more and looked at her face, his eyes locking on hers. Her first impulse was to look away. Feeling as though he was testing her, she held her head up and waited. He was better at it, though, and she finally gave in and looked away, down the hall, hoping he would start walking again.

He did.

They entered a large gym. Steve said, "The original gym, built back in the late fifties was larger and had a balcony allowing for spectator basketball games. In the early eighties, the boys' and girls' Locker rooms were enlarged, eating up a portion of the gym. Around that same time, the balcony was enclosed and turned into ROTC offices."

She absorbed the information without comment. They walked upstairs and peeked into a few classrooms, greeting teachers who were polite yet distant.

On their way back to her office, Steve said, "Unfortunately, while general building maintenance has been performed, major repairs such as replacing inefficient heaters and classroom equipment have been on hold." He looked at his watch. "Students will be arriving any minute. I wish I could stay and talk more. Unfortunately, you'll be busy and I'm supposed to meet with another principal in half an hour. I'll stop by again in a few days. If you need us, don't hesitate to call me or Frank Lawrence. He's the assistant superintendent who will supervise you."

"Thanks, Steve." She tilted her head. "You've made me feel more welcome here. I wasn't sure yesterday . . . ."

"Yeah, sorry about that. I've had time to think about it. Maybe someone young and full of energy is what this school needs." He turned to leave, glancing back, and smiled.

Claire smiled back, then turned and started walking toward the administrative office. Halfway there, the first warning bell of the morning rang. *Hmm, might be a good opportunity to see how this all works.* She changed direction, walking over to a window, and stood watching the students clamor off the lined-up busses. Some students came straight into the building, but many milled around, visiting with friends. When the second bell rang, more students came in. By the third bell, it seemed like most students were inside the building, though judging from what she'd seen yesterday, she suspected some still lingered outside.

She turned and watched the students inside. The entry hall and corridor were bustling with activity now: people pushing and shoving, locks on lockers clicking, locker doors opening and closing, voices buzzing loudly. Chaos. The halls quieted as students and teachers dispersed to their classrooms and the last bell rang.

She turned back to the window. As she'd guessed, at least a dozen students stood around in clusters outside; well, a dozen that she could see from her position. Nearly all of them wore orange bandanas and sported tattoos. Unlike yesterday, she now knew these bandanas were worn by the toughest gang in the school. Somehow she would have to figure out what to do about them, though not today.

The fourth and final bell rang, telling everyone that classes were in session. Instead of going back to her office straight away, she walked back upstairs and looked in the first open door. Students were sitting around chatting, some laughing. Others had ear buds sticking out of their ears and MP3 players in their laps or lying on their desks. Where was the teacher? Claire let her gaze move around the room until it landed on Bob Lewis, a teacher. He was sitting at his desk in the front left corner of the class, his legs stretched out and his feet resting on the edge of the desk. He was reading a magazine.

Claire gritted her teeth and moved to the next room. This one was worse. Students were out of control: throwing paper airplanes, tossing insults, flipping chairs around like balls. The teacher was shouting and waving her arms, but they ignored her.

In the next classroom, the teacher was speaking about Shakespeare and two students were actually discussing Hamlet with him. Several other students appeared to be listening, while others doodled on paper or typed messages on their mobile phones.

Oh dear. Clearly the students aren't the only problem here.

She turned and started walking back to the administration office. Inside the outer office, several students were sitting in chairs. "How may I help you?" she asked.

"I'm here for the nurse," a girl said. She didn't look like she was in dire need of assistance, so Claire went on to the next student.

"We're waiting for Mr. Baker," a boy said, motioning toward his buddies.

Claire nodded and started toward her office.

"You Ms. Constantine?"

"Yes." Claire looked around her to ascertain who had spoken. A middle-aged woman whom she didn't recognize was staring at her.

"You have the Keoghs in your office."

Claire frowned. "What are Key-os?"

"Mr. and Mrs. Keogh." The woman sighed theatrically. "They're here about their son, he was thro— told to leave the class yesterday.

"Right. Right. She looked at her office door, then back at the woman. "So, what would be the best thing with them . . . ?"

She held out a file. "This is sweet little Donny's rap sheet. He's okay, but talks, you know?" She shrugged. "The parents are okay. They like to let off steam. Talk nice, promise them he'll be back, they'll promise he'll behave, you'll both agree he's a good kid at heart."

"All right." Claire glanced at the file in her hands, then looked back up at the woman. "Who are you? I haven't seen you before. I mean, obviously, you work here, but . . . ."

"Oh, I took the day off yesterday. Name's Kim Wallace. I'm your secretary."

Thank God, thought Claire. She wasn't completely on her own. "Nice to meet you, Kim."

As soon as Claire finished with the Keoghs, a gym teacher whom Claire had met during the tour with Steve barged into her office.

"God damn students poured grease from the kitchen all over the gym floor mats."

"Are you serious?" Claire said. "How did they get the grease? Are students allowed in the kitchen?"

"How the hell should I know? I only came in here to tell you that you've got a problem."

During the next two hours, Claire rounded up the students and instructed Kim to call their parents, while the gym teacher and custodial staff cleaned up the mess. After that, Claire spent time talking with parents. After things calmed down, Claire sat at her desk, behind her closed door, and browsed through more files. Two hours into reviewing files she came upon a report from Steve about setting goals for the district. She read it, and then her mind wandered to thoughts of Steve. Despite his apparent doubts about her, she'd taken to him at once. No doubt he was attractive, and he also seemed . . . kind. That meant he was probably married. Weren't all the good ones taken? Oh, good grief! What am I doing? Maybe the loneliness is finally getting to me. Enough of this, she told herself. *He's too old for you, but more importantly, he's your boss and you don't need complications. Don't be a total moron!*

She gritted her teeth and forced herself back into reading faculty meeting minutes, browsing school yearbooks and reports, and by late afternoon a clearer picture of the school emerged, unfortunately an utterly abysmal picture. The irony wasn't lost on her: she'd done everything she'd been told to do so that she could protect herself and her son, and now it seemed she'd ended up in a den of drugs, gangs, and violence.

Claire was interrupted from her thoughts when Kim stuck her head in the office.

"Ms. Constantine, I have two students here to see you. Mr. Owens sent them with referrals slips."

The boys hesitated. Claire motioned for them to enter, and they shuffled toward her and handed her their referral slips. She glanced at the names, then looked at them and said, "Sit down boys."

They looked young. One was tall and lanky, hair styled in dreadlocks. The other was average height and sported a buzz haircut. Neither had tattoos that she could see, and neither wore the gang bandanas she'd seen other students wearing. "Are you freshmen?"

"No way. Sophomores," the tall boy said, puffing out his chest.

She nodded. "So why are you here? Why did Mr. Owens expel you from class?"

"We didn't do nuttin' wrong," the shorter boy said. "We get good grades. Don't cause no problems."

"Which one are you, Le Roy or Curtis?"

"Huh? Oh, I'm Le Roy," the shorter boy said.

"What did Mr. Owens accuse you of doing this time?"

The boys exchanged glances. Curtis, answered. "He said we was disrupting the class."

"What was happening in class?"

They squirmed and poked each other, then Le Roy said, "Teacher was talking 'bout boring junk. You know, triangles,

44

polygons, quadrilaterals. Oh, and circles and circumferences and diameters. What are we gonna do with that stuff?"

"And what were you doing during this boring speech?"

"Nuttin'. Just sittin' like I told you."

Claire resisted the urge to sigh. It was like talking to a typical five year old.

A mobile phone rang, and Le Roy pulled it out of his trouser pocket, looked to see who was calling, and then answered.

Claire hopped up from behind her desk and snatched the phone from his hand.

"Hey, that's my phone!"

She turned it off and placed it in her top drawer. "We're having a discussion. You can pick this up after school. Now, you will tell me what you were doing during Mr. Owens's lecture."

The boys stared at her with mouths gaping open. Finally, Curtis said, "We was only clowning around. Making shapes with our bodies. You know, trying to look like triangles, pyramids, circles. Everybody laughed, said math was less boring in 3D."

Claire shook her head and tried to keep her face blank. "You said you get good grades in math. Is that correct?"

They nodded their heads.

She turned to her computer and brought up Le Roy's record and then Curtis's from the previous school year since grades weren't posted yet for this semester. Both had received 'A's' in Algebra. "All right. For now I'm placing you on detention. I'll speak with Mr. Owens and decide whether further discipline is warranted. You're dismissed."

They left, and she smiled. At least they aren't all incorrigible. Maybe there's hope yet.

Another hour at work, and she could finally go home.

AFTER DINNER SHE gave Marcus his bath and toweled him off. "Time for bed, my love." She expected a fuss. Instead, he ran into his bedroom, naked and giggling. By the time she reached his room, he was half dressed in his pajamas.

"My, my, you're getting to be a big kid. I didn't know you could dress yourself so quickly."

"I gotta do it fast. You said I can try to read tonight." He picked up one of his books and climbed into bed.

CHAPTER FOUR

CALLUM FULLER LAY on his motel bed, TV remote control in hand, fingers repeatedly flicking the channel button until he came across a National Geographic program. It wasn't the sort of show he usually viewed, but he needed something to take his mind off problems. Watching animals in the wild, he figured, was better than watching cop shows with car chase scenes. He'd had enough of that in real life lately, most recently being last week when the police had spotted him leaving a train station in Chicago. He'd barely avoided capture.

Twenty minutes into the show, a mother lion was fighting to protect her cub from a large snake, and failing. Callum's shoulders tensed. Just what he needed—a reminder that his son was out there somewhere without his father to protect him. Callum avoided thinking about that. It did little good and it caused him to question his decisions and life choices. Juliet, undoubtedly, was a good mother. When it came to Aidan, she was the lioness. But when it came to the dangers of real life, she was more of a kitten.

The door to the motel room burst open, making Callum jump and nearly fall off the bed. He righted himself and then reached for the gun under his pillow. He wasn't fast enough.

Two large men stood with their backs to the window and with their guns aimed at him.

Bloody hell. He recognized them—Eddie West and Doug Fray. They worked for the Boss, Regg Kincaid.

"What are you doing here?" Callum asked.

"The woman. Your wife. Where's Juliet?"

"How the bloody hell should I know? And she isn't my wife. We were living together. She ran off and took my kid with her. Haven't seen her in ten months."

"Yeah, and I'm the pizza man. Don't lie. You're covering for her, and Regg is losing patience. I don't have to tell you what that means, do I?"

Callum ran his hand through his hair. Regg had been threatening to cut him out of the operation ever since Juliet had disappeared. Sometimes, Callum wanted out more than anything. Problem was he knew Regg pretty well. When he cut someone out, he usually meant it literally—as in, cut out his heart and delivered it to the next of kin. Even though Regg was in police custody, awaiting trial, his power hadn't decreased one bit. Callum wasn't that desperate to quit the syndicate.

As for Juliet, Callum truly didn't know where she had gone. He'd tried to find her himself and was still looking. If he found her, he didn't know what he'd do, but he didn't like the way they'd left things between them. And he certainly didn't like that he couldn't see his own son. A boy needed his father.

"Juliet won't help you anymore. You're wasting your time looking."

"We don't need her to help, moron. She's a loose cannon. She knows too much about our operation."

"I. Don't. Know. Where. She. Is. Got it?"

"Find her. Else next time we might be charging an arm or leg for your next pizza delivery."

"Hey, Eddie, you just made a funny joke."

"Shut up, Doug. Let's go."

Callum smashed his hand into the motel room wall after the thugs left.

ON THE DRIVE to work the next morning, Claire checked the rearview mirror frequently to make sure she wasn't being followed. After almost being killed once by a sniper back in Boston, she couldn't be too careful. *Ha, maybe hiding out in a den of delinquent students isn't as bad as I first thought. The people who want me dead wouldn't think to look there, would they?*

As she drove, she tried to mentally review her schedule for the day. Although she had no planned meetings, if the past two days were any indication, she could expect parents, students, teachers, or administrators to drop in for impromptu meetings. Definitely different from life at University where meetings were always scheduled in advance, and only during certain hours.

She arrived at work and was at her desk by half past six. As usual, her phone had a red light blinking on it which meant she had messages. She listened to those, took notes, and then read through the emails she hadn't had time to read the day before. Many of those were requests for meetings with parents or teachers, so meetings for next week were filling up rapidly.

Her last email, probably the most important, was from Steve Jensen. The message told her that all of the district's high school principals, the HR Manager, one of the assistant superintendents, and two of the school board members, including President John Richmond, were invited to the Superintendent's Bi-Weekly Luncheon Meeting. She stared at the screen momentarily and then leaned back in her chair. So, in a week-and-a-half she would finally meet the board President. Was that a good or a bad thing? She jotted a note in her appointment calendar to be sure she didn't miss it—if she was here that long—because although it said 'invited' the wording left no doubt that everyone was expected to attend.

By Monday Claire was falling into a routine. She checked her messages first thing, made coffee, and did as much of her paperwork as possible before teachers and secretaries arrived between a quarter past seven. From then until the third morning bell, it was chaotic with teachers using the copy machine, phones ringing, and teachers demanding to see her. She tried to leave the door open so they could come in as they pleased, except kept it closed when she had a meeting or was handling something that needed to be done immediately. This morning Nancy Palmer stopped by.

"I have some notes for you for tomorrow's advisory meeting."

"What advisory meeting?" Claire asked as she took the paper Nancy was offering.

"The Speech teacher, George Bryant, and I chair the Debate team's advisory meeting. The principal attends our meetings. Didn't you know?"

"Uh. No. I didn't see anything about that in the records I've read. Didn't know you had a debate team. When do you meet?"

"Every other Friday after school."

"All right. Thanks. I'll read this over and get back to you."

After Nancy left and Claire finished reading the notes, she did a quick walkabout. She was beginning to dread them because she invariably saw problems she didn't know how to solve.

On Wednesday, one week on the new job, Claire sat in a Subway restaurant eating lunch with her supervisor, Frank Lawrence.

"Sad to say, it's like a reform school run amok," she said. She rolled her eyes and took a sip of her tea. "Yesterday, we caught students flushing paper cups, drinking straws, and plastic spoons and forks down toilets in a boys' room on the second floor. It's unusable until we get a plumber."

"Damn," Frank said, shaking his head. He took a big bite out of his submarine sandwich.

"Oh, and this morning, someone carpeted the fourth-floor corridor with toilet paper. The entire corridor end to end."

Frank grinned and wiped his mouth. "Huh. Inventive. At least that's harmless. You know kids. They think it's cool to teepee. Pretty common, I'm afraid, though they usually do it to other kids' homes and with their own rolls of toilet paper. Can't say I've seen it inside a school. I don't like it, but I've gotta give them credit for creativity."

Claire had taken to Frank immediately when he turned up on her third day; a comfortable, slightly untidy man with a lopsided smile and a good sense of humor.

"I think they used up a two months' supply of toilet paper."

"On the bright side, they could have sprayed graffiti over the entire building, then teepeed the hall. You're lucky."

"How comforting." Claire took a bite of food.

Frank sipped his soda and studied her with such intensity that Claire wondered if he was trying to read her mind.

"Sorry." She looked down at her sandwich on the table and said, "I'm complaining too much."

"Not at all. That's what I'm here for. To listen, to help. Let it out. I've found that principals need to vent, especially those in such cushy jobs." He smiled. "So come on. Vent. Talk to me."

It could be a trap. Supervisors did that sometimes. Talk nice. Get you to let down your guard, then bite with a snake's venom. But Frank seemed genuine. Her spirits were low, frustration level high. Who else would listen to her grumbling? No one cared, not even the Superintendent, if his lack of follow-up was any indication. Frank, though, had shown up and whisked her away from the school where she wouldn't be sucked back into the dramas.

"You're right. There is something." She hesitated, then whispered, "It's hard to admit this to anyone, especially my supervisor. After only one week on the job I already have to force myself to come to work. Am I a terrible employee?"

Frank smiled and said, "Yep." Claire stared at him. He smiled, then became serious. "No, Claire, everybody goes through at least some of that. Me included. Not every day. But then I don't work at Midland."

"There are daily student fights. Most teachers stand by and watch. Only a few step in to break them up. One of these days somebody's going to get seriously hurt." She sighed, pushing wayward strands of hair out of her eyes. "And then there's the constant bullying."

She paused, took another sip of tea. "Not only do the teachers let it continue, but some also have shoved each other or argued with one another right in front of students. I've seen it happen. They're supposed to set good examples. It's taking all of my self-control not to scream 'Grow up' to all of them. Students and teachers."

"Maybe you should," Frank said. "Don't be so polite. Be tough. Don't go postal, of course. Remember, these students and teachers need to be reined in. Disciplined. Sometimes a bit of fire and brimstone are necessary. It's about time someone with guts let them have it."

"Huh?"

"Look, you can't win a war without fighting. Give 'em hell, but stay in control of your actions. And remember, I'm here. You can call me whenever you need support. Or when you need someone to listen."

And he did listen. For an hour, he let her vent, offering advice when he could. His manner was so relaxed, his comments coming at the right times, and showing unwavering interest and compassion, that Claire came away feeling like she'd gone through a counseling session. Frank talked, too, about his longtime friendship with Steve Jensen and about his own family. It was the first time anyone in the school district had engaged her in a real conversation without causing her anxiety.

However, the following day, Claire's spirit hit a new low. After her worst morning yet, she sat at her desk scoffing down a sandwich between emergencies. The day had begun with a fire that students had deliberately set in a storage closet. It went downhill from there.

Her phone rang, and she groaned. *Don't answer it. Whoever it is can leave a message.*

But when she heard Steve Jensen's voice on the answering machine, she picked up.

"How's your day going?"

She sighed. Did he already know? Had Frank told Steve about their talk? Why else would he call now?

"Well, I've had better. I'm having one of those days, the kind where you wish you'd stayed in bed even if that meant you were sick as a dog. It's pretty bad when I'd rather have the flu or food poisoning than come to work."

"Hmm, I've had those days, myself. Believe me." He chuckled.

"I guess I shouldn't complain. Things will get better. The first weeks on a new job are always hard, aren't they?"

"Absolutely. It takes time." After a brief pause, he said, "Hey, the reason I'm calling, I got a call a few minutes ago from the police chief. I heard there was a problem at Midland."

"Uh, yes." *Which one was he referring to?* "Uh, we had a student overdose on cocaine this morning. Paramedics and police came. It was a frightening scene."

"How's the student?"

"The hospital says he'll recover."

"That's good. Anything else?"

She told him about the early morning fire and about an incident involving a BB gun. "No one was hurt in either of those."

"Did you put the school on lockdown?"

"Yes. We've been in lockdown off and on all morning. I think the student body's goal is to get the school in permanent lockdown. We finally found something they're good at."

"That's gotta be tough," Steve said. "At least you're getting the chance to perfect the procedures."

"Procedures? Should I have called you or Frank about these incidents?"

"Frank needs to know. In the future, when these things come up, give him a buzz. He'll notify me if he thinks I need to be informed."

"Right. I didn't know, but I probably would have called when I had time, anyway."

"On another subject," Steve said, "I came by the school yesterday morning. Your assistant principal told me you were in a meeting. Said he'd let you know I was there."

"He didn't say anything." *Damn, he had plenty of chances to tell me yesterday and today. So what's going on?* "I'm sorry," she said. "I would have called had I known."

"Not a problem," Steve said. "I figured you were busy."

"I'm always in some meeting," Claire said. "Never a moment to spare."

"I hear you. Same with me. When I stopped by the other day, I was on my way to a meeting. Couldn't have stayed more than a few minutes anyway."

Steve fell silent and Claire waited. He cleared his throat but still didn't speak. Was there a problem? she wondered.

"Hey," he said finally, "the other reason I'm calling is to ask you out to dinner tomorrow night. As a casual get-acquainted meeting."

Alarm bells went off in her head.

"I normally do those over lunch. Unfortunately, as I said, my days have been crazy busy. I eat on the run most days."

She looked at the half-eaten sandwich on her desk. Until now, she had no idea how demanding public educators' jobs were. Apparently, it wasn't only Midland, judging from what Steve had just said. Life working at University hadn't always been easy, but it was a country club by comparison.

"Are you still there?" he asked, sounding concerned.

"Oh, sorry. I—uh, well . . . ."

"We could meet Saturday night instead if that works better for you."

She'd gone to lunch with Frank without any qualms. So why the hesitation with Steve? Of course the moment she asked herself that question she already knew the answer: Frank was married and had two children. He'd even talked about them during lunch. Frank was safe.

He'd also mentioned that Steve was divorced and childless.

And she was attracted to Steve.

Apparently, she waited too long to answer, because he said, "If you're uncomfortable with that, we could maybe meet at my office for an early morning coffee. I'm afraid it would have to be really early, though."

She shook her head, then felt ridiculous since he couldn't see her. Then, going against her better judgment, she found herself saying, "I guess dinner would be all right. Friday night."

"Good. I'll pick you up at your home around six-thirty."

"Uh, well, I'd rather meet you at the restaurant if you don't mind."

"Okay. Guess we have to decide where. How about the Applebee's restaurant near Central Administration? Do you know the place?"

"Sure. I mean, I haven't eaten there, but I've driven past it."

After she hung up the phone, she took a deep breath and blew it out. What was she thinking? She knew she shouldn't have agreed.

She'd worked for some men whom she wouldn't have dared go out to dinner with no matter what you called it. Covering her face with her hands, she tried to work out her reasoning. Frank had told her that he and Steve were best friends, and instinct told her Frank was a decent guy. Didn't that mean she could assume Steve was, too?

Resigned, deciding the damage was already done, she put shopping for something to wear on her list. Must make time this afternoon to go to the mall.

After school on Friday, Claire ordered a pizza for Marcus and Nanny Kate, who had agreed to stay late and watch Marcus while Claire went out.

While they ate, Claire brushed her hair, dressed in the new form-fitting black dress with a low-cut neckline and dozens of sparkles she'd bought for this occasion. Assessing herself in the mirror, she bit her lip. The dress that had seemed right when she'd tried it on in the store—she'd always been told you can't go wrong with black—now seemed too sexy. She went back to her wardrobe and pushed clothes around, desperately searching for something else. Unfortunately, other than her business suits and everyday clothes, this was it. Sitting on the edge of her bed, she sighed and put on her shoes. She grabbed her handbag from a chair and swept into the living room, plopped down on the sofa, and flipped through the TV channels to watch the news while Marcus and Kate finished pizza in the kitchen, talking and laughing. At six o'clock, she went into the kitchen and told Kate, "Please don't open the door to anyone. I'm not expecting visitors. Call me if anything comes up. I expect to be home by half past eight." Claire decided that Kate was a wise young woman, for not reminding her that they had gone over this more than once before.

When Claire arrived at the restaurant, the parking lot was full. As she was deciding what to do, a car pulled out of a space, saving her more frustration. Entering the restaurant, she spotted Steve right away. He grinned at her, and taking his lead, they took off coats and sat down in the waiting area.

After the query formalities regarding how each was doing, Steve said, "I put our names on the waiting list. They said it shouldn't take long to get a table. You look lovely, by the way."

"Thank you." She turned her head and glanced at the crowded dining room. Then, when she faced him again, she breathed a sigh of relief that he was looking at her face and smiling, instead of staring at her breasts or leering at her like so many men did.

A couple of minutes later, the hostess seated them in a cozy booth with a red and purple flowery tiffany lamp hanging overhead, gave them menus, and disappeared.

Claire gazed around the dining room and settled on two large photographs of a mountain. "I like those photos," Claire said. "They're lovely."

"That's Pike's Peak near Colorado Springs," Steve said. "You can drive your car up to the top of the mountain. It's more fun, though, to take the cog railway up."

"A cog railway?"

"Yeah, the track goes practically straight up, so it's a really steep ride to the top. A bit scary, to be honest. But a spectacular view. If you go on a clear day, you can even see Denver's skyline."

"Oh, that's sounds like fun. I must try it sometime."

They talked a bit about the sights around Denver, then during a lull in the conversation, Claire flipped through the menu. She decided on blackened fish, which Steve told her was a good choice. After they ordered their meals and an onion blossom to munch on, the waitress asked, "Can I get you some wine?"

Claire thought a glass of wine might help her relax. On second thought, this was supposed to be a business meeting, not a date. *Wine probably isn't a good idea.*

She opened her mouth to say no, but before she had a chance, Steve ordered a glass of Chardonnay for each of them.

After the waitress left, he said, "I hope that was okay with you? I probably should have asked first."

"That's okay." Claire bit her lip and looked away.

"How are you adjusting to Denver?"

"I'm getting used to it."

"Where did you move from?"

"Albuquerque, New Mexico."

"I've been there once. It was after a big rain storm. I remember mud everywhere."

She laughed.

"So, how are things going at work?" Steve asked.

"Busy. Always busy." She hesitated, then said, "I did want to ask you about something?"

"That's what I'm here for."

"I'm still concerned about security in the school. I talked to Frank about it. He said I should talk to you." Steve nodded assent. "First, I really think we need to have controlled access," she said, "such as locked doors after the start of the school day, security personnel assigned to monitor doors, and sign-in sheets for visitors. Also, is there any chance of getting cameras and metal detectors?"

Steve grimaced. "Tall order. But I am working on it. You wouldn't believe the red tape and hoops I have to jump through to get anything non-standard."

"Non-standard? You mean other schools in the metro don't have those things?"

"Not in our district. Even the Denver Public School District doesn't have metal detectors or cameras though they do have security guards and police liaison officers. Districts in other states take a tougher stance. Chicago and Palm Beach, for instance, have guards and cameras and metal detectors in all their schools." He scratched his head. "Our school board believes that if we installed those things, we'd be admitting to the public we have problems, like it wasn't already obvious."

They talked for a few minutes about the school and the district, and when that subject petered out, no one spoke. Claire hated awkward silences. She toyed with the cloth napkin resting on her lap and focused her attention on the song playing through the overhead speakers, but the noise level in the crowded restaurant made it difficult to hear the lyrics.

To her relief, Steve broke the silence. "What are you interested in outside of work? Do you have any hobbies? Special things you like to do?"

Should she tell him what she really liked to do, or should she make up something the way she'd been instructed to do? She'd read plenty of books on assorted topics, so she could fake interest in something she didn't like, couldn't she? But could she act? Better play it safe. "I guess I'm kind of boring, really," she said. "I'm an avid reader. Sometimes I feel like I've read every book ever written." She smiled and took a sip of wine. "I also play musical instruments."

Steve raised his eyebrows. "Really? So do I. Piano, for one. My mother forced me to play when I was a kid. I'm more of a guitar man now, though."

Claire smiled at that. "I play both also. And electronic keyboard and synthesizer."

"Do you sing?" Steve asked.

"A little. Mostly I compose."

"Now that's intriguing. And you said you were boring." He was grinning again, and Claire bit her lip. Maybe she should have made up a story. Telling him too much about herself could be a mistake.

"What about you?" she asked, turning the focus on him and hoping she might get him wrapped up in talking about himself.

"Believe it or not, I like to read, too. I suspect most educators started out as avid readers. As for music, I started playing guitar in high school. Frank Lawrence and I went to school together in Palo Alto, California. Did he tell you?"

She nodded.

"We've actually known each other all our lives. Anyway, he and I formed a rock band with some friends years ago. We played at parties for a while."

The waitress stopped at the table and told them their food would be out shortly; Steve thanked her, then looked back at Claire. "Now where was I? Oh, yeah. I also played football. Later, I got involved to snow skiing, water skiing, boating, fishing, dancing, and hiking. I like going to movies and plays, and the occasional monster truck show. Oh, and last but not least, I've been taking flying lessons. Got my pilot's license a few weeks ago."

"Flying lessons? A license to fly? Wow. No one could ever call you boring."

Conversation halted when the waitress reappeared, carrying a large tray. The conversation idled for a while as they ate, and then Claire returned to an earlier topic. "Tell me about your flying. Will you buy your own airplane?

"Oh, I'd love to do that. Maybe someday. I'm a real sucker for planes; even collected model planes and remote control planes for years. Of course owning a real plane takes a lot of time and money, neither of which is in abundance right now." He shrugged, gave a melancholy smile, and sipped his chardonnay.

She studied his face, the way the light and shadows played on his features and accentuated his eyes, warm and expressive blue eyes, a lovely kind of blue that reminded her of a Caribbean sky on a summer day. "That's fascinating," she said. "I don't know if I could ever ride in a small airplane, let alone fly one. I'm impressed that you can do that. It must be exciting."

"It really is. There's freedom in the clouds. Maybe sometime you'll give it a try—as a passenger at least." He smiled and his smile was contagious.

Although there was a brief silence, it didn't bother her this time.

"What kind of music do you like?" Steve asked, taking her by surprise.

"Oh, uh, I like a variety: classical, pop, rock, electronic, oldies. My grandfather was a musician, so I went to many classical music concerts when I was young."

"Really? A famous musician?"

Claire felt her face grow hot. *Oh bloody hell!* She definitely should have tried to make up something. She'd been so worried she would make a mistake and get caught in a lie, and instead let down her guard and let her mouth flap. "Uh, no. He was just a local musician, one who never really made a name for himself in the business. I thought he was wonderful all the same."

"I'll bet he was," Steve said. "Who needs fame when you've got a good family? I'm sure his children and grandchildren are his pride and joy."

Claire smiled, and touched the rim of her wine glass. Her grandfather wasn't ever proud of his son, Claire's father. She wouldn't go into that subject tonight.

They went on to talk about politics, history, and science. Even when their points of view differed, they didn't argue, refreshingly, but discussed rationally. It was such interesting conversation. When she got home, after Nanny Kate left, she checked on Marcus. He was fast asleep. She went to her bedroom, undressed, and then went into the bathroom. In the mirror, she was smiling broadly. She touched her lips. It was then that she realized she'd been smiling for much of the evening, and that for the first time in a very long time she didn't look or feel fatigued and stressed. This—engaging conversation with an intelligent and handsome man—was what she'd been missing. Her smile slowly faded. This was something that she couldn't afford.

CHAPTER FIVE

CLAIRE SHOWERED, GRADUALLY feeling the tightness in her muscles ease under the caress of warm water. She dried herself off, then wiped the steam from her bathroom mirror so she could survey herself. Slight bags under her eyes betrayed her lack of sleep and uneasiness. Not good on a normal work day, and more problematic today, Wednesday, when she wanted to make a good impression at her first Superintendent's Round Table Luncheon meeting.

She dabbed make-up on her face, and then blew-dry her shoulder-length golden-brown hair into a pile of natural curls. When she'd first entered the program, Brad had insisted she cut her waist-length hair, declaring that her extra-long hair made her stand out like a 'palm tree in a pine forest', and that was unacceptable for someone in witness protection. That was the first time he'd told her she needed to be a chameleon and blend-in. 'You're my responsibility,' he'd said. 'One of my chameleon projects, as I like to call them. I can teach you the ropes, but you've gotta be willing to learn and play the game.' She sighed once again at the loss of her beautiful hair. Grabbing her straightening wand, she straightened her hair and then picked up her curling iron and began curling the ends at her shoulders.

While doing so, she thought about her dilemma for the umpteenth time and again couldn't decide which was worse: feeling like a fictitious character or feeling like an impostor principal. Probably not a lot of difference between the two.

Did it really matter? She missed her old life, dearly missed teaching college students who truly wanted to learn, and most of all, she missed being happy.

Claire opened her wardrobe, pushing aside her casual clothes, and selected a dark blue business suit and a light gray blouse from the back of her closet where she'd stowed them on her fourth day of work.

She grabbed a pair of scissors from a drawer and cut-off the price tags, not because she was a shopaholic, but because she and her son had been whisked out of Albuquerque with nothing more than the clothes on their backs.

She shook her head. Buying clothes used to be fun. Funny how that changes when you're forced to shop, especially when you have no idea what to buy for a new identity and a new job. After her first day at Midland, she'd bought five more of these suits. Then, a couple days later, she'd overheard faculty whispering behind her back, saying things like 'she looks all hoity-toity in her snooty suits' or 'she thinks she's better than the rest of us'. And so back to the mall she'd gone. Of course she'd also had to go again to buy that black dress she'd worn when she went out to dinner with Steve.

The morning at school raced by. When she glanced at her watch and saw how late it was, Claire gasped. Being late for the meeting was something she couldn't afford. She dashed out the building, jumped into her car, and sped to Cameron High School, arriving only five minutes before the round-table meeting was scheduled to begin.

She walked into the school and then stopped in her tracks. The difference between this school and hers was jaw dropping. Cameron was like a fairy tale castle full of well-dressed students carrying books, looking eager to learn, while Midland was like Dracula's castle full of dark and dangerous students who, for the most part, seemed to come to school to buy or sell drugs.

Shaking off her shock, she hunted for the conference room Steve had mentioned in the email. She found an empty chair at a ten-person conference table and sat down. Porcupine came by and handed each attendee a bag lunch, after which Steve opened the meeting. He started out with a few droll opening comments and then asked Porcupine—*oops, she must stop thinking of her as that, and use her name, Helen Jackson*—to read the minutes from the previous Round-Table Meeting. When she finished, Steve had everyone introduce themselves since this was Claire's first meeting.

As they ate lunch, one high school principal after another gave verbal reports of issues, accomplishments, updates on items from the previous meeting, etc.

Some of the reports and discussions nearly put Claire to sleep, especially since she hadn't fallen asleep until two o'clock in the morning because Marcus had been hyperactive. The last two reports had captured her full attention, though, because they had garnered criticism that seemed to her unwarranted.

The current speaker, Manuel Rodriguez, the principal of Cooper High School, was reporting on their science fair competition that one of his school's star students had won. The student's project was to be featured on the local news tomorrow.

The Vice-President of the Board, Edward Malone, who was a heavy-set man with salt and pepper hair, said, "That's what we need to see. This district needs more star students and teachers. Good job, Manuel. Don't you agree, John?"

While John Richmond, the President of the Board, sipped his coffee and seemed to be pondering his answer, someone stood up and poured herself a fresh cup of coffee. Two people appeared to be checking for messages on their mobile phones, and another person was flipping through pages in a notebook.

Finally, John spoke. "An award, especially in a subject like science, is good. Don't get me wrong. It's going to take more than one award, though, to increase the district's ranking and its prestige in the community. This district's image is well below par. Manuel and all of you need to push harder on your teachers and students." He paused, and glanced at his iPad, then said, "Look at his school's record on sports, for example. They're near the bottom in every activity. What does that say about Manuel's leadership?"

Claire watched Manuel, a middle-aged man in a well-worn suit, who sat across the table from her. His smile melted, and he loosened his necktie and wiped beads of perspiration off his forehead. *That poor man.* She would talk to him after the meeting and let him know he had her support despite John's unreasonableness. No doubt John wasn't an educator and didn't know how difficult the job was.

John Richmond was white-haired and bronze-skinned, in his sixties, Claire guessed. When he'd entered the room moments before the meeting began, she'd noticed him right away because he was at least six-foot-three, attractive, and distinguished looking. He reminded her of a former colleague, a professor she'd admired years ago, but after listening to his many condescending comments this morning, she found nothing to admire.

"I have to disagree with you on that one, John," Steve Jensen said. Today, he was all business, dressed in a crisp white dress shirt, striped black-white-gray tie, and a black business suit. "In the two years Manuel has been at Cooper, he's done an excellent job encouraging students to stretch their minds and participate in scholastic competitions. This isn't the first win one of his students has achieved. And yes, the sports teams have had a rough patch, but aren't academics our number one priority, John? Manuel's one of our best leaders."

Manuel's face reddened, and then he glanced at Steve and smiled.

Steve nodded at Manuel and Claire held her breath, waiting for John's reaction. When he didn't respond, she breathed a sigh of relief for her fellow principal.

After another fifteen minutes of idle talk, she looked at her untouched coffee cup and debated whether to drink it. She'd already drunk two full cups this morning at the school. Hmm. She glanced at her watch. Probably need the extra caffeine to get through this meeting without falling asleep. She took a sip of the hot liquid. It went down the wrong way, sending her into an uncontrollable coughing fit.

All eyes turned her way, and she felt her face grow hot.

"Are you all right?" Liz Olson, another principal, asked.

Claire's eyes watered and she coughed one more time, then nodded.

"Ah, our newest principal," John said. "I almost forgot about you. How could I have forgotten someone so lovely?"

Claire squirmed in her seat like a child caught doing something mischievous.

"We haven't heard anything from you yet," he said. "Do you have any school successes to tell us about?"

She set down her cup and cleared her throat. "I've only been here a fortnight. There's not much to tell yet."

"A fortnight?" He looked around the room at the other faces. "Who uses that word these days? Didn't that go out of use at the turn of the century?"

"Well, actually, fortnight is simply a shortening of the longer 'fourteen nights'. It's used often in many countries," Claire said. Underneath the table she pinched herself for her mistake in using the British term for two weeks. *Must be more careful.*

"Okay, I guess I stand corrected," John said, with a little wink. He leaned back in his chair and put his hands on the back of his head. "You know, it seems to me like two weeks is plenty of time for you to enchant everyone at Midland with your charm and cleverness. You're telling us you haven't worked your magic yet?" He smiled and waited for her to respond.

What was his game? Was he flirting, or taunting. She couldn't tell. "I guess it's time for me to visit Ollivander's Wand Shop in Diagon Alley. Maybe they'll have something that will work."

He squinted, and said, "Huh?"

Liz laughed. "It's from the Harry Potter books, John."

Several people chuckled, including John.

"Ah. I remember that now," he said. "I saw one or two of the movies with my grandkids." He turned his attention back to Claire. "You know, we were led to believe you were somewhat of a miracle worker, that you could snap your fingers and get anything you wanted. Were we misled?"

Surprised, Claire said, "I don't really know how to answer that."

John shook his head, and Claire thought she heard a faint snicker from him.

"We'll talk later, in private." He straightened up, gave her one last look and then called on another principal.

An hour later when the meeting adjourned, she started to leave along with everyone else, until John caught up with her and took her aside, waiting for the last to leave.

John said, "I let you off easy in the meeting. I had no choice. But I want to make something clear to you. We didn't hire you for your glowing abilities. You were forced on us. Apparently, you snapped your fingers and Senator Alan Reynolds gave you what you wanted."

"Huh? What on earth are you talking about?"

"You're Reynolds's mistress."

Her cheeks now felt like they were on fire. "I'm no one's mistress."

"That's not what I was told."

At that comment, alarm bells went off in Claire's head. What had Brad and this senator done to get her this job? She bit her lip and squelched the expletive that came immediately to mind. "There must have been a misunderstanding. I've never even met Senator Reynolds."

John shook his head.

"You can play it that way if you want, but you aren't fooling anyone. We aren't idiots. And this isn't the first time I've been in this position, having to hand over a job to a man's lover because she's young and beautiful and knows how to manipulate a man into doing whatever she wants. It happens more often than most people think."

She pressed her lips together and tried to hold in her anger, but words spilled out anyway. "How dare you. It wasn't like that. Not at all. And besides, this job is certainly no prize."

John leaned into her personal space. "If you don't like it, we certainly don't want to force you to stay. Say the word. We'll gladly cancel your contract. Although the other board members aren't here, I can assure you they'll agree."

She stared at him, wordless. She felt nonplussed, and for all her intelligence, she couldn't think of anything to say to extricate herself. Even if she could, she couldn't trust her voice.

"You can muddle through for a while. We all know it's only a matter of time before you fall on your face. That's what happens when someone takes on a job they aren't qualified for."

He paused and smirked, then added, "Oh, and don't forget you have to take the PLACE test #80 for Principals required by the Colorado Department of Education and then complete the Alternative Principal Preparation Program. Helen Jackson told you about that, didn't she? Imagine your lover's disappointment, though, if it got out that his mistress couldn't pass the test or the program or messed up in a job he'd recommended her for. Not good for his re-election campaign."

Claire opened her mouth to speak, then snapped it shut. Now she understood why the school board had put her in the principal position. They wanted her to fail. And how could she fight back when she hadn't even submitted a resume? According to Brad, she didn't need one for this job, like she had for her previous jobs. His superiors had taken care of everything—but without telling her what background information they'd given the school district.

She drew in a deep breath. *Relax. Don't give the chauvinistic snake the satisfaction of seeing your distress. You can do it.* She wrapped the strap of her laptop bag over her shoulder, said "Nice to meet you as well", then turned on her heels, and walked out the door without looking back.

On her drive home all Claire could think about was placing an emergency call to Brad Meyers. He had to move her again, move her into a situation where she stood a chance of making things work. Her eyes began tearing-up, making it difficult to see. As she wiped at her eyes, she suddenly saw a car in front of her. She slammed on her brakes and barely avoided a crash. Her heart racing now and her hands shaking, she wiped her face and sat up straight. When she was calm enough to proceed, she planted her hands firmly on the steering wheel and forced herself to concentrate on her driving until she pulled up to her condo complex.

RETURNING TO CENTRAL Administration after the Round Table Meeting, Steve Jensen sat down behind his desk and began checking his phone messages. Forty voicemail messages. Good God. That always happened when he was out of the office for half the day, but the number of messages seemed to get bigger every month. He punched the message button and listened, scribbling notes on a pad of paper as he did so.

He prioritized the notes, number one being a question from the mayor, one that required research on Steve's part. He turned his chair around so that he could retrieve the book he needed off the bookshelves behind his desk. Before he found the right book, he heard a knock on his door.

Frank stuck his head around the corner. "Hey Steve, you got a minute?"

"Sure. What's up?"

"Your luncheon was today, wasn't it? Sorry I couldn't make it to this one. What'd I miss?"

Steve shook his head. "Not much. John Richmond was his usual obnoxious self."

He thought about the odd remarks John had made to Claire about her not using her magic yet. Damn strange. And he was sure he saw John wink at her once, which was something he'd never seen John do before.

"Where are you, somewhere in the Alps?" Frank asked, bringing Steve back to the present. "Aren't you going to tell me what happened this afternoon? Come on old man. I want details."

Steve smiled and shook his head. "Funny. Look who's calling me an old man. Takes one to know one, huh?"

"Yeah, yeah, come on."

Steve gave a summary of the events at the meeting.

"So why do you think John dislikes Claire so much?" Frank asked.

Resting his elbows on the arms of his chair, Steve swiveled the chair and steepled his hands. "To tell you the truth, I'm not sure. After the meeting, I stopped to talk to Manuel outside the conference room. John was talking to Claire inside the room. The door was open and I caught a snippet—something about Alan Reynolds and a mistress. She came out a few minutes later and looked really upset. I tried to talk to John afterwards, but he brushed me off."

"I sure hope she doesn't walk off the job tomorrow," Frank said. "I really like her. What did you think of her?"

Steve hesitated, remembering her shimmering light brown hair with its gold highlights. Sometimes, when the room's lighting was just right, her hair had a slight reddish tint. Oh, and her sparkling blue eyes were incredible. Yes, she was beautiful, sexy, intelligent, witty, but he damned sure wasn't going to say it, not even to Frank. He hadn't told anyone about his date with her. "I don't know her very well yet. I like her. I'm usually a good judge of character. I hope I'm right about her. Gotta admit that John's behavior toward her during and after the meeting bothers me a little. Of course he often doesn't know what he's talking about. Don't tell anyone I said that."

"My lips are sealed. You know how I feel about him, too."

Steve nodded. He knew darn well that he and Frank weren't the only people around here who didn't like John Richmond. Although most wouldn't dare say it aloud, their body language spoke volumes.

"Hey, that reminds me," Steve said. "If you find out anything about why the board hired Claire, let me know."

CHAPTER SIX

CLAIRE FUMBLED WITH her front door lock, then entered and closed the door, wanting to cry. She couldn't let her son and his nanny see her that way, though. She pulled off her suit jacket and hung it on the coat rack. Regaining a modicum of composure, she went into the living room.

"Did you have fun at work, Mommy?"

She nodded and pulled him into a hug. Kate then summarized what they'd done during the day and left. Setting her laptop, handbag, and mobile phone on the coffee table, Claire plopped onto her sofa, and stared off into space.

Marcus hopped around in front of his mother like a puppy dog, drawing her attention. "Are we gonna read a book? I've been waiting all day."

She stood up and walked over to him, picking him up in her arms. "Sorry, little man. You'll have to wait a bit longer, I'm afraid. I need to make an important phone call. Can you go upstairs to your room and play for a while? I'll read with you later."

"Okay."

She set him down, and off he went like a windup toy, spinning and rolling and giggling—the epitome of innocence.

Suddenly, she longed to be a child again, even if that meant reliving her not so easy childhood filled with long days locked in her bedroom, forced by her father to study from the time she'd get home 'til bedtime on school days and from morning 'til night on non-school days.

Claire's mother had tried to intervene, tried to tell her husband that no one needed that much studying. He wouldn't listen. He told her he envisioned his daughter going down in history as the youngest person ever to attend Oxford. Later she had indeed made it into Oxford, but wasn't even close to being the youngest, and her father never let her forget his disappointment in her. That wasn't the kind of childhood she wanted for their child, and her former fiancé, Callum, had agreed.

How sad that that part of her life had become the good old days.

For the past hour she'd been desperate to call Brad. Now that she had the opportunity, she couldn't bring herself to pick up the phone. How would Brad react? He'd told her point-blank that she called him too often with worries. Would he tell her she was overreacting again?

While she worked up the nerve to call him, she opened her laptop and googled 'Colorado Alternative Principal Preparation Program' and read through the requirements. Oh God. It was worse that she'd imagined and she doubted she would even be accepted into the program. Sighing, she leaned forward and picked up her phone, then slumped back against the sofa back and hit the speed dial number that connected her directly to Brad.

"Brad Meyers here."

"It's Juliet Powell."

"What?" Brad said in a shocked tone.

Oh bloody hell! She wasn't supposed to use that name, not even with him. That person no longer existed. "Oh. Sorry. Claire Constantine."

"What the hell? You know better than that."

"I'm sorry, Brad. I'm having a bloody miserable day. I don't know what the hell I'm doing." She sighed, and her breath vibrated with emotion as she exhaled.

"What's happened? Please tell you aren't in some kind of danger. "

"No. I mean I don't think I'm in any danger," she said. "It's not that. It's—it's this job. It isn't working. Not at all."

"Okay. Hang on a minute. You're gonna have be more specific. What isn't working? Did you blow your cover again?"

"Uh, well, no, that's not the problem." How could she sum it up and not sound like a whiny baby? "It's the school board. They—they think I'm having an affair with some senator. A Senator Alan Reynolds, I think. It's insane. Until today, I'd never even heard the name. They think he helped me get hired because . . . ."

She couldn't finish.

Brad groaned into the phone without saying a word.

"Are you going to move me?"

"Before I do anything, I want to know what happened. You've been in Colorado less than two weeks. We can't keep moving you, especially on a whim."

"It's not a whim."

"Okay, so give me the details."

She relayed the scene for him, and when she finished, he said, "Damn. They were supposed to hire you as a teacher. You were supposed to blend in, be invisible. Why didn't you tell me they'd offered you a principal position?"

"I—I thought about calling you, but I couldn't call in front of the HR Manager, could I?"

"You couldn't excuse yourself and call?"

"I thought about it. Then I remembered what you told me the day you brought me to Denver. You said, 'don't keep calling me and asking what you should do. It's been almost ten months. I can't keep holding your hand. You've gotta stand on your own'. Don't you remember that?"

"*Now*, you choose to listen to me!" He sighed. "We obviously need better communication."

"Yes, and speaking of better communication, I need to know what background information was given to this school board."

"Huh? You mean you didn't know? No one discussed that with you? You've gotta be kidding."

"Does this sound like I'm kidding?"

"Hold on, let me pull up your file on my computer." Silence followed for a moment, and then he said, "Okay, you're supposed to have taught math at two high schools, one in Indianapolis and one in Cleveland. You've taught for fourteen years. As for the other issue, I'm gonna have to do some checking, talk to some people. I'll get back to you."

Claire hung up and sat slumped over with her head cupped in her hands. Finally, she rose, went into her bedroom to change into pajamas, then flopped across her bed. An hour later he still hadn't called back.

"I'm hungry, Mommy."

She looked up and tried to smile. "Oh, Marcus, I'm sorry. I forgot all about dinner. I'll start it now. What do you want?"

"Mac and cheese," he said. "Mackie and cheesy, mackie and cheesy." He giggled and hopped, and Claire smiled in spite of her bad mood.

"That, I can do."

After dinner she read with Marcus. When he grew sleepy, she tucked him into bed, then quietly crept to the door and switched off his light. How innocent he looked, lying there under his yellow comforter, the soft glow of his night-light giving off an almost angelic aura. If only he could stay that way. Someday he would face life's challenges, and his innocence would fade away. The sudden ringing of her cell phone made Claire jump and sent her dashing from his bedroom down to the living room. She made it to the phone on the third ring.

"Sorry it took so long to get back to you," Brad said. He cleared his throat, and in the distance a car horn tooted. "I was on the phone with my immediate boss. Not an easy man to deal with, even when things are going good, so you can guess his reaction." He paused, and a clicking sound, like someone typing on a computer keyboard filled the silence.

Claire's hope sank. The pauses, the tone of his voice, his words. He was preparing her for bad news.

Oh, God. Please let it be a minor delay. I can't last here a week or two more.

"You're not gonna like this."

She plopped down onto the sofa and waited for the anchor to drop and pull her underwater.

"Okay, there's no easy way to say this so I'm gonna give it to you straight. My boss's boss is a good friend of Senator Reynolds, so when she asked him for assistance in getting you a job in a school district in his state, the senator agreed, as a favor to her. No one in the school district knows why Senator Reynolds stuck his neck out, only that he personally wanted you hired there. He vouched for you, based on info we gave him. If you quit or if you fail, it'll reflect on him."

Claire struggled to digest this new information.

"That would cause a friction between us and the Colorado state government, as well as between two friends. I don't think I need to tell you what that means, do I?"

Claire's mouth dropped open. She could hardly breathe, let alone get any words out of her mouth.

"Look, I know this isn't an easy situation," Brad said. "Personally, I'd rather bring you and your son in and start over. But it's not my call."

"But—but wouldn't it cause more friction if John Richmond follows through with his threat?"

"His threat?"

"He, well, he said that if I messed up in the job, it might get out to the public that the senator recommended me for the job because I was his mistress. That would hurt his re-election campaign. That sounded like a threat to me. I'm sure he was implying that it would get leaked out."

"Yes, I would call that a threat. Listen, he's trying to intimidate you. This was a power play. That's all. He was letting you know that he was ticked off because someone usurped his power and told him who to hire."

"I understand that. But how do you expect me to work under these conditions? He's terrible, the school's terrible. I don't think I can even do this job. It's a nightmare.

"You'll do fine. You're not gonna fail, Claire. You can't."

"But you don't understand. The school is—"

"I'm not moving you," Brad said. "I can't. Deal with it."

Tears stung her eyes. "But you promised."

"We have limitations and you've pushed them. Two moves in less than a year and you're asking for a third. Not gonna happen. No more moves."

"What about the Principal PLACE test and the principal preparation program? How can I possibly pass those?"

"How about study? I'll try to get you a copy of the test, if I can. I can't promise anything."

"Did you check out the program requirements? It says they do an extensive background check and I have to submit college transcripts. How can any of that happen? You have to bring me back in."

"Yeah, I did look at that website after our earlier conversation," Brad said. "So did my boss. He said he'll take care of those two items. It'll take some doing but there are ways around some of that when you have the right connections."

"Right, I forgot. It's all about politics and connections, isn't it?" He didn't answer.

After she hung up the phone, she wanted to scream. Throw a temper tantrum. Something. That reminded her of the few occasions when, as a child, she had thrown a tantrum. Her father had locked her inside a dark wardrobe until she'd settled down.

She rose and paced around her living room. How could she stay here in Colorado? Brad and others involved in the program had promised to protect her and Marcus. Where was the protection in that horrible school and this situation?

Ugh! She picked up a glass vase off an end table and aimed it at the wall, then stopped herself. Smashing it would wake and scare Marcus.

Claire rolled the delicate vase back and forth between her open palms, calming her nerves, and thought back over the meeting earlier in the day. Under John Richmond's scrutiny she'd squirmed like a naughty child. But John wasn't the only person who made her feel anxious. Her whole life she'd been a social misfit, especially around her so-called peers. Interactions in her past two fictitious identities reaffirmed that as well. The truth suddenly hit her in the face. It wasn't only peers that caused her anxiety; she had problems with all the politics and the rules, too.

She sighed and closed her eyes. She'd entered witness protection assuming she'd be giving herself and her son the best chance to live. But what was the ultimate cost? Politics and rules now controlled her whole life, restricted her ability to live in accordance with her own values. With so many restraints, how could she ever hope to blend in around these people, especially considering she felt like a freak? In the past, she'd blamed her freakiness on the fact that everyone knew she was a child-prodigy and thus treated her like a misfit. So if she wasn't showing her real self now, what was her excuse now? Why couldn't she fit in?

She set the vase back down on the table next to her sofa and switched off the lamp, then wandered into her bedroom. Groggy from stress and finding no answers, she decided a good night's sleep might provide a fresh perspective.

Thursday morning, Claire awoke with a terrible headache. She pulled her car out of the garage, saw the gloomy sky looking ready to dump snow, and she groaned. Didn't she have enough clouds hanging over her already? *Okay, look at the bright side. If it's going to snow, make it a blizzard so school will be cancelled.*

She waited for a while, sitting in her car in the driveway with the car's motor running. Of course not a single flake fell. *Just swell!* She covered her face with her hands—doomed to go to work and deal with problems. Bracing herself, she slowly backed out of the driveway.

School held four more disciplinary problems, two teacher complaints, and one practice fire drill before she had the chance to sit down. When she did, she took a deep breath and closed her eyes. Times like these, she really missed having a confidant, like her mother or father or boyfriend. What would they say if her mother was still alive, if her father was still speaking to her? Would they tell her to abandon ship and disappear in the night? That's something Claire had thought about doing more than once. No, her parents would probably say what she already knew in her heart. Hiding out without the government's help might be possible if she were alone. But as a mother, she couldn't risk it. Claire's one consolation in all of this was that her so-called protectors might have no choice but to bring her back in.

If she failed, that is.

But could she bear to fail? Could she even accept failure as an option? Although she was far from perfect, she hated failure more than she liked to admit. She shook herself. No, she couldn't. *That's not going to happen.* Her shoulders slumped. Yeah, right. Just because she hated failing, that didn't mean she was immune to it. So there she was, full circle—stuck, with no hope for release, and facing the fear of failure and violence that seemed inherent in this job.

She laid her head on her desk. Brad Meyers would surely come to his senses and bring her in, she told herself. Until then, best she keep busy and try to work on solving the school's problems. A challenge suddenly struck her head-on. Granted it was a seemingly impossible one, but a positive challenge, none the less. What if she could actually accomplish it? She would be making the school a safe environment and helping all those students. Perhaps she needed to stop feeling sorry for herself and start thinking of the students and the faculty.

Her spirits lifted momentarily, until the enormity of the task threatened to shove her down. She—one person—couldn't fix so many problems, especially when she didn't even fully understand how this school functioned. God! No one could do it alone. It would take the entire faculty. How could she get their support when they mostly treated her like she had the plague?

She needed a secret weapon. Ron. He was the key to her success here. With his support, she might, just might, have a chance of winning over the rest of the faculty. They seemed to follow his lead despite him being second in command. Of course that still left her with a problem. Ron remained aloof despite her best efforts to win him over. That needed to change.

For the rest of the day, whenever she caught a few spare minutes, she brainstormed ideas, researched online for resources, and jotted down notes. After school was dismissed for the day, she met with Ron in her office and laid out her plan. He didn't say anything after she finished. He looked at her like she'd lost her mind.

Claire sat in her chair, her arms spread out on her desk in front of her in almost pleading fashion. "I know it won't be easy, but I want to make Midland a place where we can all feel safe, faculty and students alike. To do that, I need your help. I need the faculty's help. One person can't do it."

He drummed his fingers on the desk for a few moments, his face turning red.

"Why should I help you? You're just like the last principal here at Midland. He left all the work to me and did nothing except kiss up to the board. He finally tried to tighten security—only after things had deteriorated so bad that he couldn't bear coming to work. By then, it was hopeless."

"It's not hopeless. We can fix the problems."

"You mean 'we', as in the rest of us. We're supposed to do your job. I've worked for a couple principals who treated their staff like slaves. I'm not going to be anyone's slave anymore."

Shocked at his vehement response, and from what she was hearing, Claire tried to see things from his perspective. "I'm sorry you've been through that, Ron. I've worked under people like that, too. I promise you, I won't delegate my work. I'm a doer. But I can't do everything. What I'm proposing is a huge undertaking, I know. To fix the problems here—and the problems are not trivial—I have a lot to do and I need the entire faculty to work together with me as a team."

He shrugged his shoulders. "That's hard to believe. From the start you seemed like another one of those 'do-nothing' types."

Claire winced. "Ron, please don't judge me yet. Yes, I didn't jump into action immediately. I've only been here a little less than a fort—I mean two weeks." She paused. "I needed to get acquainted with the school first. I'm still getting acquainted. I needed to study the situation so I could figure out what needed to be done before I initiated any plans. Like I said, I'm a doer, but I don't jump into action blindly, without facts. Does that make sense?"

He studied her face. After a few moments, he said, "I guess it does. You've got to understand my situation." He stood up and paced the floor. "I was second in charge around here. The job should have gone to me. Instead, I'm skipped over and forced to answer to an inexperienced principal. No matter what your credentials say, it seemed pretty obvious you didn't know what you were doing."

"You're wrong. I've plenty of experience." She paused, realizing what he'd just said. "Wait. You wanted the position? They told me no one wanted the job."

"Of course I wanted it. I'm stuck here and I've been doing most of the administrative work, except for budgeting and going to the administrative meetings, so why shouldn't I have the title and the money?"

"Ron, I'm sorry. Please understand that I didn't make the decision to skip over you. The board made that decision. Please don't hold a grudge against me."

He crossed his arms and remained silent for a few moments, then apparently decided and said, "I know it was because of the previous principal, Carl Robinson. He didn't like me and didn't hide that fact. He put me in a bad light with the board. This may get me fired, but I'm tired of walking around on egg shells around bosses, afraid I'll say something wrong, something that'll make him or her mad and get on my case. I'm not the only one around here who feels that way. Makes life here untenable. If we can't be honest with each other, say what has to be said, then you're no different than those other principals and I don't want to work here anyway."

She bit her lip. He was absolutely right. A year ago she would have said the same thing. Before she became a pawn in a liar's game of chess. Don't let him see how much his words sting, she told herself. "All right, look, I admit it. I may not know all I need to know about this job at this moment, but I can and will manage and I will fix this school. It'll take time for me to become proficient, so I would appreciate any help you can give me."

He snickered.

"Look," she said, "it's no surprise that you're ahead of me when it comes to knowing about this school, the faculty, and the students. I will learn about that quickly. And if you help me get there I can teach what you need to know about budgeting, finance, planning, and decision-making skills to become a principal. Have you heard of Game Theory? Working together can be a win-win scenario for both of us."

He stopped in mid-pace and stared at her. "Yeah, right. Forgive me for not kissing up. I'm not that easily swayed."

"Ron, listen to me. Please. I mean every word. I want this and I truly believe everyone at Midland will benefit. Well, with the exception of the gang members and drug-dealers, that is."

He twisted his mouth. "You want to impress the school board, take all the credit for fixing things so that you can advance your career. Isn't that what this is really about?"

Claire sighed. "No, I don't have any desire to move up in this district, Ron. I don't even know how long I'll be here. I just want to make this school safe for as long as I'm here and afterwards."

He squinted at her. "What? I'm confused. You talk like this is a temporary job for you. We were told that it's permanent."

"It's supposed to be. But, honestly, I move around a lot."

His gaze held hers. "Well, Principal, I guess that's the difference between us. You see, I live here."

"Please work with me, Ron."

"I'll think about it and let you know." He got up and walked out.

CHAPTER SEVEN

CLAIRE PULLED INTO the garage next to her condo on Sunday afternoon after shopping for groceries. She helped Marcus out of his car seat and then popped open the car's boot. Marcus, eager to help, ran to the back of the car and pulled out a bag of apples. Before she could stop him, he ran out of the garage toward their front door, swinging the bag. The bag broke and spilled apples out onto the sidewalk. He screamed and burst into tears.

Claire set down her bags and rushed over to him. At the same time, a gray-haired woman ran toward him, bent down, and began scooping up the apples and placing them back in the mesh bag.

"It's okay," the woman said. "Happens to me all the time."

"Thanks," Claire said, "but you don't have to do that."

"Pish-posh. What else do I have going on right now? I'll tell you. Nothing. I couldn't bear to watch another hour of television, so I went for a walk. I don't think we've met yet. I'm Angie Williams. I live next door to you."

"Oh, nice to meet you. I'm Claire Constantine. This is my screaming son, Marcus."

"I've met Marcus. I see him with his nanny now and then. She takes him over to the park when the weather allows. "

Claire stuffed the last of the apples into the bag. She remembered Brad telling her to act normally in her new place, not to hide away but be open with the neighbors. Unfortunately, all she really wanted to do was go inside. When she straightened up, Claire noticed that Marcus had quieted and was looking at Angie.

"I 'member you," he said. "You brought donuts and gave 'em to Nanny Kate and me. They were yummy."

Angie chuckled. "Yup. That bakery near the corner of Kipling and Wadsworth has the best donuts in town. I went over to buy one donut and in a moment of craziness came out with a dozen. I didn't dare eat them all." She padded her round stomach and laughed. "After eating two, I had to dispose of the rest so I took them around to neighbors."

Claire smiled tightly, and took hold of Marcus's hand. Besides wanting to avoid people in general to minimize the lies, she really did need to work on plans for her next faculty meeting scheduled for tomorrow morning. She needed this meeting to go better than the first one, or she was sunk. The meeting and the mention of donuts suddenly clicked together.

"Thanks for the tip about the bakery," she said. "I'm holding a faculty meeting in the morning. I think I'll stop by there and buy some donuts for the staff."

"Oh, yeah? Where do you work?"

"Midland High School." Angie opened her mouth, then snapped it shut.

"Well, hopefully it's only temporary," Claire said. "It doesn't feel safe to me there." *Oh crap, I shouldn't have said that.*

Angie nodded, and then tilted her head. "That reminds. I saw someone hanging around the building the last few days. Seemed like he was watching somebody or something. I went over and asked him what he was doing, and he asked if I knew you. I didn't know your name so I said no. But then he mentioned a little boy around three or four. "

Claire gasped. "What—what did you say, then?"

"Nothing. I just shrugged my shoulders and went back inside."

"What did he look like?"

"An average Joe. Middle-aged, wavy dark-blond hair, clean-cut, dressed in jeans and a lightweight jacket."

Her head was spinning with possibilities. *Did the people who wanted her dead already find her? Should she call Brad?*

"Thank you for telling me. I'll keep a lookout for him. If you see him again, will you call me, please?" She took a piece of paper and a pen out of her handbag which was strapped over her shoulder and scribbled her phone number.

Angie took the paper and said, "Of course."

Claire thanked her for her help and walked Marcus up to the door, unlocked it, and took him inside, where she swept through the flat to make sure no one was hiding inside. Nothing unusual, no sign of an intruder. She went back to her car and gathered the rest of the groceries, then closed the garage door and walked back toward her condo, looking around for the watcher as she walked.

When she was safely inside, she locked the door and did another ritual check of windows and back door. After that, she dialed Brad's number. He answered on the second ring and she told him what her neighbor had said.

"Okay, don't panic. Be careful, and keep me apprised of the situation. Like I said before, my bosses don't want to move you unless it's absolutely necessary. And to be honest with you, Claire, this, coming, right after they told us their stance, will make them think you're making it up unless you give us some proof there's a problem."

"You're not helping me," she said. "Why have you changed so much? I used to be able to count on you for support."

"It's complicated. Let me know if you get any proof that you're in danger."

CLAIRE WALKED TO the faculty lounge a few minutes before her second faculty meeting, this time armed and ready for battle. She set down a box with a huge assortment of donuts on a table where everyone could see them.

Claire planted herself in the corner of the room, a corner that gave her the best view of her employees, and watched as teachers straggled in, poured themselves coffee, picked through the donuts 'til they found the one they wanted, and finally sat down. She still didn't know whether Ron would help, but he'd told her he would think about it. Hopefully his decision would be favorable or her planning would be useless.

Glancing around the room at sullen faces, she said, "I've had a bit of time to familiarize myself with this school and see many things that need to change, starting at the top and filtering downward."

One of them stood up, walked by the table, and sneezed on the remaining donuts. Claire tried to hide her shudder as she wondered if it had been a deliberate sabotage. Several other teachers stood up to pour themselves coffee refills, and three teachers moved from the front, to a back corner, and began whispering together. They're already bored? She'd only said one sentence. Was it any wonder the students ignored their teachers when they had these people as role models?

"I did not meet Carl Robinson so I don't know his philosophy about being a principal," Claire said. "I can tell you mine though. A school isn't a school and can't function without teachers or without students. It can function without a principal and assistant principal though." Ron gave her a funny 'what gives' look, and she smiled. "Maybe not very well," she added, "but it could function." The people who were actually listening, laughed, including Ron.

Claire continued. "A principal and assistant principal don't make a school. Our roles are important, but in a different way. We're here to lead, support, organize, plan, and deal with problems. We're here to help you—the teachers, counselors, and the students. You are the school. We're the support and the framework that holds the school together."

She paused and looked around the room. Maybe half of them looked somewhat more attentive. She gave Ron a questioning look, and he nodded. "Let's make this school a better place for you teachers and your students. Ron and I have some ideas on what to do, which we will share with you. We need your input. We need your help and want to hear your suggestions."

Teachers looked at each other and then looked back to Claire. No one commented. Some fidgeted, others played with their cell phones or other electronic devices. Were they texting each other? She couldn't tell for sure.

Finally, someone said, "Sounds like platitudes, if you ask me. I've worked for principals who talk big. It's always the same. They sit behind their desks, collect fat paychecks, while we do all the work with no support and no recognition."

"I understand. I've been a teacher. I know how it is, how hard it can be. I'm telling you I don't function like that. What I am saying is that this school is currently broken. I want to fix it. So does Ron. And neither of us want to be the kind of leadership you have apparently been subjected to. That's not how we want to lead." Claire paused. "Midland High School can be a place where teachers want to spend their days, where they don't dread coming to work and where students respect you and themselves.

89

Ron and I want to help. But it will take all of us together to make it happen. This school and your lives will continue the way it is unless we fix it. Please give us and your students a chance."

Several teachers folded their arms, clearly dismissing her, except for one man, Ed Logan, a science teacher. He said, "Boy, that's something I never thought I'd hear coming from a principal."

Whispering buzzed through the room, and Claire wished for super-hearing.

"You can't fix this hellish place," one teacher said. "It's too late."

"It's never too late. I've researched other urban schools around the country. Many have succeeded. With your help, we can too. It won't be easy. I'm not naïve. But if we pull together and work as a team, I know we can do it."

The buzzing increased.

"What's in it for you?" Nancy Palmer, the English teacher Claire had met in the Admin office on her first day of work, asked. She was sitting near the back of the room. "A raise, a promotion, maybe a transfer to one of the good schools? Assuming you can pull this off, of course."

That surprised Claire. She'd thought Nancy was nicer than that. Disappointed though still determined, she said, "I get the same thing you do—a better environment and to feel safe. This is the scariest place I've ever worked in."

Several heads bobbed in agreement.

"Look, if we can pull this off, as Nancy said, there would be no need to transfer to a good school. This will be a good school. That's the point." Claire paused, waiting for their reactions, but when they came, she sighed.

"You can't fix this place," a teacher who was leaning against the back wall shouted. "These kids are incorrigible. Don't you know the kind of homes they come from? Go drive through the neighborhoods. You'll see you're wasting your time and ours." Heads nodded and then half the teachers rose and walked out.

Claire took a deep breath and let it out. The body language of some of the remaining teachers gave the impression they'd stayed because they hadn't the courage to walk out. Oh well. At least they're here.

"Thank you for staying. We'll create a mission statement and goals for the school," Claire said, "But we'd like your input, so please think about it and get back to Ron or me."

She turned to her secretary, Kim. "Would you please make a list of the teachers here?"

Kim nodded and began writing on the notepad she'd brought with her.

After the meeting adjourned, Claire went back to her office and closed the door behind her. Obviously, she wasn't cut out to inspire people with speeches. How was she supposed to reach the students when she couldn't even connect with more than a handful of faculty members at best?

TUESDAY MORNING, CLAIRE arrived at work early to practice the speech she would be giving later that day. She'd spent most of Monday creating the framework of a game plan for school improvement, including a building-wide discipline system, then spent a couple more hours generating her proposal speech. Now, she sat at her desk with her door closed for an hour, speaking it aloud, scribbling minor changes on a piece of paper. A knock of the door startled her and interrupted her verbal practice. The door opened and Frank poked his head around the corner. Claire smiled and motioned for him to enter.

"Good morning," Frank said. "Is this a bad time to talk?"

"No, not at all. I'm preparing for an assembly."

"Oh yeah? What kind of assembly?"

"First, to introduce myself to the whole school and, second, to let the students know about changes we'll be making and about our new expectations."

"Sounds interesting. I'd like to attend, if you don't mind."

Could she really say no without alienating him? Although she wasn't sure she wanted him there to witness her flailing around, she tried not to show it in her face. She smiled, smoothed her hair, and said, "Of course you can attend."

"Super. When is it?"

"Ten o'clock."

"Okay. I have another stop to make this morning, so I'll take off now and come back at ten." Frank stood up, but hesitated, waiting for her response.

"See you then." She stood, too, and they walked to the door together.

"Oh, you know, I might bring Steve Jensen along if he's available."

She struggled to keep her mouth closed so he wouldn't see her sudden anxiety. She liked Steve, but she had enough pressure to succeed without having to worry about what he thought of her performance. She nodded, then looked away quickly.

Later, shortly after school began, Ron gave his daily announcements over the intercom and announced the mandatory assembly schedule. "Everyone will gather in the auditorium at ten o'clock."

Ten minutes before the assembly, Claire stood up, preparing to go to the auditorium. *Just breathe. You can do this. Pretend you're in a lecture hall giving a talk to your freshman college students.*

She glanced at her watch. *Guess it's show time.* She walked out of her office and bumped into Ron.

"Nervous?" he asked.

Claire gave a half smile. "Ron, you have no idea." Although Ron's disposition toward her had warmed slightly since yesterday morning's meeting, she had discovered his general manner was a bit formal, distant with most people. Knowing that was who he was had changed her perspective, and made her a bit more comfortable with him now than previously.

Entering the auditorium, Claire resisted the urge to cover her ears. The noise inside was deafening, reminding her of the tube station back home in England and the train station in Boston at the height of rush hour. Students were supposed to be seated but half were wandering around, cavorting with classmates, or throwing things at each other. Paper airplanes floated through the air, reminding Claire of kids in a daycare, only much bigger. Despite their childlike behavior, these particular children were far from innocent.

As students began noticing Claire and Ron, they nudged each other and gradually quieted. Ron took a seat up front as curious eyes watched her walk up onto the stage alone.

Claire attached a lavaliere microphone to her jacket lapel and stood in front of a podium that had been set on the stage. She took a deep breath and let it out, looking around the crowded room.

"Good Morning. Most of you don't know me yet, so I will start out today by first introducing myself and telling you a little about me." Of course, it was the brief story made up by Brad and his superiors.

Surveying the massive room, she spotted Frank Lawrence and Steve Jensen standing with a group of teachers, not far from the stage. The expression on their faces was one of intent interest. Both men were observing the students, as well.

"Now that you know a bit more about me, I want to talk to you today about our new plan for this school. We, the faculty and administrators of Midland High School, are making some changes to make this a much better school, to improve the environment and educational opportunity for all. We are going to make that our primary goal for this year. We need all of you to work with us to reach that goal. We need—"

Boos and profanity rang out and drowned out Claire's voice. About twenty students stood up and wandered around the auditorium, some shoving each other and taunting students who were still seated.

"Quiet! Sit down," she shouted. No one paid attention. Could they even hear her over the noise?

Ron came to her side and shouted into another microphone, his voice louder and stronger than hers, but instead of helping, it seemed to add fuel to the ruckus. About fifty more students jumped up from their seats and threw hats, water bottles, and shoes into the crowd.

Claire moved, intending to get off the stage and try to intervene. Ron grabbed her shirt sleeve and shook his head.

Teachers rushed toward the students and herded them out of the auditorium, leaving Claire and Ron standing onstage helpless. Claire looked toward Frank and Steve. To her dismay, they were looking at her and whispering, and then they turned and walked out without stopping to talk to her.

Claire's cheeks burned as she left the stage and weaved through the crowd on her way back to her office. It was bad enough to lose every shred of credibility in front of the whole school, but in front of her supervisor, too?

She sat at her desk and held her head in her hands. For all her education and supposed intelligence, she apparently hadn't a clue how to proceed.

Claire dealt with minor problems most of the next day and was preparing for the next assembly to be held on Thursday. Her phone rang and she immediately recognized Steve Jensen's voice.

"The reason I'm calling is to let you know I think you're efforts at the school are commendable. Sorry we rushed out without speaking with you."

"Thanks. Sometimes I have doubts whether it's do-able. I guess it's still early in the process. This is a big task and I guess setbacks are to be expected."

"It's good to be realistic. But don't let minor setbacks like yesterday deter you. Frank might attend your next assembly. Unfortunately, my work schedule is still so insanely busy I probably won't make it. Anyway, the reason I called was to see if you'd have dinner with me Friday night."

Claire hesitated for a moment. "Uh, I—I don't know. Is that a good idea?"

"Well, I didn't bore you too much the last time we had dinner, did I?"

"That's not what I meant."

"We can discuss it Friday night, okay?"

"I—uh, I guess so. Meet at the same restaurant?"

"Sounds like a plan. See you there at six."

She hung up the phone. All right, the first dinner with him might not have been a date, but this one? Oh God. What was she doing? And more importantly, what was she going to wear this time?

When Claire arrived at home that evening, Nanny Kate picked up her handbag and college text books. Instead of leaving, Kate hesitated near the front door, looking as if she wanted to say something. Claire gave her a quizzical look and asked, "Something wrong?"

"I'm not sure. I mean, on Monday you asked me to tell you if I saw anyone acting peculiar, or watching us. And, well, there was a guy at the park this afternoon. Today was one of the few days this week when it was warm enough to go, you know, so we left here after lunch and walked there." She paused.

Claire nodded, hoping that would encourage the girl to continue.

"This guy was standing around, watching the kids play on the equipment. I guess there were about a dozen kids and half a dozen moms, and a couple of nannies. I wasn't the only one who noticed the man. Some of the moms were sitting at a picnic table chatting and then started whispering and pointing to the man. I walked over to them and asked if they'd ever seen him before. No one had."

Claire felt a wave of nausea. "What did he look like?"

"He was old, like late thirties if I had to guess. He had dirty blonde hair, I think. After a few minutes, the moms got up and rounded up their kids. They left while I was tying Marcus's shoe that had come untied. Soon as I finished, I realized the man was standing less than three feet away from us. He asked me who I was and who the little boy was. I couldn't believe it. I mean, that takes a lot of nerve, doesn't it?"

Claire's heart was racing, but she tried to remain composed. "What did you do?"

"I remembered what you'd said about strangers, and then I picked up Marcus and ran."

"Did he follow you?"

"I don't think so. Should I have called the police? And should I avoid the park?"

Claire glanced over at Marcus who was watching TV. "I don't know if we need to call the police. Not yet, anyway. If you see him again, please call me right away. I think it's definitely a good idea to avoid the park for now."

After Kate left, Claire dialed Brad's number, but he didn't answer. She left a message.

On Thursday morning, after spending the night lying awake and worrying about the watcher, Claire decided to cancel the assembly. She called Frank and let him know about the cancellation. Then, since she hadn't heard back from Brad, she called him and left another.

She didn't have time to go shopping for another dress. When Friday night came, she wore the black dress again, adding a red necklace and matching earrings and styling her hair differently, this time letting it curl naturally and then pushing the hair on the left side behind her ear. With the dress, she wore a red cashmere sweater that she'd bought when she first arrived in Denver.

At the restaurant with Steve, Claire struggled to find a safe topic to discuss. She didn't really want him asking questions about work. Nothing good had happened. She also didn't want to talk about her cancelled assembly, or explain her reasons for cancelling.

After they ordered their meals, she asked, "You told me that you and Frank grew up together and went to school together."

Steve smiled. "Yeah, we've known each other since we were in kindergarten. That's a long time. I won't tell you how long. Trust me. It's been decades."

Claire laughed. "Have you always worked together, too?"

"No, no," Steve said, shaking his head. "That's recent. After we graduated college, Frank moved to Chicago and I moved to Los Angeles. Worlds apart. We stayed in touch though. Attended each other's weddings, that sort of thing."

Silence ensued. He'd given her the perfect opportunity to ask about his marriage and divorce but if she did, he would ask about her love life. Instead, she chose the safer route. "How did you both come to work here in this school district?"

His brow creased a little and he took a sip of wine. "I'm not married anymore in case you were afraid to ask. Been divorced for many years."

She felt her face grow hot. "I—I, well Frank already told me that."

"Ah."

Again silence.

"Did both of you start working here at the same time?"

"No. I've been here a little over three years. Shortly after I started, one of the four assistant superintendents retired. I immediately thought of Frank."

"That was really nice of you," Claire said. "Friendships like yours are hard to find."

"They are indeed. Though sometimes I worry if I did him a disservice. Don't get me wrong. It's good to have a job, and as far as jobs go, the pay is not bad here. But Frank's job and my job are stressful. We put in tons of overtime and we have little time for private lives. He sometimes complains that he worries his wife and kids will forget him because he's working such long hours."

She nodded, not knowing how to respond.

"So what about you," Steve said. "I don't see a ring on your finger."

She quickly covered her left hand with her right and felt daft for doing it. Obviously it was too late. She tried to make light of it. "You're too observant. Has anyone ever told you that before?"

He laughed. "As a matter-of-fact, yes."

Before he could ask anything else, the waitress miraculously appeared with their meals.

After she left, and they began eating. Steve quickly returned to the conversation. "So I take it you're not married."

"I'm not."

"Divorced?"

She bit her lip and looked down at her plate, while she debated how to answer. Finally, she said, "No. I was engaged. We actually broke up a few months before the wedding date. I suppose now in hindsight that was for the best."

"Certainly cheaper," Steve said in between bites of food. "I mean finding out before spending the money for a wedding," he added, smiling.

They went on to talk about global warming, super volcanoes, alternate energy, and other miscellaneous trivia. An hour later, as Steve put his credit card back in his wallet, he said, "Why don't we catch a movie? I'm not sure what is playing. Maybe we can find something to see."

"That sounds nice." She hadn't been to a theater in over a year. Until now, she hadn't realized how much she missed it. She and Callum used to go every other weekend.

They left the crowded restaurant and stood in the parking lot together, trying to decide what to do about having two cars there.

"Why don't we just both drive to the movie theater and meet there?" Claire said. Steve agreed. Once there, it didn't take long to discover that most of the movies had started about a half hour earlier, but they did find one action movie that was about to begin.

It was around eleven o'clock when the movie let out, and Claire and Steve discussed the movie as they walked out to their cars. It turned out to be a much better movie than Claire feared. When they arrived at the parking lot, they stood next to Claire's car, and she kept pushing her windblown hair out of her eyes. She knew she was stalling for time more than anything else. She wasn't sure what was expected, so she said, "I had a good time, Steve."

"I had a great time. I hope we can do this again." He paused, and looked uncertain for a moment before he spoke again. "I don't know how you feel, and I don't want to pressure you. I like you and I'd like to see you again—outside of work, I mean." He hesitated, looking thoughtful, then said, "Please don't feel you have to go out with me, of course. I'd never pressure you, or anyone, that way. I've never dated someone who worked for me, and I really shouldn't do it now. But with the long hours I work, how else am I supposed to find someone, you know? It's tough finding the right person to be with."

Claire bit her lip, again stalling for time.

"I'm sorry, this is awkward, isn't it?"

She nodded. "I've never dated anyone that I worked for either."

"I hope you don't think I'm too old for you. Am I too much like your father?'

"You're nothing like my father." She would never date someone like her father, a man with sharp words and biting anger.

"I'm forty-six. Is eleven years too much of a difference?" He searched her face and she had the uncanny feeling he was trying to figure out if she really was thirty-five.

"Let me think about it? I'll get back to you in a few days."

AS SHE TRIED to get to sleep, she thought about Steve. She truly liked him—his easy-going attitude, quick wit, intelligence, and incredible self-confidence. But could she trust him? Was he setting some kind of trap for her?

She'd never been paranoid, and she didn't think she was now.

If she said no to Steve, he might assume she didn't like him, which wasn't true at all. Or worse, he might think she wasn't really available. Had John Richmond spoken to him about his belief that she was the senator's mistress? If he had, Steve might interpret her declining of his advances as evidence that John was right and that she uses men to get what she wants.

On the other hand, she could be worrying over nothing. Maybe she was sabotaging herself. Wasn't that possible? But then she thought about another possibility: that she might be afraid of getting involved with someone whom she might have to suddenly leave behind or who might hurt her fragile trust in people. Oh, bloody hell. She needed to get out of this job.

CHAPTER EIGHT

CLAIRE KEPT HEARING Kate's and Angie's words about the stranger as she dressed for work Monday morning. Her nerves were on edge driving across town, and she couldn't stop checking her rearview mirror to ensure she wasn't being followed.

She arrived at school an hour and a half before the first bell because she needed to work on a weekly report mandated by Steve. The report took an hour to finish, leaving less than half an hour at most to email her report and check her new emails. Opening her inbox, she was shocked to see thirty-six emails, far more than usual, unread and screaming for attention.

She groaned, sent out the weekly report, and began opening the unread mails one by one. In the middle of reading one from Frank, Ron stuck his head into her office, clearing his throat to let her know he was there.

"Hey, sorry to interrupt," he said, "but we've got another problem."

"What now?" Claire asked brusquely, rubbing the back of her neck with her left hand as she closed the inbox with her right hand. She sighed and glanced up at Ron, who looked taken aback at her reply. Immediately realizing what she had done, she said,

"Oh, Ron, I'm sorry. It's not your fault about the problems. I shouldn't have snapped at you."

He nodded, his face blank again. "Nancy Palmer got here fifteen minutes ago, grabbed a cup of coffee, and headed up to her classroom. That's when she discovered a mess. Spray paint. Gang symbols. All over the hall floor and on the classroom doors. But that's not the worst of it. They also hung liquid-filled condoms over all the doorknobs. At first she thought they were water balloons."

Claire's jaw dropped open. "Oh my God, please tell me you're kidding."

Ron winced. "Afraid not."

"It isn't throughout the school, is it? I mean, is the vandalism confined?"

"We thoroughly checked the second floor, and did a quick scan of the other floors. We didn't see any vandalism in the rooms themselves and no fresh vandalism on the other floors."

Ha. Fresh vandalism. That was the only way to describe the difference, wasn't it?

"Well, at least that's a bit of good news," Claire said. She tilted her head, then thought aloud. "So, why that floor? What kind of message were they trying to send?"

"Damned if I know," Ron said. "I'll call Hector Minosa. Have him get his custodial staff to start cleaning it up. I just don't know how we're going to prevent it from happening again."

An hour later, while on her way back to her office, Claire heard a noise and turned to see where it was coming from. Something was happening outside the cafeteria. She rushed over in time to see five boys, all wearing orange bandanas, shoving two smaller boys, and laughing.

"Leave them alone," she shouted. They turned at the sound of her voice, and then looked at each other.

"Did you hear what the pretty lady said?" one of the boys said.

While the gang members were distracted, the younger boys ran off.

One of the other members said, "Yeah. Ooh, I'm scared. Whatcha gonna do 'bout it, huh? You wanna take us on, mama?"

Claire struggled to keep from showing fear. She was alone with these boys and no one knew she was here. She studied them briefly, trying to keep her demeanor calm, and although she dearly wanted to take each of them by the ear, be the strict disciplinarian and march them out of the school, cooler thinking prevailed. This wasn't the right time or conditions. Finally, she spun around on her heels and walked briskly back to her office, not daring to look over her shoulder. Please let them not be following, she thought.

Later, sitting in her office, she replayed the morning's events. As she slid from one scene to another, something clicked in her mind. Teachers need a discipline plan that encompasses clearly defined rules of conduct for all their students. It would make sense to develop and follow the same plan throughout the school, train the teachers, and then inform the students of the consequences and that they would be enforced.

A while later, she walked into Ron's office and asked him to announce a second assembly. She would try again at ten o'clock today. Before the assembly, she searched through last year's yearbook to see if she could identify the gang members she'd seen bullying the younger boys. She felt like she was looking at mug shots in the police station. Soon she found four of the five boys. Although she couldn't do anything about them now, she would listen for any mention of their names among the faculty and students.

At five minutes before assembly time, Claire took a deep breath, let it out, and walked briskly up onto the stage. She'd spoken before large audiences thousands of times before in lecture halls, but most of those students had attended willingly and that had given her confidence. Facing a hostile crowd was a completely different animal.

After a brief introduction and pause, she continued. "I've learnt a lot about Midland in the short time I've been here. There are things that need to change."

There were some shouts, some of them obscene, and much whispering among students. Stay calm, she told herself.

"This morning we had an incident of vandalism. After that I witnessed some students bullying other students. If you know who is responsible for the vandalism, please come to see Mr. Baker or me. If you are a victim of bullying, or know of someone who is, please also see myself or Mr. Baker. Don't let the troublemakers ruin your education or your life. Over the next few weeks, this whole school will meet every other day in this auditorium."

Again there were whispers and the occasional obnoxious, loud wise crack. Claire pushed on, raising her voice. "People here—students and faculty alike—have not been safe or happy. We have to change that. We have to fix our school's problems. Fixing the problems is a huge task. No single person can do it alone, but with everyone working together, students and faculty alike, we can."

As in her previous assembly, a ruckus broke out and Claire was forced to stop. She strained to decipher the sounds, and the best she could surmise, was that it was a mixture of boos and cheers, with boos unfortunately still outweighing cheers.

Ron and several teachers were busily intercepting students who left their seats.

Claire steeled herself, and then spoke as loudly as she could into the microphone. "We will begin the next assembly with new procedures. Before then I want you to come forward and tell what you know about the vandalism, the bullying, the—"

Ignoring her, students jumped out of their seats and stampeded toward the doors. Ron and a few teachers prodded them like cows to go on to their next classes. Afterwards, Ron walked over to Claire and he said, "You'll never get them to rat on each other. You're a fool for thinking kids will do that. In places like this, you say nothing, you lie, you do whatever you need to survive."

Claire stared at him. "Are you giving up?"

"No, I'll do what I can to help, but don't kid yourself. Don't expect miracles."

TUESDAY MORNING, CLAIRE arrived at work groggy, having been up half the night with Marcus who'd had a nightmare and couldn't get back to sleep. She probably wouldn't have slept well anyway, still worrying about the watcher and not having heard from Brad yet.

Walking around to the front of the building from the faculty car park, she stared in horror at the building and leafless trees dressed with Maypole-like streamers of toilet paper and at the streaks of bright red spray-paint on the remnant snow blanketing the grounds in front of the building. Unfortunately, Gang symbols, ones that she'd come to recognize, were also painted on the snow-cleared sidewalk in black.

This was the worst she'd seen yet. And this coming after she started trying to fix the school's problems immediately made her believe the gangbangers were sending her a warning.

Brad Meyers's words about John Richmond popped into her head. "He was trying to intimidate you. It was a power play.

That's all. He was letting you know that he was ticked off because someone usurped his power and told him who to hire." Wasn't that similar to what was happening here? Wasn't she trying to usurp the troublemakers' power?

Don't let them intimidate. Don't let them win. Not John, and not the troublemakers here in the school. She glanced at the clock, then sent out a message over the school's intercom, advising the faculty to report immediately to the school's music room for a brief before-school meeting.

Fifteen minutes later, sitting on a stool on the music room stage, she said to the faculty, "We're going to continue the school assemblies." She'd selected this room because it had stadium-style seating and was cozier than the auditorium, yet able to accommodate one-hundred-twenty employees. Everyone faced her, allowing her to watch their reactions and also engage them in conversation. "We'll hold them every other day until we don't need them anymore. They're working. It may not seem like it yet, but what we see today is retaliation by the school's troublemakers. We've rattled them, and we'll keep on rattling them."

"And they'll keep on retaliating," one of the teachers said. "I don't want to come to work in fear."

Several other teachers nodded agreement.

"What, you don't come to work in fear now? We can't give in," Claire said. "We have to keep trying." She paused. History teacher Jerome Shaw was sitting off to the side, looking down at his lap. His fingers tapped on his iPhone, probably texting someone across the room. Claire's eyes swept the rest of the room. History teacher Jill Barnes, who was Jerome's 'friend', was doing likewise in the back of the room. They might be discussing the meeting, but more likely planning a hot date. Best let it go.

Claire took a sip of the tea she'd brought with her from her office, then said, "We can't continue to allow a quarter of the student body to run this place. We must not let them intimidate the other students or us. They are robbing the other students of a good education. They are robbing each of you the chance to educate and to have a safe work place. This school can and must change for the better. We must make it happen for everyone's sake."

About a third of the employees smiled or gave some form of approval but the others whispered to one another, or fussed with their hair, their neckties, or their phones. Clearly, she still hadn't convinced them. What would it take to get through?

"Those of you who are interested in fixing the problems, stay here and we'll discuss ways to handle school fights. The rest of you may leave, but please think about what this environment is doing to your lives and the future lives of your students." She'd done enough homework that she could give a brief lesson on school fights.

Roughly forty percent of them stayed and spent the next thirty-five minutes discussing the primary reasons teens fought in school, and the techniques for dealing with those fights: restraining techniques, getting back-up assistance, using firm nonverbal and paraverbal communication, etc. Everyone agreed that the team-restraining techniques, while usually suggested to be used as a last resort, would be invaluable at Midland. At the end of the meeting, she told them she would have another, more in-depth training session the following week.

When she returned to her office, she called Frank and informed him about the vandalism and the results of the faculty meeting.

Later in the day Ron came into Claire's office, and said, "I heard from some teachers that someone wrote a threatening message on the mirror in the ladies' faculty restroom near the main faculty lounge."

Claire said, "Crap."

She stood up, and together they walked to the restroom. Claire entered first, then stepped out and motioned to Ron that it was empty. They both stared at the large messy red lipstick message: STOP MESSING IN OUR BUSINESS OR YOU WILL DIE.

Ron looked as shaken as she felt. Her earlier resolve to not let them intimidate, to not let them win, flew out the window.

"What do we do?" she asked.

"Damned if I know," Ron said, rubbing the back of his bald head. "Think we should we notify the police?"

She sighed. "I hoped that wouldn't be necessary. But—" She looked back at the bloody-looking message. "I'll call Frank. He'll know what to do."

Within half an hour, Frank arrived and met Claire and Ron in Claire's office. They took him into the restroom and showed him the mirror, and he was angrier than Claire had even seen him. When they returned to the school's Admin. Office, three teachers were waiting for them.

"Someone slashed my car tires," Jim said. "I went out to go to lunch and couldn't go anywhere. Fucking delinquents."

"My car windows were broken out," Millie said.

"Mine, too," Charlie said.

Claire looked at Frank. He shook his head and rubbed his hand through his hair.

"Better show us the damage," he said.

Outside, they all stood in the car park looking at the three vehicles.

"Okay," Frank said, finally, "we need to get the police involved. These teachers need police reports to go with their insurance claims."

Frank, Claire, and the three teachers remained outside while an officer took down the information for their reports.

Before Frank left, he said, "Claire, I know this is difficult. Try to stay calm, okay? Keep me apprised of the situation."

"Thanks, Frank. I appreciate all your help more than you know."

He nodded and gave her a worried smile.

Claire asked the question that had been niggling at her. "Clearly the school's problems are escalating. Is it me? Am I an incompetent principal? I mean, I expected some reprisals, but this—well, it's far more than I expected."

Frank twisted his mouth and then said, "No, it's been getting worse for a while. Under each of the last few principals."

She nodded. *Not terribly comforting. I'm merely the latest in a line of incompetent principals.*

CLAIRE SAT AT her desk and looked at her calendar. The circle around Wednesday's date, with the notation 'Bi-weekly round table meeting' meant she'd been working here for four weeks now. In some ways it seemed impossible that time had gone by so quickly. Yet from another perspective, it also seemed so much longer.

Although she was supposed to attend the meeting, she didn't dare leave the school. At least that was the excuse she gave Steve via an email. She wouldn't have gone, anyway, because she would have seen John Richmond, and that was something she wasn't ready to do.

Late in the afternoon, in a brief moment of quiet, one of the teachers, Jody Simms, poked her head inside Claire's office. "I know this guy, my sister's husband's brother," she said, "who would love to meet you."

Claire tilted her head. "Why on earth would he want to meet me?"

Jody grinned, then shook her head and said, "Apparently, you haven't heard yet. I'm notorious for matchmaking. You aren't married, are you?"

"I'm not. But, well, I—"

Before Jody had a chance to respond, Ron rushed into Claire's office. "Sorry to interrupt. We've got another problem, a fight out in the entrance hall."

All three of them ran out of the admin office. Two students were on the floor, struggling with each other, punching and clawing, surrounded by a crowd of students cheering them on.

Several teachers stood on the sidelines waiting for help. Claire looked at Ron, and they both waited for a lull. When it came, she yelled at the students to break it up. Several bystanders took a few steps backwards. The fight continued.

Claire looked over at the group of teachers and motioned for them to join her and Ron. Once everyone was in position, she gave a hand signal. Ron and a male teacher grabbed one of the males and put him into a wrist-shoulder hold restraint, holding his head down. Claire and the other two teachers did likewise with the other student. They took one student to Claire's office and the other to Ron's office so they could cool down.

It didn't take long for Claire and Ron to establish that the fight was over a drug-deal gone wrong. Claire notified Frank, the police, and both boys' parents, and when everyone was there and seated in the school's small conference room, a long meeting ensued. After the police and parents with boys in tow left, Frank, Claire, and Ron sat in Claire's office behind closed doors.

Frank said, "Did the police search the boys' lockers? I don't recall them doing that?"

"No," Claire said. "Should they have?"

"Yeah," Frank said. "Or at least someone should. I guess the three of us can do that. Those kids will probably be back here. We need to see what's stashed in their lockers."

They found the boys' lockers, opened them, and looked inside. Ron pulled a gun out of one of them. He handed it to Claire, and said, "This is why you don't get the truth here. This is the new truth."

Claire stared at the gun, the first one she'd every actually held, and she fought hard to hold back tears. When she could finally trust herself to speak, she said, "Should I call the police and ask them to come back?"

"Probably," Frank said. "But if news of a gun in school hits the media, we'll have a much bigger problem, with parents and with the school board. The board, especially John Richmond, hates negative publicity. Better to lock it up in your office."

After Frank left, Claire carefully wrapped the gun in paper towels and placed it in the bottom drawer of her desk and locked the drawer, then made herself a mental note to look into the possibility of conducting a drug search of the school building and grounds.

CHAPTER NINE

ON THURSDAY, JUST another day in paradise, Claire sat in her office eating lunch, while reading emails, and generally keeping out of everyone's way, when her phone rang.

"It's Steve Jensen. Hey, I read your report. It got me thinking about you. Do you have plans for Friday? We could have dinner again. Maybe see a play afterwards."

"Uh, well—I—" Seeing one's boss outside of work was a bad idea. She opened her mouth to say 'No', but the word wouldn't come out. Her mouth went dry. She already had an enemy on the school board. It couldn't hurt to have Steve as an ally. Besides, she truly enjoyed talking to him. She closed her eyes and said, "I guess I could do that."

She pushed the receiver away from her ear a moment and bit her lip.

"Great. I'll pick you up at your home. Why don't you give me directions?"

Her heart was racing now. Shouldn't she meet him somewhere like she'd been doing? Wasn't that safest? Oh, what the hell, Steve wasn't the enemy. After she gave him the address and directions, she hung up the receiver, then picked it back up and called Angie Williams to see if she could babysit again. If she couldn't, then she would take it as a sign that she shouldn't go out with Steve. As luck would have it, Angie told her she'd love to babysit Marcus.

That evening, she went out shopping for another dress. She and Marcus ate dinner in the mall food court, which worked well, Marcus liking the idea and therefore didn't complain as much as usual when shopping.

When Steve arrived to pick up Claire on Friday night, she was dressed in her new shiny blue skirt, the color of which matched her eyes. What she especially liked about the skirt was that it would swirl if she were dancing, and swirling skirts always made her feel ultra-feminine. Her blouse, with elbow-length sleeves, matched the skirt in color and had tiny raised flowers on it. She shrugged on her coat, grabbed her handbag near the front door, then dashed outside without inviting him in. Steve raised his eyebrows, but didn't say anything. She gave a nervous smile, and said, "Sorry, my house is a mess."

At the Golden Dragon Mandarin Buffet dinner conversation proved less problematic than she'd feared, because she discovered that if she asked him questions, and kept him talking about himself, he didn't have much of a chance to ask her personal questions. That kept her from having to lie, at least for the moment.

He talked more about his carefree high school and college days with Frank, and Frank's wife, Gloria. His stories were funny and entertaining. Then, turning more serious, he told her about his father, who had been a fighter pilot in Vietnam, and later an aerospace engineer, and who had later divorced his mother. Steve's mother raised Steve and his two younger sisters alone. She sounded like a strong woman. The more he talked, the more intrigued she became. There was so much more to the man than she'd even realized.

"I've been doing all the talking," he said after his second trip to the buffet tables. "Tell me about yourself. What were your school days like? Tell me about your parents and siblings. Do you have any? Siblings, I mean."

"I don't. I was an only child. I guess I was enough of a challenge for my parents." She took a bite of food and looked down at her plate as she chewed, hoping he'd move on to another topic.

"Maybe you were everything they wanted, and they didn't need another child," Steve said.

She smiled, and sipped her iced tea, peering at him over the rim of her glass. How could she avoid lying to him without breaking the program's rules?

"Come on. Tell me more. What are your parents like? Where do they live? Are they educators, too?"

Every time she changed identities, her protectors provided her only a minimal background to go with it. It was up to her to create a more complete faux background. If Brad was whispering in her ear right now, he would tell her to outright lie. But when she'd tried that in previous identities, it had not gone well. She eventually got tripped up in her made up past and had to move on. It seemed more prudent to stick as close to her real life as possible, without giving anything that could be used to trace her.

She sighed, and carefully said, "My Dad and I, well, we haven't spoken to each other in thirteen years." She looked up at Steve and shrugged. "I guess I'm not very good at relationships."

"Are your parents still married?"

"No. Divorced. I was sixteen. When they split, my father and I went our separate ways. I've only seen him once since then, at my mum's funeral a year after their divorce."

"Why is that? Did he mistreat you?"

Claire bit her lip, thinking. Why not make up a doting father who'd made his daughter feel like she could succeed at anything?

Steve would never know. Joe Powell had pushed his daughter to excel in all academics, which wasn't necessarily a bad thing, except in doing so he had prevented her from all social activities. According to him, she didn't need socializing. Too distracting. Was it any wonder that she was socially inept? Not only had he locked her in her room the minute she returned from school, forcing her to study until she went to bed, but on occasion he'd even withheld food and drink when her performance didn't meet with his personal expectations.

"Uh, well, no," she said. "He didn't mistreat me. Not exactly. Still, he's not a pleasant man. I should probably leave it at that."

Steve nodded. She could see the wheels turning in his head. He didn't say anything for several minutes, and she excused herself to get another plate of food. She wasn't particularly hungry any longer, but it was a good excuse to leave the table. With any luck, he would forget about the conversation.

When she sat back down a few minutes later, he said, "What about your mother? You mentioned her funeral?"

Damn, the man was persistent. Claire struggled for composure. How could she talk about her mum without crumbling into tears? Her mum, Amelia, had been a beautiful social butterfly from a wealthy family. For husband Joe, that had made up for her having a lower intelligence than he had, and he'd fooled her into thinking he would be her perfect husband. Soon after their wedding, Joe had clipped Amelia's wings and forbade her visiting with friends or going anywhere without him.

"Are you all right?" Steve asked.

"I'm fine. I guess talking about her has brought back some sad memories. It's been a long time."

"I'm sorry. What happened?"

"I don't really want to talk about it. It's still hard for me, especially since she was the only family I had left. I was only seventeen. It—her passing—left a crater in my life."

"I can understand that," Steve said. "I was sixteen when my parents divorced, too. My dad married his mistress. Moved away. I guess that's why he and I aren't close. It's not the same as losing a parent, though at times it felt like he'd died because my mom wouldn't allow us to talk about him."

"Your mum was bitter about the divorce?" she asked.

"Yeah, took it pretty hard. At least she had her career. She was a professor at Stanford University. I think her work saved her from slumping into depression."

Claire bit her lip and tried not to think about her parents.

When she didn't say anything, Steve gave her a funny look. "You know, if you ever want to talk to me about your loss, your feelings, I'll be glad to listen."

"Thank you. Someday, perhaps. Sorry to be so gloomy. Can we change the subject?"

"Of course. Sorry. I noticed you were fingering your charm bracelet. Are those cats on the charms?"

"Oh, yes." She tried to smile, embarrassed that he'd noticed something she hadn't even realized she'd been doing. "Cats of all varieties. My mum loved cats and would take in any stray. My father used to tell her that if she wasn't careful she would turn into an old cat lady with a houseful of cats and crap."

Steve laughed. "So, do you share her affinity for cats?"

"I suppose, but I don't have any pets. Maybe someday I will. But more likely a dog than a cat."

"Why is that?"

"I don't know. Maybe because they're more loyal."

"I have to ask. Why are you wearing a cat bracelet if you like dogs better?"

"Oh, well, it was my mum's. I actually made it for her. I design and make jewelry as a hobby. I used to, anyway. This one," she said, touching the silver charms, "I gave to her for her thirty-eighth birthday. Sadly, it was her last birthday. This is the only keepsake I have of hers."

"That's really sad," Steve said. "At least you have that, though."

She wasn't supposed to keep it. She was told she mustn't keep anything from her past, but she'd managed to sneak a few small items into her purse. Her keychain with the ticket stub from the first time she went to see the Royal Ballet when she was nine, the cat bracelet, and her pi necklace that she'd made when she'd started teaching mathematics.

"What was your childhood like?" he asked.

"Huh . . . oh, I'm sorry. I didn't catch your question. I was thinking about something."

"Anything you want to share?"

"No. It was nothing, really." Nothing that she could talk about, that is.

He nodded, then said, "I wondered about your childhood. I've told you tons of stories about mine. What was yours like?"

"Quiet, mostly. No siblings to fight with." She forced herself to smile, hoping to lighten the mood. She went on to tell him carefully edited stories from her childhood, leaving out that fact that they'd lived in England, that her grandfather had been a musical prodigy, and that life hadn't been happy.

By the time they finished dinner, conversation evolved to the less personal and Claire began to relax. She had made it through the difficult backstory questions. Not perfectly, but Steve seemed satisfied with her answers. Everything about Steve, at least outside of work, was so open and relaxed and, while he exuded confidence, he didn't come across as conceited.

After dinner he took her to the Front Range Center For Fine Arts for a production of "Wicked", and during the play, Steve took her hand in his and they sat by side, hands entwined, and it seemed right somehow.

Afterwards, he drove her home and walked her to her front door. Taking her hands in his, he smiled and gazed into her eyes, which sent her pulse racing. She thought she saw a question in his eyes, and she looked down at their hands. He let go of her left hand and reached up, tilted her face upwards to his, bent forward and gave her a kiss so light, so gentle that she wondered if she'd imagined it.

He straightened up and gazed into her eyes. "I hope I haven't chased you away," he said. "I want to see you again, if you'll let me."

She smiled and nodded. "I'd like that, too. I had a nice time."

"Goodnight, Claire."

Closing the door behind her, Claire leaned up against the door and smiled. What a perfect date. She could actually get used to this.

Angie walked toward the door, and paused. "I thought I heard you come in," she said. "Did you have a nice time?"

"Really nice. How was Marcus?"

"We played some games, watched TV, and ate cookies," Angie said. "Not an exciting date, but I've had worse." She smiled and winked.

CLAIRE CHECKED PHONE messages on Monday afternoon, hoping Brad had returned her call. Still nothing. There was, however, a message from Kate asking her to call home. Claire immediately hit the speed dial for her home phone.

"Sorry I had to call you at work," Kate said. "Someone's been calling here and when I answer the phone, no one says anything. At first, I thought it was some jerk being rude. Then I remembered that guy in the park. Do you think he could have your phone number?"

"Oh, God, I hope not. Have you seen him around the building recently?"

"Well, no, not him. I did see a car driving slowly past here a few times. I didn't recognize the driver, though. It could have been just someone looking for an address. I've done that before. You know, got lost."

Claire was starting to hyperventilate. She took a deep breath and held it, then let it out slowly, calming her nerves. "All right, I'm going to make another phone call and then I'll call you right back."

She hung up and then called Brad. Please don't go to voicemail, she said under her breath. This time, he answered. She told him about the incident in the park, the phone hang-ups, and the car driving past the building.

"Okay, hang in there, Claire. I have to talk to my boss and then I'll call you back."

While she waited impatiently for his call, she searched online for information about stalking. Ten minutes passed, and then her phone rang. She answered.

Brad said, "Okay, I talked to my immediate boss."

Someone knocked loudly on her door, and Claire said, "Sorry, Brad, can you hold on a minute?"

Ron burst into her office and said, "We've had another fight. Two students. One was injured. Looks like a broken wrist."

"Oh, no!" Claire slumped back in her chair, her mobile phone held tightly in her hand. "What are we supposed to do? Do we call paramedics, police, parents?"

Ron rolled his eyes. "Policy says we need to call the student's emergency contact number and proceed from there. Do you want to do it, or should I?"

Claire could feel her face growing hot with embarrassment. She should have known the policy. "Go ahead and make the call,

Ron. I'm tied up here with a home emergency of my own. Will you call Frank and let him know, too?"

He nodded and turned on his heels.

Could this day get any worse?

"Sorry for the interruption," she said to Brad.

"I can't bring you in. The boss thinks you're overreacting. Says you're being a Chicken Little. You know the story, don't you?"

Claire's mouth dropped open. How dare they?

"Now you're calling me a liar? That's ridiculous. You had to move me because I'm not good at lying."

"I know that, but I'm not in charge."

"So what am I supposed to do, wait until someone grabs my son? There's no way I can bring him to work with me. If you saw this place, you would understand why."

"Can't you have the nanny watch him somewhere else for a while?"

She sighed and leaned forward. "Maybe. I'll look into it."

After she finished that phone call, she called Kate and asked if she could take Marcus to her own home for the day. Claire would pick him up after.

Kate said, "No problem."

Claire suggested Marcus pick a few toys to take with him, and then she took down Kate's address and directions. When she picked him up after work, she could check it out and decide if it was suitable for the future.

When Claire saw Kate's home, she was relieved. It was a small flat, clean and tidy and in a safe neighborhood from what she could tell. Marcus seemed fine with it, too, so she made arrangements to drop Marcus off there and pick him up, for the next week or so.

CHAPTER TEN

TUESDAY MORNING, CLAIRE was stuck in back-to-back meetings and behind in her promise to conduct assemblies every other day. She was afraid that soon no one would take her seriously because she didn't follow through on her promises. With her hectic schedule, she also had no time to worry about the watcher

After leaving a meeting with parents and a student, she rolled her shoulders to get the kinks out, then picked up her coffee mug. Time for a cup of coffee. Past time, actually. She'd tried to get a cup when she'd first arrived, but even before her first meeting at seven o'clock, she'd not had a free moment because of phone calls, emails, and interruptions by teachers. It was now ten o'clock. She grabbed her mug and headed to the coffeemaker in the outer office. She didn't get that far. She stopped at her office doorway, seeing Jorge Perez coming at her, red-faced and eyes blazing.

"Jorge, what's wrong?" she asked, guiding him into the office and closing the door.

"One of my students, Lizzy Morgan, slapped me in the face a couple minutes ago, at the end of my second hour Spanish class."

Claire stared in disbelief. When she looked closely, she could see red finger marks on his right cheek. "Oh my God! Why would she do something like that?"

"She was angry because I gave her a zero on her test. She blames me for her failure. She left the whole second half of the test blank. 'Lazy Lizzy', sorry, that's what the other kids call her, thought I should give her credit for the few questions she answered."

Claire frowned. "Why didn't you? Were they incorrect?"

"Not all of them. Only she had copied those answers off the student sitting next to her."

"Are you sure? That's a serious allegation."

He ran his hand through his hair and paced. "Yes, I'm sure. I saw her. The other student was called away to the nurse's office and gave me her completed test before she left. After that, Lizzy sat there and did nothing. And the answers were the same as the other student's, even the two wrong ones."

"I'm not saying you're wrong, Jorge. I'm trying to understand the situation. Are they friends? Maybe she was just worried about her."

"No. They rarely talk to each other."

Claire looked up the girl's schedule and asked her secretary, Kim, to call Lizzy to the principal's office. At first the girl denied the attack. After they contacted her father and he confronted her, she finally admitted it.

Claire looked at her wristwatch as soon as her office cleared out. It was now half past eleven. So much for coffee and checking phone messages. She would love to grab a quick lunch, but she needed to visit a few classrooms, which she'd hadn't had time for since Friday. On her way upstairs she ran into a teacher, Jody Simms, on her way down.

"Oh, Claire, I've been hoping to see you. We didn't get to finish our conversation the other day. Have you considered a blind-date with Roger?"

"Who?" Claire asked.

"Roger. The guy I told you about. Don't you remember? He's single, mid-thirties, and not bad looking. I told him about you, and he's interested."

Claire sighed, and gave her a half smile. "I appreciate the thought. Unfortunately, I don't think it's the right time. Maybe later."

Jody's forehead wrinkled in question.

"I—I recently ended a long-term relationship," Claire said. "I need more time." At least it wasn't a complete lie, she thought. She really did end a relationship—with the father of her child. But she wasn't going to admit she was now dating her boss.

"Oh, sorry. I guess I can understand that. Okay, I'll check back with you in a week or two."

Claire rushed up the remainder of the steps and walked through the corridor, intending to visit a couple of science classroom at the end of the hall. Halfway there she heard heavy footsteps pounding behind her. She tensed her shoulders, and kept walking. Would she ever feel safe in this horrid place?

"Claire, wait up." *Huh, was that Ron's voice?*

She turned around and saw him rushing toward her.

"I've been looking for you," he said, between ragged breaths. "You won't believe this. Bob Ryan caught two students engaging in sex in one of the restrooms."

"What? Please tell me you're not serious." Claire grimaced.

"No such luck. Makes you wonder how often that happens without anyone finding out, doesn't it?"

"I don't even want to think about it. Have the students' parents been contacted?"

"Yeah, I called their parents and we're waiting for them to arrive."

"Where are the students?"

"Sitting in the counselor's office. He and the nurse are talking to them. Lotta good that's going to do."

So much for lunch, for coffee, and for visiting classrooms. Now she really did feel like a computer with legs—everyone seemed to think she didn't need food or drink. Claire walked back to the Admin offices with Ron. While they walked, she told him about Jorge and Lizzy. He told her about two other students who had disrupted their classes and/or argued with their teachers. He also described several fights that had broken out in classrooms and in the public areas.

Claire said, "You think that's bad. In Nancy Palmer's class, she caught three students sitting in the back of the room snorting cocaine. They didn't even try to hide it."

"Good God," Ron said.

"I'm going to see about getting the police to conduct a drug search of the school building and grounds. I'll let you know what I find out."

That afternoon she did some checking online, then called Frank for advice. He told her he'd look into getting a police search and he'd get back to her.

Before she left work, her phone rang.

"Hey, Claire," Frank Lawrence said, "I've arranged for the local police to conduct a scheduled search activity in the school Thursday morning. They'll call you right before they arrive so you can meet them in the parking lot."

"You did that for me?" Claire said. "I didn't expect you to set it up for me. I was prepared to do that myself. But thank you."

"You're quite welcome," Frank said. "I know you could do it yourself, but I also know you've got plenty to keep you busy. One less thing to worry about."

"Frank, you're a lifesaver. Well, maybe not literally. You know what I mean. I don't know what I'd do without you. If you were here, I would give you a big hug."

He chuckled. "Maybe I should have driven over there instead of calling. No, scratch that. My wife would skin me alive if a beautiful woman, other than she of course, hugged me. So, I guess I did save a life—mine." He chuckled.

"You are a big ham, you know," Claire said. Even with all the drama surrounding her, Frank could make her laugh, and she needed that more than anything right now.

As promised, the Denver police called Claire at eight o'clock on Thursday morning to confirm their appointment for two hours later.

"We'll need you and a couple of your employees to meet us in the parking lot to assist," the detective said.

The police arrived on time and brought dogs trained to detect chemicals in enclosed areas. Claire stood next to the officer in charge. "I wasn't sure if a search like this was legal without a search warrant."

He nodded. "That's a common misconception. Fact is this type of search is commonly conducted at high schools throughout the country. We use them to identify students who are in possession of chemicals on school property. Not only does it get immediate results, but it also increases awareness in students that possession and use of alcohol and illegal chemicals is not tolerated at school."

"What happens if you find something?"

"If we find something? More like, when we find something. I have no doubt we will."

Claire twisted her mouth and felt her face burn. "Of course. I knew that. Drug use and drug sales are rampant here. That's why I requested this search. But I didn't want to give you the impression I was biased."

He grinned. "We know all about the drug infestation at Midland. It's not new."

"Then why hasn't anyone done anything about it?" Claire asked.

"Good question. You're the first principal here apparently to give a rat's ass, if you'll excuse the term."

The school was placed on soft-lockdown, meaning everyone was required to stay in their classrooms while the search was in progress, and no one was allowed to use cell phones. It took an hour. The police dogs sniffed out drugs in numerous vehicles in the student parking lot. Then came the task of identifying the drivers of those cars. Two dozen students were called into Claire's office and were asked to open their vehicles for police inspection. Some of the students—those whose cars were found to contain large quantities of drugs—were taken into police custody. Their parents were phoned. More than half of the students who were caught were believed to be members of one of the school's biggest gangs: The Varrio Crisps.

After everyone had gone and only Claire, Ron, and Frank were left, Claire asked, "What will happen to those students?"

Frank said, "Can't say for sure. I suppose some will be given warnings, others might be arrested. The one thing they all have in common is that they'll face possible expulsion when the school board reviews their cases at the next board meeting. As of now they are at least suspended."

Later that afternoon during passing period, Claire noticed a mob of students hovering near the first flight of stairs. They should have been moving, heading to their next classes, not standing around. She watched and listened, and though they were speaking loudly, the sounds of all the other students moving about muffled most of their words. She edged toward them, hoping to hear more of what they were discussing.

"Did you guys see the friggin' drug dogs here during third period? Before that new principal showed up, you could do any drugs you wanted 'round here. Look at this fuckin' place now. She's trying to turn this into a prison."

Claire was so intent on listening that she didn't watch where she was going and crashed into something. She caught herself, and stepped back to see what she'd hit. An overweight black girl, tears running down her cheeks, stood in front of her. "Oh, no," Claire said, "did I hurt you? I'm so sorry."

The girl shook her head and wiped the back of her arm over her face. "You didn't do nothin'. It was Padma and Maria and Shanna. Those bitches. They—" She turned her head slightly to her right, and clenched her hands.

Claire looked around. Three girls stared at them, hatred in their eyes. "You're dead meat, Tyeesha," one of the girls said. Another spat on the floor before they all turned and walked away. The group of loitering students, who had been watching, spread out in all directions, like ants scared away from a picnic.

Claire turned her attention back to the girl, and reached out, touching the girl's arm. "Did they hurt you?"

The girl bit her lip and looked down at her feet.

"Why don't we go somewhere quiet where we can talk, okay?"

The girl jerked away. "I got nothin' to say to a principal. I done said enough."

"It's all right. I can help you," Claire said. "Don't be afraid of me. Tell me about those girls. What happened?"

"Oh, no. I can't. You heard them. They'll kill me." She turned, intent on escape, but Claire was faster.

"Let's go to my office." She put her arm around the girl's shoulders and guided her toward the admin office. "We'll talk confidentially. You can trust me."

In her office Claire motioned for the girl to sit, handing her some tissues, and sat in a chair across from her. "You're okay now. What's your name?" she asked.

The girl sniffled, and slumped in her chair, arms crossed over her plump stomach. Claire wondered if she would speak. She wore jeans and a hooded sweatshirt. Her long hair was a mass of braids. The girl sighed in resignation and said, "Tyeesha Moore."

"What grade are you in?"

"Tenth." She squirmed. "I can take care of myself. I gotta go. I'm missing science."

"I'll write you a pass. Don't worry about that."

"Like I told you, I can't talk to no principal."

"Please tell me why you're so scared. Maybe I can help."

"You can't help. They said no one leaves the gang. Anyone who tries will pay. Big time. And they mean business. Last year, right after I joined up with them, this girl tried to leave. Aurora. She died." She raised her hand to her head, made it look like a gun, and clicked her trigger thumb.

Claire put her hand over her mouth. It sounded too much like what Callum had said about trying to leave the syndicate.

"Tyeesha," Claire said, leaning forward and placing her hand over one of the girl's hands, "I won't let that happen. I promise you. I'll find a way to get you out of the gang, safely."

"You can't do nothin'. Nobody can." Tears flowed down her cheeks.

Claire handed her more tissues. She knew about the district's no tolerance policy. Gang members could be suspended, but Claire needed help with that. She would discuss it with Frank. Unfortunately, even if they could eliminate the gangs from the school, the bigger problem remained: how to prevent gang members from retaliating outside of school.

"I don't know how yet," Claire said. "Please trust me. I'll figure out how to protect you. Hang in there, okay?"

Tyeesha looked up and gave her a timid smile. "Thanks. I never had nobody stick up for me before." She stood up, then swung her backpack over her shoulder.

"I'll get you that hall pass," Claire said.

Now, all I have to do is figure out how to follow through on my promise.

AFTER PUTTING MARCUS to bed, Claire collapsed on her sofa, her mind returning to all the problems at school. Somehow, she desperately needed to figure out how to help the poor students who weren't unreachable, and also deal with the rest. In the morning she resolved to go in extra early again and do more research online.

Weary and not finding any real solutions coming to mind, Claire drug herself off to her bedroom, undressed and prepared for bed. Once in bed her mind solidly refused to settle down, continuing to plague her, replaying the day's events. Eventually though, tired to the bone, her thoughts drifted off randomly and precious sleep claimed her.

CHAPTER ELEVEN

CLAIRE FELT CHILLS through her body as she entered the school Wednesday morning, wondering why it was so cold in the building. She checked the thermostat and realized it was on an automatic timer and wouldn't turn on the heat for another half-hour. Ah, she'd never arrived this early before. She manually increased the temperature setting, then went into the admin office and began brewing a pot of coffee.

While the coffee machine performed its magic, in robotic fashion Claire unlocked the door to her office, hung up her jacket on the coat rack in the corner, and switched on her computer. She then picked up her ceramic mug from her desk and carried it to the coffee stand. With a steaming cup in hand, she was ready to get down to business. She closed her office door, sat down, and brought up the internet while she sipped coffee.

Gangs, how they operated, their codes and lingo, their initiations, their strengths and weaknesses—those were questions she needed answers to, and today she began searching the internet to learn everything she could about the school's number one enemy.

She read an article from the local newspaper. It stated that Colorado was home to 110 gangs and 12,741 members. It went on acknowledging the obvious, that there was a serious gang problem in the Denver metro area. Another article talked about police liaison officers being placed in many Denver high schools. An article on Wikipedia gave history of gangs, current numbers, and info on who's at risk.

Claire typed two letters of a new search word and jumped at a loud noise in the outer office. She raised her head and listened. Had Ron come in early? She remembered him complaining yesterday about not having enough time in the school day to get his work done, because of all the fights and recent problems.

She waited, expecting him to peek in her office, but nothing happened. Probably overreacting to what she was reading, she decided. Returning her attention to the computer, she typed in "how to leave a gang", and clicked enter.

Several loud thumps followed by multiple deep voices raised hairs on the back of her neck. Ron might come in early, but whom else? None of the other employees came in this early.

The sounds were coming directly from the other side of her closed door.

Claire's mouth went dry. She stood up and moved around her desk, her mobile phone in hand so she could dial 911 if needed. She edged toward the door and when she was close enough, she reached out for the doorknob. Before her hand touched it, the door swung open with a force that made her jump backwards and drop her phone. She reached down and picked it up.

"Get her," a male voice said.

She jerked back upright, dropping the phone in the process, and froze. Facing her were three students wearing orange bandanas, students who had been among the group bullying the two boys in the corridor last week. She hadn't known their names until yesterday when they'd become agitated because of the drug search, and Ron had identified them.

The student closest to her, the tallest of the three, was Jose Rodriguez. He lunged at Claire and she stepped backward. Ricardo Black and Darius Lorenz followed him into the office and closed the door, blocking Claire's only exit. Her mouth went dry and her heart raced. Jose stood towering over her, so close she could smell his foul breath. He lifted a hand and she caught a glimmer of steel. She tore her eyes away from the steel to glance at Ricardo and Darius through a daze, then gasped as two more knives came into focus. She backed up further until she bumped into her desk. With nowhere else to go, she put her arms in front of her in a feeble effort to keep the students away. If they were trying to scare her, they were doing a bang up job of it.

She stared at their legs. Their intimidating stance made her blood run cold. She jerked her attention up to their faces and immediately regretted it because the contempt in their eyes left little doubt in her mind: she was going to die.

Jose grabbed her arm. She struggled to get free from his grip.

"Please don't do this. You won't get away with it. You must know that. You'll accomplish nothing." She sounded desperate to her own ears and she hated that. *Be brave. Don't give them the satisfaction of seeing you cower.*

Jose was twisting her arm now, twisting it so hard that tears welled up in her eyes. She tried to pull away. Darius grabbed her shoulder in a steel grip as Ricardo tore at her clothes.

She struggled, but the more she fought, the rougher they treated her as she learned after she kicked one of them in the groan and he struck back harder and with intense anger. With three pairs of hands now restraining her, she knew she didn't stand much of a chance of escaping. A cold knot formed in her stomach and she felt sick.

She tried to scream, but someone's hand was glued over her mouth, and then in a flash she was being forced down, backwards. Desperate, she kicked upward. She didn't have enough leverage to do any damage so she tightened her hands and clawed at them like an animal. One of them yelped in pain.

"Get the bitch," he yelled.

Shaking and scared witless, she tried to roll over, hoping to break their grip. Somehow, without her realizing what was happening, one of the gang members had sprawled on top of her. His weight crushed her, making it difficult to breathe, but nothing could keep her from screaming. She was going to die, she thought. So much for witness protection.

UPON ENTERING THE school building, Ron heard a bloodcurdling scream followed by another and another. He ran toward the sound, and quickly realized the screams were coming from the admin office. Claire!

He sped up, yanked open the door to the admin office, yelling out her name at the top of his lungs. Someone rammed him and knocked him down. He landed hard on his side and groaned. Momentarily stunned and out of breath, he watched two more men run past. He pulled himself up and took off in pursuit. By the time he made it outside, the men were driving away in a beat up Chevy Impala low-rider. He thought he recognized one of them but not the car. Trying to read the license plate number, he caught only the last two numbers, and waved his arms in frustration.

He ran back into the building to find Claire. The sight of her lying on the floor in a crumpled heap, her clothes torn and barely covering her, her hair in wild disarray, with strands stuck to her tear streaked red face, sent waves of nausea through him.

"Oh, my God!" he said. He froze, perspiration beading up on his head. She was bleeding. He could see it from where he stood. He moved closer and crouched. She was conscious and semi-alert, probably in shock. Taking her hand in his, he said, "Claire, can you talk to me? I'll call 911." He tried to let go of her hand so he could get the phone on her desk, but she held on tight.

"No!" she wailed. "Please don't call the police." Tears glistened on her pale face, and she struggled with her free hand to pull together her torn clothing. He took off his coat and draped it over her.

"I've gotta call them, Claire. They'll catch the creeps that did this to you."

"Please don't! I'm begging you." Her voice was fragile and shaking. "Don't call them. You can't tell anyone."

Letting go of his hand, she buried her face in her hands and cried.

Ron sat down with his legs sprawled and stared in disbelief that she didn't want to report the crime. She'd never hesitated to call the police or paramedics before. What the hell was he supposed to do? His normal reaction would be to hold her and soothe her like he would a frightened child, like he had done when this happened to his youngest sister, Celia. She was only fourteen at the time. Celia hadn't wanted the police either, but he'd called them. He'd thought he was doing the right thing. He was wrong.

He struggled to keep his voice under control. "You need to report this, and then get medical attention."

"No! You can't call the police."

He rubbed his beard. "Okay. Then Frank. I'll call him. He'll know what to do."

"Please don't call them. Don't call the police or Frank." Tears were blinding her eyes and choking her voice. When she

Susan Finlay

spoke again, Ron had trouble understanding her words. "Plea—please don't tell—tell anyone."

"They stabbed you Claire, and raped you. You need medical attention."

She was unable to speak for a moment, and the tormented look on her face was wrenching. This was his fault. He knew the school, he knew the gangs and how they operated. He'd been in a gang when he was in middle school, before his family moved out of Chicago. He should have expected some kind of retaliation for the drug search. He shouldn't have let her be alone in the school. He should have insisted on a buddy system where they'd get to work at the same time. He could have prevented this.

He was jolted out of his own thoughts when she spoke again.

"They didn't rape me! They would have, I'm sure, but you arrived before . . . Ron, please, no one can know about this." Although her eyes were red and swollen, and a wound on her abdomen was bleeding, she continued. "If the school board finds out, they'll remove me from here, and those gangbangers will win. That's what Jose and the others want. I can't let that happen." She paused, and half sobbed. She stopped again and swallowed hard, then looked up at him pleading.

"You know who did this and you're still refusing to report them?" He couldn't believe she would let them get away with it. "You say you don't want them to win. Then let me call the police."

"Do you think that will stop them? Won't others in their gang retaliate against me or against the school? I know I've failed so far, but don't make me run away in shame."

He saw her agony, and he could understand to some extent. His sister's shame had ruined her. Yet the thought of letting those creeps get away with this was too much. "Claire, I can't do that."

"It's my decision to make. Please. Help me."

"You're in shock. I get it, but I'm afraid you'll feel different when you calm down."

"How can you know how I'll feel? You've never been in this position." She looked at him, pleading, and he wasn't sure he could speak. Celia had looked at him the same way. Although only nineteen at the time, he had been the man of the family. The police had shown up with their flashing lights and two days later Celia was dead. She'd slit her own wrists in the family's bathtub.

Ron took a deep breath. He couldn't force Claire to report it. He could try to reason with her, tell her she needed to get out of her job. Of course that would sound like he wanted her out of the way so he could have the job. He sighed and shook his head. God, he hoped he was making the right decision. He lifted her gently up in his arms and walked toward the door.

"My keys," she said, reaching out toward the desk. "Must get my school keys and lock this door. Get my handbag, too. The keys are inside it."

Probably a good idea to lock the office. Keep people out. Safeguard any evidence, in case she changed her mind about notifying the police. He found her purse lying on her desk, took out the keys and locked the door, then drove as fast as he could to St. Joseph's Hospital's emergency room. At the hospital the doctor, a middle-aged woman, instructed a nurse to bring over a rape kit test.

Claire said, "That's not necessary. I wasn't raped. Ron arrived before—"

The doctor looked at Ron. Ron squirmed, then looked at Claire and said, "Please let the doctor do her job. The test is standard, isn't it, doc?"

The doctor nodded.

While she was being treated for the stab wound and bruises, Ron called the school and let their secretary know that they would both be out of the office all day. He told her they were in an offsite meeting.

"What meeting is that?" Kim asked. "I haven't heard anything about it?"

"We're meeting with the police department. We need to talk about security, drug enforcement, that sort of thing."

Kim was silent for a moment. "Both of you? Who's going to run things here? I hope you don't expect me to talk to students and parents."

He hadn't thought of that. Now what?

"Tell Ed Logan he's in charge today. He can pull a few teachers out of the classrooms to help. Call in substitutes for the teachers. Oh, and will you please announce that today's assembly is cancelled?"

"Okay. Will do."

A short time later, when the doctor came back into waiting room, Ron asked, "Is Claire okay?"

"She'll be fine. I stitched up the wound and I'm giving her a sedative. She shouldn't be alone for the first 24 hours."

Ron nodded. "She wasn't raped then?"

"No, but she was traumatized. I talked to her and tried to convince her to report this."

"Yeah, I know. I tried, too. She's so damned stubborn."

The doctor nodded and said, "Would you try again? She's been through a lot. I don't want to upset her any more. Maybe as her friend you can reach her. She seems to trust you."

Trust him? He wasn't so sure about that. One thing he'd learned about her was that she was as aloof and distrustful as he was. "I'll try, but I doubt she'll budge."

The doctor led Ron into the exam room to talk with her.

"I can't do it," she said. "I know you must think I'm crazy, but you don't know, you can't know, how it is. I've made up my mind. It has to be this way."

The doctor and Ron exchanged looks, and finally conceded to her wishes. The doctor sent her home with instructions for changing the bandages covering her wound, where the attackers had stabbed her. "If you have any problems or develop a fever, call me here at the hospital." She gave a pamphlet to Claire, and added, "Read this. And please consider making an appointment with a counselor."

Outside, Ron helped her into his car and when she was comfortable, he said, "I'll drive you to your home. I need an address."

She sat next to him, his coat wrapped around her like a blanket, slouching so that she was half-hidden, and her purse was lying on the floor near her feet. "I don't want to go home yet. Could you take me to your home? For a little while."

He raised an eyebrow, and was about to ask why, but changed his mind.

He started the engine and drove to his apartment in south Denver, and helped her get up the stairs. "You can lie down there on the sofa while I go in the kitchen and make some hot tea, okay?"

She took off her shoes and grabbed a plaid blue and white blanket that Ron kept on the sofa for cold evenings when he watched television.

While he was in the kitchen, he peeked into the living room at her. She was still sitting with her legs curled under her, the blanket around her shoulders, and her bare feet uncovered. She looked younger than ever, and vulnerable. He'd never really thought of her like that before.

He handed her a warm cup and she responded with a feeble smile and pulled the blanket tighter around her neck. Feeling awkward, he stood up and went into his bedroom and came out with an old sweatshirt and sweatpants his former girlfriend had left behind. "You can change into these," he said. "There's a bathroom down the hall."

"Thank you, Ron. I owe you more than you can possibly imagine."

After she changed clothes, they sat together, drinking their tea. As the sedative the doctor gave her took effect, she fell asleep. Ron puttered around the house and tried to keep quiet so he wouldn't wake her. When she awoke a couple hours later, he said, "Will you be okay alone if I leave you for a little while? I need to go to the school and check on things."

"You're right. I should have thought about that."

"No. I'm acting principal today. You're supposed to be resting."

She gave him another of those half-smiles, then said, "I'll be fine. Go. I'm going to sleep some more. I think the doctor gave me horse tranquilizers."

He grinned, and pulled the blanket up over her. Before he left her, he said, "Call me if you need anything. I'll come back in a while to check on you."

She nodded and said, "Go."

"Okay, I'm going. But can I at least call Frank? He's been great, helping with other problems. He should know about this."

"No! Please, don't. Please promise me you won't tell him, or anyone."

He nodded, and left. Damn, she could be frustrating at times.

STEVE JENSEN SAT in the conference room at Cameron High School, along with the school board's president and four of the six high school principals, waiting for the remaining two principals to arrive so that he could begin the Round Table Luncheon Meeting. Steve glanced at his watch again. Three minutes had passed since the last time he checked.

John was tapping his pencil on the table, clearly annoyed at the delay. "Well, it looks like they aren't going to show." He looked at Frank, and said, "They know they're supposed to be here today, don't they?"

Frank leaned forward in his seat and said, "Oh, definitely. I talked to both of them on Friday."

"Well, then I suggest you get on the phone and find out what's holding them up. Tell them to get over here. But we're not going to wait any longer."

Before John had a chance to say anything more, Liz Olson burst into the room.

"Sorry I'm late," she said, taking her coat off and draping it over the back of an empty chair.

John glared at her, then said, "That's it? Sorry I'm late. No particular reason for your tardiness, Liz?" His voice had an edge to it that signaled to Steve that this was going to be a difficult meeting. John was not an easy man to get along with even when he was in a good mood.

"Believe it or not, I had another meeting prior to this one. It ran a little longer than expected."

Frank left the room to call Claire. When he returned, he was frowning.

John asked, "Well? Did you talk to her?"

"Midland's secretary said that Claire and the assistant principal, Ron Baker, are in a meeting off premises. She didn't have any more information."

John shook his head and said, "What the hell! These meetings are mandatory."

Frank nodded, then looked down at his notebook on the table in front of him.

141

As John turned his head and stared momentarily at Steve, Steve clenched his jaw. Whether or not John was right about Claire and the Senator, it was obvious John believed it and was not going to let it go. The man had it in for Claire. Sooner or later, Steve would need to talk about the issue with her.

WHEN RON ARRIVED at the school, Kim told him that Frank had called.

"Claire's supposed to be at the Superintendent's Round Table Luncheon," Kim said.

Ron sighed, and rubbed his head. "Sorry. We both forgot about that meeting. I should have called in to let them know she went home sick. I'll call Frank."

"Huh? She went home sick? I thought you were both at a meeting."

"Yeah, we were. But she got sick and left."

Kim nodded.

"Any problems here today?"

"Not so far."

After Ron called Frank, he returned to his apartment at lunchtime to check on Claire. When he opened the door, she jumped.

"It's me. Ron. Don't worry." He stuck his keys back in his trouser pockets. "Are you okay?"

"I'm fine. What's happening at school?"

"Believe it or not, it's relatively quiet there today."

"You mean if I'm not there, they behave. Is someone trying to tell me something?"

"Believe me, they were misbehaving before they ever met you. It's not you. What you do or don't know makes no difference."

"Oh, that's comforting."

Ron winced. "Sorry. That didn't come out the way I meant it." He set his keys down on a table. "Can I get you something to eat? I haven't had lunch. Would a sandwich be okay?"

"I'm not really hungry."

"Won't you at least try to eat something? You need to keep up your strength."

"I guess. I'll try."

He went into the kitchen, returning a short time later with two plates and two cups of tea. After lunch he returned to school and sat in his office, thinking about the situation. He'd done the best he could with Claire under the circumstances, but was that enough? He didn't think so. He certainly had failed with Celia. A female would know what to do; someone totally different from Ron and from Celia's mother, someone stable and comforting. Decision made, he went to the faculty lunchroom to talk to Nancy Palmer, the English teacher whom he trusted and Claire liked. They went back to his office and Ron told her in strict confidence what had happened. Nancy assured him she would keep their secret.

After school let out for the day, they went to Ron's apartment together. When they arrived, Ron hesitated outside his own door. God, he hoped he was doing the right thing bringing Nancy here.

When Claire saw Nancy with Ron, she cried out, "You promised you wouldn't tell anyone. How could you betray me like that?" She jumped up from the sofa, and paced, wringing her hands.

Ron grabbed her and tried to calm her. "Claire, I only told Nancy. I needed someone else to help. I'm not equipped to deal with this. You need a woman to talk to. Please don't be angry."

He coaxed her back to the sofa and she calmed down. Then he and Nancy talked to her at length and Ron was relieved that his decision to bring Nancy proved right.

Late in the afternoon Ron said, "I'll make us some sandwiches for dinner." He stood up to head into the kitchen but stopped when Claire shouted "Oh no!"

He stared at her. "What's wrong?"

"I didn't know it was dinnertime. I have to go home."

"Huh?" Ron said. "You don't have to leave. If you don't want sandwiches, I'll go out and get some takeout. Nancy and I planned to stay up with you all night, if you need us too."

"I can't stay here," Claire said. "I have to get home to my son. He'll be expecting me now."

Ron and Nancy exchanged glances. "Your son? You never told us you had a child."

"I'm sorry. I don't like to discuss my personal life at work. Besides, it's not like I have a lot of free time at the school."

Well, she was right about that. They had little time to discuss their private lives, but still, most of the faculty members knew the basics about each other. Until now, he hadn't realized how little they knew about Claire.

"Where is he?" Nancy asked.

"At his nanny's house."

"His nanny? How old is he?"

"He's three-and-a-half. I'm supposed to pick him up by six o'clock. The nanny goes to college classes on most weeknights and it's a quarter past five now. I don't have my car. It's at the school." Claire was back on her feet, pacing like before.

Ron said, "I'll take Nancy back to the school so she can get her car, and I'll take you to your nanny's house to pick up your son. Then I'll drop you off at your home."

Nancy said, "Someone should stay with her tonight. Do you have anyone who can stay with you, Claire?"

Claire's face reddened. "No. But I'll be all right."

"I'll stay," Nancy said. "You can drive both of us back to school. We'll take my car to Claire's. That way, if we need anything, we'll have transportation."

Ron pulled up next to Nancy's car and watched until they drove away, then he leaned his head on his steering wheel and wept, thinking about Claire and Celia.

CLAIRE WENT INSIDE the nanny's house to get Marcus, while Nancy waited outside in her car. When they came out and Claire opened the car door, Marcus looked up at his mother and said, "This isn't our car, Mommy." Claire put her hands on his shoulders and said, "It's all right. This is my friend, Nancy. She's going to drive us home and spend the night because I'm not feeling well. She's going to help out."

Claire made the introductions, and then helped Marcus climb into the car.

"Mommy, where's my car seat?"

"Oh, I forgot about that. We'll have to make do without it tonight."

"Okay."

As Nancy pulled away from the curb, she said, "If you don't mind, I'll make a quick stop at my house. I need a few clothes, toothbrush, and other necessities. We can stop and get something for dinner to take to back to your home on the way."

After dinner Marcus fell asleep on the sofa next to Claire.

A while later, Nancy came over to the sofa, scooped him up, and carried him upstairs to his room. When she returned to the living room, she and Claire talked for a while, about kids and growing up mostly. Nancy had three grown kids of her own, and she shared some of her own experiences in child rearing. Claire was glad for the distraction from her own thoughts. Around eleven o'clock they decided to call it a night. They gathered up sheets and blankets and prepared the sofa bed for Nancy. After saying their goodnights, Claire retreated upstairs to her room and shut the door.

Alone again, Claire tried to push away pictures from her mind. She almost succeeded until she laid down and her mind flooded with fragments of memories, ancient and new. Her body still ached, but it was the mental anguish that was almost unbearable. How would she ever be able to go back to work? She knew she didn't really have a choice, but the thought was terrifying. Even walking into that office felt impossible. Her mind played games with her, tormenting, ridiculing, and blaming. Why did they do this? Why didn't she see it coming? She was supposed to be brilliant, and yet she hadn't anticipated this. She felt like a fake, not so smart after all. She hated them for the attack.

She hated herself, too.

Tossing and turning for what felt like hours, she looked at the clock on the nightstand, and sighed. Would she ever get to sleep? She began to doubt her effectiveness as a leader. Had John Richmond been right about her failing? Maybe she was living in a dream world. Maybe she couldn't fix the problems at the school.

The logical thing to do would be to call Brad again and tell him everything. He wanted proof, and she had that now: the hospital emergency room could verify it. He would take her back to the center and erase her identity. What choice would Brad and his bosses have? And hadn't that been what she wanted?

She sighed. Why couldn't anything be simple?

Her thoughts argued on and on. She needed to get out this horrible job. She wasn't doing anyone any good, especially not to herself. But leaving now would be admitting failure. Was she prepared for that? It wasn't like before, when she'd blown her cover by slipping up. That was nothing compared with failing at a job. She'd never done that before. And could she really abandon ship and leave the school to the gangs and bullies? She hadn't ignored the crime that Callum was committing. She'd gone out of her way to make sure he and the others didn't get away with it, though of course she had other reasons as well. Was this any different?

She rolled over in bed, wincing from pain in her side, where she'd been stabbed. Turning once more, the pain dissipated somewhat and she closed her eyes again, still trying to fall asleep. Then another thought occurred to her. If she stayed in the job, could she make a difference, or was she nothing more than another incompetent Midland school principal?

Slowly, and with care to avoid causing herself pain again, she pulled her legs up and curled into a fetal position, the safest position she could think of—but three unwanted faces, each with a set of brown eyes, stared fiercely at her in her mind.

A shiver ran through her. She hid her head under the fuzzy pink blanket on her bed, trying to blot out the images, and it worked. Only now her thoughts shifted to another memory, one that had occurred in England long ago when a group of male students in her high school had followed her and cornered her in the girls' lavatory. She was the only thirteen-year-old in the school prepping for A-Levels, which had made her a target of ridicule for the older students. "If you want to be an adult, you haveta start acting like one," they'd said. "You gotta do what other girls do with blokes." Luckily, a couple of girls had shown up, and the boys had run off before they had a chance to do anything more than taunt. She'd never forgotten the fear.

Stop it! Don't let any of those jerks ruin your life. She pushed away the mental pictures and tried to imagine going back to Midland and acting as though nothing had happened. The memories would probably diminish with time. But she knew the fear would haunt her for a lifetime.

CHAPTER TWELVE

IN THE MORNING, on Thursday, Nancy phoned Ron, telling him that Claire would be staying home for the rest of the week. Claire listened in on the phone call.

"She's doing better, but isn't ready to go back."

"Are you staying with her, or coming in?"

"I'll stay here today and try to be at work on Friday. We'll have to see how it goes. She's been sleeping a lot, which she apparently needs."

"Thanks," Ron said. "Do whatever you think is best."

Claire stayed in bed all day on Thursday, not by choice but out of necessity. Her body ached even more than it had the previous day, and the pain meds and tranquilizers the doctor had prescribed made her sleepy. She would sleep a while, and then awaken when a nightmare made her sit up a scream out in terror.

Nancy attended to Marcus. Claire would occasionally hear laughter coming from the living room. Several times, when Marcus ran upstairs and into Claire's bedroom, Nancy guided him away, and said, "Sorry, Claire."

Claire tried to get up at noon. When she lowered her legs over the side of the bed and tried to sit up, her side hurt fiercely and she felt nauseous. She would never have guessed that the day after her stabbing would be worse.

Nancy brought Claire's lunch into her bedroom. Claire nibbled at it and then set the plate on the nightstand. How could she eat when she kept choking up tears? She was worthless. She'd done nothing to fix the school and she'd let everyone down, including herself.

She rolled over with her back toward the window, and closed her eyes.

She awoke later to the sound of her mobile phone ringing in the living room.

Nancy poked her head in the doorway and whispered, "Are you awake?"

Claire nodded and rose up on one elbow.

"Steve Jensen is on the phone for you. He wants to know if you're okay. He said you weren't at the round table meeting yesterday and Kim said you were out sick."

How could she have forgotten Steve and the meeting? He'd told her she couldn't miss two meetings in a row.

She tried to think but her head was spinning. "Uh, I don't think I'm up to talking with him." She started to lie back down, stopped, and looked at Nancy. "Did he ask you what was wrong with me?"

"I told him you have the flu. I hope that's okay."

Claire nodded. "That was quick thinking. Thanks for covering for me. Did he ask who you were and why you were here?"

Nancy twisted her mouth, chuckled, and then said, "Yeah, he thought I was you, at first. I told him I'm a neighbor and I came over to check on you."

Had he unwittingly given Nancy a hint about their relationship? Claire tried to read Nancy's expression, but Nancy was giving her a poker face. That, in itself, probably said it all.

Claire tried to hide her sigh. "Thanks, Nancy. Please tell him I'm fine, that I'm sleeping and I'll talk to him on Monday?"

Alone again, Claire wondered why everyone except her could think quick and come up with easy lies. She was supposed to be the genius and yet she undoubtedly would have blundered if she'd taken the call.

In the evening Claire forced herself out of bed and wobbled into the living room.

"Mommy, you're up!" Marcus rushed over to her and wrapped his arms around her legs.

She patted his head. She didn't dare try to pick him up or squat down to hug him.

"Are you feeling better?" he asked, looking up at her.

She tried to smile. "I am. What have you been doing?"

"We read books and played games. Nancy's nice. We're watching TV. Do you wanna watch with us?"

"Sure."

After everyone went to bed, Claire lay awake, still trying to push images of the attack out of her mind. The best way to do that was to think about something else, she kept telling herself. One of the biggest moments in her life, her move from England to the U.S., came to mind. The move had been both exciting and stressful—months of planning, getting work visas, sending out resumes, interviewing. By the time they actually were on their way to the U.S. and their new life, she and Callum had momentarily felt homeless and free like gypsies. He'd suggested they sell all of their furniture and most of their belongings and start over.

"This is going to be fun," he had said as they made their way to Heathrow Airport in a taxi. "I already rented us a posh flat. We'll decorate it with furniture and pictures that we'll pick out together. No more his-and-hers, you know."

She'd smiled, and nodded. They'd had plenty of arguments about what should stay and what should go when they'd first moved in together two years earlier.

"You're going to love the place. Thanks for agreeing to the move. You won't regret it. The university is prestigious and you'll get to rub elbows with the best faculty in the world."

A porter smiled at them, and asked which airline they were going on. He then loaded everything onto a cart and took it to the ticket counter. Once they finished with the check-in, they headed to the gate and an hour later boarded the Boeing 747.

She wouldn't regret it. Ha! Trusting Callum was the first of many mistakes.

Claire flashed forward to another flight—her first one with Marcus when she'd fled Boston right after someone had tried to kill her in a drive-by shooting. That was back when she was still Juliet and Marcus was still Aidan. *Callum should have been there to see his son experiencing something so big and exciting! Callum should be here now to see his son grow and learn. But he doesn't deserve to see.*

The flight attendant had pointed out their seats, and Juliet had helped Aidan into his seat and then settled into the seat next to him. After she sat down, she made sure Aidan was comfortable and safely tucked under his seatbelt. She had seated him next to a window and he was straining to see outside, so interested in seeing everything that was happening. He smiled and watched everything with bright eyes, and Juliet smiled at his eagerness. She felt herself relax a little, and settled into her own seat.

When she was situated, she couldn't resist peeking through the window herself to see what the two-and-a-half-year-old was so interested in. They watched luggage carts being wheeled around, and saw men tossing suitcases and bags into the baggage compartment. Inside the airplane, she heard the throaty roar of the plane's engines, and the whisper of the air conditioner. A man in front of her reached up to adjust the air direction, and Juliet decided to follow suit and adjust hers and Aidan's vents, too.

Once everyone was seated, the flight attendants came around to check that seatbelts were fastened and tray tables were in their upright position. A few minutes later, the pilot welcomed his passengers via the intercom and told them they would be departing for Minneapolis-St. Paul soon. Ten minutes later the plane began to move, first backing up, turning, and then maneuvering its way down a long runway.

When the plane took flight, every muscle in Juliet's body tensed momentarily. Flying wasn't so bad, she thought, once they were at cruising altitude. It was taking off, landing, and flying through turbulence that frightened her. But apparently not Aiden, who reveled in every acceleration and bump. Once the airplane stabilized, the attendant conducted her safety procedure demonstration, and the fasten seatbelt signed was turned off. Juliet leaned back then, closed her eyes, and tried to relax.

Juliet was finally calming down when Aidan began to chatter enthusiastically about how they were 'eagles flying in clouds'. Although he was mostly a well-behaved child, he was already squirming in his seat. He unfastened his seat belt and scooted to the edge of his seat, so that his short legs, with hints of baby fat remaining, hung over the edge, and the toes of his sneakers tick-ticked against the seat in front of him. He giggled and smiled and asked a hundred questions, undaunted by his limited vocabulary, taking Juliet's mind off her fear of flying for a while.

After his fourth trip down the narrow aisle to the lavatory, Juliet finally told him he would have to stay seated because she was growing weary of escorting him back and forth. She knew that he didn't really need to go to the bathroom—he was only recently toilet-trained—he just liked to walk through the plane and to go into the tiny closet-like room. Once used to the sounds and motions of the plane, he quieted and played with some small toys that Juliet pulled out of his carry-on bag.

When he was finally settled in, Juliet sat back and closed her eyes again, hoping to sleep for a while. Sleep evaded her though and her mind drifted from place to place as she contemplated what she would do once she arrived in Minneapolis. She hadn't a clue if she would find a job, but she couldn't stay in Boston and wait for someone to take another shot at her or her son, nor could she wait for the police to come and arrest her for her inadvertent role in Callum's criminal activities. Her biggest worry was for Aidan, her sweet, innocent boy. He'd already lost one parent—she couldn't let him lose another. Looking over at him and watching him play with a toy, she thought about her life. She hoped things would work out; she would probably never again be a professor—she knew that—but couldn't imagine herself unemployed. Her work, she hated to admit, was her life, her identity.

Claire rolled over in bed and tried to push away those old memories. That flight had ended with an FBI agent handcuffing her and taking her in for questioning. She'd handed over Callum's laptop computer and entered the program. She punched her pillow hard. It's no use, she thought. No matter how hard I try to fix the problems in my life, I can't. She hadn't jumped ship, and yet she was drowning. She pulled her blanket over her head and let the tears roll down her cheeks.

In the morning Nancy said, "Are you sure you'll be okay on your own today? I can stay another day."

"I'm fine," she lied. "I will be all right alone." She made an attempt to smile, and hoped it was convincing. Then, as an afterthought, she said, and really meant it, "I appreciate everything you've done. I couldn't have made it through this without you. And Ron. Please go back to work. I'll see you there on Monday."

"I'm glad I could help. I know Ron feels the same. Should I drop Marcus off at the nanny's apartment on my way?"

"You wouldn't mind doing that?"

"It's not a problem. I already know where she lives."

"Yes, then. Thank you. I'll call her and let her know you're coming."

Before Nancy left, she stuck her head back into Claire's room. "I just got off the phone with Ron. Your car is still at the school. If you give me your car key, I'll pick up Marcus after work in your car and drive him here. Ron will meet me here and then drive me back to the school."

"Oh, thank you, Nancy. I'm sorry I'm so much trouble."

"No problem, just feel better."

Claire called the nanny and told her about Nancy dropping off Marcus and picking him up, then she walked downstairs and hugged Marcus before he left with Nancy. When they were outside, Claire closed the door and locked it. She double-checked the deadbolt, then sat down on the floor, covered her face with her hands, and cried herself to sleep. She woke up later on the hard floor. She pulled herself up and padded into the kitchen. The digital clock read 10:33. How could so much time have passed already?

She sat down on the sofa. Her back and necked ached, probably from lying on the floor, she decided. Picking up the remote control, she turned on the TV and flipped through the channels, but finding nothing of interest gave up and turned it back off. She picked up her mobile phone lying on the coffee table and looked at the message list. Steve had called twice yesterday. She carried the phone upstairs, placed it on her nightstand, and lay down on the bed. She thought about dinners with Steve, how he'd made her laugh; his jokes and his stories about his growing up. They could intelligently discuss almost any topic. Did he know how rare it was for her to find someone with whom she could do that? She pictured his face, his warm blue eyes, and smiled. She was pretty sure she was falling in love with him. That brought up a new dilemma. It was bad enough having to hide her real identity from him, but how could she not tell him about what had happened today? She couldn't tell him and she couldn't not tell him. Their relationship, like her life was a doomed conundrum. She sighed and then groaned as images from the attack pushed their way back into her mind.

What could she have done to prevent it? Frank had told her the previous principals were incompetent, yet they hadn't allowed something like this to happen. What did that make her? She glanced at the bottle of prescription pills on her nightstand. How many of them would she have to take to end it all?

She rolled over and pushed that thought out of her mind. Eventually, she fell asleep, but several times over the weekend, especially as her back-to-work day grew closer, she glanced at that bottle.

BY MONDAY MORNING her physical pains had eased. Claire surveyed herself in the bathroom mirror. While her clothing hid most of the black-and-blue marks on her body, other marks weren't so easily hidden. She stared at her face, which reminded her some piece of fruit, a nectarine or plum perhaps, bruised in several places from falling off a tree branch prematurely. She wrinkled up her face and puckered her mouth. Now she really did look like a prune! She would have laughed at the comparison under better circumstances. Taking her makeup kit out of a drawer, she began to work on concealment.

An hour later she bit her lip as she studied her work. It looked dreadful. Her mum would never be have allowed herself to be seen in public looking so artificial. Claire took a moist cloth and blotted away some of the powder, the dark-circle-diminisher, the foundation, and the blush, and then smoothed and blended the remaining spots. Most women could probably have worked magic, but not her. Applying makeup was decidedly not one of her talents—another notch to add to an ever-growing list.

Turning from the mirror, she left the bathroom and went to Marcus's room to help him get ready to go to Kate's. Half an hour later she pulled their coats from the closet, and bundled up Marcus. It was snowing outside.

He fussed and squirmed, and it was nearly impossible to tie the string on his hood.

On her drive to the school, after dropping off Marcus at the nanny's apartment, she chided herself for not going for the gun that she'd confiscated and locked in her desk drawer. She shook her head. Wouldn't have done any good anyway. What did she know about guns? Nothing. And was the gun even loaded? She'd locked it up without checking. What an idiot.

She parked in her normal space in the school car park, and sat there, trying to find the nerve to get out of the car. Ron had sent her a text message this morning telling her that he and Nancy had cleaned up her office over the weekend. Still, the thought of entering her office was making her sick to her stomach. Ron would be there soon. Best to wait for him. She sat there for fifteen minutes, constantly turning every which way to make sure no one was lurking about. By the time she saw Ron's dark blue SUV pull into the car park, her neck was hurting again.

Ron parked next to her and waited for her to get out of her car.

"You made it," he said. "I wasn't sure you'd be here. How are you feeling?"

"I'm fine," she lied, making her best attempt at pasting on a smile.

"Glad to hear it. Are you ready to go inside?"

She nodded and matched his pace as they walked so she wouldn't get left behind, especially while they were on the side of the building where the evergreen bushes were.

He unlocked the front door of the building and turned on the lights. She hesitated, and he gave her a questioning look. She took a deep breath and followed him inside.

"You don't have to do this today, you know," he said when they stood outside her office. "Maybe you should wait a few more days. Give yourself more recovery time."

Her mouth was dry and she wasn't sure she could speak, but she had to try. "No. I'm ready. I'm fine."

Unlocking her door, he opened it, reached inside and flipped the light switch. He handed her the keys. She stood frozen, staring into the office.

"Are you sure you're ready? Do you want me to go in with you, keep you company? I can set up my laptop in your office."

She wasn't sure of anything except that she didn't want to be here. *Don't tell him that. He'll think you're a baby. Remember the magic word—fine. Everyone accepts 'fine'. Marcus, Nanny Kate, Nancy, Steve.*

"I'm fine. You don't need to stay. I'd rather be alone, anyway."

"Whatever you want. If you need me, you know where to find me."

She stared a moment longer, then turned her head to look at him. He was already gone. All right, then. Time to take the plunge. She stiffened her back, bracing herself, and entered the office. Why hadn't she asked Ron to check it out first, make sure no one was hiding? Get a grip. The door had been locked. It's safe.

Slowly, she walked over to her desk chair, peeking around the furniture and under the desk to be sure, but stopped where she'd dropped her mobile phone. Her eyes filled with tears and she had to force herself to stop them. Finally getting to her chair, she plopped down and stared at nothing, only seeing the visions inside her own head.

A century later someone knocked on her door. Claire stared at it, afraid to move or make a sound. The door slowly opened and she stifled a scream.

"Ron told me you were back. I hope you're feeling better." It was Kim.

"Thanks. I—I might still be contagious so I'll stay in here and get caught up on paperwork. I don't want to expose anyone to the flu. If anyone needs the principal, please send them to Ron."

"Will do. Let me know if you need anything."

A couple minutes later, Kim returned. "Would you like some coffee? It's fresh."

"No. Thank you. I'm fine. I just want to be left alone."

Kim gave her a questioning look before turning and pulling the door closed behind her with a loud click.

By ten o'clock Claire had answered most of her emails, except for the ones she forwarded to Ron or to Bill Wilson. She looked at her calendar. A budget report was due on Wednesday. That was something she could handle. She'd barely begun working when her phone rang.

Ron said, "We have an emergency in the gymnasium. I need your assistance."

She hung up the phone and stepped out into the outer office, then made her way through the corridors which were filled with students rushing between classrooms. She tried to avoid physical contact as she passed through the crowd.

In the gym she learned that two students had brawled and one of them was injured, possibly a concussion. Paramedics and police were on their way. She stood around watching. What was she supposed to do? When the police arrived a few minutes later, she glanced at Ron. He looked her way and she mouthed 'I'm in the way. You can handle this,' and then carefully walked back to her office.

RON FINISHED HIS report with the police, and went back to his office. He glanced at Claire's office on his way. The door was closed.

He exchanged glances with Kim.

She shrugged her shoulders, and asked, "Has she come out of her office today?"

"I saw her once," he said.

"Is something wrong? I know she's been sick, but she nearly bit my head off when I asked if she wanted coffee and again when I tried to send a boy and his parents to her office. You were busy. What was I supposed to do with them?"

He kept his face blank, although he was worried. Clearly, Claire wasn't ready to be back. What was he supposed to do about that? Damn. He didn't want to go over her head to Frank. Okay, give her a couple days, he told himself.

"What did you do?"

"I apologized and told them I'll have to reschedule."

Over the next couple of days, he kept a close eye on Claire— at least when she was out of her office. Most of the time, she kept herself closed off, literally, and when she was out of her office, she walked around like a zombie. It wasn't until late Wednesday afternoon that she finally met with two teachers and with one student and her mother. Again this morning she met with a small group of teachers. That was a good sign, wasn't it?

After lunch, he stood near Kim's desk discussing the student who was taken to the hospital on Monday. Claire rushed by and went into her office, slamming the door behind her.

Kim said, "What was that about?"

"Damned if I know."

"I'm getting worried," Kim said. "Parents are pissed because she set up appointments with them yesterday, and now she's cancelling them. What is going on?"

"Huh? I hadn't heard anything about that."

"I've gotten four phone calls in the past hour from parents complaining. Your schedule's already full. What am I supposed to do about the meetings?"

"I'll try talking to her."

He knocked on her door, then opened it and stepped inside and closed it.

"We need to talk, Claire."

She didn't respond.

"Have you tried talking to a counselor? You've been through a trauma. You need some help."

"I don't need anything. And I don't want to talk. Now, if you don't mind, I have work to do."

AFTER RON LEFT her office, Claire started shaking. She picked up her mobile phone and called Brad.

She told him about the attack, choosing her words carefully because she was afraid she might fall apart.

When she finished, he groaned. "Why didn't you tell me sooner?"

"I—I don't know. I thought I could deal with it, but I can't. I need you to bring me in, Brad. I can't eat, I can't sleep. This is a bad place and I'm getting more frightened to come to work. I can barely drag myself here.

"Before I do that," he said, "I need a copy of the police report to show my boss."

She didn't respond.

"Claire, are you still there?"

"There isn't one. A police report, I mean. I—I didn't report it."

"You what?"

She explained what happened, how Ron had taken her to the hospital and helped her. She tried to explain why she kept it a secret.

"You expect me to believe this? I believed you when you said someone was watching you, even though my boss didn't buy it. But you've gone too far. I might have believed it if you'd called me the day it happened, but a week afterwards? No way."

"I'm telling you the truth. You know me. I'm a terrible liar. I couldn't make up something like this."

"Sorry, Claire."

"I can't take this anymore. If I stay, I'll get fired. I can't do this." She didn't tell him how close she was to taking a whole bottle of pills and ending it all.

"You're gonna have to make the best of your situation. You taught at Oxford and Weymouth University for Christ's sake! You don't have any excuse for not being able to handle the job."

"It's not the same."

After she hung up, she remembered the visit to the hospital. Surely he would accept a report from them as proof. She dialed Brad's number again. He didn't answer.

Twenty minutes later, her phone rang and she grabbed it. It had to be Brad. He must have seen that she tried to call him back.

"Hello."

"Hi, Claire, it's Steve. I've been calling you all week. I've been worried about you."

Her heart stopped. She'd been dreading this call. She bit her lip, took a deep breath and let it out. "Oh, Steve. Sorry I didn't return your calls. I've been busy. Uh, I have someone in my office."

"Okay, I won't keep you, but I want to see if you'll have dinner with me again on Friday night."

"I'm still not feeling well. I'll have to pass. Maybe another time."

Steve was silent for a moment, then said, "Did I do something wrong?"

"No. I can't talk right now. Like I said, I have someone in my office."

She hung up the phone and hid her face in her hands.

Ten minutes later she packed up her laptop and stood up. She grabbed her handbag and started to walk toward the door. Remembering the gun in the desk drawer, she went back to her desk and unlocked the drawer. She took the gun and dropped it into her handbag, then walked out of her office, locking the door behind her. She walked by Kim's desk and said, "I'm going home."

Kim looked at her as if she thought she'd lost her mind.

On her way home, as she was sitting at a stop light, she looked around and waited for the light to change. In a park on the corner she noticed a teenage boy sitting on a picnic table bench, his gangly legs sprawled. He looked familiar. The light changed. She flicked on her turn-signal and made a right-hand turn giving her a closer view. Was that Curtis Browne, one of the boys who were sent to her office on her second day of work?

Oh bloody hell! Keep driving. Pull up to the driveway on the left, turn around and drive home. But she didn't. She pulled into the car park, got out, and walked toward him. He looked almost as miserable as she felt. He apparently saw her coming and twitched as if he would bolt. But he didn't. She sat down next to him on the bench and glanced sideways at him. He looked younger than she remembered—a little boy in a big body.

"Why aren't you in school, Curtis?"

He looked at his feet and didn't answer.

"Please talk to me, Curtis."

He turned his head and looked up at her. "Why aren't you in school?"

"Fair enough. I'm having a really bad day. I had to get away."

He didn't say anything. He looked back down at his feet. "I'm having a bad day, too."

"What happened?"

"I don't wanna talk about it."

They sat quietly for a while.

"You know," Claire said, "It's really cold out here. Would you like to get something warm to drink? There's a coffee shop down the street. It'll be on me."

He looked around, then said, "I guess that'd be okay."

After the waitress brought drinks, Claire said, "You can talk to me. I'm a good listener. Although I'm not good at much else, I am good at that."

He looked surprised.

"The other kids, well, they've been teasing me. A group of jerks stuffed me in my locker yesterday. I couldn't get out. I kept banging and screaming. Finally, another student heard and let me out. It must have been fifteen minutes later. I got a tardy slip from Mr. Owens. He sent me to Mr. Baker. I got detention and my mom yelled at me for causing trouble."

"Did you tell Mr. Owens or Mr. Baker what happened?"

Curtis bent his head. "No," he whispered.

"Why not?"

"Because you don't rat on bullies like that."

"Didn't you want to make sure they didn't do that to you again, or to anyone else?"

"They woulda got detention and that woulda pissed them off. They already stuffed me in a locker. What do you think they would do if they were really mad at me?"

Claire studied the boy. She had so many questions she wasn't sure which one to ask first. Finally, she said, "Why did they stuff you in the locker if they weren't mad at you?"

He looked up again, this time making eye contact.

"Smart kids mess up the grading curve. That's what they said."

"Are you a smart student?"

He nodded.

"Straight-A student?

He nodded.

"What are you best subjects?"

"Math and science. I love numbers and theories." He paused and then said, "You won't tell anyone, will you? People already think I'm a nerd."

"I won't tell anyone at school. But I will drive you home. Maybe I can talk to you mom or dad. Would that be all right?"

"I guess so."

At his house, his mother raised her eyebrows when she saw Claire.

"Hello, Mrs. Browne, I'm Claire Constantine, the principal at Midland High School. Could we talk for a moment?"

"What did my boy do? He got detention already. You expelling him? He's not a bad kid, maybe goofs off sometimes, but he never does anything mean or disrespectful. I'd smack him upside the head if he did."

"No, no. Nothing like that. I'm worried about him, actually. He tells me he's having some problems with bullies. They're teasing him for being smart."

"Oh, that. Curtis takes after his daddy. Smart never did him any good, either."

"I really don't like the way the other kids are treating him. We need to nourish his strengths. He has the potential to go to college and make something good of himself."

"Yeah, what are you gonna do about it? Who's gonna take care of him? You?"

"Will you come into the school next week and speak with our assistant principal or maybe the school's counselor? Maybe they can figure out a way to help your son. I can arrange the meeting for you."

"I don't go into that school. Besides, there's nothing anybody can do to help."

"Shouldn't we try, Mrs. Browne? His future isn't already written."

The woman stared at her disbelievingly, and said, "Oh, yeah?"

AFTER TALKING TO Curtis's mom, Claire drove to the nanny's home and picked up Marcus. They ate an early dinner, she read to him for a while, and then she put him to bed early. She needed time to think.

Sitting on the sofa, she sighed and closed her eyes to think, but her mind veered back in the direction of the attack, which morphed into a rehash of her problems at school and her being stuck in the witness protection program. This time, though, instead of blaming herself entirely, she blamed Callum, too. If not for him, she would still be a respected mathematician and none of her problems would ever have happened.

She remembered vividly how it had all started. She'd opened her computer one morning, a Wednesday morning, and went to her documents folder to work on a file for her latest project. It wasn't there. Instead, she saw oddly named folders. What the bloody hell, she'd thought. Further investigation revealed she had taken Callum's computer to work by mistake. Her first impulse was to close it up, but something about those file names nagged at her. She found her way into one and immediately knew something was wrong.

When she'd questioned him about it at home that evening, he'd explained it and said she was so unworldly that she didn't understand these things. He'd called her naïve.

That memory almost made Claire laugh. She certainly couldn't be called naïve any more. She would give almost anything to go back to the way she was. Life sucked. For the first time, she now understood why her mother had taken her own life. Joe Powell used to call his wife, Amelia, naïve, too.

The vision of Claire's—Juliet's— mother on the day she'd died, popped into her mind. Her mother sitting in the driver's seat of her rusted-out Bentley that she'd bought second-hand after her divorce from Joe.

Emancipated minor, Juliet, had arrived home from work that autumn day thirteen years ago, had opened the garage door, and found Amelia's car there. Nothing unusual in that since Amelia had been practically hibernating in Juliet's leased house for two months because she was too depressed to do anything. But as Juliet had driven her car into the garage, she'd realized the other car's engine was running and saw old rags stuffed into the tailpipe. The car was filled with smoky fumes. She'd jumped out of her own car and rushed to the driver's side. It was too late. The sight of her mother's cherry red skin and lifeless eyes had sent Juliet into hysterics.

Her mother had given up, and Juliet now understood why. Joe had clipped Amelia's wings soon after their wedding and kept them clipped for eighteen years. He wouldn't let her visit with friends or go anywhere without him. Only when he was out of town could she have a social life, and after all those years she had decided she couldn't stand it anymore. Not confident enough to ask him for a divorce, she had gone in a different direction and had started taking advantage of that small opening in her cage by going out to parties while he was away. During one of those parties she'd met a man and had started an affair. Juliet had discovered it by accident. Amelia had begged her to keep her secret, and Juliet had tried.

Of course back then, Juliet had been an even worse liar than she was now. When Joe had come home early from one of his trips a few months after Juliet had made the promise to cover for her, he'd questioned Juliet about where her mum was. Juliet had made up some story about her having gone to the doctor. Joe had drilled her, because he didn't believe her, and Juliet had run to her room. When Amelia had returned that evening, they fought. Her mother screamed, and fearing for her mum's safety, Juliet had taken her mum away. Amelia moved in with her lover and she seemed happier than Juliet had ever seen her. Months later, after the divorce, Amelia had caught her man in bed with another woman and her fairytale romance had vaporized.

She'd given up on life. She hadn't been perfect, but she had so much to offer. What a tragedy, what a shame.

Claire opened her eyes and sat up. Was she really thinking about giving up, too? What would happen to Marcus if she took out that gun and ended her own life? She couldn't do that to him. Her stomach knotted up. All these years she'd beaten herself up repeatedly over her role in her parents' divorce and her mother's suicide. The guilt was almost unbearable. Maybe Marcus wouldn't suffer from guilt, but he most definitely would suffer loss. He'd already suffered the loss of one parent. She jumped up and went into Marcus's bedroom. He lay there wrapped in blankets. So peaceful and innocent. She had done everything she could to shield him from harm, and here she was, about to give up. She shook her head. No way could she do that to her son. She thought about Curtis, too, and his mother. The woman clearly loved her son, though she didn't seem the kind of mother who would fight for him. Who was going to do that? Maybe Ron, but he didn't have the time or the resources.

She reached down and patted Marcus's head, tucked his blanket around him, and left his room. When she entered the hallway, she caught her reflection in a wall mirror. She stared, taking a good long look. Well, Claire Constantine wasn't doing too well. She was no speechmaker, no great leader. Maybe it was time to go back to who she really was. Dr. Juliet Powell.

CHAPTER THIRTEEN

AFTER CLAIRE DROPPED off Marcus at his nanny's apartment Friday morning, she sat in her car in the car park outside Nanny Kate's building and called Ron.

Having made a decision, Claire said, "I'm taking the day off, but I'll be back at work on Monday."

"God, Claire, we thought you'd walked off the job yesterday," Ron said. "I wasn't sure whether to call Frank and tell him, or not."

"Oh, no! You didn't call him, did you?"

"No. I didn't have the time, to be honest."

"I'm really sorry. I was in a really bad place. I needed more time to think, without interruptions. I hope you understand."

He didn't answer.

"Ron, I will be back. I haven't given up yet."

"Well, that's good to hear."

The tone of his voice didn't exactly match his words. Was he disappointed that she was coming back, or was it something else? Better let it go for now.

"Will you let Kim know?"

"Sure."

After she ended her phone call, Claire pulled out of her parking space and drove to an office supply store on East 120th Avenue. She had put together the beginning of a shopping list last night. Now it was time to take action. She started with a Quartet Inview Magnetic Whiteboard identical to the one she'd used in her office at Weymouth. Next, she found, a dry erase eraser, dry markers, magnetic clips, a lightweight presentation easel, a 60" by 30" white folding table, a 25" by 30" flip chart and markers, and a plastic file tote. What else? She stood motionless in the middle of an aisle momentarily, thinking. Oh, yes, printer paper, highlighters, sticky notes and flags. That should do it.

She paid for her purchases, which set her back almost three hundred dollars, and drove home. Making several trips back and forth between her condo and car, she carried everything inside and set it in a pile near the front door. Now came the hard part. Where was she going to put it all?

The living room was really the only possible place for a makeshift office, the best spot being in the front corner near the window where her furniture sat. Seeing no choice, she slid the coffee table over, and then moved the loveseat out of the way. She then struggled with the sofa which was almost impossible to budge. Eventually she managed. Although the new arrangement was rather cramped, she could live with it.

First thing after setting up her makeshift office, she placed her computer and printer on the table, pulled up a chair from the kitchen table, and brewed herself a pot of coffee.

Tired from her labors, she plopped down on the sofa with a cup of coffee and took a break. All right, she thought. I have everything I need. Now what?

Ideas began swirling around in her head. As usual, though, her mind soon drifted back to her banishment. Her genius with numbers, analysis, and logic had put her into this situation. Of course, when you got down to it, Callum's corruption was the root cause, but if she hadn't been so good with numbers and algorithms, he might have given it up, or at least she might not have contributed to the crime.

It had really begun, not just by her inadvertently taking Callum's computer to work with her, but by her digging around on it and finding a suspicious looking folder. In the first document she'd opened, she had seen columns of figures and blocks of equations. Meat and drink to her and almost without consciously thinking she began seeing patterns emerge. She'd started to see amounts she recognized, sums given in grants to the University, which she had heard discussed; other sums which had been reported in newspapers. All these entries represented vast amounts of money, manipulated, and transferred, page after page. There were dates, too, and some also meant something to her both from the news and from her own life. She had that kind of memory, that kind of ability to see links and relationships between numbers.

She'd questioned him about it that evening at home.

"You're so unworldly," he'd said. "You don't understand these things. You really are an innocent when it comes to business, honey."

She'd hesitated. Maybe he was right. What did she know about business? Still, she couldn't get the numbers out of her head.

"But it's the University's money I saw and it was being manipulated. I know you handle their finances, but it doesn't look right. I know numbers."

"Juliet, I know how you are with figures. But you're not equipped to understand my situation. My work is complicated. Leave it to me."

Only she couldn't let it go. They'd argued, and he had tried to bully her into forgetting about it, which was unlike him. She'd cried and eventually gave in. "I guess you're right. I must have been mistaken." Throughout the next day, she'd tried to tell herself she'd made a mistake. Callum was intelligent, basically honest, and he was a nerd, as was she. He wasn't the kind of man who'd get caught up in something unscrupulous. There was no way she could have misjudged him all those years they'd been together.

The next evening, Callum didn't come home from work at his usual time and she had worried that he was still angry with her. She did her best not to let Aidan see that she was upset. After she had put him to bed, though, she sat up all night, waiting, biting her fingernails, and listening for Callum's key in the lock. During those dark hours she had recalled odd conversations she'd overheard, phone calls she'd answered only to be hung up on, nights when Callum had to leave to run some errand. He'd sometimes be gone for two or three hours and would return long after she'd gone to bed. He thought she was asleep. She wasn't. She'd suspected an affair. The numbers, the money, the dates pointed to something entirely different, though.

Something else had niggled at the back of her mind. She had looked back through the files on her computer and found the program she'd written six months earlier for Callum. He'd told her he was working on a presentation for his department—a presentation on accounting fraud—and he'd asked her to create an algorithm which would transfer funds from accounts and deposit them into other accounts in such a way as it would be hard for anyone to notice. Like an idiot she'd done as he asked and given it to him without question, believing it was part of his presentation.

She shook her head at the memory. The other thing he'd called her—naive— had been right. It was hard to believe she'd ever been that gullible. She returned to the memory.

He finally returned very late that night. She was awake and pressed him for the truth. He eventually admitted he'd gotten involved with a syndicate.

"You can give up your job and drop all ties with the syndicate," she'd told him. "I'll quit my job, too. We'll move our home and start again. It's not too late."

He shook his head and squeezed his eyes closed. "I can't tell them I want out. It doesn't work like that. They'd never let me walk."

"You got me involved, too. I can't let them continue stealing, Callum. You know me better than that. You know what happened with my parents."

He sighed and shook his head. "Bugger. Why did I have to go and fall in love with the Pope? Problem is, now that you know about the plan and refuse to look the other way, you put yourself and Aidan in danger. These guys aren't amateurs. This is bigger than you know."

She searched his face. What was he saying?

"You and the baby have to go away."

"No. We'll all go. We'll go together. Tonight. Pack a couple of bags. Take the baby, and go back to England."

He opened his eyes and stared at her. "You're not listening. I'm not leaving. I can't. And England is the last place you should go. Go to Taiwan. Or Singapore. Or South Africa. But not England."

"Then we'll go to the authorities. We'll tell them everything. They'll give both of us immunity. They'll protect us."

"It's not that easy for me. You can go to the authorities. Get protection for yourself and Aidan. Or you can take your chances and run. It's your decision."

"Why can't you go to the authorities with me?"

"I can't do that," he said, pacing across their living room. "It's a lot more complicated than you think."

173

"You can't continue with their plan. Please tell me you're not going to help them steal."

He became more agitated, running his hand through his hair as he paced. "There's one thing I can try. But I'm telling you, if it doesn't work . . . you'll have to run or go to the authorities. Give them my computer. Tell them what you know."

Before she had a chance to let his words sink in, Callum grabbed his coat off the back of the sofa and dashed to the front door.

"What are you going to do?" she screamed. "You're scaring me. Callum. Please don't do something foolish."

He hesitated, and she thought he would turn around. He didn't.

In the morning she had driven to work and stopped in his office in the university's finance department. His co-workers told her he hadn't come in and hadn't called, either. She went through her work day, anxiety ridden, as best she could, and then got in her car to drive home. Five minutes into her commute a dark sedan pulled up beside her and someone shot at her window. She'd sped up and the shooter had missed her, but hit the back seat. She panicked, lost control of the car, and slammed into another car. Fortunately no one was hurt, and luckily she hadn't picked up her son from daycare. She was thankful for that, but wanted to kick herself for not getting the license plate number as the sedan sped away.

She pulled her thoughts back to the present and refocused on her school problems. Callum had been wrong about her not being equipped to understand his situation. She certainly had understood his situation, and knew what he had done. He really was manipulating money, embezzling and, according to the FBI, was still involved with the syndicate. They just hadn't caught him yet, because he moved around so much.

Now, she was in a situation in her job that she understood, but wasn't really equipped to deal with. Her government protectors having abandoned her, she somehow had to fix this school, fraught with money problems, dangerous student gang elements and educators who had given up, or quit and go off on her own. Claire decided that Dr. Juliet Powell was not going to be a quitter. Could she use her genius with numbers to change things?

She gulped down the last of her coffee, then remembered the gun in her handbag. She took it out and locked it inside her file cabinet. That done, she strode to the whiteboard, wrote Aims as a heading and created headings for three columns: Students; Faculty; Community. As she began populating the columns she realized this work paralleled her study at Weymouth and a rush of excitement coursed through her.

After she had the basics listed, she turned to her computer. Now she was ready to get down to business. Public schools, school operations, and how to fix troubled schools—those were the questions she needed to answer. She searched the internet and learned everything she could about ways other educators had turned around their troubled schools.

She read an article from a major newspaper describing how to target and respond to troubled students. An article entitled 'How to Get Principals to Think Like Managers' caught her attention, but when she clicked on she found a message that the page no longer existed. She read several more articles and then tried a different approach, typing in 'improving school safety' in the search box. Numerous other results popped up, and she clicked on one. This was a large site with useful information, safety checklists, and links to other resources. *Wow! This is what I need.*

She opened up a safety check list. *Must be twenty to thirty items here. Good.* She began reading:

- The school building and its entrances, parking lots, and grounds are monitored and/or supervised at all times.

We've definitely failed this one.

- The school's policies and procedures strive to inhibit weapons from being brought into the building, and outline consequences of any violations.

Obviously not.

- Gang-related identifiers and activity are prohibited on the school campus, and the staff is periodically given in-service training to keep them abreast of what to watch for.

Oh, my God. Are we doing anything right?

- Strategies for ensuring structured passing periods are in effect. These strategies include maximizing staff visibility, monitoring hallways, teaching students what the school's hallway expectations are, and outlining consequences for inappropriate hallway behavior.

Not even that.

- The school's policies and procedures include an Anti-Bullying program.

Nope.

- The school has a positive discipline model for all teachers to follow, and teachers receive appropriate training, allowing for 80 to 90% of disciplinary actions to be handled in the classroom.

We definitely have that one backwards.

Claire continued reading through the remainder of the safety check list, printed it out and appended notes and questions to checklist items.

Over the remainder of the weekend, she read more articles, making additional notes and printing out much of the material. She found more safety checklist items on other websites and compiled them and made modifications to tailor them for

Midland High School. Her next step was to put together a team to oversee and manage her plan. If they were going to have a chance to fix the school's problems, they would need to get everyone involved.

Late Sunday afternoon, Claire called Frank, Ron, Nancy, and the school's counselor, Bill Wilson, at their homes and told them she wanted to meet with them on Monday at three o'clock. She wanted to give them some advance notice. After she finished the last call, she stood with her back to her living room window with a cup of coffee in her hand, debating whether to also call Steve. Frank had suggested it, but she knew Steve's schedule was crazy.

A car horn tooted and Claire swung around. Although the car was gone, a man wearing a baseball cap stood on the sidewalk, staring at her building. She grabbed her mobile phone and went to call Brad. Then she remembered their last conversation. She looked outside again and the man was walking away. Maybe he wasn't the man Kate had seen. Better send a text message to Brad, anyway.

CHAPTER FOURTEEN

CLAIRE RUSHED INTO the school building, carrying her whiteboard, presentation easel, flip chart, and the plastic tote filled with papers, markers, and her meeting outline. Dumping it all off in her office, she brewed a pot of coffee, took a steaming cup into her office, and closed the door. As usual, the light on her phone was blinking, indicating she had messages. As she listened to her messages, she sipped her coffee, took a few notes, and read through the emails from Thursday afternoon and Friday. Many of those were the usual requests for meetings with parents or teachers.

Better talk to Ron and Kim before scheduling any of those meetings in case they've already taken care of some of them. She hoped they had, because she needed as much time as possible to practice for her afternoon meeting so she could make her presentation perfect. Selling her plan to Frank, Ron, and the others was her prime focus today.

While reading over her meeting outline for the second time, people began arriving, talking and laughing. Doors opened and closed, and desk drawers rattled. A glance at her watch confirmed that it was indeed time for employees to begin preparing for their day. That meant Kim was probably at work.

Claire went out into the outer office and found Kim standing next to the coffee stand. Kim looked directly at Claire but said nothing.

"Good morning, Kim."

She didn't answer.

"How was your weekend?"

"Fine."

"Were there any big problems here Friday?" Claire asked.

"Why do you care?"

Taken aback, Claire responded with, "Excuse me, but why wouldn't I?"

"You walked out. We figured you quit."

"Didn't Ron tell you I called Friday and said I would be back?"

"Yeah." Kim poured herself a cup of coffee and walked away.

"Kim," Claire said, following her. "I know I was snippy with you last week, and I was withdrawn. I'm sorry. I was going through a rough emotional time. But I'm back now and feeling much better. Things will be better now. I promise."

"Glad to hear it." Kim was looking at her computer when she said it. A cartoon with dancing dogs filled the screen.

Claire hesitated, then entered Ron's office, closing the door behind her. Ron looked up.

"You're here," he said. "What's up?"

"Did something happen here on Friday?"

"The usual. Why?"

"Kim's clearly angry with me. I wondered what's going on. "

"Well, sorry to say this, but to be honest, a lot of people thought you'd abandoned us. Even before you walked out you weren't really here."

"Agreed, but you know what I was going through. You didn't expect me to bounce back instantly, did you?"

"No, of course I didn't. I knew you were having trouble, but you wouldn't talk to me or to anyone here. We understood. We were worried and concerned for you. You withdrew from everything and then you just left."

Claire plopped down in a chair and looked at Ron. "I needed time to pull myself back together. Things will be different from now on. I promise."

He remained silent.

"I've made mistakes and I understand what my walking out must have looked like to all of you. I admit it. But I feel much better now, ready to re-engage. Something happened while I was out that set things straight for me again. Call it an epiphany. I have a real plan for what I, we, need to do to fix this school. That's why I scheduled an afterschool meeting."

Ron shrugged. "You may be fighting an impossible battle, but you should do what you think you need to do. I'll help if I can."

"Thank you, Ron. And thank you for everything you did for me after . . . well, you know."

He nodded and smiled.

Back in the outer office, Claire approached Kim and waited for her to look up.

"I'm forming a new committee," Claire said "and we're holding our first meeting today at three o'clock in Nancy Palmer's classroom. I'd like for you to be on the committee."

"Me? I've never been on a committee before."

"You've been working here longer than anyone else. I looked at your personnel file. You have firsthand knowledge of this school's history."

She pursed her lips a moment, obviously intrigued at being included for once, then said, "What's the committee for?"

"It's a surprise. I'll explain everything in the meeting." Claire turned and walked to her own office, leaving the door open this time. Next, she sent emails to three more faculty members and asked them to join the committee.

At a quarter past four Claire carried meeting supplies upstairs to Nancy's empty classroom and set up the easel and whiteboard. When everything was ready, she sat down and waited, resisting the urge to go over her speech again, having done that all day, every chance she'd had. Instead, she tried to relax and randomly gazed around the room. Posters of famous books adorned the walls. *Catcher in the Rye*, *The Great Gatsby*, *Hamlet*, *Of Mice and Men*, *The Vampire Diaries*, and *Twilight*. Claire smiled at the last two and shook her head. *Dracula*, she understood, but the Vampire Diaries? She supposed some catering to student popularity was to blame.

Low two-shelf bookcases sat against the walls all the way around the room chaotically half filled with assorted paperback and hardcover novels, some on their side, upside down or backwards. Above the bookcases on one wall were four large windows so dirty and smudged that little light actually came through.

"I'm not late, am I?"

Claire turned her head. Frank was standing in the doorway.

"No. You're actually the first one here. Come on in."

A few minutes later, the rest of the group gradually filed in and were busy milling and chatting. Deciding everyone was present, Claire motioned for people to take a seat. Frank sat in the front, off to one side. Ron and Kim sat next to him with two empty chairs between them and him. The counselor, Bill Wilson, and teachers Nancy Palmer, Bob Lewis, Louisa Rodriguez, and Jorge Perez sat in a row behind them.

"Thank you for coming. I asked you here because I have generated a plan of action for resolving some of the problems at Midland that I want to share with you. I would like to form a committee to review, expand, and modify this plan, and turn it into action. You've all been tentatively selected for this committee because I believe each of you is capable and has positive skills to offer."

Ron sat with his arms crossed. Kim, Bill, and the teachers were all frowning. Frank, dear Frank, smiled and nodded. She could always count on him.

"After resolving not to let my prior incident with the school board, of which you are all well aware, deter me from performing my responsibilities to you, to our student body and to the school board. I spent the weekend researching what other school districts and urban school officials are doing to improve performance and safety. I pooled these notes and ideas, and added them to what I already knew about Game Theory."

The people in the back row were glancing at each other and shrugging their shoulders.

"As you may or may not know, Game Theory is largely about desired and preferred outcomes. In regard to schools, we must consider the desired outcomes for our students. It's also about identifying crucial decision points."

Ron said, "You're talking about a wish list. That's not realistic."

"I believe it can be. Realistic, I mean. Closely related to Game Theory is Systemics. That's essentially the idea of seeing things holistically, as systems. You can't change academic achievement simply by looking at students, say, deciding to provide better textbooks; all sorts of factors become relevant. In mediation and restorative justice concepts, it is the community you are seeking to restore and the involvement of parents that becomes crucial. If they become involved, they help set standards of behavior and commitment."

Frank said, "I think I understand where you're going with this. If we can involve parents, the community, and faculty, we'll have a stronger support system."

"Precisely. Here, I've printed out some pages I'd like you to read through. Some are research, some are charts and checklists I've created. I'd like your feedback and ideas. What I've come up is meant only as a starting point."

She handed out the papers and then sat down and waited to give the attendees time to thumb through them.

Nancy was the first to look up. She glanced at Claire and then looked at the others.

"Okay," she said. "It's obvious you've done a lot of work, and some of this looks good. The checklists you generated already tell me we have some serious problems that I never thought of, but I don't see how we can do all of this. We barely have time to do our work as it is."

"I agree," Bob said.

Ron shook his head. "Some of this is good, but it doesn't go far enough."

"I don't claim to have all the answers. That's precisely why we need a committee," Claire said. "Make copies of the plan as a starting point and mark it up with your ideas. Tell me what you think we need to do. Everyone's opinions count here."

Kim said, "Why am I here? I'm not a teacher or administrator?"

"But you see a different side of the problems. You see the referrals, the parents coming in, the students getting detention, the police calls, and the like. You are on the front line, Kim. Your input is important."

Kim raised her eyebrows, then nodded. "Yeah, I guess I've seen it all. I know the drugs and gang problems are getting worse."

Claire looked around the room again. "I see that, too. We might not be able to rid the school of them entirely, but we can clean up much of it. That alone will go a long way toward improving our school."

Jorge said, "What do you know? You've been here like five minutes compared to the rest of us. You're a newbie and you're clueless."

"You are correct, Jorge, I am new here. But the problems have not been solved so far, have they? You have become inured to the problems, believing this is the way it has to be. Perhaps a new perspective is what we need. I know THIS," she said, pointing at her research and the board, filled with math equations.

"I don't have any clue what math has to do with solving behavioral problems," Kim said.

"I'll explain it all to you at our next meeting. There's a whole science behind it. Think about Maslow's theory, too. It ties in with what we're trying to do."

"I don't know what that is, either," Kim said.

"American psychologist Abraham Maslow devised a six-level theory of human behavior known as Maslow's Hierarchy of Motives. He ranks human needs as 1), physiological; 2) security and safety; 3) love and feelings of belonging; 4) competence, prestige, and esteem; 5) self-fulfillment; and 6) curiosity and the need to understand. Correct me if I'm wrong. Don't gangs use some of those needs to recruit new members?"

Frank jumped in. "Good point, Claire. I think this is worth pursuing. The next step, I think, should be a faculty meeting. See if we can get the rest of the faculty onboard."

Ron said, "Okay, I agree with that. It couldn't hurt to try, right Claire?"

What did he mean by that? Was that a jab?

"Look," Claire said, "I know we're going to severely ruffle specific feathers. The problems might actually increase for a time until we change behaviors. My personal experience is a stark reminder that the gangs can be dangerous. We'll have to be very careful, support each other and anticipate retaliation. If we do our job right, and perhaps we can get some help, then we can obviate negative outcomes. Frank, do you know anyone who we might get involved?"

"I'll look into it. Maybe contact the police department and the university. I know someone in the Education Department over there and I believe they have a Violence Prevention Program."

Ron's face lit up. "You've given me an idea, Frank. I know someone who might help. Few people know this, but I used to be in a gang, back when I was in eighth-grade. Where I lived, you joined a gang, or you might not make it to ninth grade. I learned all the lingo: Popping, C's up cuzz, what dat red be like. That was back in Chicago. When my best friend refused to join, they shot him in the head in front of his house two doors from ours. That's when my parents packed up the family and moved us to Colorado."

"Oh, my God," Claire said. "Why didn't you ever tell me?"

He shrugged. "This guy I know is the first friend I made after our move. He works as a mediator."

Frank said, "Why don't you talk to him, Ron? And Claire, you should talk to Steve. Let him know what we're doing."

Claire nodded. "I'll do that."

"So, when do we want to meet again?" Frank asked.

"Wait a minute," Nancy said. "Don't the rest of us have a say?"

"Sorry, Nancy. Of course you do," Claire said.

"You think it's this easy?" Nancy was leaning forward and waving her hands.

Claire frowned. "Oh no, I don't think it's easy at all. This will put a strain on all of us. But we live here and good students live here. Is this the way we want our lives and the lives of these kids to be? Our only other choices are to live with the status quo or quit and get jobs elsewhere. But our students have no other choice. Their lives are on the line here, too. No, this will not be easy. Our task will be easier, though, if we follow this, a kind of map. You're the ones out there, you know the landscape. What we need to do now is get the rest of the faculty involved."

Nancy was shaking her head, clearly not sold.

"Look," Claire said, "First we need to understand and acknowledge the desired outcomes for the students, staff, parents, community, and school board. Those outcomes need to be analyzed and not regarded as simple. To take an obvious example, the school board wants academic success, sporting success, certain behavioral standards, budgetary outcomes, and absence of detrimental news items."

"Okay," Nancy said.

"To accomplish these outcomes, we need systems that work. It's no good cracking down on gangs if there is nothing to replace them; there is a reason kids are in gangs, one of which is safety. It is no good punishing gang members if there we cannot provide safety. Safety is necessary to create a culture of openness. Students aren't simply items, they have family and community context needs; school is a factor in their community and vice-versa. In schools where these factors are in proper supply there is no problem. But here, these factors are in short supply. If you want students to learn, you must give them a reason to, and you must make it possible for them. There's no point teaching Shakespeare without focusing on basic literacy skills, and no point doing either without a sense of the cultural and social contexts of the students and how they relate to the cultural and social contexts of the staff."

"I think I am starting to get an inkling of where you're going," Nancy said.

Claire said, "Read through the research material I handed out when you have time. You'll see that this is all interconnected."

"The ideas make sense," Bill Wilson said. "But you haven't demonstrated any expertise in dealing with people. Why should we listen to you?"

"Fair enough. I admit I'm lacking in people skills. But I am an expert in strategic planning. Each of you has strengths, too. I'm asking all of you to combine our skills."

Bill nodded.

Frank said. "Does anyone have any objections to giving it a shot?"

No one answered. "Okay, then," Frank said, "we should touch base again on Wednesday, after school. Hopefully, we can plan on a faculty meeting for Friday and, if all goes well, we could hold a school wide assembly on Monday or Tuesday."

CHAPTER FIFTEEN

CLAIRE SMILED AS she cooked dinner. Today, for the first time since she'd arrived in Denver, something had gone the way she'd hoped at work. She hadn't flubbed her lines, and she'd won some support, tentative though it was. If they could get the outside help that Frank and Ron had mentioned, she thought, they had a great chance of success. Well, maybe that was stretching it. A good chance.

She talked with Marcus who was sitting on a chair near the stove, watching her cook. They laughed and played a word game that he loved.

When dinner was served and Marcus began eating, he exclaimed, "This is my favorite, Mommy. Better than mac and cheese. What's it called?"

"Lasagna. And I have a surprise for you. Chocolate ice cream for dessert. We'll eat it while we watch television."

"Yay!"

After dinner, she put the last of the dirty dishes into the dishwasher and turned it on, then walked into the living room and plopped down on the sofa near where Marcus sat on the floor, playing with toys. Claire watched him for a few minutes, then closed her eyes, relaxing. Steve popped into her head. She missed him, and yet after the meeting today, she'd emailed him about the committee's plans instead of phoning him as Frank had suggested. It was the coward's way. But she wasn't ready to talk to him.

Her mobile rang, and she reached down to the coffee table and picked it up. The caller ID showed Ron Baker.

"Hey, I've been talking to some of the teachers about the ideas we discussed earlier today," Ron said.

"Already? What did you do—call everyone?" Claire leaned forward.

"No. The Debate team's advisory meeting was tonight. After the students on the committee left, the rest of us stayed and talked. Looks like Nancy and I talked some more teachers into getting involved."

"Oh, Ron, that's great news. Thanks."

"We did it for the school."

And not for you. He had to get that in there, didn't he?

"I also called my friend. You know, the guy who works as a mediator with juveniles who are in trouble. His name's Shaun Bales. He says he'll come to our faculty meeting on Friday, and if that goes well, he'll come to our first assembly. Maybe even speak to the student body if we want him to."

"That's wonderful."

Ron didn't say anything.

"Are you still there, Ron?"

"Uh, yeah. There is something else I wanted to tell you. This isn't so good."

Claire slumped back against the sofa's back.

"This afternoon three students came to my office while you were in a meeting with parents. I didn't get a chance to tell you at the school—it slipped my mind by the time I saw you in our after-school meeting. Anyway, these students reported that on

Friday morning someone was at their bus stop, asking students about you. I took down their descriptions of the guy."

"What? Why would someone do that?"

"Damned if I know. It gets worse. A little while later, Kelly Jacobs, came in and said she was coming back to work after a doctor appointment and she saw a man lurking on the sidewalk in front of the school. The description of him fit the students' description."

"What did you do?"

"I ran outside to talk to him. I wanted to know what he was doing. But he'd left."

"Did you call the police?" She held her breath waiting for his answer.

"Well, no. I didn't think there was much they could do since he was gone."

"Why didn't you come and get me?"

"By then, you were upstairs getting ready for the committee meeting. I figured I would tell you after the meeting. I forgot."

Claire rolled her eyes. *How could he forget something like that?*

"Thanks for calling and letting me know. I'll watch out for this guy. Can you give me his description?"

After she jotted down the information, Ron said, "Should we call the police? Do you think it's somehow related to your attack? The gang members aren't going to give up easily."

"I know they won't. Let me think about this before we do anything."

The moment she hung up, Claire ran to the front window and looked out, but she couldn't see much. It was dark out. She put on her shoes and coat, unlocked the door, and opened it.

"Where are you going, Mommy?"

She turned around. "Marcus, stay inside. I want to check something." He nodded, and she went out. She walked to the sidewalk and looked in one direction and then the other.

Nothing unusual. No sign of the man Ron had described. She walked back and shut the door behind her. Think. Brad won't do anything. Would the police do anything? Would she have to tell them she was in witness protection?

She went into the kitchen to find a telephone book to look up the police department. Maybe she could ask a few questions without actually filing a report.

The doorbell rang, and she looked up, then set down the phonebook down. The bell rang again. She walked into the living room and found Marcus standing in the open doorway talking to someone. Oh, my God! She'd forgotten to lock the deadbolts.

She lunged forward, grabbed Marcus, and looked up in surprise.

"Mommy, let go. Put me down." He was kicking and squirming.

"Steve. What are you doing here," she said as she released Marcus.

His eyebrows drew together, and he said, "I have a better question. Why didn't you tell me you have a son?"

She tried to speak, but the words somehow stuck in her throat. She coughed and then said, "I . . . probably should have told you sooner. I . . . ." She paused, searching for the right words. "I don't really know why."

Marcus, who had been standing next to Claire watching, walked up to Steve. "Who are you?"

"I work with your mother. My name's Steve. What's yours?"

"Marcus. Do you wanna see my room?"

Claire put her hands on Marcus's shoulders. "Not right now, sweetie. Why don't you go play in your room so Steve and I can talk, all right?"

"Okay." He hesitated, looking back and forth between them, and then turned and ran up the stairs.

Steve stood awkwardly with his hands in his coat pockets. His cheeks were turning pink and Claire could feel an icy chill radiating from him.

She took hold of the door's edge. Part of her wanted to send him away and close the door. "Do you want to come in?"

Steve didn't respond. He studied her in silence, a silence that grew steadily more uncomfortable. After a few moments, he took a step forward, and she backed up to make room for him. Once he was inside, she closed the door.

Steve turned to her and said, "I don't understand why you kept this from me. I've told you all about myself, but you kept this from me. Don't you think I might have wanted to know that you're a mother?"

"I—you're right, I should have. I didn't want us to end, and I didn't know if you liked kids."

"Huh? Why the hell would I be an educator if I didn't like kids? That's a sorry excuse, Claire. You must have known the right thing to do was tell me."

"Well, yes, but not at first. I mean, we were only friends at first. Then, I wasn't sure what we were. I didn't know when to tell you, or how, and I was afraid."

He sighed and ran his hand through his hair. "Okay. I'll accept that for now. But then why have you been avoiding me? What the hell did I do wrong? I thought things were going great between us, and then you just pulled away?"

What could she possibly say? Of course he hadn't done anything wrong. He was great. It was her. She'd had enough trouble keeping her story straight before the attack. She couldn't build a relationship on lies. Not one that would be worth anything. Telling him the truth wasn't an option, either, no matter how much she wanted it to be.

"It wasn't you. It was me, all right? I've been going through some things."

"At school?"

"Yes." That wasn't entirely a lie.

"I got your email about the plan. It sounds great, Claire. That's one of the reasons I came over here tonight. I think I can help. I can make some phone calls. See if I can find some professionals to assist you and your staff. This could be a pilot program. If it works in Midland, we can use it in other schools."

She nodded.

"Look, I want to try again with you, Claire. Please don't keep pushing me away. Will you give 'us' a chance?"

He didn't get it. There couldn't be an 'us'. But how could she tell him that without hurting him?

"The timing is all wrong. As I said, it's not you. Maybe when school's out for the summer. Right now, I have my hands full. A relationship isn't in the picture."

"You don't think I have my hands full, too? I'm swamped at work. I go home at night, sometimes not getting there until nine or ten. I miss dinner, or have to eat it in my car on the way to a meeting. That's life. I don't see my job getting easier. I have to make time for relationships where I can; otherwise, I'll put it off until it's too late."

She didn't know how to respond. He was lonely. So was she. But they couldn't be the ones to fill each other's need for love and belonging. She wouldn't be here long enough.

"Claire, don't push me away. Let's make time for each other."

Looking into his eyes, she could feel the weight of his loneliness, the same loneliness she'd been feeling for the past year. How could she say no? She took a deep breath and let it out. "All right. But you'll have to be patient. Let me get through these next couple of days at least. It's going to be very hectic."

"I can do that. And I'll make those calls and do what I can to help you and your faculty with your plan for the school."

"Thanks."

He stepped closer to her, pulled her into his arms, and kissed her. "I should be going. I was on my way home. Haven't eaten yet. Say goodbye to Marcus for me."

"Okay. Goodnight, Steve."

She watched him leave from the front window, then opened the door again, and said, "Wait!"

He turned around and walked back.

"I have some leftovers from dinner. It's not much—some lasagna and fresh Italian bread. If you'd like, I can heat it up for you."

He smiled. "Now that sounds great."

They talked about her school plans while he ate. After dinner, she served each of them a bowl of ice cream. Marcus took his into the living room and watched television.

Half an hour later Marcus ran into the kitchen and said, "Can I show him my room now?"

"I'm sorry, sweetie, it's your bed time."

Steve stood up. "I should be going anyway. But I'd like to see your room. How about next time, okay, Marcus?"

Marcus nodded and smiled. "Okay. Bye."

Claire followed Steve to the door, they kissed, and said goodnight. When he was out of sight, she closed the blinds and locked the front door and deadbolts. She picked up her mobile phone and called Brad. He didn't answer. Of course not. His voicemail picked up and she said, "I need to talk to you A.S.A.P. She needed to know what to do, whether she should get the police involved because of the watcher, or whether that would compromise her cover.

GROGGY FROM A restless night's sleep, Steve stumbled out of bed on Saturday morning and started a fresh pot of coffee, hoping it would rejuvenate him and get him out the doldrums. While the coffee brewed, he stepped outside on his front porch dressed in a plain white t-shirt and plaid cotton pajama bottoms. He looked around at his neighbors' houses. No one was in sight. Then he stepped out onto his driveway and picked up his newspaper.

He sipped his coffee and attempted to read The Denver Post. It normally held his interest, but not this morning. Dinner at Claire's had been great, and as usual, he'd enjoyed talking with her. He'd gone home tired, and for a change, fairly happy. During the night, however, after waking up several times feeling anxious, he began to question himself. Why did he have to go and fall in love with Claire? He hadn't realized how he felt until last night. What else would turn a man who prided himself on fairness and objectivity into a complete idiot?

No matter how hard he tried to push his thoughts aside and just read the newspaper, he couldn't. Giving up, he let the newspaper fall across his lap, and closed his eyes, remembering his surprise when he'd rung her doorbell and her little boy answered.

How could he have been so clueless? He'd convinced himself that he knew her, and that John Richmond was wrong about her. Although he had planned to ask her about John's accusation about an affair with the Senator weeks ago, he hadn't. He'd convinced himself that John had made it all up because he was angry that the Senator had asked them to hire her.

Throughout the day, thoughts intruded on Steve's activities. They were there when he took his shower, when he threw a load of laundry in the washer, and while he sat in front of his TV, scanning through the channels with his remote control. When he realized he wasn't even noticing the scenes passing by, he clicked it off and sat there, slouching and rubbing his temples. This lousy headache that had been sneaking up on him all afternoon was gaining momentum.

He dragged himself out of his chair when the buzzer on his washer alerted him to move the wet clothes into the dryer. After turning on the dryer, he slogged into the kitchen, where he made a ham and cheese sandwich for lunch and grabbed a can of Pepsi from the refrigerator. He carried everything into the living room.

Was he such a bad judge of character? He'd always prided himself on having sharp senses and spot-on evaluations of people. But what if he wasn't as good a judge of character as he'd thought? Had she tricked him?

He closed his eyes and folded his hands behind his head. Claire hadn't exactly lied to him, yet she hadn't really been open and honest either. She'd misled him by letting him believe she was a single, available woman with no family and no commitments, completely unattached. But he'd known she was keeping secrets; she hadn't really disclosed much about herself. He hadn't missed her use of the word 'mum' on several occasions. Yet he'd let it slide, telling himself that he shouldn't push her. He'd told himself that they had a strong attraction between them and that was enough to start with.

Did that make her deceitful, untrustworthy?

It wasn't entirely her fault, he conceded. He should have asked more questions. Damn. If he was really being honest, he shouldn't even have gotten involved with one of his employees, something he'd never allowed before. He especially should have steered clear of her when he found out she was already suspected of being in an inappropriate relationship with a State Senator.

He shook his head and took a swig of his beer, the only alcohol he had in the house, and sighed.

He already knew the answer as to why he'd allowed himself to get involved. Claire was his counterpart, a strong and intelligent woman with whom he could talk about any subject. A woman to whom he was attracted, and with whom he wanted to start a family.

Admitting that to himself led him right back where he'd started. He didn't know enough about her to make a commitment. She didn't know everything about him, either, but she sure as hell knew more about him than he knew about her. It should have occurred to him at some point that she might be hiding something big from him.

When the dryer buzzed, he trudged back to the laundry room. He removed the clothes from the dryer, sorted and folded them, and carried them into his bedroom to be put away. He didn't like the chore, though he liked the scent of freshly washed laundry.

The distraction didn't last long though. Soon he was back on his sofa with thoughts flooding his mind again. Something else that he'd pushed aside swung back into the forefront. She'd told him that her mother had died thirteen years ago. But in the next breath said that she had given a bracelet to her mother for her thirty-eighth birthday. And then, she added that it was her last birthday. He didn't have to be a mathematician to figure out that meant her mother would have only been sixteen when she had Claire, if Claire was really thirty-five. Okay, some girls had babies at that age. Still, it seemed unlikely.

He searched within himself for answers, and ultimately realized, in anguish, that he wasn't going to have all the answers; that he was going to have to decide whether to trust her and let her explain, or walk away and close the door on their relationship before it was too late.

The following morning, cooking his breakfast, he found himself humming. He wasn't going to give up on Claire. His instincts might occasionally be off, but he was rarely completely wrong about a person. Claire obviously had some secrets, but she was a good person. He would bet his life on it.

CHAPTER SIXTEEN

CALLUM FULLER FOUND his seat on the Delta Airlines jet, stuffed his carry-on bag in the overhead compartment, and sat down, looking out the window at the flurry of activity on the tarmac—luggage cart trains wheeled around by big engines, bag after bag hoisted onto a conveyer, a plane at another gate being eased away. In a few minutes the plane he was on would do the same and then get in line to take-off.

He contemplated the tip he'd received last night, indicating that Juliet was living in Albuquerque, New Mexico. It might be a waste of time and money to fly there without verifying the information first, but he didn't want to wait and give her a chance to run again. After a year, he couldn't wait to see his son again. How big was he now? Was he in preschool?

Of course the biggest question was, would he remember Callum? God, he hoped so. Aidan had been two-and-a-half when they'd last seen each other. Surely, he would remember his father. The problem was how he would get to see Aidan when Juliet would probably try to block him. She'd been so angry with him the last time they'd spoken on the phone and she'd blamed him for her almost being killed by a sniper. She'd sworn that she would never let him near their son again.

The Pilot welcomed the passengers on board the airplane on the loud speaker as Callum buckled his seatbelt and turned off his mobile phone.

FRIDAY, AFTER SCHOOL, Claire and her new committee set up six easels and flip charts in the school cafeteria. Claire chose that location for the full faculty meeting because of its long picnic-style tables, allowing all of the faculty to spread out the worksheets she would be handing out. Bill set up a slide projector and screen.

The worksheets, seating arrangements, and presentation had all been worked out by the committee during a meeting on Wednesday. Before the meeting began, Claire checked for messages on her mobile phone. It had been four days since she'd left a voicemail message for Brad, and he still hadn't returned her call.

Frank and Steve walked in and stood in the back of the room, as planned.

Once everyone else was seated, Ron and Nancy handed out a packet of papers and a pencil to each person while Claire introduced the topic for the meeting and explained the associated theories, much like she'd done in the first meeting with the committee. Throughout her speech she noticed people typing text messages, falling asleep, or doodling on the papers in their packets.

Ron took over for part of the presentation, while Bill ran the slide projector for him. Some teachers were inattentive for his presentation as well, but less noticeably. They at least attempted to show him a modicum of respect. Claire sighed, making notes for future reference to let Ron be in charge of the meetings as much as possible. Unfortunately, they'd already planned out how this meeting would go.

Ron finished his section and turned the meeting back over to Claire. She talked about Maslow's theory and about getting the community involved in their plan. Again, teachers fidgeted and some even started whispering to each other.

One teacher, Eric Johnson, interrupted Claire. "We're only asking for more trouble. Didn't you learn that a couple weeks ago?"

Claire frowned. *What did he mean by that? Did he know about the attack?*

She took a deep breath and let it out. "I know there will be retaliation if that's what you mean." She went on to repeat what she'd said at the first committee meeting.

Some teachers nodded, but others sat with their arms crossed.

Moving on, Claire asked them to open their packets and take out the materials. "I'd like you to take fifteen minutes to read through the papers. After that, Ron and Nancy will hand out questionnaires. You'll be asked to answer them, and then we'll break up into groups, each table making up a group."

After everyone had presumably read the paperwork and completed the questionnaire, Claire instructed each assigned group leader to take their place at the head of the seven tables to facilitate discussion.

Frank, Steve, Ron's friend, Shaun Bales, and Claire walked around the room and listened as the faculty members read the school goals they'd written on their questionnaires and discussed them. The group leaders jotted down notes with markers on their flip charts.

Several times, shouting caught everyone's attention. Steve would rush over and find out what the teachers were arguing about and would calm them down.

At one point Judy Cartwright said, "I'm not stepping into the middle of a student fight and you can't make me. I'll quit before I'll put myself in that kind of danger. I'm too damn close to retirement to take that chance."

"Everybody has to get involved," Bob Johnson said. "We have to send a message that we're united."

"And get knocked on the floor. Do you have any idea what a fall could do to someone my age? I could get a broken hip. That's happened to friends of mine. I'm not doing it." She crossed her arms and glared at him.

Claire waited for Steve's response.

"We're only getting ideas right now, people. We're weighing all of the possibilities. If we come up with a mandate that all teachers must step in to break up fights, it will be carefully thought out and people will be trained. No one will be fed to the dogs."

Ron said, "Sorry to butt in, but I would like to add something. We've already done a little training on fight intervention. Claire led the training. Only a few of us were involved in it because there weren't many people interested. We tried out the techniques we learned, and they actually worked. I want to also stress that no employee should intervene alone. You do it as a team of at least three."

"That's good, Ron," Steve said. "Thanks for telling us about that. You've reiterated a primary point that we need to take an organized approach to fixing the problems."

At the end of the meeting, Claire told the committee, "We'll compile all of your notes and put together a more detailed plan in the coming weeks. We'll hold our first school-wide assembly on Tuesday at ten o'clock. Several guest speakers from outside will also be there, including today's guests and someone from Restorative Justice.

TUESDAY MORNING, CLAIRE, Ron, the team, and guest speakers, including Steve, entered the auditorium. Everyone except Claire sat down in chairs that the head janitor had set up onstage. It should be obvious that the assembly was now ready to start, but the students were either clueless or didn't give a damn. Probably the latter, thought Claire. Paper airplanes flew through the air, students were turned around talking loudly to friends. Some stood up and shouted at friends higher up in the stadium, while others wandered around the auditorium. Claire shook her head, clearly frustrated.

She pinned the microphone lavaliere to her blouse and checked to assure it was live. She was supposed to give the opening remarks and then turn the microphone over to Ron. First she shouted, "I need your attention. Please settle down and take your seats." That reduced the noise slightly. She repeated the command, and added, "Quiet down."

Finally, the noise was reduced to a buzz and Claire began. "In the short time I've been here it's obvious to me that Midland's students and faculty aren't safe or happy. We're going to change that."

"You're wasting your time, Bitch!" someone shouted.

Claire gasped. Did she really hear what she thought she heard?

Laughter broke out. Someone else yelled, "You can't change anything. You're fucking stupid if you think you can."

Claire couldn't tell who the speaker was. She glanced at Ron and the guests.

Ron stood up and walked over to Claire. He whispered, "Why don't I go ahead and speak first?"

She nodded, took off the lavaliere, handed it to him, and took his vacated seat.

"Everyone needs to shut up and sit down. NOW!" Ron said. "No more crap. Anyone else who disrupts this assembly will be removed and immediately suspended."

That was met with guffaws, but no one said anything more.

"Now. We've put together a plan and a team to make changes. This school will become a place where everyone is safe and everyone is treated with respect. There will be no more drug dealing and drug use, no more gangs and no more fighting or bullying."

Coyote-like yells rang out and reverberated, and from where Claire was sitting on stage, she still couldn't pinpoint where they were coming from.

"Over the next few weeks, this whole school will meet in the auditorium every other day. Today, I'm going to tell you about the basic plan and introduce the people who will be working with us. The first thing you need to know is we've established core principles that this school WILL meet. They are: Cooperation, Pride, Safety, High Expectations, and Success. We've also established some core values that we are committed to: Respect, Responsibility, Compassion, Integrity, and Appreciation of Diversity. These principles and values are all topics that we'll discuss in depth beginning the day after tomorrow."

Boos and foot stomping made it impossible for Ron to continue.

Steve and Frank glanced at each other, then stood up and flanked Ron.

Ron nodded at them and then shouted at the audience, "SHUT UP."

When the audience was reasonably quiet, he said, "We will no longer tolerate this kind of behavior. Beginning with our next assembly, we're implementing new procedures. Students will be assigned seats with their classmates and teachers. The teachers will sit on an aisle and in a position to see all of his or her students. Any student who disrupts will be removed and receive detention. At the end of assemblies, students will return to their classroom with their teacher, and roll will be taken." He paused and then added, "Before the next assembly, your teachers will discuss with you proper behavior. Any disrespect to that teacher will result in the student receiving after school detention."

On that note, Ron concluded the day's assembly. He hadn't introduced the guest speakers, but Claire understood why. Students burst out of the huge auditorium in a stampede, and the teachers prodded them like cows to proceed to their next class.

After the assembly, Ron and his friend, Shaun Bales, went to Ron's office. Steve left to go back to Central Administration, but Frank accompanied Claire to her office. "I have to tell you, Claire, I'm impressed with what you and the committee are doing."

"Thanks. We aren't exactly off to a good start, though."

"No. It takes time. I would have been shocked if the first assembly had gone as planned."

Claire gave him a half smile.

"Hey, I was wondering if there's anything else can I do to help."

"Well, yes, there is actually something."

"What's that?"

She gave him a conspiratorial smile. "Is there anything you can do to get some building improvements done?"

"What kind of improvements are you talking about?"

"For starters, we could sure use a better heating system. We need more lighting for the hallways and stairs, new paint throughout, and better locks on the lockers. . . ." Claire paused and stopped herself. "Probably too much, right?"

"Hmm. I can't really promise you anything, but I'll certainly see what I can do. I have to warn you though, it might take some time."

"I understand. That's fine. I appreciate any and all help I can get." She was beginning to realize how much Frank's support meant to her. He was a lot like Steve, and yet different.

As he turned to leave, Claire added, "Oh, there is one more item. I hesitate to mention it because I know it's not popular."

"Go ahead."

"Surveillance cameras."

Frank winced. "That one is doubtful, to be honest. But I'll throw it in with the others when I ask for approval. Maybe it will force them to give in on the less controversial items, you know."

While Claire was walking upstairs to visit a classroom Monday morning, her mobile phone rang. *Please let it be Brad.* She still hadn't heard from him. She grabbed the phone from her pocket and answered.

"Hey, it's Frank."

Her shoulders slumped, and she leaned back against the stairs, one foot on one step, and one on the step below that.

"I got approval for a new heating system. Wasn't easy, but they gave in."

"Oh, Frank, that's fantastic," she said. "And quick. How did you do that?"

"I was able to sneak into a budget committee meeting this morning. Couldn't have sold the request if Steve hadn't pushed it, too."

"Ah. Thank you so much, Frank. I'll have to thank Steve, too. You two are marvels."

He was quiet for a moment, then cleared his voice and said, "Ah, I also have some bad news to share."

Claire held her breath.

"I wasn't able to get approval for any of the other items. They were a no-go. I'm really sorry."

Claire wasn't surprised and didn't expect to get everything on her list. She remained delighted that Frank and Steve had gotten approval for the most expensive item. She could always work on other items later. "Frank, it's all right. I figured that might happen. Thanks for trying and thank you for the good news."

When she disconnected the call, she checked again for messages, thinking she might have missed a call from Brad. Nothing.

CHAPTER SEVENTEEN

STEVE ARRIVED AT Cameron High School at noon on Wednesday for their Round Table Meeting. He looked for Claire. Not seeing her, he looked to see if John Richmond had arrived yet. Steve's cell phone rang and he answered. A few minutes later, Frank rushed in, glanced around, and then walked over to Steve.

"Oh thank God, I was afraid I'd get here late," Frank whispered, "and expected Richmond to chew my ass. I didn't see his car, though. Does that mean he's not coming?"

"Afraid not. He just called a few minutes ago. He's on his way and wants us to wait to start the meeting until he gets here."

"Crap. I was hoping he wouldn't show."

"Speaking of no shows," Steve said, "have you heard from Claire? She can't miss another meeting.

"I called, but she wasn't in her office. I left a message with Ron and he said he'd remind her."

Steve's jaw tensed as John Richmond strode into the conference room.

Everyone took their seats. *Come on, Claire. Get here before John notices.*

John looked around the table. His face turned to stone. "We seem to be missing someone again."

"She's on her way." Steve and Frank said it in unison.

"She'd better show up if she knows what's good for her."

Steve clinched his jaw, opened up his notebook, and began the meeting.

TWENTY MINUTES LATER, the door burst open and Claire rushed in, breathless. She slid into the only empty seat at the table and blurted out, "I'm sorry for being late."

John clenched his jaw, knowing he should be glad she'd shown up. Why wasn't he?

She shrugged off her coat and draped it on the back of her chair.

Pointing laser eyes in her direction, John said, "You think you can waltz in here whenever the hell you feel like. No wonder your students are so irresponsible. Look at the example you're setting."

"I'm sorry. I tried to get here on time and would have been on time, if I hadn't been pulled over by a police officer for speeding. It was humiliating, so go ahead and yell at me, but believe me, even you can't rival a cop when it comes to intimidation."

There were chuckles around the room.

John bit back the insult that found its way to the tip of his tongue. He couldn't let the others know how deep his hatred went. "Leave on time next time and you won't have to speed. That's what responsible adults do."

"Look, John, I was late leaving because two students had gotten into a fight. I am the principal. I had to deal with that first. I tried to make up the time and would have until I saw red lights swirling in my rearview mirror."

Several people laughed and John gave them a warning look.

"Oh, and by the way," Claire said, "it's not true that male officers take pity on women and don't give them tickets."

By now, everyone was laughing, except John. Claire's face reddened once again, but she smiled apologetically, making John want to take a rag and wipe that smug smile right off.

Instead, he just leaned forward and said, "Speaking of students fighting, I've seen troubling reports about problems at Midland. Vandalism, including tires slashed on teachers' cars, violence, and drugs on campus. What the hell are you doing over there? It's worse under your leadership than Carl's, and everyone knew he was incompetent."

Claire's face turned beet red. "We're in a transition period right now. We're working on taking back control of the school. We've put together a plan—"

John said, "Don't give me excuses."

"It's not—"

Steve said, "Frank and I are working with Claire and her faculty to fix the problems over there. We only started working on it last week."

"Hold on there. You two have your own jobs to do. Neither of you has time to devote to one school. What about all the other schools in the district?"

"Don't worry, John. We have everything under control."

"Hmph. We'll talk about this more later," John said, turning to other meeting topics.

AT THE END of the meeting, Claire waited for a chance to sneak out to get back to work and away from John.

She heard John saying, "I'd like to see this school. Cameron is one of the few high schools in the district that I've not toured."

"Well, come on. I'd be happy to show you around," the principal said.

"Mind if I join in," Frank said.

"And me," several other principals said.

Claire listened politely and then slipped out without anyone noticing.

In the parking lot, she heard someone call her name and she looked up. Steve had followed her outside. *So much for slipping out unnoticed.*

"I've been dying to catch you alone for a moment. Tell me the truth. Did you really get a speeding ticket?"

Claire grinned sheepishly and nodded.

"Sorry to hear that. However, since you did arrive late, I'm glad it was a funny entrance. Put John in his place for once. Hey, I also wanted to talk to you about us. We haven't had much time lately. Are we still okay?"

"Uh, are you talking about our dating?"

"Yeah."

"We're okay, I think. I'm just focusing on the school right now. I'll have more time, soon. I promise."

"Please know that regardless what John says, I'll help with the school as much as possible. I really do wish you'd trust me more."

"Thanks. And I do trust you, Steve."

He smiled. "Glad to hear it. But I can't always tell with you. Back to the dating. I've arranged for us to go on a picnic Saturday, if it's okay. I thought perhaps the Garden of the Gods in Colorado Springs. It's a beautiful park with huge red rock spires and hiking trails."

"That sounds lovely, but isn't it still too cold for a picnic?"

"They're predicting warm weather—fifty-five degrees. Can you believe that in Denver at this time of year? I figured we should take advantage of it. What do you say?"

Claire's mobile phone rang. She pulled it out and checked the caller ID: Brad. Finally! She said, "Excuse me, Steve. I have to take this call."

He nodded as she answered the phone and walked a few feet away, turning her back to Steve.

"This is Leo Paulson, Claire. I'm taking Brad's place. We need to meet and talk about new procedures. This evening—at a restaurant. I know a quiet place not far from where you live."

"Uh, I don't know what to say, Leo. I mean, what happened to Brad?"

"Brad is no longer your handler. He's not here anymore."

"What do you mean 'he's not here'? Where did he go?"

"Meet me at The Cove. It's a hole-in-the-wall café on—"

"I can't meet you tonight. And I don't even know if I should anyway. I don't know who you are or if you're legitimate."

"Okay, okay. You can check to see I'm genuine by calling the arranged number. Meet me tomorrow, then. Same place."

"Give me the address."

He gave her the information.

"I can't come in the evening. What about lunchtime? Is one o'clock all right?"

"That'll work."

"I'll see you then, if you check out." She hung up and turned back around. Steve was watching her, one eyebrow raised.

"Is everything okay?"

"Oh, sure. Sorry about that. Where did we leave off?"

"I was inviting you on a picnic on Saturday."

"Actually, that sounds really nice."

ON THURSDAY, CONSULTING friends of Ron and Steve were at the school talking to teachers and arranging meetings. Claire began preparations for an evening meeting for the following week, and sent out a robocall to all students' parents inviting them to the Thursday evening meeting. Her goal was to get the parents involved in the school.

She tried to stay focused on work, but she couldn't shake a feeling of dread. Though Leo Paulson had checked out when she called the prearranged number, no one would tell her what had happened to Brad. Sure, they hadn't always gotten along well, but he understood her and she could count on him to be honest, if nothing else. What would having a new handler mean?

CHAPTER EIGHTEEN

CLAIRE LEFT THE school at half past noon on Thursday. Luckily, it had been a quieter than normal day as far as problems go, allowing her to actually leave the building early without feeling overly guilty. Sitting in her car, she typed the address Leo had given her into her car's GPS and waited for the on-screen map to appear.

As she drove the displayed route, she wondered what to expect of Leo. Would he be allowed to move her to another city or would his hands also be tied, like Brad's had been? Of course that thought brought up the question of whether she was ready to move again, considering Steve and her school plans. Could she really leave both of them hanging?

Claire maneuvered slowly through midday traffic, half watching the road ahead and half watching her rearview mirror like usual. Near the entrance to Lakeside Mall she noticed a grey sedan behind her. It was following her closely. Her heartbeat sped up. A second later she shook her head. *Probably just an impatient driver.* Normally, she would speed up so as not to irritate the other driver, but she wasn't about to risk another speeding ticket. Instead, she turned onto another street. The sedan followed. She bit her lip, then gave the car a more in depth look.

It was familiar, or not? *Why do all these bloody American cars look the same?* She sighed. Was there ever going to come a time when she didn't think she was being followed? *Not bloody likely. After someone shoots at your car, you can't ever feel safe.*

The steering wheel felt slick under her palms. She wiped one palm on her jacket, then switched hands and wiped the other hand, while her eyes flicked back and forth between the rearview mirror and the road. She muttered under her breath, "Was he there when I turned at the lights—well, was he? Think, think."

The front of the sedan seemed suddenly to loom over her rearview mirror—it was so close. Back off, she wanted to shout. She glanced over her shoulder. He was a middle-aged man, nondescript, and she didn't recognize him. Her heart pounded in her chest and she could hardly breathe. Maybe she was being paranoid like Brad said.

The voice on the GPS spoke, pulling her attention away from the other car. It was recalculating, after her unplanned turn off, directing her to turn left onto a small side street, the kind that almost no one used. She could finally get out of the car's way and not worry about him anymore.

The sedan made the same turn, and she began hyperventilating and freaking out. *Take a deep breath, hold it, let it out. Now think back. How long has the car been following? Was it behind me when I was on West 64th Avenue? Think.*

Yes, she'd noticed the car on 64th when they were stopped at a red light, but another car had pulled in between them and she'd dismissed the grey car. All right, the guy could be simply heading in the same direction. Bloody hell, it could even be Leo for all she knew. She didn't know what Leo looked like. Surely he wouldn't pull a stunt like that on someone in witness protection. If it was him, she was going to be really pissed.

Making a split second decision she spun the steering wheel and the car whipped into another side street. The calm voice of the GPS rang out into the tension, "Recalculating." Tears sprang into her eyes, blurring the view as the car sped forward. She made another right turn and another. Her breathing quickened, and she felt her gut clench as the sedan appeared round the corner. Still there. Crap!

Out of the corner of her eye, as she made another sudden turn and sped onto the main road, she spotted a blue pulse of lights atop a police car that was parked on the shoulder of the road. The police car pulled away from the shoulder and caught up to her.

Claire slowed down and pulled over as the grey sedan slid past. The driver glared through his side window. Angie's description flashed into her mind: "An average Joe. Middle-aged, wavy blond hair, clean-cut, dressed in jeans and lightweight jacket."

It was him, the man everyone else had seen.

The officer stepped out of his car, walked over to her, and motioned for her to roll down her window. "Did you know you were speeding?"

Shaking, Claire replied, "I—I did, Officer." She wiped away tears and tried to compose herself. "I'm sorry, but I had a good reason. The gray car that turned behind me and just passed you was following me. I was attempting to get away from him."

"Someone you know?"

"No. I don't know who he is. I do know that he's been watching my home and my son, and he has been stalking me for days. He must have followed me from work."

The officer studied her a moment. "I'll fill out a report, but I will need to see your driver's license, vehicle registration, and proof of insurance."

She gave him the documents and waited as he walked back to his squad car. A few minutes later he returned.

"I see you were cited for speeding yesterday."

215

"I was. I was on my way to an important meeting and I was late."

"Uh huh. I'm giving you another citation." He handed her the ticket and told her to drive safely and have a nice day.

She sat there with her mouth open. He obviously thought she'd made up the story to get out of a ticket. Nothing to be done about it. She started up the engine, pulled away, and followed the GPS's directions again, this time without anyone following, as far as she could tell.

In the dark café, Claire told the greeter that she was meeting someone. Before the woman had a chance to ask for the name, a man jumped up from his seat and motioned to Claire.

He looked totally different from Brad. Instead of a balding older man, Leo was young, with dark brown slicked-back hair and brown eyes. Claire reached out her hand to shake hands. His grip was firm, almost too firm.

"We finally meet," Leo said. "I've heard a lot about you."

"Really? I've heard nothing about you."

"Didn't you call to verify?"

"Yes. They confirmed that you're my new—wait a minute. Could you please identify yourself? I need to see your badge, please."

"Fair enough." He pulled out his badge and held it out for her to see.

"Forgive me for being cautious but someone was following me on my way here. I tried to lose him, and he chased me. I ended up getting a speeding ticket. I'm pretty sure he's the man who was seen watching my home and my son and asking about me at a school bus stop."

"I read Brad's notes. He mentioned your paranoia."

"My paranoia? It's really happening. Many people have told me about the man and gave descriptions. The man today matched their descriptions. I can give you names and phone numbers of people who can verify my story."

"Did you tell the police officer that you were being chased?"

"Yes. He didn't do anything except give me a citation."

"Why didn't you call me?"

"When? While I was being chased or after the policeman pulled me over?"

"When you got pulled over."

"How could I do that? Should I have said, 'Excuse me a minute, officer, while I call my handler and ask him what I should do?'"

"Do you always come up with excuses for why you can't think quickly? I read your file. You're supposedly a genius. Seems to me you're not any smarter than the rest of us. Hell, you might be less smart. I sure as hell can think on my toes.

"Just because I can't think fast on my feet doesn't mean I'm stupid." Claire paused to calm down, then continued. "All right, I think we haven't gotten off on a good note. That's partially my fault and I apologize. Can we start over?"

"I don't see any problem between us. This is a typical introductory meeting. In case you need to contact me you can call me at Brad's old number. Also, I have a temporary office in the FBI building in downtown Denver. I'm meeting with another new witness in the metro. In a few weeks, I'll return to Virginia and take Brad's old office. Nothing else has changed regarding your case. I can't move you and you'll have to make do in your situation for the time being."

Claire leaned back in her chair. All right, she wasn't sure she was ready to move again, anyway, but what about the watcher? Why wasn't Leo paying attention to that?

"What happened to Brad? I can maybe see why he isn't on my case anymore. But you say he's gone from his office and his cell phone. Why?"

"It's not something you need to know."

"Where were you before this? How long have you been a handler?"

"That's not really any of your business, either."

"You seem young for this position. I can say that because people say it to me all the time."

"I'm old enough to know my job. I started in the Department of Justice fresh out of college and I've been there five years. My recent move into the U.S. Marshals Service will put me on the fast track up the ranks. I do my job, follow rules, keep my nose clean, and in no time I'll move up."

"Is that what happened to Brad?"

"Brad didn't follow the rules."

SATURDAY MORNING, CLAIRE dragged herself out of bed. Worries about Leo and the watcher kept her tossing and turning all night long. She made a pot of coffee, and after finishing a second cup, she remembered her date with Steve. The digital clock read 8:30, and he would be here in an hour and a half. Steve hadn't mentioned bringing Marcus along and she'd forgotten to arrange for a babysitter.

Maybe she should cancel. But it wasn't fair to Steve to cancel at the last minute. And she really could use a distraction, especially since the weather was exceptionally nice for this time of year. All of the snow was melted off, and the temperature forecast was upgraded to reach sixty degrees. More importantly, she really wanted to see him. No sense pretending otherwise.

She stood and went into the bedroom to retrieve her mobile phone, then dialed Angie's phone number.

"Of course, I'd love to watch the little tike," Angie said. They talked for several more minutes. After Claire hung up, Marcus came out of his bedroom rubbing his eyes.

"Who were you talking to, Mommy?"

"The lady from next door. Angie. Do you remember her?"

"Yes."

"Well, I'm going out for the day and I've arranged for you to spend the day at her house."

"At her house?"

"Yes. She promised to teach you how to bake cookies, as long as you promise to help her eat them."

"I can do that," he said, all smiles and nodding his head. He pulled a chair away from the kitchen table and sat down, dangling his bare feet.

"Oh, and she said she's taking you out to McDonalds for lunch and to play in their playland."

"Yay!" He wiggled and then wiped the sleep from his eyes. "But I'm hungry now."

"What would you like for breakfast?"

"Cinnamon toast. That's my favorite. Nanny Kate sometimes makes it for me."

"I know she does," she said. "Cinnamon toast coming up."

During breakfast, Marcus told her that he liked Angie a lot better than Kate. Claire tried to find out why, but he wouldn't say. She'd heard a few minor complaints from him over the past few weeks, though nothing notable.

After breakfast, she helped him dress. Then, looking at the clock, she decided there wasn't time for a shower. She dressed in a comfortable pair of blue jeans and a red plaid cotton blouse, and then looked in the mirror at her messy hair that had begun to curl overnight. She gave it a quick brush through, not worrying about straightening it, and decided it looked presentable enough for an outing.

Claire had to admit she was more eager about seeing Steve again than about sightseeing.

Ten minutes before Steve was due to pick her up, Claire walked Marcus over to Angie's condo and thanked Angie again for watching him on short notice.

This time, when Steve knocked on her door, she greeted him with a warm smile and invited him inside. He glanced around her living room, and smiled. "If it's okay with you, I figured we'll stop and get chicken and fixings in Colorado Springs to take to the park."

"Of course. That sounds good. Let me grab my handbag and jacket and then we can go."

"Where's your son?"

"Oh, he's next door. My neighbor, a retired lady, is watching him for the day."

Steve nodded, pulling the door shut behind them.

They entered Steve's Jeep Cherokee, and once they were seated and ready to pull away from the curb, Steve asked, "Have you ever been to Colorado Springs?"

"No. I'm not even certain where it is."

He smiled. "It's about an hour's drive south of here. The scenery along the way is beautiful, though population sprawl has taken its toll the last few years. Do you snow ski?"

"I've been a few times, but I'm very much a novice."

"I love skiing. Maybe we can go up to one of the ski resorts together sometime. Your son could even try skiing on the bunny slopes. They have good ski instructors for kids up there."

"I'm sure he would love that," she said, pleased that Steve was thinking of including Marcus.

As they turned onto the freeway, Steve told her about his summer vacation driving across the U.S. She was fascinated listening to him described the places he'd been. When they arrived in town, the 'Springs' as he called it, they stopped momentarily to purchase their picnic lunch, then got underway again. Steve told her their destination was just a few minutes away.

When they arrived at the entrance to The Garden of the Gods, Claire was enthralled with the scene. The mountains in the background were picturesque, but she'd seen mountains before; but the stunning red rock vertical monoliths, stretching skyward here in the park, took her breath away.

After Steve parked and gathered the food and a blanket, they exited and walked a short way. They were not the only ones taking advantage of the warm day. Apparently many other souls had come out with spring fever driving them to enjoy a respite from Colorado's long harsh winter.

Claire loved standing in the midst of this garden of rocks, soaked in the scenery around her, smelling fresh pine in the air, enjoying the deep blue sky backdrop against the red-orange rock pillars, making the panorama look like some artists surreal oil painting.

"What do you think?" Steve asked. "Should we eat first or explore first?"

"I'm fine either way."

"In that case, let's eat first. I'm starved. Looks like a good spot over there." He pointed to a cottonwood shade tree.

"That looks inviting," she said.

Standing under the tree, Steve handed Claire the red and blue plaid blanket. She unfolded it, shook it out, removed a few small rocks from the target area, and then laid it down on the sparse grassy ground. She knelt on the blanket, smoothed it out, and then looked up at him with a smile.

"Looks perfect," Steve said, smiling. He handed the basket with the food to her, and then he dropped down next to her as she began spreading out their meal. While they ate, Steve pointed out Pike's Peak in the distance, and related some of the history of the area. He'd learned a lot about Colorado in the few years he'd lived here. He'd learned a lot about the geology of the area, too.

Steve said, "Geologists claim the story of the Garden of Gods began nearly 300 million years ago, when sediment from the Ancestral Rockies was carried eastward and spread out into great alluvial fans. This sediment was then reddened by ferric iron and long covered by a shallow inland sea." He was pointing to the beautiful red rocks a few hundred feet from where they were sitting.

Claire shielded her eyes from the bright sunshine as she looked at the rocks. "I love the red rocks."

Steve continued. "I've read that some sixty million years ago—when the modern Rocky Mountains began their upward thrust—the horizontal sedimentary rocks were elevated and tilted. Later, the forces of wind and rain gradually stripped away the softer layers, sculpturing each rock into the forms we're now seeing."

"That's fascinating. You must have been a great science teacher. Do you miss it? Teaching, I mean."

"Sometimes. I like what I'm doing, of course, but I have to admit I'm a science junkie. I love talking about science, especially geology."

She laughed, and said, "I do understand. Although much of my career was in teaching mathematics, I started out teaching science. I've always been torn between those subjects."

He grinned and said, "Yeah, I suspect we're both kind of fanatics when it comes to science, facts, and teaching, in general."

Again she laughed. "I think that's probably a true statement, I'm sad to admit. I shouldn't tell you this, but I'm also a science fiction nerd."

He laughed so loud that she felt her face growing red. He reached out and touched her hand. "I'm sorry. I wasn't laughing at you. I don't know anyone who's as big a sci-fi nerd as yours truly. If people at work knew my passion, they'd tease me to no end. So don't tell them, okay?"

"My lips are sealed, as long as you don't tell on me," she said, and then laughed.

After they finished and cleared everything away and packed it back into Steve's vehicle, they set out on a long hike, wanting to climb on some rocks, especially those known as Balanced Rock and Sleeping Indian, but Steve told her it was now prohibited, because of the damage people were causing to the soft sedimentary formations. Meandering through the little hills and gullies, they laughed, played at hide and seek, and sat on boulders soaking in the rare sunshine. He took her hand on several occasions to help her climb up onto the a few higher boulders, and she was conscious of where his warm flesh touched hers. As they meandered on, Steve took her hand in his and for the first time in a long time, Claire almost forgot about her problems.

She was interested in everything here, and she asked many questions that Steve seemed happy to answer. He told her about the plants—the Mountain Shrub, Ponderosa Pines, and Pinion Junipers, and about the animal life and history of the area.

Steve said, "I can't wait to show you some of the other places in Colorado. You'll love it here. I think you'll love exploring up in the mountains. In spring and early summer, the wildflowers are spectacular. If you're interested, we could even go snow skiing up at Vale. And in late spring or early summer, there's river rafting up in Glenwood Canyon."

Claire smiled and said, "I can't wait. It all sounds wonderful. In many ways this place reminds me of Albuquerque, where I lived before moving here. Seeing this makes me a little less homesick."

"I remember you told me you lived there."

By late afternoon, their legs were beginning to ache and their feet were tired, so they started back home. On the drive, Steve said, "Why don't we stop for dinner? I know a little hole-in-wall pizza restaurant on the way. They have the best pizza around." He gave her a sideways glance, and then added, "If you like pizza. I guess I should have asked, first, huh?"

She laughed, and said, "I do like pizza. But this time I'm buying."

He smiled, and said, "Fair enough. We're not far from the restaurant."

"Oh, I do need to call the babysitter though to make sure it's not a problem."

"We're almost to the restaurant. Why don't we go in, get a booth, and then you can call her. If it's not okay, we'll leave."

After they were seated at a booth in the restaurant Claire went to the ladies' room and pulled out her mobile phone. She made a quick call to Angie. Angie sounded happy and told her they would make sandwiches and watch TV together.

At dinner Claire and Steve chatted for a while and then Steve paused and gazed at Claire, looking like he wanted to say something. She took a deep breath and asked, "Is something wrong?"

"Well, I've told you a lot about my past, but I've noticed you're holding back from me. Last week when I asked you about trust, you said you trusted me. I can't help wonder if that's true."

She bit her lip. How could she answer that? For that matter, did she really trust him? If so, then maybe she could open up a bit more.

"I don't talk much about my past. Not with anyone, really."

"Not even with Marcus's father?"

Claire smoothed back some hair from her eyes. "I did talk to him about it. I guess I don't like to talk about my childhood because it . . . well, stirs up bad memories. I'm sorry. I don't like to admit some of the things my parents did."

"You can tell me, Claire. It'll help me understand you better."

She sat silent for several minutes, staring off in the distance, without really looking at anything. Finally, she took a deep breath and let it out. "My dad was a disciplinarian. Strict not only with me, but also with my mother. He would lock me up in my bedroom after school and force me to study. He didn't lock up my mother, but he severely restricted her. She wasn't allowed to go anywhere without him."

"Didn't he leave the house to go to work? What did your parents do for a living?"

"When I was young, my father worked on an assembly line in a car factory during the day but worked on inventions at home the rest of the time. He pushed himself hard. My mother worked in the same factory answering phones and doing clerical work."

Steve nodded.

"Later, my father quit his job and worked on his inventions full-time. He used my mother's inheritance money to support the family. Sometimes he would travel to try to sell something he'd designed and built. During his away time, my mother took advantage and, well, let's just say she did some things she shouldn't have done."

"While the cat's away, the mice will play?"

Claire tilted her head and gave a half-smile. "Something like that. I discovered she was having an affair and she begged me to cover for her. I was torn. I was sixteen and I understood how it was between my parents, but I didn't approve of her affair."

"What did you do?"

"About a month later, my father left on a four-day trip. Two days later, he came home unexpectedly. His sales pitch hadn't gone well. My mother wasn't home. He questioned me about where she was and I tried to lie but botched it. I'm a terrible liar."

"So what happened?"

"When she returned that evening, they argued. It was horrible. I'd heard them quarrel before. This was different. He hit her and she screamed. After the third scream, I was certain my father was going to kill her. He might have, too, but I escaped from my bedroom by smashing through the hollow-core bedroom door with my desk chair. When I reached my parents, he had her on the ground, trying to choke her. I pounded on my father's back, surprising him and releasing my mother long enough for her to get out of the house."

"Wow! Where did you go?"

"We went to a neighbor's house and stayed two nights. After that, we moved into Jack's house. Jack was the guy she was having an affair with. I stayed for a few months and was able to find a decent job. Once I had enough money, I became an emancipated minor and rented my own place."

"So your parents never got back together?"

"No, they divorced. My father has spoken to me only once since."

"Because you covered for your mother?"

"Yes. I helped her and left with her. He said I lied to him and betrayed him."

"That's sad. What happened to your mother? Did she marry the other guy?"

Claire looked down at her empty plate. Steve placed another slice of pizza on it.

"Things didn't work out between them. Karma maybe. Six months later she caught him with another woman. Mother moved in with me. She was depressed, and got fire from her job because she wasn't concentrating on her work. After that, she would stay in bed half the day. One day, when I returned home, I found her in her car, dead from asphyxiation. She'd given up and taken her own life".

Steve reached out and placed his hand over Claire's.

"That's really sad. But I'm glad you confided in me."

When the conversation idled, Steve looked at her for a long moment, and then said, "Can I ask you something else?"

"Okay."

"A while back, I overheard part of a conversation between you and John Richmond. He said something about you being Senator Reynolds's mistress. Is that true?"

"No. I've never actually met the senator. I hadn't even heard the name until John said it. I don't know why he thinks I'm involved with the man."

Steve nodded. "John gets something in his head and hangs onto it whether it's true or not. Makes it hard to work with him sometimes."

"He seems to have taken an instant dislike to me."

"Yeah, it's not the first time he's done that."

Steve told her a couple of short stories about working with John, while they finished eating. Claire paid the check and they left the restaurant.

They arrived at her home around eight o'clock and stood near her door gazing at each other. Steve pulled her close to him, leaned down to kiss her, and then stopped.

He looked at her, and Claire felt heat rising and her heart racing. She knew what he was asking without him speaking aloud, and she had to fight her own desires, as she said, "I had a wonderful day. I want to invite you in, but I need to get Marcus, and I'm not sure I'm ready." She gave him a shy smile, and hoped that he wouldn't be angry with her.

He sighed, then said, "I understand. I don't want to push." Smiling, he added, "I'll be calling you again soon."

After a long passionate kiss, he turned and left.

She watched him get into his car and pull away. It had been such a wonderful day, and she realized how lonely she'd been over the past year. Don't get too used to having him around, she told herself. It can't last. But she wanted it to.

As she lay in bed later, she thought about their date, about the nature park, and about her parents. Steve's comment about Marcus learning to ski got her to thinking about her childhood and how little she'd done outside of school. She thought, too, about Marcus's childhood so far. She hadn't really taken him out to parks and other fun places in more than a year. She used to take him on weekend outings all the time when they lived in Boston. Steve was right. Marcus would love to learn to ski and deserved to get the chance.

CHAPTER NINETEEN

CLAIRE TOOK VARIED routes to Nanny Kate's apartment and to the school in the week that followed, watching through her rearview mirror for signs of the sedan. She didn't see the car or the man again, but was afraid to let down her guard. Her new handler worried her, too, especially since he wouldn't tell her what had happened to Brad. Work was so busy, though, that she had scant time to think about it.

Standing on the auditorium stage Wednesday evening, Claire studied the disappointing group of about fifty parents sitting in the audience. She'd hoped for a much larger turnout for the first parent meeting. Steve, Frank, and about a dozen teachers stood along the sides of the room. After introducing herself and Ron to the group, Claire said, "Students here at Midland are struggling. Many have failing grades and are in danger of not graduating. Equally alarming is the fact that many students here are afraid for their safety. Some are continuously being bullied or threatened, some are exposed to drug usage or drug dealing on campus. Almost none will come forward and file complaints, for fear of retaliation. We also have a gang problem, one we believe to be our biggest threat. Some members want to leave their gangs but are afraid—afraid to leave because doing so places their own lives at risk with that gang." She paused and looked around at the faces in the audience. "Teachers here are also being bullied into suboptimal practices and are at risk and in danger daily. There is no doubt in my mind that the majority of failing students are failing due to the conditions here at Midland." She watched their reactions before continuing.

"We have created a plan to solve these and other problems so that our students and faculty can be safe and thrive. This plan has required our faculty to engage in special training and to implement specific enforcement and engagement tactics to terminate undesired behaviors and improve school conditions. But our staff cannot wholly solve these problems on their own. Part of this plan requires the involvement of parents and the community. We need your support and your help."

She paused again, waiting for any response from the audience. Other than a few coughs, the room was silent. Continuing, she said, "One way you can help immediately is to talk to other parents of Midland High students, encouraging them to also become involved."

"What is it you want people to do?" someone yelled.

Claire looked for the speaker.

A plump middle-aged woman was standing up and waving her arms. "We got jobs to do. How we s'posed to help out in a school?"

"Good question. There are many things you can do. Some could volunteer during school if they have time, others can tutor students after school or in the evening. All of you attending more of these parent meetings and talking about your concerns and your ideas for improving things will help."

Ron stood up and walked toward Claire. He held another microphone. He said, "We could also use guest speakers at some of our school-wide assemblies. We're trying to open up the lines of communication between students, teachers, administrators, parents, and community leaders. What we'd also like from you, as parents, is to talk with your kids. Maybe you have some real life experience you'd like to share, such as mistakes you've made and learned from. You likely don't know this, but when I was in eighth grade, I was in a gang for a short time. I wasn't a bad kid, but I was coerced into joining. I'm going to talk to the students about that experience and try to get them to open up."

A man stood up. "I was in prison for five years. Did time for drug dealing. Clean now. I could talk to 'em."

"We would appreciate your talking to them. Sharing your experience with them, sharing the consequences you suffered and what you learned would be great."

Several more parents spoke up and offered help.

Claire noticed that many were still frowning or sitting with their arms crossed. It'll take time, she told herself.

Steve walked her out to her car after the meeting, and they stood outside talking for a few minutes about the meeting. "I think you're doing a great job," he said. "It's not easy, even for someone who's been there for a long time, and here you've only been at the school less than two months. I'm very impressed."

"I didn't think I could do this. I can't tell you how close I came to giving up. And we still don't know if what we're doing will help."

"No, we don't. It's too soon to tell, but that fact you've gotten this far is amazing."

As she got into her car, Steve leaned in and said, "And if I forgot to tell you, I really enjoyed our day together in Colorado Springs. Let's plan something again, soon, okay? I have a funeral to go to out of town this weekend. My uncle. I told you about him the other day. But next week?"

At the second parents' meeting two days later, on Friday, the turnout was larger, perhaps ninety attendees this time, not including teachers. Before the meeting officially started, Frank came and sat at the back of the room. Claire walked over and sat next to him for a moment.

"I'm glad you came. Why don't you sit up front?"

He smiled. "This is your party. I'm just here for moral support. Go get 'em."

"Thanks." She got up and walked toward the front of the room, but glanced back once, with a smile.

After the first parents' meeting she and Ron had discussed many of the initial ideas proposed by parents and teachers, the most ambitious and the one they ultimately chose being a face lift of the school by employees, students, and parents. This involved painting the interior, cleaning and waxing the floors, general cleaning up of classrooms and washrooms, and trimming the bushes around the exterior of the building.

After her opening remarks Claire said, "We need your help. We want to give the school a face lift, but cannot afford to hire outside help to do the actual work. We propose a community team building project, getting all of us involved, employees, faculty, students, and parents. By all working on this together, instead of trying to fund raise to hire outside help, the project can build team spirit, camaraderie, and pride in both our community and our school. Not only that, but by having students and faculty take part in the work, they'll be more likely to keep it nice looking. If we can get your support and help, we can pull this off. This can be a win-win scenario for all of us."

"How you gonna get the money to pay for all that?" a parent asked.

"Great question. We've already spoken to a couple paint store managers and owners. Two of them have generously offered to donate supplies, including paint, brushes, rollers, drop cloths and other materials needed. We also talked to one of the major hardware chains and they agreed to donate mulch for around the exterior of the building. We were hoping, too, that parents and teachers might also have some extra supplies at home, like brushes, rollers, roller pans, ladders, rakes, trimming tools, etc. that they could bring in and use or loan to students to use."

"I've got a painting business," a man said. "I'll help, as long as you can get some of those lazy kids to help. I'm not doing it for them."

"Thank you. Our goal is to get everyone involved—students, teachers, and parents; especially our students. Most of our staff have already volunteered to help. We'll be proposing the plan to the students on Monday. We must get at least twenty-five percent of the students to volunteer, or we won't go forward with the plan. That's something we all agreed on. We plan to do this over a weekend, so it should not interfere with most work schedules. A few of the local pizza places have agreed to provide pizzas for lunch. The superintendent and I have agreed to provide soft drinks and hot dogs for everyone working. Perhaps some of you can volunteer to head up the food committee and we would love for some of you to bring a dish, cookies, chips or other food to share. We can make this fun."

"If that's true, you can count me in." At least twenty more parents chimed in with their commitment.

"Thank you. That will be wonderful." Claire wrapped up the meeting with a few timing details and initial assignments, then thanked everyone again for coming and for their support.

She drove home, thinking about the meeting and about Steve. He'd called her earlier in the day to say he was still out of town, but asked her out again for the following week when he would be back from his trip. For the first time in months, she wasn't worrying about anything.

Over the weekend, Claire packed Marcus in the car and drove up to Rocky Mountain National Park. She'd been too busy lately to give him the kind of attention he needed. Since he'd recently indicated an interest in science, she figured he'd enjoy getting out and learning about nature. The thought of the stranger who'd been watching them was an added reason to get out of town for a while.

At the student assembly on Monday, approximately one-third of the students seemed enthusiastic about painting and fixing up the school from what Claire could tell. They would have a better idea of participation later in the week, as she'd given all teachers a sign-up sheet for homeroom classes. They would start getting students to sign up and commit to volunteering for the project beginning Tuesday morning.

After the assembly, Claire went to Mr. Owens's classroom. She'd spoken to him about her talking to one of his math classes. She slipped into the room and waited in the back while the teacher finished speaking to his students.

By way of introduction, Mr. Owens said, "Ms. Constantine is here this morning to talk with you about something related to math, but don't worry, you won't be tested on it."

"Thank you, Mr. Owens." Claire walked to the front of the room. "Have any of you ever heard of Game Theory?"

No one responded, other than with shuffling of feet and books.

"Well, basically Game Theory is a mathematical analysis of any situation involving a conflict of interest, where the person analyzing is trying to find the optimal choices that, under given conditions, will lead to a desired outcome."

Students were looking at her with a dazed look on their faces.

"Have any of you ever played checkers or poker or tick-tack-toe?"

Almost everyone nodded.

"All right, then. You have actually already had some exposure to Game Theory. I won't bore you with the background of the theory, except to tell you it was first explored by a French mathematician. During World War II military strategists used game theory to help them win the war. After that, the theory was picked up by people in the social sciences."

Six students in the back of the room began whispering. Three students near the front were texting on their mobile phones. Someone on the left side of the room let out a wolf whistle. Claire couldn't tell where that came from. All she knew for sure was that she was losing the students' interest fast.

Looking closely at the students, she recognized many of them. Some she had dealt with in her office for some problem or offense, some others were students who had been on suspension for drugs found in their cars during the police department's search.

That gave her an idea. It might not be the wisest thing do, however, but it might get the idea across.

"Have any of you ever heard of the famous game known as the Prisoner's Dilemma?"

The whispering stopped, and the students turned to look at Claire. She'd captured their interest.

"In this game two players are partners in a crime. They have been captured by the police. The police have evidence to convict the two for auto theft, but not for their suspected robbery. Each suspect is placed in a separate cell away from one another. Each is offered the opportunity to confess to the crime.

"If one of them confesses to the robbery and the other does not, the deal was that the confessor would go free and the other would incur a ten year sentence in prison. If both confessed, then each would be given a reduced six year prison sentence."

A few heads nodded. Students were sitting up now, clearly interested.

"If neither suspect confessed, they would both be convicted of car theft and receive a three year sentence."

One student said "So they are better off promising each other to not confess."

"Not really. You see, even though keeping silent offers the lowest dual sentence for both, for each individual criminal, their best outcome is to shoot for freedom and no prison sentence, and therefore to break any made promise and confess. Each criminal must assume that the other will be tempted by the chance of no prison sentence and will therefore confess. The solution is that the criminals will look after their own best interest, will confess, and take the police department's deal."

Several students nodded.

"There is a simple mathematical game theory logic for this behavior. Each criminal has two choices, either remain silent or confess. If criminal one confesses and two remains silent or confesses, criminal one receives either zero or six years in prison. But if criminal one remains silent, then criminal two remains silent or confesses, resulting in either three years or ten years in prison. This is also true for criminal two. The choice is either zero or six on the one hand, or three and ten on the other."

"I get it," a male student Claire recognized as Johnny said. "So it's about calculating odds. Is that it?"

"You've got it."

"What happens if a suspect has no idea what his partner is going to do?"

"It's always best to confess. The only way you can come out better is if neither of you confesses, which is taking a really big risk."

Several students nodded.

Claire continued. "I've often heard students complain that math doesn't apply to real-life, but it does. You'll use basic math to manage your finances, figure out budgets, figure out percentages, etc. You can use more advanced math if you go on to study Game theory, which I briefly introduced you to. Game theory is the study of probability, a branch of mathematics focusing on the application of mathematical reasoning to competitive behavior. It's used in economics, psychology, biology, political science, philosophy, logic, and computer science. Businessmen even use it in setting prices, say for bids on contracts."

"Hey, it can probably help drug dealers who are competing with other dealers," one student said.

Claire sighed. *Yeah, they have the idea. I guess that's something at least.*

ON MONDAY EVENING when Claire went to pick up Marcus, Kate said, "I'm sorry to tell you this, but I can't watch Marcus anymore."

"What? Why not? Is something wrong?"

"No."

"Is it because you have to watch him in your home? We could try back at my home if that's the reason." She didn't like the idea, with the watcher getting bolder, but she hated to lose Kate and she would do whatever was necessary.

"I can't. I'm sorry."

Claire gave Kate her final daycare payment and whisked Marcus into the car. What was she supposed to do on such short notice? She was so preoccupied with her worries that she didn't notice Marcus was crying until they were halfway home.

"It's all right, Marcus. I know you'll miss Nanny Kate, but it'll be fine."

In the rearview mirror she saw him raise his tear-streaked face. "She doesn't like me, Mommy. She called me a freaky little bastard."

What? Oh, bloody hell.

"Did she say why, Marcus?"

"She said I'm not like other kids." His voice dropped to a whisper and Claire had to strain to hear him. "I ask too many questions."

That could mean more than one thing. Maybe Kate was doing things that he questioned, that he suspected were wrong. Or it could mean that he pestered her with questions she didn't know how to answer. That seemed most likely.

"What kind of questions?"

"You know, Mommy. Like why do some clouds make rain and some make snow? Or, why do some letters make more than one sound? "

Yes, she did know. She'd been the same way when she was young. At age four, she'd been the youngest, smallest kid in class and the other kids had made fun of her because she was always either answering all the teacher's questions or bombarding the teacher with more questions.

"I'm really sorry, my love. Unfortunately, people can be cruel, especially when they don't understand you. You are different from most kids. Not freaky, but unique, sweetie. So am I. I understand you more than you could possibly know." She fought back tears and paused a moment, hoping that she could speak without betraying her emotions. "Sooner or later you'll have to get used to some people not understanding and being mean. Perhaps it's time to enroll you in a preschool. That way, you can play with other kids and learn, too."

His face lit up. "School? Yes."

Great. Now she had to find an acceptable preschool, one that would accommodate a special little boy. God, she hoped she could find that—and quickly.

The following morning, Claire called Ron and told him she would be late to work and explained why. It took her half of the day, but she did find a preschool/daycare that she felt comfortable with and that would accept a new student. Marcus had been a bit shy at first, when the director introduced him to the other kids, but he quickly made friends with several boys. She interrupted their play for a minute to say goodbye. "I'll pick you up after work, okay?"

CHAPTER TWENTY

A WEEK AND a half after Claire had announced the school facelift plan at the second parents' meeting, final preparations for the big day were underway. Parents, students, and faculty would begin work at nine o'clock Saturday. That, of course, assumed everyone who signed up actually showed up and brought with them what they had agreed. Recognizing that was a pretty big assumption, Claire was keeping her fingers crossed in hopes that her fears wouldn't come to pass. Steve wouldn't be there. She wasn't even sure if he knew about the remodeling project. She hadn't seen him in two weeks and he hadn't attended the second parent meeting. He had even cancelled their date for last week, saying he had to take time off from work and travel to Massachusetts to visit his mother who was in the hospital undergoing surgery.

Claire had left color schemes for classrooms up to the students and teachers to plan together, while she, Ron, and the others in the Admin office had picked the colors for offices, hallways, and the main lobby. Paint and hardware store owners had donated much of the paint, but Claire had bought the rest of the paint with her own money.

By Friday afternoon, she had obtained estimates for a new heater and had scheduled the installation of the new heating system for Wednesday of the following week. She'd also spoken over the phone with a parent who owned a lighting business about replacing several damaged lights in the building hallways. He said he'd be at the school Saturday, since he and his daughter, Jenny, planned to help with the painting. "I'll ask Jenny to introduce us while we're there," he'd said, "and we can go over options."

Frank and his family were among the first to arrive early Saturday, after Claire and Ron. Frank's wife Gloria was an attractive blonde with flaxen blond hair halfway down her back. She was a bit heavy, but not much, maybe fifteen pounds overweight. Amy was a slender, pretty fourteen-year-old with waist-length blonde hair. Kyle was a football-playing sixteen-year-old, and a charmer with light curly brown hair and an adorable smile. Both kids sported their father's blue-gray eyes.

"What grades are you in?" Claire asked.

"I'm a freshman," Amy said, "and he's a junior."

"Where do you go to school?"

"Wilkins High School," Kyle said, "but I'm beginning to wish I went here."

They talked and laughed for a while until others arrived. Soon the building was a madhouse, bustling with activity. Claire was delighted. She had been expecting three-hundred-fifty people total, but by ten o'clock, she suspected there was closer to five-hundred-fifty. Ron was in charge of directing and assigning tasks to avoid total chaos. Claire was responsible for answering questions and resolving any problems that might arise.

While Claire was painting in the faculty lounge, she heard a familiar voice talking to Frank. She looked up and saw Steve in the doorway. He and Frank were joking around. When they finished, Steve approached her and smiled.

She looked around. No one was watching them, and she said, "I thought you were still out of town. I'm really glad you could make it. I've missed you."

"I wouldn't miss this for anything. Frank told me about it. What can I do to help? Oh, and by the way, I've missed you, too."

"Grab a paint brush or a roller, your choice."

An hour later when Ron made an announcement over the intercom that pizza, hot dogs, sodas, and other foods had arrived, compliments of local pizza restaurants, the faculty, and parent donations, there was a mad rush for the cafeteria.

After lunch Jenny introduced her father to Claire. He'd brought with him several options for replacement lights. Claire made her choices, and he promised he'd have replacements installed next Tuesday.

It was a costly improvement she'd have to pay for out of her own pocket, but the employees and students had earned a reward. Claire was grateful she could afford it. Having improved lighting in the school halls would be worth its weight in gold. Fewer dark hiding places meant less crime. At least she hoped so.

By the end of the day, the whole school was a cheerier place. Although it was too cold really enjoy being outdoors, volunteers did manage to trim back the bushes, making them less conducive to hiding. They also shoveled and raked in several yards of mulch that had been delivered the previous day. Everyone was tired, but pride showed in all their faces as they appraised their work. It looked good, inside and out. Claire felt an overwhelming pride, too, not only in the work, but also in these people who were laughing and enjoying themselves.

After almost everyone had gone, Claire and Steve stayed to move bags of trash left behind to the school trash bin. As they walked through the building, Claire had a better chance to really take in and assess all the changes to the building. The main entrance was immaculate and bathed in light. The walls would hold the fresh paint smell for a while, but even without the smell no one could miss the abrupt change from its prior dingy gray to the now bright creamy yellow.

Incredible. Even the lockers in the long hallway visible in the distance shined from their fresh coat of tan paint coordinating with the original gold-flecked tan linoleum floors, scrubbed cleaned and waxed to a glistening sheen. Large plants set in brightly colored adobe clay pots had been donated by a local nursery and arranged in strategic places, giving lively splashes of red and orange and blue and green.

Doors to the various offices and classrooms were painted a warm, burnt orange as a splash of bright color, while the trim around the doors and windows was painted the same calming tan as the lockers. The stairs still had their original walnut risers and concrete treads, but the old, black wrought iron railings were now painted the same tan color as the lockers.

The overall effect was warm and welcoming.

After locking up, Steve and Claire left and walked around the side of the building toward the faculty car park adjacent to a side street lined with old two-story houses and tall oak trees whose roots had over the years lifted up the sidewalk in many places.

"Where are you parked?" Claire asked.

"Down the road on this street." He pointed straight ahead. "I'm about a block down. That's what happens when you get here late. Both parking lots were full. I'll walk with you to your car, though."

"That's all right. You don't have to do that. It's been a long day and we're both tired. No sense walking more than you have to."

"Okay. I'll call you later. I'd give you a kiss before I leave, but it's probably not a good idea. Could be some students lingering around."

"True. Good night. Thanks for all your help." She waved and turned to the right and walked across the car park. When she reached her car and took out her keys, she felt someone standing next to her. Steve must have changed his mind. She turned to speak to him and gasped. The man with wavy blond hair was standing two feet from her. She backed up and bumped up against her car.

Was he going to kill her? She glanced right and left. Could she make a break for safety?

"Don't bother running," he said. "I was on my high school track team and my college's track team. You won't outrun me."

She took a deep breath to calm herself. "Why have you been following me? Who are you?"

"I'm doing my job, which is to find out about you."

"Who hired you, and why?"

"That's privileged information."

"Not good enough," she shouted. "You made me drive recklessly when you were chasing me, and if it weren't for that police officer who pulled me over, you probably would have caused an accident."

"Not my fault you're a lousy driver."

"I'm not. Anyone would drive too fast if they were being chased. Don't try to put the blame on me."

"Have it your way. But there's something you need to know, I saw you in that café with Leo."

"What? How'd—" She clamped her mouth shut. How did he know Leo's name?

"He's a U.S. Marshall. I've seen him before. After I saw him, I put everything together. You're in WITSEC. I'm sure there are people who will pay big money for knowledge of your whereabouts. But I'm willing to keep your secret—for a price."

"I—I don't know what to say. I need time to think."

"Don't wait too long."

"How do I contact you?"

"I'll be around, Claire."

Her mouth dropped open and her heart was beating so fast she thought she would pass out. She fumbled with her keys and somehow unlocked her door. As she tried to open the door, her hands were shaking, but she managed to get into the car and quickly lock the door. He was still standing there. She pulled straight out of her parking spot and sped out of the lot. In her rearview mirror she saw him walking toward a grey sedan parked against the back of the building.

STEVE HAD REACHED his car and gotten in, and was turning the car around so that he could drive back to the main road when he saw Claire talking to a middle-aged man. They were clearly arguing. Was he a disgruntled teacher? A parent maybe?

He pulled over to the side of the road and watched. She got into her car and pulled out of the parking lot without looking, her tires screeching in the process. Something was wrong.

The man was walking toward the only car in the lot. Steve pulled in, stopped crossways behind the gray car as the man was getting inside. Steve got out of his car and approached the man.

Almost instantly, the man jumped out of his car and waved his arms at Steve. "What the hell are you doing? You're blocking my car."

"We need to talk."

"Oh, yeah. About what?"

"Claire Constantine. I saw you two talking. It looked like you were arguing."

"What business is it of yours?"

"I'm the district's superintendent. You're on school grounds and arguing with my employee. It's my business."

"I don't have to talk to you."

"Yeah, you do. I'll call the police if you don't."

"I don't think your boss would like that very much."

"Why's that?"

"Because I'm working for him. You better talk to Richmond before you go threatening me with getting the police involved."

"What kind of work are you doing for him?"

"Let's just say you don't really know anything about Claire Constantine. Now get out of my way."

Steve glared at him, but decided he should take this up with Richmond in the morning.

CHAPTER TWENTY-ONE

CLAIRE STOOD BY the front window of the entrance hall and watched as students arrived for school. The stunned looked on the faces of students who hadn't participated in the remodel of the school was priceless. She wouldn't have missed it for anything.

She returned to her office and smiled to herself. At least something good had happened over the weekend. She didn't want to think about the encounter with the watcher. She should call Leo and find out how she should deal with the threat, but she procrastinated. Listening to Leo chiding her and accusing her of making up another story was not productive.

Half an hour later, while working on a budget report, her phone rang. It was Steve.

"Hey, I wondered if you'll have dinner with me tomorrow night. I actually have some free time in the evenings this week and I'm dying to see you again."

"That sounds great. Oh, but I can't. Not tomorrow. I'll be here for another parents' meeting."

"Okay. How about Wednesday?"

"That should work."

"Great! Oh, and don't forget the Round Table Luncheon on Wednesday."

Later in the day she visited classrooms and saw a distinct change of attitude in many students and in teachers. For the first time they actually seemed happy to be there.

On Tuesday the lighting was installed as planned, and then on Wednesday morning the heating and plumbing guy, Manny Rodriquez, showed up to replace the heater. Claire was getting ready to head out to the Round Table Luncheon when Manny stuck his head into her office and told her they had a problem.

"I need to show you in the furnace room. Then you decide what you want me to do."

"All right. Let's go."

PHIL SEGER TOOK off his coat, threw it on the floor, and plopped down in his desk chair. Looking around his dark office, he wanted to scream. This was not the kind of investigator's office he'd envisioned for himself. He'd expected a bright office with a huge cherry wood desk, leather chair, photographs of Tahiti or Hawaii on his walls, an outer office with a sexy secretary who would schedule his appointments and screen his new clients, selecting only the most interesting cases for him.

Yeah, right. What he had was an office the size of a walk-in closet with one window, scenically overlooking a brick wall, a crappy desk from the second-hand shop, and a small secretary chair, but no real secretary. He did it all. Wasn't hard considering he didn't exactly have clients lining up to hire him.

Right now, gathering information on Claire Constantine was his only job. And John Richmond, who acted like he was paying him in gold, was in actuality a cheapskate. But what choice did he have, with no other paying customers? Disgusted, Phil picked up the stack of bills he'd accumulated over the past month.

Richmond's payments weren't going to be near enough to even cover expenses, much less provide any profit.

Some P.I. he was. He'd discovered Claire's affair with her boss. He'd even thought of blackmailing her over that. But big freaking deal! If she hadn't jumped at the deal he'd offered her, of keeping her secret about being in WITSEC for a price, she certainly wasn't going to pay him to keep quiet about her affair.

Thinking along those lines, he regretted telling that nosy school superintendent whom he was working for. The man had rattled him, plain and simple. Richmond was going to be pissed. Nothing he could do about it now. Damn, he hoped Richmond wouldn't fire him.

Phil didn't want to turn Claire over to criminals, but he figured if she was in WITSEC, somebody might not want her to testify. That somebody might be willing to pay for information about her whereabouts. Problem was, he still didn't know who she really was or who might be looking for her.

After seeing her with that Federal agent, Leo, he had followed the guy and saw him make several stops, one of them at a gun shop. The next day, Phil had gone back to those places. In the gun shop, he hit pay dirt. An employee wearing a name tag— Jim Miller—was willing to let his tongue wag for a price. The guy said Leo was looking for information about someone who had bought a gun from him a few days before. The kicker was that Roger Simons—a dirty cop whom Jim occasionally saw in the neighborhood and in his store—had been in a couple of days earlier asking about the same buyer.

Phil handed over his last hundred dollars, and Jim gave him Simon's phone number.

Phil had called Simons and set up a meeting. Simons wouldn't say much about the case at first—not until Phil told him he was working a case involving a woman in WITSEC. Simons suddenly opened up, telling him the few bits he knew about the case involving a syndicate, which he suspected would be willing to pay big bucks to get their hands on the prosecution's main witness. If Phil's subject was indeed that witness, they could perhaps strike a deal with the syndicate and split the proceeds. Of course Phil had readily agreed to work with him, the smell of quick money in his nostrils. They exchanged business cards, and both agreed to poke around and call if either found out anything more.

Simons had also given him a name—Juliet Powell.

Phil sat down at his desk and turned on his computer. *Okay, time to get serious*, he told himself. Time to dig in and see what he could find out about this Juliet Powell. Was Claire Constantine the same woman? Could he connect the dots? Claire was previously a math teacher—at least that was her cover story. And after actually speaking with her, he thought he detected a hint of a British accent. He'd worked a case a while back that had taken him to London. He'd gotten a snout-full of the accent, enough that it had been permanently etched into his brain.

Searching online for the name Simons had given him, along with the word England, he actually found something. Oxford. Weymouth. A search of her name again along with the word Boston brought up an article about an arrest warrant for one Callum Fuller. His brow furrowed as he skimmed the article. Then he saw it; Juliet Powell, a math professor, the girlfriend of the suspect.

Excited, Phil looked at the piece of paper with Simon's phone number. Before he got a chance to dial, his phone rang. It was Roger Simons.

"Hey," Simons said, "I got the name of the top boss in the syndicate, but you're not gonna like it. Seems the case is connected to one Samuel Peters." Phil choked. "Yeah, that's the guy. Anyway, one of his syndicates started some scheme that landed him in trouble, and somehow Powell is connected."

"Thanks." Phil scribbled the name on a scrap of paper.

Silence. The sound of cars in the background gave Phil the impression Simons was in his car or outside instead of in the police station. Made sense. No colleagues around to listen in.

Phil said, "What do we do now? Do you have any connections to Samuel Peters?"

"That depends. What did you find out about your subject?" Simons asked. "Is she the woman we're looking for?"

"Think so. Still need to verify it." Phil didn't tell him that he wasn't at all sure. His only real clues were math teacher, WITSEC, and slight British accent. It would not go well if she was the wrong woman.

"Good. I've got another name for you. Someone who might be willing to pay for the information. But I need to confirm our deal. We're in it fifty-fifty."

Phil said, "Why should I give you fifty percent? I'm the one who knows where the woman is."

"Yeah, well, I'm the one with the name and phone number of the guy who might be willing to pay for the information."

"Fine. Fifty-fifty. Give me the name and number."

Simons gave him the information, then said, "Double-cross me and you won't live to regret it."

After Phil hung up, he groaned. Samuel Peters was hardcore. He was a well-known mob boss who dipped into everything from finance to gunrunning to supporting terrorists. Did he really want to give up this woman with a kid to Peters and his men? She's be dead meat for sure.

His phone rang again and he figured Simons had forgotten something. Nope. This time it was Richmond.

"Damn it, Phil," Richmond said. "You told Steve Jensen you're working for me. That was supposed to be secret. What the hell are you doing? Now I've got him breathing down my neck."

"Sorry about that. It wasn't planned. He cornered me. I had to say something."

"So you did tell him! I wasn't sure, but he acted strangely when I talked to him this morning. Damn. At least tell me you've got something on Claire and the Senator."

"Not yet. I'm working on it."

"Better speed it up. I'm getting damn impatient."

Phil hung up again, and looked at the name he'd written down. He picked up his phone again and dialed.

SHORTLY BEFORE LUNCHTIME on Wednesday, Steve looked at his office wall clock and gritted his teeth. *Time to go.* The last thing he wanted to do today was attend his own Round Table Luncheon. What a sad state of affairs. He'd begun to hate them after John Richmond got involved.

The luncheons had begun as casual get-togethers, meant to bolster a community atmosphere and allow principals to discuss topics that interested them. But John had injected himself and insisted they needed formal agendas, mandatory attendance, and a rigid format. Damn the man. It was called the Superintendent's Round Table Luncheon, not School Board President's Luncheon.

To make matters worse, he'd already had one argument with the bastard this morning, and he hadn't even told John yet that he knew about that private investigator.

He steeled himself, gathered up his paperwork, and drove to Jackson High School, the site of this meeting. When he entered, most of the attendees had already arrived and were milling about. Steve looked around for Claire. She wasn't there.

He surveyed the room again. Nothing. He strained to hear the voices mingling in the hallway outside the conference room, hoping to hear her voice, but she didn't seem to be in the hallway, either. He'd reminded her of the meeting when they'd spoken on the phone. Well, there's still time, he told himself. After glancing at his watch and noting that it was two minutes until start time, he pulled Frank aside.

He whispered, "Where is Claire?"

Frank shrugged. "I don't know. She promised she'd be here."

Steve ran his hand through his hair, looked across the room and spotted John Richmond talking to another school board member, Peter Williams.

"Call her and get her over here."

Frank made a quick exit.

Upon Frank's return a few minutes later, John asked everyone to take a seat and then motioned for Steve to start the meeting. Frank sat down, glanced at Steve, and shook his head. Steve's jaw clenched and his eyes narrowed in response, but he quickly recovered and began speaking.

Things moved along well for about an hour, until John began asking about the various schools. When he finally realized Claire was missing again, his voice hardened and his eyes became cold and dark. "I see Claire thinks she's too good to join us. What's her excuse this time?"

Frank squirmed in his seat. "The school's new heating system is being installed today. She'd planned to leave her assistant in charge of that. Unfortunately, there were some decisions to be made, things that required her personal attention. That's what her secretary told me. I left a message for Claire."

Damn, thought Steve. He'd forgotten about the heating system installation. She'd told him about it.

John's voice snapped his next words. "There's no excuse for her missing these meetings. She seems to think she can do whatever the hell she feels like."

Whenever John was angry with someone, he behaved like a bear with a thorn in its paw. Steve wasn't in the mood for placating the grizzly.

When the meeting ended, three long hours after it began, John dismissed the principals but asked Steve to stay. Steve's shoulders tensed up as he waited for the room to clear.

John said, "I want to know what the hell is going on at Midland High School. What do you know about it?"

"Things are going well. Claire and her staff have been working to fix the school's problems. There have been some minor issues, but all in all, it's going great."

"You and Frank are still helping her?"

Steve kept tight control of his expressions. He knew John was watching him. "Yeah."

"Didn't I tell both of you to stick with your assigned job tasks? You have other schools to deal with and you shouldn't be giving special attention to one school."

"Look, John, Midland is the worst school in the district. It needs special attention. It's about time someone did something to fix the problems over there."

John's face turned red. Steve thought of the Devil.

Steve added, "Neither Frank nor I are neglecting our work if that's what you're worried about. We're putting in extra hours on our own time, which we aren't getting paid for, by the way."

John waved his hand and said, "I need to make a few phone calls, so I'm leaving, but I'll catch up with you in your office, shortly."

Great. Just what I need. Another meeting with Richmond.

An hour later, John showed up in Steve's office as Steve was getting off the phone with the principal of one of their elementary schools.

"We're holding a special board meeting tonight. Be here at six-thirty." He turned on his heel and left without giving Steve a chance to respond.

Damn. What's he got up his sleeve now, the asshole?

Steve picked up his phone and dialed Claire's number. She didn't answer, so he left a message that he couldn't make it to dinner tonight.

AT FIVE-THIRTY, CLAIRE'S mobile phone rang.

"Hello, I'm John Richmond's secretary. He instructed me to call you and let you know there's a special school board meeting tonight. You need to be there at six-thirty, at Central Administration."

Claire called Angie and asked her to babysit. "I'm sorry it's such short notice. I just found out about a meeting."

"No problem. Send the little tike over whenever you're ready."

Claire had to catch her breath as she entered the Central Administration Building. She fussed with her clothes and hair, took a deep breath and let it out, straightened up, and walked up to the reception desk.

"I'm here to see Mr. Richmond."

"And you are?"

"Claire Constantine."

"Ah, he's in the board room. They're expecting you. Do you know where that is?"

"No."

"Okay. Follow me."

She paused outside the door. As the woman walked away, Claire fussed with her own clothes and hair again, took a deep breath and let it out. When opened the door and stepped inside, she was stunned to see a courtroom style board room, with what appeared to be the whole school board in session. Steve was sitting next to the board members in what was evidently his assigned seat based on the name plaque in front of him.

"I'm sorry. Am I interrupting something?"

"Not at all," John Richmond said. "We've been waiting for you. Have a seat."

She looked around, unsure where she was supposed to sit. All the audience seats appeared vacant. What did that mean? Was she the only non-board member here?

She decided to take a seat up front. That's when she saw Frank. He was sitting in one of the audience seats, facing the board. She sat down beside him.

John introduced her to the rest of the board. One member, Ed Malone, she'd already met.

"Since you failed to show up at today's Round Table Luncheon I did some checking and found out that you've given Midland High School a major overhaul." John paused for effect. "Apparently, since you told Frank and Steve that you were trying to fix the school's problems, they let you do whatever you wanted." He gave Steve an admonishing look. "Steve is responsible for your performance, whether he's your direct supervisor or not," he said, his voice heavy with sarcasm.

Claire looked at Steve. She couldn't read him, his face was a stone mask. Her attention was drawn back to John when he spoke again, "And Frank is your direct supervisor. He should be fired for this."

"What?" Claire asked. "Are you insane?"

Steve gave her a warning look, but she couldn't stop. She couldn't let it go.

"He's been a great supervisor. He's been at Midland at least three times a week for the past few weeks, and—"

"You're telling us he knew about all of what you were doing?" John said, waving his hands.

Claire snapped her mouth closed.

John seemed to make a decision. He stood up and snapped, "I want all of the film footage from the security cameras we installed at the beginning of October. You may leave now. After we review it, we'll call you back here."

Claire was flabbergasted. "What film footage? What security cameras?"

John said, "The board had a few cameras installed in case any problem arose that needed investigation."

"I—I haven't seen any cameras. In fact, I talked to Frank about installing cameras on my second day here." Her forehead creased as she looked at John and then at Steve for some sign.

"Since you so aptly pointed out earlier," Frank said, "I'm her supervisor. So why wasn't I informed of this?"

John squirmed. "That would have defeated the purpose because you might have told her about the cameras. We couldn't take that chance."

Claire snapped, "Huh? You were afraid I'd inform the students so you wouldn't catch any drug dealing? And why put surveillance cameras in now, when the school has had problems for years?"

John smirked. "Because the school didn't have a brand new, inexperience principal before now."

Claire's mouth dropped open, but she regained her control and said, "So you were expecting what? To catch me doing something wrong?"

John didn't answer. He crossed his arms and stared at her.

She was speechless. Taking a deep breath and letting it out, she forced herself to stay calm. "Where are these spy cameras?"

"I'm not at liberty to say right now."

Oh God! Was there one in her office? She glanced over at John and to her horror everyone was staring at her with puzzled looks on their faces. Oh crap. It must have been written on her face. It was then that she realized her mouth was hanging wide open with her shock. She snapped her mouth shut, and struggled to compose herself. "I—I don't understand. I haven't seen any cameras. Who changes the tapes? Where are these tapes kept?"

John gave her a smug look, and said, "They're special CCTV video surveillance cameras, small black spheres barely noticeable when placed near the top of high ceilings."

"And you've recorded conversations as well? Private conversations?"

"The cameras don't record audio. Video images are sent to a hard drive on a central computer in a locked room here in the building. The head of your custodial staff was trained on maintaining the cameras and computer."

Hector Minosa? He wouldn't have hidden this from me, would he? We have a decent working relationship. Why would he take part in a spy campaign against me?

John made no attempt to hide his enjoyment of this, and she could feel her anger rising.

"Hidden cameras don't sound legal," Claire said.

"Well, not exactly hidden but inconspicuous, you might say," John said, and his mouth twitched ever so slightly with amusement.

Claire felt heat creeping up her neck and into her face. She dug her fingernails into her thighs trying to control her anger before she spoke again. She turned to Steve, and asked, "Did you know?"

"I did not," Steve said. He turned and spoke to John now. "Regardless what you think, I should have been apprised of something this big. I'm not an idiot. I know there are government requirements pertaining to use of surveillance cameras in schools. What you've done leads me to question whether you've followed those requirements."

The Vice-President of the board, Ed Malone, said, "These cameras aren't meant to be permanent. You can call them a test. If they prove effective, then we'll consider using them in other schools. At that stage, we'll draw up written policy and procedure manual.

Peter Williams and Mary Hammond agreed.

"Are these cameras from your company?" Steve asked. "You've always said you couldn't supply surveillance cameras to the school district, either by selling them or donating them, because it would give the impression of a conflict of interest."

"They are neither a gift, nor a purchase," John said. "They're only here on loan. Like Ed stated, we're testing them out. If we find we want to install cameras in Midland or any of the other schools, we'll purchase them from a competitor of my company. That way, it clearly won't be a conflict of interest."

Steve grimaced and glanced over at Frank and then at Claire.

John said, "I've already instructed Hector Minosa, Midland's head custodian, to retrieve the computer's hard drive and bring it over here. I have it ready. We'll hook it up to our computer system. That way, we can use multiple computers to access the videos. Peter, I need you to bring in four computers."

Peter left the room, and Claire struggled to control her rising panic. Worry, anger, agitation, fought each other inside her and she couldn't let anyone see any of that right now.

John looked back at Claire, who was standing in the doorway, and said, "You can go home now. We'll let you know when we're done viewing everything."

She struggled to make her face a poker face, but the grin on John's face told her she'd failed. As she left the building, she was wringing her hands and replaying the footage that she prayed no one would see.

Maybe Hector hadn't done his job properly. Maybe he messed up and accidentally deleted some files. It was possible, but unlikely. Hector was too good at his job.

She prayed that if there was a camera in her office, they would tire of watching the videos long before they reached the scene she wished she could erase from existence.

When she got home, she called Ron at home and told him what had happened.

"I could understand why they might put cameras in the school," Ron said, "but they wouldn't put one in your office, would they?"

She sighed. "I think it's very likely." She told him about the confrontation she'd had with John at the first Round Table Luncheon.

"That's not good," Ron said. "Sounds like he wants to get rid of you."

After she got off the phone, she walked next door to pick up Marcus. She gave him a bath and helped him change into his pajamas, then read him a short story and put him to bed. While running warm water into the tub in the master bathroom, she undressed and then got into the tub and tried to relax before she had to face a day that she dreaded more than a root canal.

STEVE COULDN"T BELIEVE what was happening. He'd known for some time that John had it in for Claire, but this went beyond anything he would have imagined. This was bullshit.

John said, "This is going to be a long evening. Anyone who can't stay should let me know now. I'll order pizzas for those staying."

Steve wanted to leave, to show the bastard what he thought, but he needed to be there to defend Claire if they found anything questionable. He couldn't squelch his increasing uneasiness as he prepared to review videos. How could he invade Claire's and her staff's privacy in this way? She had said it didn't seem legal. He agreed. Still, John and the other board members were his bosses. He had to follow their instructions, for now.

John split the group into pairs, each pair assigned to certain categories from the file menu. When Steve and Mary Hammond were instructed to view the videos from Claire's office, Steve said, "She should be present while we look through these since these videos were made in her private office."

"Her private office?" John said. "She doesn't own the office. It's a space that we allow her to use to do a job which we hired her to perform. We have every right to know what she does in that office."

Steve clenched his jaw and tried to control his mounting anger, but couldn't stay silent any longer. "What the hell? I thought you were so worried about morals, standards, rules, and ethics, John. How can you justify what you're doing?"

"We need to know what this woman is up to," John said. "The surveillance devices that my company makes are used by law enforcement and other institutions to investigate suspicious activity. They're meant to protect the public. That's what we're trying to do here. Protect our students."

"You can't tell me you think Claire is doing something illegal or dangerous," Steve said. "You're pissed at her because Senator Reynolds forced you to hire her. This is—"

Steve stopped when he noticed Mary Hammond, standing nearby and waving her arms to get his attention. He looked her in the eye, saw a warning look, and clamped his mouth shut. Mary was arrogant and condescending, and she and Steve didn't get along well, but he knew she was right in warning him to say no more.

This was going to be one hell of a night.

As it turned out, they were there until eleven o'clock and Steve was bone tired. Everyone else looked as bleary-eyed as he felt. John finally told them to pack up for the evening. "We'll meet here again at eight o'clock in the morning," he said. Steve grimaced, and he wasn't the only one.

Well, so much for getting any of my real work done, Steve thought as he dragged himself out to his car. He was worn out and irritable. Not only did he have to endure John's company all evening, but he was tortured watching Claire, too, because the videos made him miss her even more than he already did.

CHAPTER TWENTY-TWO

ON THURSDAY MORNING around nine-thirty, as Claire and Ron walked out of the admin office toward the faculty lounge, Kim came running after them out of breath, calling for Claire. "Frank's on the phone. He needs to talk to you right away."

"He wants me to call him back right away?"

"No. He's holding for you."

Claire looked at Ron. "Go on ahead without me. I'll catch up later." She followed the receptionist back inside, then went into her own office to take the call. She sat down and took a deep breath, letting it out slowly, before she picked up the phone.

"We need you to come here to Central Administration right away."

Frank's voice sounded strained, giving Claire goose bumps. "Is everything all right?"

"You need to get over here. Expect to be out the rest of the day, so make arrangements with Ron before you leave."

Her heart sank. "All right," she said. "Uh, is there anything I need to bring?"

"No. Just get here as soon as you can."

She could barely breathe as waves of apprehension swept through her. "I'll be there in about twenty minutes." Once she hung up the phone, she scribbled a quick message, grabbed her handbag, and then dropped the message off with the receptionist, instructing her to get it to Ron right away.

As she drove to the meeting, she replayed recent events in her mind. After she'd found out about the cameras, it hadn't taken long for her and Ron to locate each one. The final one, the one she'd dreaded finding, was the camera in her office. She'd stood there in the doorway frozen, hand clasped over her mouth, staring at the tiny black sphere hanging near the ceiling in one corner. Ron had told her not to worry. But she'd seen him studying the camera and knew he was trying to figure out the angle, trying to figure out how much of the attack it might have captured.

Once she arrived at Central Administration, she raced inside and after a few inquiries, she was directed back to the board room. The receptionist said everyone was already there and she should go right in. Pausing outside the door, she closed her eyes. *Take a deep breath. Don't let them bully you, no matter what.*

She reached for the door knob, thinking she was ready. The muffled voices she heard drifting through the heavy door rattled her and made her hesitate. She took a deep breath and let it out, opened the door, and walked into the room.

"Have a seat, Claire," John said. His face was red and stern.

Looking away from him, she perused the other faces but couldn't read their expressions. It took all her effort to get her legs to cooperate. She finally made it over to a chair next to Frank, who was sitting with Steve, and sank into it. She tried to sneak a look at Frank, hoping to catch his eye, but he was looking down at the pad of paper in front of him. Probably pissed at her. Why else would he avoid her gaze?

She didn't say anything. She didn't know what to say, and she couldn't trust her voice at this moment. John didn't have any trouble speaking, though.

"I'm sure you've figured out why we called you here. We didn't watch every video, and those we did watch weren't watched in detail, but we saw enough." He paused for dramatic effect, his accusing gaze riveted on her as he waited for her reaction. She was frantic inside, but she was determined not to give him the satisfaction of seeing how upset she was. Still watching her, he said, "We were impressed with your most recent assemblies. Without audio, we had to use our imaginations. It wasn't too difficult to see you, or at least your faculty and guest speakers, have affected the students and faculty in a positive way, but . . . ," here he paused again, and the look on his face turned somber. His eyes bore down on her and her breath caught in her throat. "We have some extremely serious problems with you, despite your attempts to fix the school."

Her body went rigid and she tried not to look directly at anyone.

"I don't even know where to begin, Claire. You've broken so many rules. You changed the school's curriculum and added these assemblies without getting approval from this board. You added lighting to the building after your request was declined, and you made other changes to the building without approval." He paused to catch his breath, then continued. "You allowed hundreds of people to work on the building. That's a liability to this school district. If someone had gotten hurt, we could have had lawsuits to deal with. We have a district-wide maintenance department for building improvements, but you didn't use them. They're bonded, licensed, and insured."

"I tried to get the district's maintenance department to make the improvements," she said. "They wouldn't. They said they wouldn't step foot in Midland. Told me it was too dangerous. I tried to tell them it was different now, but—"

"It was too dangerous for them. So instead, you decided you'd bypass them and put parents, students, and teachers at risk. We can fire you for that alone."

"First off, if it was too dangerous for them at Midland, which I do not agree was the reason, how is it not too dangerous for the faculty and the students themselves? Look, it was something that everyone was excited about, including the students. If I can say so, this was a great idea in many ways. It's created a bond between students and faculty, and even the parents, and made them proud of themselves and their school. I'm sure they'll be more likely to take care of it now that they've put a bit of themselves into it and it was a good start toward making the school less dangerous. I do apologize, though. I didn't think about the liability aspect."

"And the additional lighting?"

"I thought the board didn't authorize it because of the cost. It was something I felt strongly about, so I paid for it myself, out of my personal funds. It was a gift to the school."

"Of course you didn't bother to find out why the request was denied. You presumed you knew."

Claire squirmed. She didn't have an answer.

"What about the assemblies?"

"I didn't know I needed approval to hold assemblies as it falls under my purview as the school's principal, especially since Steve and Frank—" She snapped her mouth closed. She'd already gotten Frank into trouble once.

John leaned back in his chair, looking silent and deep-in-thought. The room fell quiet. Then he said, "The state has requirements regarding curriculums. What do you think your Senator Reynolds would say if he knew you weren't adhering to them? Hmm?" He stared straight at her and lifted an eyebrow.

Claire bit her lip and stayed silent.

"No answer, huh? Don't you know there are state education standards?" John said. "Midland High School is a low-performing school, and has been for years. Those kids need more classroom lessons, not less. You've taken away precious time from their schoolwork, and you didn't think it mattered? You thought your own agenda was more important?"

Claire flinched at his words and the harsh tone of his voice. However much she despised him, she couldn't deny he had a point. She'd started out with the assemblies because she'd needed to make the school safe for herself. But that had changed once she'd become familiar with the students and faculty. They'd become her first priority.

She cleared her voice and then said, "Yes, the students needed more classroom lessons, but without motivation, without hope, without desire to learn, and without appropriate controls and order, all the classroom lessons in the world are a waste of time. I knew that I needed to reach them and get them motivated and enthusiastic first, then the lessons would be more effective and valuable. I began the assemblies intending to supplement the class work, not take away from it. If you look at our recent test results in almost all of our classes, you'll see that grades are actually beginning to improve."

"What concerns us most is that you seem to think you're autonomous," John said. "You act as if you can do whatever the hell you feel like. You seem to think you don't have to answer to anyone. You take everything into your own hands, even the law."

Claire could feel Frank's body, next to hers, tense at those words. They'd seen the video. She held her tears back with great effort, waiting for John's next words.

"You are supposed to report to Frank, and ultimately to Steve. They report to this board. You're required to report any and all crimes committed on campus no matter who the victim is. You bypassed everyone. That's unacceptable. You can't make all the decisions at your school. You don't have the experience or the power to make the kinds of decisions you've been making." His voice was getting louder.

"We've already placed Frank on probation for allowing the assemblies, his involvement with the painting of the school, and for allowing you to purchase the extra lighting, all without reporting them to this board. Steve has also been disciplined for not reporting the assemblies."

Claire turned and looked over at Steve and Frank. "I'm so sorry. I never meant to get either of you in trouble."

"As for you, Claire, you're still new which means you're probationary. We're perfectly within our rights to fire you and that's what we're doing. As for the school, they will be required to follow the state's curriculum. No more special assemblies."

She looked around the room. Half of the attendees were looking away, avoiding her and the other half looked at her with unreadable expressions. She thought she would suffocate.

Gathering herself together as best she could, she said, "I understand. Fire me if you think you must. But you're making a mistake about cancelling the assemblies and discontinuing the work that has been accomplished. Someone has to do something to fix Midland High. Significant progress was being made on the students' behalf. If you stop the programs we've set up, you're sending the message that the district doesn't care about Midland. Things will return to the way they were, with gangs dominating the whole school and intimidating everyone into submission. The gangs will win. I beg this board; please don't let that happen."

"She's got a point," Ed Malone, the vice president of the board, said. "I'm also not sure about firing her. She needs better guidance, sure, but firing her may be too drastic. It may not be in the district's interest. Something does need to be done about Midland and nothing has been improved until now. Perhaps we should discuss this further."

Several other board members agreed. John grimaced, then abruptly stood up and said, "For now, you're on suspension. We'll take the firing decision under advisement. This meeting for you is in recess for thirty minutes." He picked up his iPad, turned on his heel, and walked out of the room. The other board members looked at each other askance and then stood and followed John.

Steve and Frank remained seated for a few moments, looked at each other, then stood up as well.

Claire stood up, too, and said, "Again, I'm so sorry for everything. I never meant for any of this to happen, especially to both of you. You have been such good friends to me and so supportive." She waved her hand.

"We know," Steve said. "Don't fret about it. We'll survive. Go home and get some rest. We'll be in touch later."

She nodded, and slinked away to her car. Once in her car, with no one was around, she broke down and let her tears flow.

STEVE, FRANK, AND the school board reconvened the meeting after Claire left. It was a tense couple of hours and at some point, someone, Steve wasn't even sure who, brought in the district's legal counsel. After getting a few readings from the council, things cooled down somewhat and they resolved much of their issues—at least for the moment.

By the time the meeting with the board adjourned and Steve walked back to his office, it was already around one-thirty. He cornered John Richmond after the meeting and asked him to follow him back to his office to speak in private, deciding it was time to confront him.

In his office, Steve sat behind his desk while John sat in one of the guest chairs facing him.

"So, what more did you need to talk to me about?" John asked, sounding disturbed at being summoned by an underling.

Steve stared at him and said, "I met your new employee."

"What. What are you talking about?"

"The private investigator you hired to check out Claire."

John glared at him and said, "I didn't hire anyone to investigate her. You're wrong."

"Am I? Phil Seger seems to think you hired him."

John's mouth gaped open.

"Yeah, I talked to Seger when I caught him spying on Claire on school grounds. Are you still going to deny it?"

"Okay. Yes, I hired him. If you must know, this was my own unofficial probe. I'm trying to figure out what's going on with Claire because you and I both know there's something fishy."

Steve rubbed his forehead and told himself to remain calm. "What makes you so sure about that?"

"I have my reasons."

"Something to do with Senator Reynolds? I know you accused her of an affair with him."

John's eyebrows shot up. "I did no such thing."

"Give me a break, John. I overheard part of your conversation with her after her first Round Table Luncheon. You mentioned him in yesterday's meeting as well. You can't just deny it."

"Fine. I did accuse her because I think it's true."

"Why?"

John hesitated, then asked, "Did she tell you why the senator insisted we hire her?"

"No," Steve said, "and I didn't ask."

"You're her boss. I know Frank's her immediate supervisor, but you've been working with Claire, too. Didn't you ask her about that? That's one of the first things I would have asked."

"Don't bullshit me, John. From what I can tell, you didn't get a resume and you didn't interview her. You didn't ask her anything until you met her for the first time at that meeting, and when you did, you didn't believe anything she said."

John stared at him, his face growing red.

Steve continued. "So why did you cave in and hire a stranger? Because the senator asked you to? Does he have some hold over you or the board? Is that why you're pissed at her?"

"No, of course not. It was simply politics and you know at that point we didn't have a choice."

Steve sneered.

John said, "Look. At the beginning of September the mayor invited Edward Malone and me to lunch. When we arrived at the restaurant, the mayor and Senator Reynolds were already waiting in ambush for us at a table. They told us about Claire and said she'd been teaching for years, first in Indianapolis and most recently in Cleveland. The mayor said he'd already checked with our HR Department and found out we had several open positions in the district. But they didn't ask us if we would consider hiring her. They told us that one of those must go to her. We weren't given a choice."

Indianapolis and Cleveland? Claire had never mentioned either city. In fact, she'd told him she'd moved here from Albuquerque. Steve licked his lips, and debated whether to say anything about the discrepancy.

"Can they really do that?" Steve asked. "We have our own hiring policies. Can they force us to violate our own policies?"

"The mayor is our boss. We don't have to like it, but we have to follow his orders. You know that."

"Didn't they give you a reason? I did ask Claire about her relationship to Reynolds. She denied ever meeting him."

"So, what's the deal?" John asked. He stood up and began pacing. "Does she have something to hold over them? Logic just suggested to me they were having an affair. If she's telling the truth, though, and she's never met him—"

"I don't know, John. I've wondered about it, too. In the scheme of things, does it really matter? I mean, Claire is a good person and apparently a great principal. You can't deny all the good she's doing for Midland."

John sneered. "And that means we should turn a blind eye? Ignore all the questions?" Still pacing, he didn't speak for a moment. "I spent the early morning hours searching her name on the internet. You know what I found? Practically nothing, other than on Midland's website. I searched on your name, my name, other employees' names, and found articles, etc. about each of us. But nothing else about Claire."

Steve rubbed his beard. There had been the age issue and a few other odd things, such as her using some British terms. "What about your investigator? Did he find out anything?"

"Not the answers I'm looking for, at least not that he's told me yet."

"Okay, John. Let me think about this awhile," Steve said, "and I'll get back to you. But you need to think about something, too. If Reynolds wanted you to hire her, what do you think he'll say about this situation if he gets wind of the board trying to fire her? If this is political, do you really want to piss off the senator and the mayor?"

Later in the day, Steve sat at his desk thinking. Until now, he'd only questioned whether or not Claire had a relationship with the senator. Looking at the bigger picture, however, posed more questions. If she was telling the truth and really hadn't ever met the senator, why would the guy insist the school board hire her, a stranger? Was it a political maneuver of some sort?

Damn. He still loved her and he wanted to trust her, but now he needed answers.

AT HOME ON Thursday afternoon, Claire sat on her sofa and tried to read a book, but finally gave up and just sat there, replaying scenes from the meetings earlier in the day. She was miserable about the outcome. Her only consolation was that no one had specifically mentioned the attack, even though it was obvious they'd seen the video footage.

She got up around one o'clock and called Ron to tell him she had been placed on suspension, and to discuss which of her meetings he could do and which he should cancel.

"Did they watch the videos?" he asked.

"Yes." She proceeded to tell him everything that had gone on during the meeting.

When she was done, he said, "Well, at least they're reconsidering their decision. That's a good thing, isn't it? Try to keep your hopes up. If it's any consolation, I think they're wrong. You have really put yourself out there for the kids and faculty. They should be appreciative and supportive, not hiding behind some misplaced rules. We need you here."

Claire thanked him for his supportive words before ending the call.

Around three o'clock her phone rang. She answered, expecting it to be Ron needing to talk to her about something.

Instead, she heard Steve say, "Claire, it's me. Are you okay?"

"Well, honestly, I've been better."

"Actually, I'm calling because I wanted to see if we could talk. Do you have a few minutes?"

She smiled to herself as she plopped onto her sofa, dressed in jeans and a sweatshirt. "Yes, I'm just home with all the time in the world right now."

"I thought you would want to know that the surveillance cameras are being removed this afternoon. The school district's counsel told them they had to be removed and the tapes destroyed. "

Claire said, "Well, at least that's some good news. But I'm really sorry about all the trouble I've caused you and Frank. I only wanted to help."

"I know," Steve said. "On another positive note, the school district's legal counsel also told them that not only would it be a mistake to fire you right now, but also instructed the board to remove your suspension after I pointed out they violated several state laws in order to entrap you. You actually have a case against them if they take any action against you at this point."

"Are you serious? You did that for me?"

"Well, yeah. Even the meetings to view the videos and to talk to you about their concerns were violation of the state's sunshine laws. To quote, 'All meetings of three or more members, at which any formal action is taken, must be open to the public at all times except for periods in which the Board is in executive session.' That means they're supposed to announce special meetings publicly."

"I didn't know that," Claire said.

"I also considered what you said about not letting the gangs get away with intimidation. About not letting them win. That doesn't only apply to gangs, you know. In case the board wouldn't give up, I took Richmond aside and applied a little pressure by asking him what he thought Senator Reynolds might say about this situation. You know, if he got wind of it."

"You didn't?"

He chuckled. "Damn, that felt good. I wish I'd thought of it sooner. Like before they called you into the meeting."

"Oh, Steve, you have no idea how relieved I am that they've reinstated me," Claire said, tearing up, "but do you really think this is over? I mean, won't the school board still try to get rid of me somehow?"

"Well," Steve said, "I wish I could tell you that they'll leave you alone. Unfortunately, they're not happy and I know two of the board members will hang onto this like a dog with a chew bone. Fortunately, they can't really take any action, you know, fire someone, without a majority vote and they probably couldn't get the others to agree with them so you're probably okay for now."

"I'm glad you know them so well," Claire said. She hesitated, then asked, "Is it true what John said about the buildings—that I put the district at risk by letting people paint the interior?"

Steve sighed. "Yeah, I don't know why that didn't occur to me. I'm to blame for that. If one of the volunteers had gotten hurt, they could have sued. It's different when dealing with contractors who are self-insured. I admitted it to them and assured them it won't happen again."

"Are you in trouble?"

"Not any more than usual. John and I have never been on good terms. Did I ever tell you how much I dislike this job sometimes?"

"No. I didn't know, but I do know you're under a lot of pressure. I know it's a huge responsibility. I have a hard enough time being a principal. I can't imagine trying to deal with the stress of your job."

He was silent for a moment.

"Oh, I forgot to tell you they're hiring a security guard for Midland. I pointed out that we couldn't allow another incident such as the one you suffered. The legal counsel quickly agreed."

"Thank you, Steve. I'm forever grateful to you."

"Does that mean you forgive me?"

"Forgive you? For what?"

"I cancelled our dinner date and didn't tell you why?"

"I understand. You were doing your job?"

"Does that mean you'll have dinner with me tonight then?"

She smiled and said, "I'd love that."

"Great. I'll pick you up at six o'clock if that's okay." He looked at his watch then, and said, "Oh, sorry, I need to go now. I've got a ton of work piled up and no time to do it."

She hung up the receiver, but picked it back up almost immediately and called Ron to give him the news about her being reinstated.

ON THURSDAY EVENING John Richmond sat at his desk in his home office, sipping coffee, his jaw twitching as he thought about the meeting. After leaving the building at the end of the board meeting and his 'private' talk with Steve, he'd strolled out to his car. But once he started up the engine and pulled away, his anger resurfaced and he had a hard time controlling it. Not paying much attention to his driving, he didn't realize he was speeding until he saw the red lights swirling on the police car behind him.

That speeding ticket nearly sent him over the edge. He had to sit in his car for a while after the officer left, and calm himself down before he started up the engine again. Damn! He was sixty years old and had never gotten a ticket in his life—until now. The thought was making him mad all over again.

He got up and paced around the room. He understood why they had to back down on firing Claire because they hadn't followed proper procedures and had left the door open for lawsuits. What he couldn't understand, was why he had been so careless. He prided himself on sticking to standard operating procedures and to the rules and regulations, whether at work in his company or in his position on the school board.

The problem, he concluded, was Claire. She was a loose cannon causing havoc all around her. That had riled him to the point that he'd cut corners to catch her. Well, he'd be more careful from now on. Eventually she would do something that even the district's legal counsel couldn't let her get away with. Until then, he would contact Seger and find out if he had any new information.

AT FIVE-THIRTY, Claire was in her bedroom preparing for her date. She brushed her hair until it shone, pulled on a new cashmere lavender sweater with a low neckline and elbow length sleeves, and stepped into a long mid-calf length flowing darker-lavender skirt, and high-heeled shoes. While she primped, she thought about Steve and her situation.

She'd missed Steve and wanted things to work out between them, but the original problem at the root of it all loomed large. Could she continue lying to him, giving him a fictitious history? How could she base a romantic relationship on a bed of lies? He'd certainly proven himself trustworthy, and yet she couldn't ignore the program's rules that had been pounded into her head: Trust no one! Don't reveal your real self to anyone! But her parents had been destroyed by a lie. She and Callum had also been destroyed by a lie—his lie.

And then there was the other problem. She and Steve were both lying, by non-disclosure to the school board, about their dating. That private investigator might already have found out and told John Richmond. So, even though the problem with the board had been resolved, supposedly, she wasn't out of the woods and neither was Steve.

Claire sat down on the sofa, trying to push those nagging thoughts away as she waited for Angie to arrive. She looked at the clock on her mantle and bit her fingernail. Angie should have been here by now.

The phone rang, sending an alarm through Claire. *Please don't cancel. Please don't cancel.* It was Angie calling to let her know she was running a little late.

Ten minutes later, the doorbell rang and Angie and Steve were both standing there, looking at each other and smiling. They looked at Claire, and Steve's smile widened in approval. He laughed then, and said, "Angie and I bumped into each other on the way here and we introduced ourselves."

Angie laughed and told her, "He's a keeper. I know a good one when I see him. "

Claire laughed too, and then Marcus ran to greet them both. She talked to Angie, giving her some final instructions. When Claire saw Marcus looking up at Steve, she stopped for a minute to listen.

"Do you wanna see my room?"

"Sure," Steve said.

Marcus took hold of his hand and led him upstairs to his bedroom. Curious, a few minutes later Claire tiptoed into Marcus's room to see how they were doing. The two of them sat on the floor together, engrossed in the small display of dinosaurs that Marcus was showing him. Steve was so patient and showed so much interest, she was moved by the scene. Apparently sensing her presence, both males turned their heads towards the door and smiled at her.

She smiled and said, "I'm sorry to interrupt. Are you ready to go, Steve?"

He laughed and said, "Sure, if I can manage to get up." He pushed himself up to a standing position, while Marcus jumped up and down giggling. Claire laughed.

Steve looked at both of them with mock anger, and asked, "Are you two conspiring against me?"

The restaurant was crowded, and they were told the wait was almost forty minutes to get seated. Claire thought the wait would give them a chance to talk, but it was actually too noisy for conversation. Finally, the waitress seated them in a booth. The noise didn't lessen much. They enjoyed their meal, kept their conversation light, and then decided they'd go somewhere else better to talk after dinner, leaving the restaurant more than two hours after they initially arrived.

"Where should we go?" Steve asked, sitting in his car in the restaurant parking lot.

"I have no idea."

Steve turned on the engine and started to drive.

"Where are we going?"

He grinned and said, "You'll see."

About fifteen minutes later, he pulled into a driveway, turned off the engine, and opened his car door, but hesitated half-in, half-out of the car. "I hope you don't mind coming to my house."

Claire followed him and looked around while he unlocked the house door. It was an older brick home, well maintained and from what she could see in the night lighting it was a pretty house in a nice neighborhood. Inside, the entrance was large, with a beautiful bamboo tree in a large green pot sitting on warm maple flooring that looked as if it went through the entire house.

While he hung up their jackets in the entry closet, she walked into a large living room. One wall of the living room was lined with floor to ceiling maple bookshelves filled with books, CDs, a stereo, and a collection of model airplanes. She studied the airplanes, many of which were military.

"Were you in the military?" she asked.

"No. Not me. My dad was."

"Oh, that's right, I forgot. You told me that before." She moved from the display to a large fish tank full of exotic fish.

"I got my first fish tank when I was twelve," Steve said. "It was barely bigger than a gold fish bowl. As you can see, my tank has grown up along with me."

She laughed and continued looking around.

In one corner of the room, a big screen TV sat on a shiny black cabinet. Facing the TV and filling the space was a plush black leather sofa, a gray recliner, a pair of striped black and gray fabric chairs, a maple coffee table, and a matching end table. All were arranged in a comfortable conversational setting. Red, black, and white striped drapes appointed the windows and behind the drapes, which were pulled back to the sides, were ivory colored pleated blinds. Lamps with airplanes on the bases topped in red lampshades completed the look.

"I love your home, Steve. It's very warm and inviting."

He showed her around the rest of the house. The master bedroom had a king-size bed and a dresser and armoire. The guest bedroom had a full-size bed, dresser, and rocking chair. The third bedroom was set-up as an office with a large computer desk and a double bookcase full of books.

He said he wasn't going to show her the laundry room, as it was currently occupied with mounds of his unwashed clothes, but he told her it was between the garage and kitchen. The spacious eat-in kitchen was lovely, boasting exquisite black granite countertops and center-island, modern dark maple cabinets accenting the warm maple flooring that had indeed run throughout the home.

Steve opened the refrigerator, extracted a bottle of wine, and poured them each a glass. They carried their glasses into the living room and sat down on the sofa.

"I have to ask you something and I hope you won't get angry," Steve said.

Claire nodded, suddenly growing concerned.

"I saw you in the school parking lot Saturday arguing with a man, so I confronted him after you left. He's a private investigator hired by John Richmond. I confronted Richmond and he confirmed it."

"Oh my God. The man told me he was working for someone, but he wouldn't give me a name. Why would John hire an investigator?"

"He's upset about being forced by the Mayor and Senator Reynolds into hiring you. He thinks there's something fishy going on."

He looked straight at her and she struggled to keep from looking away.

"I've tried not to think about that, Claire. I really have. But Richmond told me something I didn't know. He said they told him you'd been teaching for years, first in Indianapolis and most recently in Cleveland. You told me you'd taught in Albuquerque, New Mexico. That got me questioning things so I did some checking of my own. I could not find any trace of you living or working in any of those cities. I need to know the truth."

She covered her mouth with her hand. What could she say?

"Claire, I know you're hiding something. I should have said something in the beginning when you lied about your age, but I let it ago. I'm not trying to get you in trouble or cause trouble between us. Please trust me and let me help you with whatever is going on. I'm in love with you, and I want to be a part of your life. I can't do that unless you're open and honest with me."

Tears welled up in her eyes and she couldn't stop them flowing. "I've wanted to tell you the truth. But I couldn't. I was sworn to secrecy, and it's such a long story."

"I'm listening. You can trust me. I hope you know that about me."

She nodded. "About a year-and-a-half ago I was living in the Boston area with my boyfriend, Callum. He's Marcus's father. We both worked at Weymouth University. I was a professor, he was the Assistant Manager of the Finance Department."

Steve raised his eyebrows, and Claire forced herself to continue.

281

"One morning, I'd opened my computer and went to my documents folder to work on a file for my latest project. It wasn't there. Instead, I saw oddly named folders. Further investigation revealed that I'd taken Callum's computer by mistake. They were university issued so they looked identical. Normally I would have closed it up, but something about the file names nagged at me. At least that's what I told myself." She paused, and Steve squeezed her hand.

"Deep down, maybe I was looking for something to explain why Callum spent so much time away from home. He'd get phone calls at odd hours and then rush out the door. Sometimes he'd be out all night."

"An affair?"

"That's what I thought at first. But once I found my way into one of the files, I knew something else was wrong."

"What was it?"

"Callum handled donations that the university received. He invested that money, and he also advised clients about academic investments. That's what he did at Oxford and that's how we first met."

"Oxford University, as in Oxford, England?"

"Yes."

Steve nodded.

"I was a math professor. Numbers and equations are second nature to me. In his files I saw columns of figures and blocks of equations. Almost without consciously thinking, I saw patterns emerge. Then I saw amounts I recognized, sums I'd heard discussed because they were given to the University as grants. I saw other sums which had been reported in newspapers. All were vast amounts of money being manipulated and transferred, column after column. There were dates, too, some of which I recognized from the news, newspapers, and from my own life experience. I have that kind of memory, that kind of ability to see links and relationships between numbers."

"He was embezzling?"

"He was. I began to recall overheard conversations, too. There were other people involved. I confronted Callum that evening. He told me I was naive, that I didn't know anything about business. I tried to let it go, but the next day on my way home from work, someone followed me and shot at my window and caused me to crash."

"Were you hurt?"

"No, but I saw the shooter in the passenger seat. He had a professional rifle with a sight, and he had clearly singled me out. He either was trying to kill me, or send a message."

"What did you do?"

"After the police came and my car was towed away, I took a taxi home and picked up my son. I took us straight to the airport and flew to Minneapolis, thinking no one would find us there. I was wrong. The police were waiting for me when I got off the plane. I was taken into custody and told that I would be prosecuted as an accomplice—unless I gave them information and became a Federal witness."

"Wow, that's scary. But why would you be prosecuted?"

"It turns out Callum was working with a crime syndicate. They lured financial wizards like Callum into their group and then sent them out to universities and large corporations to steal either directly from the company or to embezzle the way Callum was doing—skimming money from the large donations to the university and from investor clients."

"You're sure about this?"

"Since the investigation began, the FBI has compiled data from banks—Suspicious Activity Reports and Currency Transaction Reports (for cash transaction exceeding $10,000). They found many of these reports filed on Callum and others believed to be in the syndicate. Some of the criminals have been caught and a few have given investigators some important information confirming what I told them."

"What were they doing with the money? Do you know?"

"I was told some of it was lining the pockets of the syndicate members, but the rest was being used for activities like bribery of officials and politicians."

"Was Senator Reynolds on the take?"

"I don't think so. Not that I've heard, anyway."

"Why would Callum leave all those files on his computer?"

"We think it was his personal records and that he was keeping them for his own protection."

"Where is he now?"

"Still on the run as far as I know."

"Why did the police think you were an accomplice?"

"Six months earlier Callum had told me he was working on a presentation for his department—a presentation on accounting fraud—and he asked me to create an algorithm which would transfer funds from accounts and deposit them into other accounts in such a way as it would be hard for anyone to notice. Like an idiot I did as he asked and turned it over to him without question."

"Oh, my God. You wrote the program that helped him embezzle?"

"Yes. I didn't know that's what I was doing, but I'm still responsible."

"Why did Reynolds force our school board to hire you?"

"Over a year ago, I went into the Federal Witness Protection Program, or WITSEC as it's sometimes called. Since then, they've moved me around, given me new identities and new jobs. Those haven't worked out so well. It was my fault, I should add. For my latest identity, my handler talked to his superiors.

Someone knew Reynolds and asked the senator for a favor. I didn't even know that until after John Richmond told me."

"So Claire is not your real name. What is your real name?"

"Juliet Powell. It's ironic, but I was able to figure out Callum's password on his computer because he used 'Romeo'." Tears welled up again.

Steve pulled Claire into his arms and stroked her hair. "I'm so glad you finally trusted me enough to tell me. I knew something was wrong. I thought it was me, that you didn't trust me, or something, because you were always holding back."

"It's not you. I've wanted to tell you."

"Promise me that from now on there will be no secrets between us."

"I promise." She pulled back slightly and looked up at his face. "There's something else I need to tell you."

They spent the next hour talking about the attack at school. Of course he already knew part of it since he'd seen the video. He understood why she'd kept it a secret.

When Claire had finished telling him all her secrets, she asked, "What about your ex-wife? How did you two meet? Do you ever see her? Talk to her?"

"Oh, well, that's a whole different story," Steve said. "We met in grad school, through my mother believe it or not. I had been teaching for several years but had taken some time off to go back and get my master's degree. I was twenty-eight and was almost finished with my second round of school." He paused and looked pensive.

"Janet was a law student and mom was one of Janet's law professors. Three months after we started dating, we both graduated. She got a job first, in a law firm in Hartford, Connecticut. I accepted a job near hers and we got married."

Steve glanced at Claire and she gave him a hint of a smile, hoping he'd keep talking, that he'd tell her more about his life.

"Things were good for a while, but a few years into her job she became obsessed with working her way up in her law profession. She had to have designer label business suits, perfect hairstyles and makeup, and the most prestigious car we could afford, anything really that would scream out to the law firm's partners that she was ready for the big leagues." He sighed, and swirled the liquid in his glass, watching it swim around for a few moments. "Thing that made living with her so difficult was that obsession with perfection."

"Did you do something wrong? Is that why she left you?"

"I didn't cheat on her, if that's what you think."

"I'm sorry. I didn't mean to imply that."

He shook his head. "No, I sometimes think she might have preferred it if I had. I wanted kids. She didn't. Her career was her top priority and taking time off for a pregnancy was not a consideration. Not only that, but she was horrified at the thought of gaining weight even for nine months of carrying a child." He took a swig of his wine. "It's probably just as well. She wouldn't have changed diapers, gotten up for midnight feedings, or stayed up all night with a teething baby anyway. It wasn't her."

"So what happened?"

"I guess for a while I still hadn't accepted her refusal to have kids. I naively thought she would change her mind, or that her mothering instincts would kick in, so I kept working on her, trying to persuade her. After ten years of marriage, she found someone else who shared her obsession and who hated kids. They began an affair. I didn't know until she said she was divorcing me. Six months after the divorce became final, I heard that she made partner at the law firm."

"Are you sorry it ended?"

"No. It took me a long time to get over it, but I've come to realize it was the best thing that could have happened. After the breakup, I took two years off from work, went back to school, got my doctorate degree, and eventually became superintendent. I could have been trapped in a miserable life. Instead, I'm happy, have a good job, and I have a beautiful young woman sitting here in my living room."

Claire smiled and pushed her hair behind one ear.

"Any more secrets you need to share?" he asked.

She bit her lip as she remembered something else. "All right. Well, I know this sounds weird, but I only attended high school for about a year and a half, and yet now I work in a high school. Guess I'm making up for what I missed, huh?"

He raised one eyebrow.

"I skipped quite a few grades. I graduated high school shortly after my fourteenth birthday. When I was four, only a few months older than Marcus is now, I started kindergarten and within two weeks I was moved into first grade. At that point, the school gave me a test. Numerous tests. They said I was gifted. From there, they put me into an accelerated school program."

"A child-prodigy. I'm impressed, though not surprised. Why didn't you tell me sooner?"

She sighed again. "Well, for one thing I might have blown my cover. But it's more than that. Haven't you ever wanted to be known for your actions in the now, rather than known for some label that someone had attached to you?" She looked into his eyes and saw confusion. "I'm not saying this very well. I grew up with that label, child prodigy. It opened doors, certainly, but it also came with another label which I hated. Freak. After I went into the program, no one knew about me and I had the chance to start out with a blank slate. I didn't have to be a freak. I didn't have to wear 'child-prodigy' on my forehead. I could be normal. Does that make any sense?"

"Sure. It explains a lot."

She smiled. "It turned out to be not quite that simple for me, though. Being stripped of the label left me confused. I hadn't realized how it would affect my self-identity, and it's been a tough road. I'm only now beginning to figure out who I really am."

"Interesting. I knew from the very beginning that you were special. It showed even when you were trying to hide it. I mean it's obvious you're intelligent. How else could you accomplish so much in the school in such a short time?"

"I almost gave up trying to fix the school. I'd lost confidence." She looked into his eyes, and said, "As a grad student, I taught a math and a science class. But I was a terrible public speaker, at least partially because I didn't have much socialization and, consequently, I didn't know how to relate to the students."

She sighed, and whispered, "One day, in a packed lecture theatre, I blundered and made a fool of myself. I ended up in tears. I rushed out, and ran straight to the dean's office. I told him I couldn't do it. I wasn't cut out to be a teacher. I told him what had happened, and he laughed. He nearly fell off his chair laughing. After he recovered, he told me to 'buck up' and get myself back to work."

"Yikes," Steve said. "That was harsh. I've never really thought about the difficulties child-prodigies face, trying to fit in an adult world. It probably made you a stronger person, I imagine. But I feel for you."

"It did, for a while. I finished out my graduate program and then taught math full-time. I learned how to talk to students and how to speak in front of an audience. But coming here and trying to be a principal, especially while hiding who I am, really threw me off."

After that, she told him how she worried about Marcus having to deal with some of the same problems that had plagued her.

"So, is your dad a genius, too? What about your mom? Grandparents? I mean, it sounds like it runs in the family."

She sighed, and wondered how much she should say. "My father is highly intelligent, a genius I think, but he didn't go to college. He didn't finish high school either. For some reason I've never understood, he's never been willing to seek the knowledge he wants."

"Lack of self-direction? Maybe he needed someone to push him?"

"Possibly. Or maybe he lacked self-confidence. I don't know. His father saw extreme musical talent in him and pushed him toward music, which he disliked. He wanted to be a scientist or inventor. His father wanted to send him to Julliard or the Sorbonne. They quarreled so often that my father quit school altogether and left home at fifteen."

"That's sad to waste all of his talent. Did he ever go back to school?"

She shook her head. "Over the years I think he came to regret his choice. Maybe that's why he pushed me so hard to excel in all academics. He wouldn't accept anything less than my best. He even withheld food when I didn't perform as he expected." She looked up at Steve and gave him a half-hearted smile. "He wouldn't let me socialize at all because he thought I'd get too distracted. He wanted me to succeed where he had failed."

"And you're afraid of doing the same with Marcus?"

"I won't do the same with my son. If he wants to learn and wants to go through school at an accelerated rate, I'll help. But it will be his choice. I already see signs that Marcus has plenty of self-direction."

"That doesn't surprise me," Steve said. "He obviously seems gifted. What about your mom?"

"It's hard for me to talk about her, you know. She was of average intelligence but more social than my dad, at least when she was young." Claire paused, then added, "Sadly, she never measured up to his standards, intellectually or morally."

"Then why did he marry her?"

"Because she was everything he wasn't. Beautiful, sexy, a social butterfly."

Steve nodded. "A beauty and the beast kind of relationship?"

Claire laughed. "Well, not exactly. My father wasn't gross or anything. He was average-looking. But he was, probably still is, uptight and stringent. I already told you about her suicide, didn't I?"

"You did. That's really sad." He hugged her. "What about your grandparents?"

"I barely remember my mum's parents," Claire said. "They lived in New York, and I never had a chance to visit them after we moved away. My grandmother was a dancer and theatre actress, apparently lovely and talented. My grandfather was a producer. My father wasn't on good terms with his parents, but I was allowed to visit with them. My father's mum died when I was ten. She was a lovely and sweet person, smart and perceptive. My grandfather, my father's father, was the genius. He died five years ago."

"A musical genius?"

Claire nodded. "I think father and son shared the same talents and intellect. Either of them could have excelled in any number of areas. Unfortunately, they didn't seem to recognize how alike they were."

"I think you're a combination of your grandparents, from what you've described."

Claire smiled. "I like that. Though I don't think I'm much like my maternal grandmother. If I had her acting ability, things would be much easier."

Steve hesitated, then said, "Most of the time when you talk about your mother, you say mum. That's British and I wondered about it but didn't want to push you. You grew up in Oxford, England, near the university?"

She brushed her hair from her eyes, and said, "I was born in the U.S. but raised in England."

"It doesn't really matter. I want to know everything about you. I'm so glad you shared all of that with me," Steve said. "It fills in many of the missing blanks and really helps me understand you."

She gazed into Steve's eyes, so gentle and non-judgmental.

"I think I understand you better now," Steve said. He set down his empty wine glass and patted the spot next to him. "Come over here." He pulled her to him, and wrapped his arms around her, then whispered in her ear, "None of the secrets matter anymore. I'm glad we're finally sharing our lives."

Tears flowed again and stung her cheeks. She brushed them away. When she pulled back enough that she could look at his face, she was stunned to see his eyes brimmed with moisture. She told him of her worries concerning John.

"His anger with me might spill over onto you, especially if he discovers we're dating."

"I can handle John. I've had enough of his power play, his intimidation. Don't worry about him, okay? Let me deal with him if it becomes necessary."

"I don't want you to protect me. I can take care of myself," she said, "or face the consequences if I fail. Please watch out for your own backside, all right? I don't want to drag you down with me."

He smiled and nodded. "Fair enough. You are a stubborn woman, aren't you? You sure surprised the hell out of everyone when you stood up to John."

"Hey, I've been dealing with hoodlums for a long time now. I'm tired of getting bullied. I tell students to stand up for themselves and not let bullies get to them. I have to practice what I preach, don't I?"

"I guess you do," Steve said, laughing.

She wanted to stay and talk more, but it was getting late and she needed to get back home so that Angie could go home. He drove her home then, and on the way he said he wanted to see her again on Saturday. He told her there was still much to talk about and he didn't want to waste any more time.

When he walked her from his car to her condo, they made plans to spend Saturday afternoon together and take Marcus out for lunch. Steve suggested a pizza restaurant with a play area for kids. They'd never been there, but Steve said he was sure Marcus would love it. When they arrived at her door, he pulled her close and kissed her, at first gently, and then passionately and at length. He pulled himself away and said goodnight. As he walked away, she heard him humming, and she smiled. She was tempted to call out his name and get him to come back, but she hesitated a moment too long. He was out of sight.

FRIDAY MORNING CLAIRE returned to work and planned to call Leo and tell him what had happened with John Richmond and with Steve, but the day was so hectic she didn't have time. The following morning, she had to do laundry and run a few errands. By the time she finished, it was almost time for Steve to arrive. She had waited to tell Marcus about their outing because she knew he'd be excited, and she didn't want him to get overworked with anticipation.

When Steve arrived and told Marcus where they were all going Marcus jumped with joy. On the way out to the car, he grabbed hold of their hands and asked them to swing him in the air, which they did, over and over again, until they got to the car.

They spent three hours in a pizza restaurant, eating pizza, watching mechanical singing bears, which mesmerized Marcus, and watching him play in a large pen filled with multicolored plastic balls. Claire thought they must have put almost four dozen tokens into the slots of rides and games for Marcus. They didn't actually get much opportunity for talk, but she didn't mind. Being together and watching Marcus having fun was fabulous.

They left the restaurant and strolled around the Southwest Plaza Mall, window-shopping, browsing in bookstores and computer software stores. When they came across a toy store, Marcus dragged them inside and Steve bought him his first toy airplane. Although Steve didn't know it, Claire knew that he'd already endeared himself to Marcus as no other man had ever done.

When they returned to Claire's home, she began cooking dinner while Steve and Marcus talked in the living room. After dinner, Claire helped Marcus into his pajamas, and kissed him goodnight.

"Can Steve read to me tonight?"

Steve, who was standing in the doorway watching, said, "I'd love to read to you, Marcus, if it's okay with your mom."

Claire smiled and handed him a children's book, then left to clear away the dinner dishes. After she loaded the dishwasher and began wiping off the kitchen countertop, she glanced back at the vase of roses in the middle of the dinner table. What had she done to deserve Steve? How many men would bring roses to his girlfriend and then read bedtime stories to her child?

"That's one great kid you have there," Steve said, re-entering and interrupting her thoughts. He wrapped his arms around her from behind as she folded her kitchen towel and laid it on the countertop. He pulled her close to him, and stroked her hair, then turned her around and cupped her chin in his hand. "I love you, Claire."

She didn't say anything right away. Looking up at him, her heartbeat was so loud she was afraid he'd hear it. "I love you, too." Where did that come from? It must be true because she didn't think it. The words came from her heart, not her head.

"Can we retire into the living room?" Steve said.

"Sure, you go ahead and I'll be in there in a minute."

She poured them each a glass of wine, and carried the long-stemmed glassware into the living room.

"Ooh, now that looks splendid," Steve said as he reached out and took his glass from her. "I think you read my mind. That's not part of your high I.Q. is it?"

"Ha, ha," Claire said. "Very funny. If I had that kind of ability, I sure as hell wouldn't have had the problems I've been having, now would I?"

He laughed and nearly spilled his wine.

Claire smiled, set her glass down on the coffee table, and sat next to him on the sofa. She slipped off one shoe using the other foot, and then switched feet, and when both feet were bare, she tucked her legs under her, reached over and picked up her glass, and leaned back against Steve. Steve put his arm around her shoulder. They talked about trivial things for a while, but she sensed he had something else on his mind.

She was starting to feel a little anxious, not knowing what he was thinking, and finally took the plunge and asked, "Is something bothering you? You seem a little distracted tonight. "

"Well, actually I want to ask you something." He cleared his throat, and fidgeted. What was he up to? Should she be nervous?

"I don't know how to say this. I planned out a speech, even practiced it. Now look at me. I can't remember the speech, so

I'm just going to come and say what's on my mind." He seemed nervous and excited at the same time.

"I want you to be my wife. I know we haven't known each other long, but I love you and don't want to risk losing you. I've given it a lot of thought. This is right." He stopped and looked at her and an uncertainty crept into his face. He looked so vulnerable and she didn't know what to say.

"Will you marry me, Claire?" His face was flushed and he reached out and took her hand in his.

She was dumbfounded, certainly not seeing this coming. She struggled through emotions. She loved him, wanted him in her life, and wanted to have a real family again. Marcus adored him already. Didn't a boy need a father? But it was all so complicated.

Continuing, Steve said, "I've been thinking about us a lot, and thinking about the school board. We made an agreement not to keep secrets from each other anymore. I think we shouldn't keep secrets from the board or our friends, either. I want us to get married. We'll tell them afterwards."

"How can we get married? I'm in witness protection, remember?"

"And they prohibit you from getting married?"

"Well, no, I don't think so. But what if I have to move again and change my identity? What if the mob finds me? It could happen. Have you thought of that? What would we do?"

"We'll deal with that. I'll move if I have to, Claire." Before she realized what she was doing, she nodded her head, and he let out a big breath and then laughed. He hugged her so hard she thought she'd burst. She laughed, too, and they kissed.

Steve said, "I don't know how you feel, but I want to get married right away, maybe in Las Vegas this weekend. It'll be a long weekend because of the holiday. Frank and his family could come with us so they can be at the wedding. Hey, maybe we could talk them into watching Marcus while we're there."

He seemed to be waiting for her response, and she thought he looked nervous. She wanted to agree with whatever he wanted, but she couldn't squelch her fears altogether. "Shouldn't we live together first? We've only known each other since early September."

"That would never fly with the school board," Steve said. "They could fire both of us for that if they found out. And with the private investigator watching us, John would find out."

"What if the private investigator knows we're dating?"

"If he does, I'm guessing he hasn't told John yet." Steve leaned forward and said in a soft voice, "I know I'm rushing things, but the sooner we get married, the better. The board, especially John, won't like us getting married. However, they can't fire us for that. If they find out before we marry, they'll try to stop us. If you want a big wedding, we can wait. I know that's important to a lot of women. Tell me what you want."

"A big wedding is certainly not something I want. I suppose a simple wedding in Las Vegas isn't a bad idea. But are you sure the school district will allow us to work together after we're married? Don't they have policies against that?"

"Frank and Gloria work together. She teaches in one of our schools and he's an assistant superintendent. It's allowed. He can't supervise her. Some board members won't like it that you and I will be married. They might feel threatened. Like I said, I'm pretty sure they would try to stop us from marrying if they found out ahead of time. That's why we're not going to tell them until later."

Claire bit her lip. Though she wanted to marry Steve, she didn't want to keep another secret or worry about another deception. But when she looked into his sparkling eyes, and at his grinning face, she knew she'd keep silent about her fear.

Steve spent the night, and in the morning Claire said, "I thought of another problem."

"What's that?"

"The private investigator threatened me at the school. He said that there were people who would pay for the information he had about my location."

"Does he know who you are?"

"He knows I'm in witness protection. If he's any good, he will find out."

"Does he know who the syndicate members are and how to get hold of them?"

"I hadn't thought of that. He might have been bluffing."

"Most likely he was. I wouldn't worry too much about him."

"What if he tells John Richmond?"

Steve looked pensive. "I don't know. I guess we'll have to figure that out if and when it happens. Worse case, we have to move and start over, right?"

"You're really sure you'd be okay with that?"

"I am."

They spent all day Sunday together and making plans for the trip. After reviewing the calendar and making some online flight inquiries, they decided on the dates and also decided to move Claire and Marcus into Steve's house two days before their flight on Wednesday, the day before Thanksgiving. They would fly to Las Vegas, get married at one of the little wedding chapels that day, have Thanksgiving in Vegas with Frank and his family, and have a mini honeymoon there. They would come back Sunday night.

Steve said, "I'll talk to Frank tomorrow and see if he and his family will go with us." He stood up, yawned, and stretched. "Well, I guess I better get home and get some rest. Tomorrow's gonna be a busy day at work, lots of meetings and appointments. And I'm gonna be making calls to make the hotel and airline reservations, assuming they aren't all booked up."

FRANK WAS IN his office on Monday reading a report when Steve walked in. He looked up and smiled at his friend, surprised to see him at this time of day. "Hey, Steve. Been one hell of a week. Sure glad things are back to normal."

Steve stuck his hands in his pant pockets and hesitated. "Well, kinda back to normal."

Frank raised his eyebrows. "Uh oh. What happened now? Please don't tell me the board changed their minds again."

Steve chuckled. "No, nothing like that. But I do have some news. Probably should have clued you in sooner. Don't be mad that I kept it a secret."

"Okay. You've really got my attention. What secrets have you been keeping?"

"I, uh, well, Claire and I have been seeing each other for a while. And we're engaged now."

Frank opened his mouth wide, as if shocked, then smiled and said, "Just giving you a hard time. Don't you think I know you well enough by now? I already knew something like that was going on, what with the way you two look at each other when you think no one's watching. But engaged is a bit of a surprise."

Steve chuckled. "I should have known you'd figure it out." He sat down in a guest chair facing Frank. "You know, I'm usually not secretive, but, well, I'm not in the habit of dating employees either. I wasn't sure what you'd say about it. And I do have a pretty good idea what the school board would say."

"Oh, yeah. I can hear them now," Frank said, pausing, thinking about the board. "Screw them. Anyway, I guess congratulations are in order, pal."

"Thanks. Are you super busy right now? I could use some food."

"I'm busy, yes," Frank said. "But I'm hungry, too. Let's go out to JayJays Café. Celebration is in order."

They walked a block to the café and continued talking over lunch. Frank agreed that he would love to go to their wedding and he was sure Gloria and the kids would feel the same way. He would call Gloria right away to confirm.

Frank was surprised, though, when Steve told him that Claire had a son. He hadn't expected that at all, but he told Steve that he didn't think it would be a problem for them to take care of him on the trip. He'd let him know for sure after he talked to Gloria. Steve and Frank both agreed they shouldn't tell anyone else about the wedding plans.

Late in the afternoon, while Steve was sitting at his desk working, Frank peeked into his office and said, "I wanted to give you a head's up. I talked to Gloria and she's thrilled. Says she wouldn't miss it, so you can count us in."

"Thanks, Frank. This means a lot to both of us, all of you being there with us when we get married," Steve said. "I'll book the flights to Las Vegas right away. You'll bring Amy and Kyle, too, right?"

"That's okay with you?"

"Of course it is. They're my godchildren after all."

CLAIRE COULDN'T BELIEVE they were getting married. She loved Steve and she was excited about marrying him, but it also felt more than a bit scary. Callum had proposed to her, too, and they'd been planning a big wedding until that fateful fall day in Boston.

She tried to imagine what it would be like living with Steve. Her mind was so occupied with thoughts and daydreams about it that she couldn't concentrate on her work. She found herself smiling all the time, and forgot about a few appointments. Staff were beginning to ask questions, wondering what was going on with her. Worrying that they would become too suspicious, she tried to push the thoughts out of her head at work and concentrate as best she could. It wasn't easy.

Frank stopped by Claire's office Tuesday morning, shutting the door behind him, and smiled. "Congratulations, Claire," he said. "I'm really happy for both of you."

"Thank you. I'm grateful for your approval. Your blessing matters to me. I know it means a great deal to Steve, too."

They chatted for a few minutes about the wedding plans, then Frank got up to leave. He smiled slyly at her and said, "We'll be happy to watch Marcus while you two lovers consummate your marriage and take a mini honeymoon," making Claire immediately blush. Frank's smile turned more casual as he continued. "I thought you said you weren't good at keeping secrets. Your son was almost as much of a surprise to me as you're engagement. Seems to me you're pretty good at it."

Later, when she told Marcus about the marriage and about their trip, he jumped up and down giggling in excitement. He asked lots of questions. Where would they live? What was Steve's house like? Would he still go to the same preschool? Would he get to see Angie? He wanted to know if he would get to take all his books and toys, or if he would have to leave them behind the way he did when they left their last home.

Claire assured him nothing would change except they would become a family with Steve and they would live in his house. He looked relieved and smiled broadly again. Claire gave him a giant hug and kiss and Marcus said he was the happiest he'd ever been.

STEVE AND FRANK were in Steve's office on Tuesday discussing the wedding and trip plans, when a voice broke in and said, "You're getting married? When?"

Both men turned and looked at Jim Halloran who was standing in the doorway. Steve's jaw tightened. Now he'd done it. It had been his idea to keep this a secret and he'd blown it almost immediately by talking about his private life at work. He should have waited to talk to Frank. Damn. Unless he flat out lied to Jim, which he didn't want to do, he would have to come clean. The only saving grace was that it was Jim, instead of one of the other board members. Jim Halloran was the only board member with whom Steve had developed a friendship. *Hmm. Actually, if Jim doesn't have a problem with it, this could work in our favor. Having a board member on our side could be a great help.*

"Come on in and close the door, Jim. Can I trust you with something confidential?"

"Of course. We've got a pretty decent relationship, don't we?"

Steve took in a deep breath and said, "I think so, too, and that's why I'm going to let you in on my secret. I'm eloping in Las Vegas over Thanksgiving break."

"Yeah, like a teenager," Frank said, smiling.

Steve laughed. "Yup. Frank and his family are going with us. We'll come back the Sunday after Thanksgiving."

Jim smiled and said, "Congratulations! I'm happy for you. Who is the lucky woman," he joked. "Do I know her?"

"Yeah, you know her. It's Claire Constantine."

Jim's mouth twitched in secret amusement. "Thought so. You're really going to frost John. You know that, don't you?"

Steve nodded.

"Well, I'm happy for you both. And I don't give a damn about John's reaction." Jim shook hands with Steve and then patted him on the back."

"Thanks," Steve said. "Hey, how did you know?"

"Well, I wasn't sure, but I saw your reactions when we all watched those videos, you know which ones I mean."

301

Steve nodded again.

Jim coughed and then continued, "Is anyone else from work invited to the wedding, besides Frank?"

"To be honest, everything has happened so quickly and we are trying to keep it secretive to avoid John finding out, knowing how he'll react." Jim nodded assent. "And well, most people already have plans for the holiday. If you don't have plans and want to go with us to Vegas, we'd love to have you there."

Frank looked surprised at first, then Steve detected a slight smile twitch at the corner of Frank's mouth. Jim's face beamed and he said he'd love to go.

Steve grinned. "That's great, Jim. I'm sure Claire will be happy, too. I'll call up the airline and see if I can get you a ticket on the same flight."

After Frank and Jim left the office, Steve sat at his desk and picked up the telephone. He hoped Claire wouldn't be mad at him for inviting Jim.

CHAPTER TWENTY-THREE

MOVING CLAIRE'S BELONGINGS turned out to be a rather large and tiring task. She was thankful to have help from Frank, his wife Gloria, and their kids, Kyle and Amy. Steve's basement was mostly empty, so they put excess furniture they didn't need down there. When the move was finally finished, they all collapsed in the living room for coffee and sodas. Having rested a while and finishing their drinks, Frank announced that they needed to get home and give the soon-to-be couple some alone time. Claire and Steve thanked the Lawrence's profusely, and then the family of four departed, leaving the new family to their thoughts. Claire walked around surveying the living room and Marcus's bedroom and concluded, "It looks amazing. I already feel as though we belong. Thank you, Steve."

He smiled and pulled her into his arms.

"I love our new home, Mommy," Marcus said. "We have a big screen TV and fish and a big backyard and a basement."

"We have a lot of kids in the neighborhood, too," Steve said. "In spring, after the snow ends, I'll put up a swing set in the backyard so you and your new friends can play."

Marcus jumped up and down, then ran over to Steve and hugged his legs. "Can we get a dog? Or a cat?"

Susan Finlay

"Whoa. Slow down there partner. We can talk about that later," Steve said, smiling.

CLAIRE SAT IN the seat next to the window on the Boeing airplane and fastened Marcus's seatbelt while Steve stowed their bags in the luggage compartment above their seats. Claire was experiencing what she knew were typical pre-wedding jitters in spades. The fact that flying also made her very nervous was not helping. Was she doing the right thing? She and Steve barely knew each other. She'd known Callum much longer and look what had happened. Obviously, she wasn't the best judge of character. But hadn't she learned more about people since then? Thoughts just kept spinning around in her head, making her anxiety level soar.

She watched Steve and couldn't help but smile. When he finished dealing with their carry-on luggage and sat down next to Marcus, a commotion coming from the row behind them made them turn and look over their shoulders.

Frank was grumbling and huffing. He'd apparently put his and Gloria's bags in their overhead compartment, next to Jim's bag, and slammed the door only to have it bounce back open. This went on for three more rounds. "There's too much damn crap in one of these bags," Frank said, "and it's not mine. Did you have to bring the whole damn house? Either someone is going to have to learn to pack less, or the airline is going to have to make the storage compartments bigger."

Steve and Claire laughed, and Gloria rolled her eyes.

"I vote for making the compartments bigger," Steve said.

"Wise ass," Frank said.

After he closed it, Frank sat down next to Gloria, and then Jim squirmed and stood up. "Hey, Frank, switch seats with me, will ya? I should sit near the aisle. Got a bad bladder. Getting old really sucks."

Frank grimaced, stood up again, and grumbled while he, Gloria, and Jim moved out into the aisle to make the switch. They were about to sit back down when Gloria said, "As long as we're all standing, I want the window seat, if you don't mind."

"Oh, for Christ sake, will you people make up your minds," Frank said.

Steve and Claire chuckled, then Steve stood up and leaned over the seat, and said, "All right now, settle down kids. Do you need me to referee?"

"Oh, very funny," Frank said. "I don't know why everyone calls me the wise guy. You're being a bigger wise-ass." He sounded mad, but gave a teasing smile after he said it.

"Ha, ha, ha," Steve said, laughing.

After Steve sat back down, he and Claire fastened their own seatbelts and prepared for their flight. Then, in the row in front of Steve, Claire, and Marcus, Amy and Kyle fought over which one of them would get the window seat. Marcus giggled, and shouted, "Maybe your dad should sit in-between you two."

"Hey," Kyle said, as he stood up, and turned around to look down at Marcus. "Maybe you should sit up here with us. The grownups are having a bad influence on you."

Marcus giggled harder and Claire shook her head and smiled.

When the plane pulled away from the gate and headed toward the runway, Claire tried to divert her nerves about takeoff by looking out of the window, noting that a light snow had already begun falling, and smiled, knowing they would soon be out of winter and into warm, sunny Nevada. She and Marcus were excited about their first trip to Las Vegas. She considered it a bonus that they'd be escaping the big snowstorm that was predicted for later in the day in Denver.

As the airplane taxied toward the runway, everyone quieted. Every bump in the runway and every noise the plane made set Claire's nerves on edge. She dug holes in the armrests with her fingernails gripping them tightly, as if that effort would control the plane and lessen her anxiety.

Marcus said "What's the matter, Mommy, isn't this exciting?"

"Yes, dear, it is," she said as she smiled and mussed Marcus's hair. Steve, noting her discomfort, took hold of her hand to try to help calm and comfort her.

After a flawless takeoff, Claire settled down a bit. The plane reached cruising altitude and the flight attendants pushed their food carts down the long aisle to serve drinks, distracting Claire and lessening further her fear level. In truth, it was the coffee that helped. Claire loved the smell of the freshly brewed coffee that filled the confined space of the airplane's interior.

Soon, the flight attendants picked up the cups, cans, and napkins and the pilot announced their impending approach to Las Vegas International Airport. Claire was amazed at how short the flight was, and she watched eagerly while the airplane descended toward the spectacular city.

Upon exiting the airport, Claire was assaulted by the sudden dry heat of the city. She knew it would be warm, but the intensity and dryness of the air was something she hadn't expected. When they all arrived at their hotel, using the hotel's shuttle bus, it was only ten o'clock in the morning and too early to check-in so they left their bags at the front desk to go exploring.

They were intrigued by the enormous hotels/casinos, and everyone had their own ideas of where they wanted to go. After several minutes of arguing, they agreed on a direction and set out to explore the strip. They wandered in and out of casinos, and Claire's senses were overwhelmed by the ever present clanking and jingling of slot machines, bells and whistles when someone hit a jackpot, changes in lighting when they went from bright sunlight into dark casinos filled with colorful flashing lights, and the smell of exhaust from the massive amount of torturously slow automobiles traveling up and down the strip.

The hardest thing to get used to, though, was the crowd. Throngs of people everywhere, filling the sidewalks, casinos, and the shops. Claire and the others were bumped into more times than Claire could count—and it wasn't even noon yet.

"Can we at least go to a show?" Amy asked, as they walked through the Treasure Island Casino. "I can't go back to school and tell my friends I went to Las Vegas and didn't do anything."

"We'll see," Frank said. "I don't even know what kind of shows are playing here. We'll have to check it out."

"Can I go too?" Marcus asked.

"I certainly hope so," Steve said, laughing. "You can't stay in the hotel alone."

Marcus laughed, and Claire looked at Steve and smiled.

"I'm hungry," Kyle said. "Can't we stop and eat?"

"Kyle, you're always hungry. You were born hungry," Frank said, as he clapped Kyle lightly on the back of the head. "Good thing you have a good metabolism or you'd weigh a ton."

It took almost an hour for the small group to agree and find the right place to eat, but when they finished eating, they all agreed they'd made a good choice. After lunch, Steve and Frank checked out the list of shows that were playing in the theatres on the Las Vegas strip. They found a family show they decided to see on Friday afternoon. On Saturday night, the adults would see Celine Dion while Amy and Kyle babysat Marcus.

When they left the casino, Steve looked at his watch, and said, "I guess we should get back to the hotel and check in. We'll want a little time to get cleaned up and change clothes before the wedding."

"Yeah, this place is a lot hotter than I remembered," Frank said. "I don't know about the rest of you, but I need a shower."

"Boy, I can agree with that," Jim said.

"Hey," Frank said.

Everyone laughed, and Jim said, "That didn't come out the way I meant it. I meant that I need one, too."

"Sure you did," Steve said.

Jim laughed, and said, "You two never quit, do you?"

At the hotel, it took a while to get everyone checked in but once accomplished, they agreed to meet in the lobby in two hours.

Claire hadn't been sure if she should wear a wedding gown since it was going to a simple ceremony, so she had selected and was now adorned in a lacy white tea-length dress with short bell-shaped lace sleeves with a low-cut neckline. She accessorized the gown with a simple pearl necklace and matching earrings. She finally finished styling her hair and placed a few blue flowers in it.

Someone knocked on her door. Claire's heart started racing. It must be time. Momentary jitters struck, unwanted, again. Was she doing the right thing marrying a man she barely knew, and dragging him into her nightmare? She loved him and wanted to marry him, and it felt right. But what if she was wrong? She didn't always make the right decision. *Well, too late to turn back now.* She took a deep breath, blew it out, and shook her hands, hoping to relieve some of her nervousness.

When Steve saw her, his face beamed approval and her nervousness suddenly vanished. He looked so happy and relaxed. She'd never seen him in a three-piece suit before. How distinguished he looked. His dark brown suit looked perfectly fitted. The blue dress shirt brought out the blue of his eyes and was appointed with a tie in the same blue and accented with darker blue stripes. His beard was neatly trimmed, and his eyes simply sparkled.

When everyone was ready, the entourage proceeded to the reserved wedding chapel. It was a charming little chapel, perhaps not the most romantic place for a wedding, but she was satisfied with it.

During the ceremony, Claire felt as if she were drifting along on a cloud, everything seeming so unreal, watching and listening to it all it a dream-like state. When the minister asked her if she accepted Steven Alexander Jensen as her lawfully wedded husband, she didn't respond and had to be prodded. Stunned back into reality, she enthusiastically said, "Yes". Steve slipped a beautiful diamond ring on her finger and kissed her, as everyone cheered them on.

After the ceremony, they exited and strolled to a fancy restaurant set in Roman décor, complete with Roman centurion waiters, for a celebration dinner. During the meal, Frank, Gloria and Jim toasted to the new bride and groom, clanking their pewter wine mugs, and the kids laughed and joined in with their ginger ale filled counterparts. Claire was ecstatic. She looked around the table, feeling a sudden wave of emotion as she realized she was surrounded by wonderful friends—and family. She knew, better than anyone, how lucky she was to have them all in her life. Her only minor regret was that Ron and some of the other faculty members couldn't be here.

As the evening wound down, Steve and Claire left Marcus with Frank and his family for the night to have some wedding night privacy. Claire was a little worried about leaving him, until Marcus said he was excited about his 'slumber party' as Amy and Kyle called it.

CHAPTER TWENTY-FOUR

BACK AT HOME, and sorry to have to end their mini honeymoon, Claire and Steve procrastinated in bed, enjoying precious moments together, then rushed to get ready for work. During breakfast, Steve announced, "Next week, Tuesday night, is the next school board meeting. I'll tell them then about our marriage while we're in executive session. I'd rather not announce it in front of the public, in case the board gives me flack."

"All right," Claire said. "When should I tell my staff?"

"Hmm, better wait until just before I tell the board. We don't want someone on the board to hear about it before I formally tell them. So, I guess after school on Tuesday would be best."

"Sure. Are you going to call your mother and tell her?"

"I will. She'll be thrilled."

TUESDAY MORNING, SHORTLY after Claire sent out notices to the faculty telling them there would be a meeting right after school, Ron stuck his head in her office and said, "What's going on? A special meeting on short notice? Don't we need to talk about it? I mean, you usually give me a heads-up."

"Oh," she said, rubbing the back of her neck, "it's . . . well, it'll just be a brief meeting, nothing that you need to be advised of ahead of time. I just have something I want to tell everyone at the same time."

He frowned, gave her an inquisitive stare, then turned and walked away, hands in pockets and perhaps a bit unhappy. She considered calling him into the office for a private chat, but her phone rang and he had already disappeared.

WHILE EVERYONE MADE their way into the faculty lounge for the meeting, Claire entered, filled a paper cup with water and sipped. When everyone was seated, she sat at one of the tables and set down her cup. "This is just a very quick meeting. I want to inform you about something personal." Her palms felt sweaty and she hid them behind her back. "I—uh—I'm not really sure how to begin." She paused, took in a deep breath, and then tried again. "I—" Although she had planned what she was going to say, when she looked at them, her mind blanked.

Ron asked, "What's wrong, Claire?"

"Sorry, everyone. It's hard for me to talk about my private life. I can talk about practically anything else, but talking about my life is hard for me. Be patient, I'll get there." She cleared her dry throat, then coughed several times and had to sip some more water. Finally, she said, "Most of you know about the problems between the school board and me, right?" Heads assented around the room. "They wanted to fire me, yet they couldn't. Not then. I believe they are keeping a very close eye on me." She hesitated, then resumed her speech. "What you don't know is that I've been keeping a secret from them." Some murmuring and whispering ensued. "From almost everyone, actually. I—

uh—well, I'm just going to say it. Our school superintendent and I just got married. I'm now Claire Jensen."

There were more pronounced surprise murmurs and whispering. Ron, who had been standing against the back wall, crossed his arms, and his head and shoulders seemed rigid. Claire studied his face but it was unreadable, the same poker face she'd seen on the day they'd first met, and it felt as though all their time spent together had been erased, like the equations she used to wipe off a chalkboard in her classroom. She shouldn't have told him about the accusations John Richmond had made. Too late now.

"When did you get married?" a teacher asked.

Claire turned in the direction of the teacher and, "Over Thanksgiving Break."

The room was quiet for a moment, and then most of the faculty offered their congratulations. As they filed out of the room after the meeting, she noted that Ron and Nancy conspicuously hadn't said a word.

AFTER WORK, STEVE stopped at home for a quick bite to eat before the school board meeting. Claire told him about the meeting with her staff.

"So most of them were fine with it," Steve said. "But you think Ron and Nancy are upset? Why would they react that way?"

"I don't know. I thought we were developing a good relationship."

"Well, I guess you should try talking to them in private," Steve said. "I'll be telling the board the same news in a couple of hours."

Two hours later, sitting through an hour of standard board meeting agenda, Steve asked the board to go into executive session. He motioned for Frank to follow.

"What's he doing here?" John asked, staring at Frank.

"I asked him to join us," Steve said.

In private chambers, Steve cleared his throat and said, "I have an announcement to make." He looked around the table and understood why it had been so hard for Claire to tell her staff. He was having trouble, too. He braced himself and continued. "I got married over Thanksgiving Break."

Everyone, except Frank, looked stunned. Jim Halloran looked down at his cell phone, and Steve assumed that was so no one could watch his expression.

"Well, congratulations, Steve," Mary Hammond said. "I had no idea. Why didn't you tell us you were getting married? Who's the lucky bride?"

Steve took in a deep breath and said, "Uh, well, I married Claire Constantine."

Mary's mouth dropped open and she leaned back in her chair.

Jim Halloran feigned surprise and said, "I think that's wonderful. You make a great couple. Congratulations."

"I'd like to congratulate you too," Josie Perez said.

"Are you all idiots?" John said.

Edward Malone said, "John, I don't think I like your tone. I don't like the fact that they kept their relationship hidden, but personally, I don't have a problem with them being married. Hell, would you rather have them continuing to just date in secret?"

"I guess I don't care if they're together, either," Peter Williams said. "If that's what they want, what's the problem, John? Would you want us telling you who you could or couldn't marry?"

"The problem is that he's her boss and he shouldn't be involved with her at all," John said. "We have policies that say teachers can't marry administrators. You know that. All of you." He waved a pointed finger.

"She's not a teacher."

"That's irrelevant. It's the same situation—she's an employee who married an administrator, her boss."

Actually, I'm her boss," Frank said. "Well, at least I'm her immediate supervisor."

"And Steve's your boss," John said. "That's a problem."

"Well, I supervise the principal at the school where my wife, Gloria, teaches and that principal is my wife's boss," Frank said. "Is that a problem, too?"

"Yes."

"That's ridiculous," Frank said. "Does anyone agree with John?"

"No," Jim said. "Look, I think we all agree that it's inappropriate for a manager to supervise his or her own spouse. Our policy prohibits that, but I'm not aware of any policy against someone supervising his or her spouse's boss."

"I disagree," John said. "We have a problem here."

Steve rubbed his temples. "Actually, I've done some checking on my own. There have already been court cases on this subject. Bottom line, the courts have ruled that a school district that prohibits an employee from supervising a 'near relative', can transfer one of them to avoid the 'perception of favoritism on the part of other members of the teaching faculty. But the policy cannot deny people the right to marry."

"Where could we transfer her?" John asked. "You're the damn boss."

"That's the point. I am not her boss. I am Frank's 'boss'. Frank is her supervisor. Frank is not a 'near relative'. I invited him here today for you and he to witness me saying that if he believes any of my direction shows favoritism, he may go directly to you with his concerns, and I answer to you."

"Look," Mary said, "we can't sit here all night arguing. We have people waiting in the board room. Can we agree to move on for now, and debate this issue at another time?"

"I second that motion," Jim said.

John opened his mouth, but before he could get a word out, Jim said, "By the way, are you all aware that John Richmond's daughter is a teacher in this school district? Just thought I'd point that out."

John clamped his mouth shut.

CLAIRE WAS RELIEVED when Steve told her about the school board meeting.

Steve said, "You know, it's my fault that you didn't tell Ron and Nancy about us. I'm the one who said to keep it a secret from everyone. I'll go to the school and talk to them. I'll explain."

"No, please don't. I can't have you coming to work to fix my problems. I would seem like a child. No. I have to figure this out on my own." She leaned forward on the sofa and gave him a hug, and whispered, "I appreciate the thought, though."

The next morning, Claire knocked on the door to Ron's office and said, "Can we talk?"

"Whatever," Ron said. He didn't even look up from the paper he was working on.

"You are angry with me?"

"You picked up on that, huh."

"Please, Ron. Please let me explain."

He looked up, his mouth taut.

"We're friends," she said. "Friends have disagreements, squabbles, but they can usually work things out. If you'll let me explain, we can work it out, too."

"I don't really want to talk to you."

"Then don't. Just listen."

He ignored her.

"I wanted to tell you about Steve. You have no idea how many times I started to, but then I wasn't sure. Not because I didn't trust you, because I do. At first I didn't even know whether or not Steve and I had a chance at a relationship. After the attack, I avoided him for a while."

"If you'll excuse me, I need to talk to Nancy about a student." He stood up and brushed past her, leaving her alone in his office.

Now what was she supposed to do? She'd meant what she'd said to Ron. He was her friend, and she didn't want to lose him. They'd been through a lot together and she realized now, possibly too late, that she may have taken his friendship for granted.

Claire fought the urge to stay home the following day, but she had to go to the damn Round Table Luncheon in the afternoon.

She left school extra early this time, telling herself that it was because she didn't want a repeat of the previous meeting. To her surprise, on the way there, she admitted to herself that she wanted to escape from her school. She entered Cameron High and waved at Steve, who was standing near Frank and a principal, Liz Olson.

Steve excused himself and walked over to Claire and she said, "It's a miracle. I'm actually early."

"I see. I'm glad you're here."

She gave him a tentative smile."

"I wish there was something I could do to help. Did you talk to Ron again?"

"No. I'll try later."

He smiled, then said, "I wish I could stay and talk with you more, but I have to mingle. Sorry."

"Don't worry about it," she said. Frank walked in and seeing her, walked over and chuckled. "Well, well, I didn't think I'd ever see the day when you'd beat me to a Round Table Luncheon. What happened?"

She laughed, and said, "I needed to stir things up a little around here. It was getting too boring."

Several principals walked up and one of them, George Williams, said, "I hope the laughter means this meeting is going to be lighter than the previous meetings."

Frank said, "I sure as hell hope so."

Before long, the room filled up and when the last of the group arrived, John told everyone to take their seats. He looked around the room, and Claire felt his gaze rest on her. "Some of you may not have heard the latest news," John said.

The principals looked around the table, and Liz Olson, the principal of Webster High School said, "What news?"

John continued. "At the last school board meeting, Steve Jensen announced that he and Claire Constantine got married."

"What? Are you serious?" She looked perturbed. "I thought you didn't date employees."

Claire looked at Liz and then at Steve, and wondered what that was about. The group was silent for a minute, and Claire fidgeted under their speculative gazes.

Dan Greeley, the principal of Southwest High school, said, "Boy, you sure fooled me. I didn't have a clue any of this was going on."

"Yeah, Steve and Claire are pretty good at keeping secrets," John said. "They seem to be masters of deception."

Claire felt her face getting hotter as her temper flared. She looked at Steve. His eyes pleaded with her to stay calm.

Looking directly at John, Steve responded. "I wasn't aware of a change of policy. What happened to keeping our private lives separate from our work lives? Hell, I don't know everything about employees' lives, or school board members' lives for that matter. I don't think I really want to know."

Several people chuckled, and Manuel Rodriguez, one of the principals, said, "Did you know that John Richmond's daughter teaches at my school?"

Everyone in the room turned and stared at Manuel.

Steve raised his eyebrows. "That, I just found out. How long has she been there, Manuel?"

"Funny you should ask. She started three years ago, right after her dad became school board president."

Heads turned and all eyes were now staring at John. He shuffled papers and didn't respond.

Steve glanced at Frank and they smiled conspiratorially. Then Steve opened his notebook and started the meeting.

CHAPTER TWENTY-FIVE

LONNY CORRELLI TOOK one hand off the steering wheel of his rented Toyota Corolla, unzipped the bag sitting next to him, shuffling around in it to find his sunglasses. *Damn, where the hell are they?* He took his eyes off the road momentarily to seek the illusive target, heard a sudden honking, looked back up and swerved the car back into his lane to avoid a head on collision. *God, that was close,* he thought, shaking. Calming himself for a few seconds and being more careful this time, he quickly looked into the bag and spotted the damn eyewear sitting right on top in a corner. He pulled the sunglasses out of the bag and put them on.

Who woulda thought he would need them in Denver in winter? He'd only brought them on the plane by accident. He'd been wearing them on his drive to the Miami airport. Getting there late, he'd parked in the long-term lot, grabbed his bag from the trunk, and dashed into the airport. It wasn't until he was inside that he realized he was still wearing the dark glasses. Now, driving away from Denver's airport, the intense sun glaring off piles of hard-packed snow made him glad to have them.

The car in front of him slowed down and Lonny veered into the passing lane and gave the other driver the finger. *Asshole.* He hated slow drivers. Last time Lonny was in Denver must be two and a half years ago, during summer, with bicyclists and joggers everywhere. But nobody was stupid enough to be out jogging now. When his boss told him he was sending Lonny to Colorado in winter, his first impulse was to flat out refuse. But then he got an idea. Rent a car, do his work, and take a side trip up to Aspen. He'd heard he could rent skis and ski boots. Why not squeeze in some R&R since the boss was paying for the air fare?

Lonny stopped at a red light. He reached over to the side pocket of his bag again and pulled out his Denver map. Opening it up, he looked at the big circle he'd drawn before he'd left Miami. He looked at the street sign at the intersection to confirm he was where he thought he was, then mapped out the three turns he needed to make. Someone honked. The light was green. He looked in his rear-view mirror and gave the woman behind him the finger. His foot slammed the gas medal. Tires spun, and the car went nowhere in the slick intersection. He swore, let off the gas, then accelerated more slowly this time and moved into the intersection, skidding sideways.

Damn, damn, damn. He managed to get the car back on track in time to see the woman pass him by and give him the finger. If he knew how to drive in the snow better, which apparently he did not, he would have taken off in pursuit of her.

He drove more carefully the rest of the way. Arriving at his destination, he parked next to a six-foot high mountain of snow that had been plowed from the parking lot of the old brick building. A big, ugly dumpster sat half buried next to the pile. *Hmm, might come in handy.*

He got out of the car, checked his coat pocket, pulled out a winter hat, and stuck it over his head and ears. Then he snatched the small briefcase sitting on the floor of the car and walked into the building, almost slipping on his ass on the way. *Crap!* Studying the tenant list, he finally saw the name he was looking for—Phillip Seger, PI, Suite 301. He climbed the stairs two steps at a time. When he reached the third floor, and began searching for the office number, he shook his head. *They call these suites. More like hovels.*

Pulling the door open, he stood looking around a dingy space. He'd expected to see—well, he wasn't sure what he'd expected. An outer office with a secretary, or at least two desks. A curly-haired man with wrinkled clothes stood up from where he'd been squatting in front of an open file cabinet, a file folder in hand.

"May I help you?"

"Looking for Phil Seger. That you?" The man nodded. "My boss sent me. Said you had information about Juliet Powell."

Seger's face lit up. "That I do."

He rushed to his desk, sat down, dropped the file he'd been holding and picked up another file. "Before I hand this over I need to be paid. Your boss and I agreed on a sum. I assume the money's in that briefcase you're carrying."

Lonny nodded, set down the briefcase and opened it, then turned it around for Seger to see. "It's all there. Now give me the file."

Seger's eyes grew wide and he smiled. "Here you go, buddy." He handed the file to Lonny.

Lonny opened it and scanned the paper. It was all there. He closed the file, nodded, and pulled a gun out of his coat pocket. Seger looked up from the case full of money in time to see the trigger pull, the bullet smacking into his forehead, and flinging his head into the wall behind him.

Seger's head rebounded and he toppled over onto his desk face down. Lonny bent down and made sure the idiot was dead, then snatched the briefcase and closed it. He calmly walked down the stairs and to his car. A quick glance at the dumpster, and he smiled, deciding it wasn't worth going back and dumping the body. Let somebody find him in his sorry ass office.

JOHN WAS GLAD Claire had finally shown up on time to one of the meetings, but it stuck in his craw that she was getting too powerful. Not only was she making progress at that school, but Frank was always coming to her defense, and now she'd latched onto Steve.

He didn't know what he was going to do about her. She had to go, that he was sure of. Since the school board meeting when Steve had informed him about the marriage, John had thought long and hard about what to do. Before he decided anything, though, he needed to know what was going on in Midland High School. He didn't want any more surprises.

He got into his car and drove over to Phil Seger's office. The jackass hadn't been answering his phone calls.

When he arrived and saw three police cars, lights swirling, and an ambulance, his heart thumped hard.

He parked, approached one of the officers and said, "What's going on?"

"Who are you and why are you here?"

"John Richmond. I came over to talk to Phil Seger."

"The Captain is going to want to talk to you. Seger's been murdered."

John opened his mouth in disbelief, shocked.

WHEN CLAIRE RETURNED to the school Thursday, she tried to talk to Ron again, but he avoided her all day. At the end of the day, she called him into her office and he stood in the middle of the room, a look of contempt in his eyes. Although she motioned for him to sit down, he stood like a statue with his arms crossed.

"I know you don't want anything to do with me, but we have to talk. We work together. We're a team. We need to clear the air. Talk to me. Scream at me. Something."

"I put in for a transfer this morning."

"What? I didn't sign a transfer."

"I had a long talk with Frank. He signed the request."

Claire felt as if someone had slapped her in the face, and she wasn't sure who it was that made her sting more—Ron for abandoning her, or Frank for signing the transfer request without even discussing it with her.

"I get why you're mad at me, I do. But I need you here. The students need you."

"Well, you should have thought about that before."

"Before what? Before I tried to have a life outside of work?"

A frown flitted across his face. "You think I'm mad because you found someone, because you got married?"

"No. Because I kept it from you. I get that. But don't you see? I'd already laid too many of my problems on you. I didn't want to involve you in all my problems. And, though Steve and I have worked things out, it was a bumpy road getting there. You didn't need to go along on that ride."

"I put my faith in you. I was there for you after the attack and I did everything you asked of me, yet you treat me like an outsider. You expect me to be loyal to you after you lied and kept me in the dark."

"I didn't lie to you."

His glance was clearly skeptical. "You didn't invite me to the wedding. I'm good enough to take you to the hospital, to look after you and cover a crime scene for you, yet you still couldn't trust me? That's bullshit, and you know it."

"Oh, Ron, I'm so sorry. You're right. I should have invited you. You aren't just my assistant. You're my friend. We've been through a lot together. Can you forgive me? Please?"

"Why should I? You've damaged our relationship, you've destroyed the trust I thought we had."

"I trusted you with a lot that got you into trouble, which I regretted. After that, I wanted to protect you from the school board as much as I could. I was afraid that if I told you about Steve and me, and the board found out that you knew, they might accuse you of helping me hide my relationship. I didn't want to get you fired. I need you."

His look softened somewhat, but he still frowned.

"Oh, Ron, this is a big misunderstanding. Can't you see that? Can't you please forgive me? I don't want to lose your friendship. If you really want to transfer, I won't stop you, but please don't stop being my friend."

He lowered his arms, slumped his shoulders, and sighed. "I don't really want to transfer. But promise me you won't keep me in the dark again. Trust me."

"I promise. And I do trust you."

Claire and Ron talked for about an hour, and then they called Nancy into the office and smoothed things over with her, too. After that, they called Frank and cancelled the transfer request.

The next afternoon, Ron and Claire sat in her office. Ron said, "I heard some students talking in the hallway this morning. Seems Jose and the other two gang members who attacked you are plotting something. I don't know the details and I don't know if it's true."

"They haven't come back to school, have they?"

"No. But they've apparently been in contact with some of the students."

"Damn."

Claire's phone rang.

"Ms. Constantine, this is Janna Collins, the Director at Happy Days Preschool. Sorry to bother you at work. Something came up, and I thought I should check with you. Marcus's dad picked him up an hour ago. The teacher who signed him out is new. She didn't know the proper procedures so she didn't check Marcus's file. I called you as soon as I found out. She'll be disciplined for not calling you first, before releasing him to anyone other than you. I'm really sorry."

"His father picked him up? Did he give a name?"

"Uh, no. I checked. He signed the log, but I can't read it. The employee doesn't think he gave his name verbally."

"Oh my God! I'll be there in a few minutes." She tried to hang up the phone, but her hands were shaking and it took three tries.

Ron said, "Are you okay? You look like you've seen a ghost. Is it something to do with Jose?"

She shook her head. "I don't know yet." She grabbed her handbag from a desk drawer. As she started to stand up, she thought of Steve. She reached for the phone again, her hands still shaking, and managed to dial Steve's mobile phone number. One ring, two rings, three, and he finally picked up.

"Where are you? Did you pick up Marcus at preschool?"

"What? No, why would I do that? I'm still at work?"

"No, oh God no."

"What the hell is going on? Something's happened to Marcus?"

"Yes. I have to go to the preschool."

"I'll meet you there."

Claire stood up, red faced and eyes suddenly teary, then looked at Ron who was staring at her.

"What's going on?"

"I have a family emergency. If I don't come back, please continue all the work we've been doing to make the school better, okay? Will you promise me that? Don't let the school revert back to the way it was."

Ron looked as if he thought she'd gone overboard. He finally said, "Let me know if you need me to do anything. I'm here for you."

"Thank you." She grabbed her coat and dashed out of her office. She sped along the snow-covered streets, driving as fast as she dared, until she got stuck behind a snowplow. She moved slightly to the left, hoping she could pass him, but pulled back into place. Traffic was already heavy, though it wasn't quite rush hour yet. Adding to her frustration, the traffic light wasn't working right, flashing red, causing everyone to treat the intersection up ahead as a four-way stop.

She glanced at the car's clock, and smacked the steering wheel. Don't panic, she told herself. That was easier said than done. Marcus was missing. WITSEC would have to move them now, no matter what the outcome.

When she arrived at the preschool, she jumped out of her car and dashed across the parking lot, narrowly avoiding a slip on some ice. She rushed inside and looked around for the preschool's director.

Janna Collins came forward and said, "Again, I'm really sorry about the mix-up. I know the employee should have called you first."

"I need to talk to the employee who saw him," she said.

"Okay, I'll get her."

By the time Janna returned with the employee, Steve was rushing through the doors, bringing with him the cold air from outside. He put his arm around Claire's shoulders.

"This is my husband, Steve. He's Marcus's father. I need to know who picked up Marcus. Describe him to us." The director blanched, realizing the situation unfolding.

"He was tall, probably six feet," the young woman said. "He had short-cropped brown hair and green eyes."

"Did he have an accent?"

"Yes. English, or maybe Australian. I don't know. Could have been Irish. I'm not good at identifying accents."

"What time was he here?"

Janna brought the sign-out log over quickly and showed it to Claire. The time logged out was '3:10 P.M.' and the name was unreadable, but the signature looked like Callum's and the description fit him perfectly.

Claire's mind was whirling and she was confused, and angry at Janna for her shoddy security. How had Callum found them and why had he taken Marcus?

She turned and whispered to Steve, "We need to call Leo."

They left and Steve said, "Let's go to my car. You can call him from there, and find out what we're supposed to do."

She followed him and they both got into Steve's car. Pulling out her mobile phone with shaking hands, she autodialed Leo's phone number and told him what had happened.

"Don't call the police," he said. "I'll handle it. Go home and wait for me."

CHAPTER TWENTY-SIX

CLAIRE SHOOK AND cried as she hung up the phone after talking with Leo. Steve pulled her into his arms, and when she calmed down a bit, he asked, "Do you want to leave your car here? You can ride home with me and we'll pick up your car later."

She shook her head, and got out of his car. Steve followed her home and they walked into the house together.

Once inside, Claire broke-down, collapsed to the floor next to the sofa, and sobbed. Steve pulled her onto the sofa and held her tight until she quieted. They sat in the living room, waiting to hear from Leo for three-quarters of an hour, neither of them speaking, while the clock on a nearby shelf ticked like a metronome.

Breaking the silence, Claire asked, "What if they can't find Marcus and Callum? Callum's managed to avoid capture all this time. He could be on a flight to another state. He might even be in another state by now."

"Don't let your mind go there, Claire. They'll find him. Yeah, he's avoided the police, but he's traveling with a child now. That will slow him down. It will make it harder for him to run and to hide."

She nodded, wiping fresh tears from her eyes. They talked about the watcher—the private investigator John had hired. Then she told Steve about Brad and about her meeting with Leo. "Do you think Leo is really doing anything to get Marcus back? It worries me that I don't know anything about him. He could just be blowing it off, like both he and Brad did when I told them about the watcher."

"I'm sure he is," Steve said, trying to assure Claire, but she could see the worry lines on his forehead. "Even though you barely know the guy, it's encouraging that he has a local office. That's at least one promising thing."

"I'm not sure if he's still here, though. He said it was only a temporary office and that he'd be back in Virginia soon."

"Why would Callum come looking for his son?" Steve asked. "It doesn't make sense to try to take a little boy on the run with him."

"I know. It's driving me crazy. I keep thinking it wasn't really him. Maybe the private investigator is impersonating Callum to scare me into paying him to keep him quiet."

"I suppose that's a possibility."

Claire began crying again, and leaned against Steve who stroked her hair and whispered in her ear, "It'll be okay. They'll find him."

She remembered the gun she'd brought home from the school. After she and Marcus had moved into Steve's house, she'd locked it inside a drawer of the desk Steve had bought for her. She got up and retrieved it. Steve's eyebrows shot up when she walked back into the living room and handed him the gun.

"Where did you get this?"

She explained how she'd come to have it in her possession.

"You should have turned it over to the police. It could be stolen for all you know."

"Oh, I guess so. Sorry."

"Well, we should leave it out for now, considering the situation, but we'll take it to the police after this is over." He set it on the coffee table in front of where they were sitting.

Late that night, Claire was curled up on the sofa, her head on Steve's lap. Both were trying to sleep and neither was having any luck. A loud knock on the front door startled them. Claire jumped up and ran to the door.

She unlocked and opened it, hoping to see Leo and Marcus, but gasped as she stared into the face of Jose Rodriguez. She caught something—a movement—out of the corner of her eye. Her attention shift down to his hand and saw a shiny knife, probably the same one he'd used when he and the others had attacked her in her office. She screamed, and tried to close the door. It wouldn't move. Confused, she instinctively turned her head to see what was stopping it.

Steve. He had grabbed hold of the door. He pulled the door out of her grasp, opening it wider, holding up the gun she'd left on the coffee table. Before he had the chance to shoot, the boy crumpled.

"What the hell?" Steve said. He looked around, but finding no initial answer there, bent down to better see the boy.

Claire stepped onto the porch and bent forward to get a look. Blood was oozing out of the boy.

"He's been shot. Go back in the house, Claire."

A loud noise across the street caught their attention and they both looked up. A car was parked alongside the road across the street from their house, with a man slumped over in the driver's seat. Another man was standing next to the car.

"Oh, my God," Claire said. "That's Leo standing by the car." Moments later, several uniformed agents appeared, seemingly out of nowhere. Within a couple of minutes, police cars and emergency vehicles began arriving, swarming the neighborhood and filling the night with sirens and flashing lights.

Leo came to their door step and said, "We need to talk in private."

Claire introduced him to Steve. Leo frowned.

After they all went inside the house and sat down in the living room, Leo immediately said, "You should have called me and told me you'd gotten married and moved."

"I guess I should have told you but, honestly, it didn't occur to me. I mean, why would you need to know that?"

"Why? I'll tell you why, damn it. We need you alert and clearheaded, not all wrapped up in love, thinking nothing else matters. It makes people do stupid things."

"You don't have other married witnesses?"

"Of course we do. Just not newlyweds," he said. "And especially not before a trial. Even during trial we discourage any romantic entanglements. Once everything is done, case closed, and everything has cooled down, then it's safe for witnesses to do what they want. That was a really stupid thing you did." He paused, then continued. "Did you at least tell him you're in WITSEC?"

"Yes."

He shook his head. "I don't know what to do with you, Claire. You know the rules."

She looked at him, her pent up anger finally bursting the dam. "No matter what I do, handlers are always on my case for what I say or don't say. I'm like a puppet. Why don't you just give me a script? Maybe then I could get it right."

He looked surprised for a moment, then seemed to reconsider. "Well, it's done. "

Everyone was silent for a few moments. Then Claire pointed her head toward the door and asked, "What is going on out there? You obviously withheld information from me, too."

"I couldn't tell you. It was all part of the investigation. When I took over as your handler, I did some checking into this watcher you'd told Brad about. I sat in front of your condo building and saw the guy. Took a few pictures, showed them to my boss. From that point, we brought in watchers of our own and planted some information, hoping to catch some of the syndicate members."

"You mean you used me as bait in a sting operation?"

"Something like that. The private investigator who was tailing you is known as a man who plays dirty. We figured he would sell your information."

"He threatened to do that if I didn't pay him."

"Well, he did sell it."

"How did he know how to find the people who wanted the information?"

"He's an investigator. He's a criminal but he's good at his job, just stupid. After he contacted them, the syndicate hired a hit man to retrieve the information on you. He killed that PI for it. The hit man is in the car across the street wounded, and he's already beginning to talk to the agents questioning him right now."

"I can't believe you put Claire at risk like that?" Steve said, his anger evident.

"It isn't our normal policy but sometimes you have to take some risks. She wasn't in any real danger. Not after I joined the case. I don't leave my charges hanging out to dry like Brad did. "

"I don't understand," Claire said. "When I first met you, you said that you follow the rules and Brad didn't. Now you're saying you took risks and did something that isn't WITSEC's normal procedure?"

"Brad was close to retirement. He wasn't really doing his job anymore because he didn't care. He was getting sloppy and lazy. That's what I meant about him not following rules. As a marshal you have to be on the ball, twenty-four seven. You have to see the bigger picture and analyze it, then take appropriate action. You can't sit on your butt and play phone tag with your charges."

Claire nodded, then asked, "Who shot Jose?"

"The hit man. Jose just got in the way. He had to shoot Jose because he needed to kill you, Claire, or he wouldn't get paid."

Claire gasped and Steve put his arms around her. She leaned into him and let him pull her closer.

"What about Callum?" Steve asked. "Did he take Marcus, or was that a trick?"

"We didn't expect Callum to show up. But our watcher first spotted him near the high school and followed him to the preschool. He waited outside. When Callum came out with the child, he grabbed Callum and took him in."

"Where's my son?"

"We have him. He's fine. He's outside in one of the vans."

Leo stopped and called someone on his phone. Minutes later a woman brought Marcus to the house.

Marcus rushed into Claire's arms. Claire looked up at Leo. "Why did Callum take him?"

"Seems he'd been looking for you for a while. Claims he missed his son. Then he heard about the hit man. He said he was trying to protect his son."

When Claire released Marcus, he ran into Steve's arms. Steve held him tightly and stroked his hair.

"We have a vehicle en route to pick up you and your son. You know the drill. You can get your purse and coats. We're moving you to a secure location until we have permanent arrangements."

"But I'm not ready. I have work to do at the school."

"They'll have to manage without you."

"What about my husband?"

"I don't know, since we didn't even know about him until now." Leo looked at Steve, and said, "We need to talk about whether you're going into the program, or whether you're going to end the marriage. You have a lot of things to consider."

"I know," Steve said. "Claire and I have already discussed it."

CHAPTER TWENTY-SEVEN

RON AND KIM stood next to the registration desk in the admin office and re-read the note Claire had sent them:

'I'm sorry I had to leave without saying goodbye in person. Maybe someday I will be able to explain why to you. I'm going to miss you, all of you at Midland. I'm so glad to hear that you've been appointed principal, Ron. You're going to be great in that position. Keep going with the plans we started and don't ever give up. Midland is going to be a great school. Good luck.' CJ.

"I still can't believe she's gone," Kim said.

Ron shook his head.

"Back when she first started I wouldn't have believed I would say this, but I'm really sad she's gone. You know, she did tell me once that she doesn't stay long in one place. I thought she was saying it to placate me. I guess she was telling the truth."

"I'm going to miss her, too. The whole school will."

CLAIRE STOOD IN the middle of the living room in their new house and tried to picture the room with the furniture they'd purchased at the Home Furniture store, being delivered this afternoon.

Steve finished dressing for work and joined Claire in the living room. They'd all slept on air mattresses the last few nights.

"Well, I guess I'm ready to head over to the university. Wish me luck."

She kissed him, and said, "You'll be great. I can easily picture you speaking in front of a packed lecture hall. Are you sure you're all right with this?"

"I'm actually excited, Claire. I mean, Amanda. Wow, it's really going to be tough getting used to new names."

"It always is. You'll get used to it, Joe."

He laughed. "I always liked that name. I'm glad they gave us an easy last name. Sinclair is pretty good."

"It is."

Joe said, "How is Eric dealing with the name changes? See, I'm getting better. I remembered."

"I worry about him. He usually adjusts quickly, although now that he's older I think he's going to have a harder time. We practiced it all day yesterday before he started his new preschool this morning."

"He'll be fine. You worry too much."

"I know, but I can't help it. You know what worries me the most? What if the syndicate finds us again?"

"Then we'll proceed with our backup plan, okay?" He pulled Amanda close and kissed her.

"You sure you don't regret staying with me and entering the program? You don't regret leaving your job?"

"Of course I will miss family and friends. That's the toughest part. But I would have missed you and Marcus more. Besides, I don't mind changing jobs. I'm getting too old to deal with the pressures and stress of the Superintendent's job. I'd much rather have decent hours and time for my family." He paused, and studied her face. "Remember, we'll survive because we have each other and we have a plan."

She looked into his eyes and smiled. He hugged her and kissed her again, then left for work. She stood by the window, with the curtains pulled back slightly, and watched him back out of the driveway. He was right. They had already discussed the future and came up with their own plan—Plan B, as they called it—because neither of them wanted to continue with witness protection if they were attacked again. Trying to get fake identification on their own and traveling to Europe or some other foreign locale wouldn't be easy, especially now that they were expecting a baby. She hoped they wouldn't have to resort to that plan. But they would do whatever was necessary to protect their family.

When Joe was out of sight, Amanda sat down on a folding chair in front of the desk they had bought and assembled the day before. She opened up her new laptop computer and turned it on. While she waited for it to boot up, she thought back on the two months they'd recently spent living in WITSEC headquarters while Steve—now Joe—was being processed into the program, and then the transfer a week ago here to Bloomington.

Four days ago, she and Joe had both met with the local university's Board of Regents. Although their new handler and his boss had helped with the introductions and interviews, Joe had insisted they obtain jobs on their own merit and with the potential employers knowing their situation and true backgrounds.

Yesterday, Joe was offered a full-time job as a Professor of Education. Amanda was also to be affiliated with the university, but as an adjunct visiting professor. She would teach part-time for now, giving her time to continue her research which she'd begun while at Weymouth. If everything went well, she would publish under a pen name.

Late in the afternoon, Amanda heard the rumble of a truck outside. She peeked out the window at the furniture store delivery truck. After a few minutes, two men got out and walked to her front door. She held her breath as she braced herself to face the strangers.

"We have some furniture to deliver to a Mr. and Mrs. Sinclair."

"Yes, we've been expecting you."

After they unloaded everything and assembled the beds, one of the men brought a clip board over to her.

"I just need your signature here to confirm your receipt of your furniture."

"Sure." She signed her new name and handed the clip board and pen back to the delivery man."

"Are you new to town, mam?"

"Yes, we are."

He nodded and said, "Welcome to Bloomington."

After they left, she walked around the living room, running her hand over the seat of the tan leather sofa, then looked up at the lovely painting of Pike's Peak hanging on the wall above it. The same tan color was reflected in the painting, along with grass-green and sky-blue, reminding her of her first date with her husband, when he'd told her about the mountain and the cog-rail train. She smiled, sat down on the sofa, and closed her eyes. Everything was going to be okay.

The sound of a rumbling truck out in front of the house again made her open her eyes. Then the doorbell rang again.

They must have forgotten something. Ah, they didn't give me a copy of the delivery receipt. That must be it!

She opened the door and stared in shock at the barrel of a gun. *Oh God! What do I do?* Her heart pounded so hard she could barely think straight. She tried to slam the door closed, but the man was standing in the doorway. The door hit him hard, knocking the gun out of his hand and he groaned in pain.

Not waiting around, she turned and ran toward the kitchen in the rear of the house, hoping to reach the back door before he caught up to her. Her bare feet tore across the living room's wooden floor and onto the kitchen's ceramic tile. As her hand reached out for the doorknob, she thought—*yes, I'm going to make it*—and then she felt something pierce her in the back as she flew forward and hit the door and her feet gave out from under her. As the doorknob faded from view, and an intense pain shot through her, she rebounded back onto the hard tile, her last thought being—*Guess I'm not going to make it*— and then everything went black.

STEVE—NOW JOE—sat at his wife's bedside, holding her hand and hearing the nearby machines make their periodic beeping sounds, monitoring and apparently providing life support to his damaged wife. He'd driven like a madman to the hospital the moment he'd gotten the call from the police.

The air smelled of antiseptic, reminding him briefly of years ago when his grandmother had lain in a hospital bed hooked up to similar machines, tubing in her nostrils and wires going everywhere, scaring the whole family. He rubbed his eyes and tried to hold back tears. *Amanda's a fighter. She'll pull through.* He couldn't allow himself to think otherwise. The numbers on the machine seemed to look okay to his untrained eyes. His eyes followed the wires back from the machines down to Amanda. She looked almost peaceful until one noticed her sallow features, the grey around her sunken eyes and her shallow breathing. The wires attached to her hands momentarily brought to mind a puppet. *God, how many times had she told him that she felt like a puppet because her life was not hers to control?*

Trying to push that thought from his mind, he turned his attention to the nurse, who was standing at the foot of the bed, writing something on a clipboard. The doctor had already told him that the surgery had been successful, not causing any major internal damage. But now it was more the head trauma they believed she had suffered from impacting the door and then the tile floor after being shot, that was the problem. "Is she going to be all right?" Joe asked. "Has the doctor given you any news?"

She looked up. "The next twenty-fours will tell us more. We're waiting for the swelling to subside." She scribbled something else on the chart, then looked back at him. "You know, she may be able to hear you. Stay with her and talk to her. Maybe she'll respond. Does she have a strong will to survive?"

He glanced at Amanda, squeezing her hand. "Yes, she does."

AMANDA SMILED AS Joe helped her ease into the front passenger seat of their car, grateful for his gentleness with her, both this afternoon and during her two week hospital stay. Several nurses, over the past week since she'd awakened from the coma, had nothing but praise for her husband, how he'd sat beside her every day, holding her hand, talking to her, and reading to both her and their son.

He rushed around to the driver's side and entered.

"Dad packed our stuff and said we're going on a trip," Marcus—now Eric—said from the backseat as they drove away from the hospital.

"That's right, sweetie." She glanced sideways at Joe and gave him a half-smile, knowing they were launching Plan B, for better or for worse.

31239214R00195

Made in the USA
Charleston, SC
11 July 2014